HIGH

HEELS

AND

LOW

BLOWS

A NOVEL

HIGH HEELS
AND
LOW BLOWS

JILL VALENTINE

P❉PCORN
P R E S S

First published in 2024 by Popcorn Press, the fiction imprint of Fair Play Publishing
PO Box 4101, Balgowlah Heights, NSW 2093, Australia
www.fairplaypublishing.com.au

ISBN: 978-1-925914-88-7

ISBN: 978-1-925914-89-4 (ePub)

Cover design and typesetting by Ana Sečivanović

This is a work of fiction. Names, characters, businesses, places, events, locales, and incidents are either the products of the author's imagination or used in a fictitious manner. Any resemblance to actual persons, living or dead, or actual events is purely coincidental.

NATIONAL
LIBRARY
OF AUSTRALIA

All inquiries should be made to the Publisher via hello@fairplaypublishing.com.au

DEDICATION

In loving memory of my mum, Claire Bennett Valentine.

Sorry for the swearing and drug references.

"Not all psychopaths are in prison—some are in the boardroom."

Dr Robert Hare,
Canadian Psychologist and
Co-Author of Snakes in Suits

Prologue

London, December 2002

This year's annual Christmas party theme was *Hollywood*, and level ten of the London investment bank was buzzing with excitement. Day-to-day work tasks had been replaced with conversations about what everyone was wearing and who would end up shagging whom.

On her way back from collecting four Pink Lady costumes from the fancy dress shop for herself and three young women co-workers, Bee Bloom stepped into the elevator and pressed the number ten. Ben Taggart, a male colleague who worked on the same floor, followed her. They both stood facing the lift doors in silence until Ben said, "I didn't see you earlier this week. Did you have a day off or something?"

She was surprised he had noticed. They'd had an unpleasant exchange at a recent client cocktail party, and he had been ignoring her, until now.

"I was on a course," she replied, turning her head slightly to meet his eyes.

"For what?" His eyebrows quirked in a way she didn't like.

"An introduction to investment banking. It's the first in a series." As soon as she finished her sentence, he erupted into laughter so loud that it sounded forced.

"Stop. That's the funniest thing I've heard in weeks," he mocked.

"Well, I missed the joke." Her voice cracked a little as she spoke. She felt ridiculed.

"You? I mean, no offence, but that's just bonkers. You're here to look good, get coffees and organise a few meetings." He chuckled to himself.

1

"You're not robust enough, and you certainly don't have the killer instinct and pedigree that's needed to be an investment banker. I mean, seriously. Someone's throwing you a bone because you've got a nice face and nice tits."

Totally taken aback, she was left speechless, unable to find the words to counter his rudeness. How dare he laugh at her and assume that she isn't 'robust' enough. He didn't know her from a bar of soap!

"Anyway, what's in the bags? Something revealing for tonight, I hope," he said while peering at the white garment bags hanging over her shoulder.

She felt his eyes crawl slowly up her body then linger on her breasts. Her heart started beating a little faster. Refusing to answer his crude question, she gritted her teeth and kept her eyes on the lift doors. The ten-second ride to the tenth floor suddenly felt like ten hours.

When the doors opened, he got out first. *A bully and no manners*, she thought. Then, he turned back and said in a mocking tone, "I'll be looking for you tonight."

She shivered internally. He was giving her the creeps now. She didn't get why he had it in for her. One thing was for sure, she wasn't going to let him burst her bubble, because she was looking forward to the party. She reassured herself that she could hide from him among a sea of two thousand employees in fancy dress.

By 8pm, the party was in full swing. Dressed in matching pink satin bomber jackets, black neck ties, black shiny leggings, black stilettos and hair in high ponytails, the Pink Ladies strutted into the Leicester Square nightclub hoping to take out the prize for 'best-dressed group'.

Bee was blown away by the extravagance. No expense was spared. There were food stations with every type of global cuisine, free-flowing cocktails served by shirtless waiters and gorgeous women in tiny sequin dresses handing out free cigarettes.

Three hours later, with at least ten margaritas under her Pink Lady belt, she swayed off the dance floor. Her least favourite song in the world, 'Love Shack', was playing. She searched for the ladies' toilets and panicked when she clocked a queue that was easily fifty people long. Her bladder cheered when she noticed an empty disabled toilet down the corridor. As she grabbed the door handle, she felt a big strong hand come over the top of hers. She was then shoved inside. It took her a few seconds to focus under the fluorescent lights, but when her eyes adjusted she saw it was *him,* Ben bloody Taggart.

"What are you playing at?" she snapped. "You almost pushed me over." Even in her intoxicated state, she was shocked *and* confused by his heavy-handed approach. She remembered his early comments about 'looking for her'. Had he been watching and waiting until she was alone before pouncing?

"Ah, don't be so dramatic." He waved her off while turning to lock the door.

Her shock and confusion turned to fear. What was he going to do with her? As he faced her, she saw his eyes zoom in on her breasts. Having worked up a sweat on the dance floor, she had tied her bomber jacket around her waist leaving her in a black shoestring-strap singlet. She glanced down at her partially exposed double D cleavage and suddenly feeling vulnerable, she swiftly slipped the jacket back on and zipped it all the way up.

"Who did you come as?" She decided to mask her internal panic by asking an obvious question.

"I'm Indiana Jones, of course," he said. He started rummaging through the costume satchel that hung across his body.

"Oh Indy, you're like a bad penny, you always turn up," she slurred. Perhaps if she just kept things cordial, she could sidestep to the door and do a runner.

"Ha ha, very funny," he replied as he removed a small piece of white paper from his satchel. "Want some coke?"

She noticed he was sweating profusely, his eyes were wide with huge pupils and his jaw was jerking. He opened the paper, tipped the white powder out onto the shelf of the toilet roll holder, cut up two lines with a credit card, then handed her a rolled-up twenty-pound note.

She shook her head. "'ll give it a miss, thanks. I'm so pissed." Cocaine wasn't her thing, but she knew some bankers loved it.

"Oh don't be like that. It's a fucking party," he said angrily. He stepped forward, closer, and she stepped back and hit the wall behind her. He stepped forward again and now she had nowhere to go. He was easily a foot taller than her. Her heart was beating in her mouth. She was no longer nicely drunk; she was panicked. "Don't you like having fun?" he spat. His breath smelt stale and white foam frothed either side of his mouth.

"Yes. But I'm just not up for some of that." She looked up at him.

He leaned in and whispered in her ear, "Wrong fucking answer." Then he pushed her head down towards the white lines. "Just have a quick sniff, then I'll let you get back to your pack of slags." The note had fallen out of his hand and onto the floor. He looked down at it and said, "Pick it up."

She couldn't believe this was actually happening. What would he do if she refused again? Too afraid to find out, she did what he asked and picked up the note from the putrid floor, rolled it up and snorted the line. When she stood up, he laughed.

"That's a good girl. Now move. It's my turn." He pushed her to the side and bent down to snort the second line. When he finished, he tilted his head back, rubbed his nose furiously and made a disgusting grunting sound.

Their eyes met. She froze. She tasted the bitterness of the cocaine as it slipped down the back of her throat and felt a numbing sensation on her tongue. He stepped towards her, and she held her breath, fearing what he might do next.

"Off you go then," he snarled. Then he unlocked the door and motioned with his head for her to exit.

She didn't need telling twice, and she bolted.

As she weaved her way through the crowded dance floor, she saw her mentor, Savannah Silva, talking to another managing director. She wanted to tell her what had just happened, but something stopped her. Knowing how competitive this business was, she didn't want to jeopardise the opportunity she was being given. So instead, she headed for the exit and as soon as she was outside, alone, in the cold evening air, she vomited.

The entire weekend was spent hiding beneath her duvet, overwhelmed by feelings of panic and shame. By the Sunday evening, she made a pact with herself that she would go back into the office and not say a word to anyone, just pretend it never happened. She wasn't going to let Ben Taggart crush her spirit and ruin her promising career. But that all changed on Monday morning when she was called for a 'random drug test', which she failed. Although she couldn't prove it, she suspected that Ben had dobbed her in. After all, nobody else knew.

Savannah became her lifeline when she not only believed Bee's story but wielded her influence to save her from being ousted.

"So here's what's going to happen, Ben," Savannah said. "You've repeatedly tried to intimidate Bee. Now maybe you were bullied at school, or your mum didn't show you enough love, but it stops today. Otherwise, you'll be flipping burgers at McDonald's. Got it?"

Ben never even glanced in Bee's direction again. One year later he left the firm.

Chapter 1

The Financial Report, *Monday, December 1, 2022*
Max Magnifico returns to his roots

Today marks a new era for the Australian investment bank, Curban Capital, with the arrival of Max Magnifico in the newly created role of chairman. 'The Gladiator', as he's known, will work alongside CEO Bee Bloom to further grow the business which, under her leadership, has been a huge success.

Kindness. Respect. Integrity. The three words bounced around the screen of Bee's Mac, first up and down then side to side before disappearing and reappearing one by one. Did these 'company values' still hold true after all these years? She wondered this as she sat, elbows resting on her glass trestle desk, hands clasped. She swivelled her cream leather chair around and gazed out the floor-to-ceiling window of her level-forty-one office. A classic Sydney postcard stared back at her: the gleaming white sails of the iconic Opera House, the famous Coat Hanger bridge, the expansive harbour sparkling under a scorching summer sun, a collection of shiny office towers shaping the city's skyline and a cloudless, azure sky as the backdrop. She watched as the green and yellow ferries made their way in and out of Circular Quay. *What a way to commute; beats the London Tube any day.*

She closed her eyes and took a deep breath in and out as instructed by the American narrator of the *Managing Anxiety* podcast she was attempting to concentrate on. Her mind kept jumping to the approaching board meeting. She always got nervous before a board meeting but today she was particularly apprehensive because she was meeting *Him*. They had held a few teleconference and Zoom meetings in the lead-up to his arrival, but today was their first meeting in the flesh.

"Now take a nice, long, deep breath in for four, hold for four, then out for four, and hold for four."

"Oh shut the fuck up!" she snapped at the podcast, irritated and unable to focus on this seemingly straightforward exercise. She couldn't decide if it was the ultra-slow pace of the narrator's voice or their weird American accent that wound her up most. Either way, this whole meditation podcast thing, recommended to her by the Human Resources department, was failing to "boost well-being, promote positive thinking and reduce emotional reactivity" as they'd claimed. In fact, it was having the opposite effect.

She hit pause and tossed her AirPods and iPhone across the desk. The phone made a loud crashing sound as it collided with her monogramed stainless steel water bottle.

"Everything all right in there?" called out her assistant, Stuart Sanderson, from his desk directly outside her office.

Her office door remained open most of the day, allowing her and Stuart to bark information at one another while also encouraging staff drop-ins. She wasn't one of those 'ivory tower' CEOs who loved the seclusion of their own glass-walled office. Some days it could make her feel like a solitary goldfish. However, due to her misophonia, an intolerance to certain sounds, sitting in the open-plan floor wasn't an option. After enduring years of sitting amongst serial sniffers, snorters, throat clearers, lunch scoffers and open-mouth gum chewers she had concluded that having a separate office was the best solution.

"Yes, all fine," she lied.

She struck the keyboard with her index finger and the screen instantly came to life. There it was. The secret email that was causing all her tension and anxiety; the reason she was even giving these meditation podcasts a go in the first place.

It had arrived in her inbox six months ago from an unfamiliar name with the subject 'It's important you read this'. At first, she thought it was one of those spam emails. The type that, she'd been told, could bring the entire firm's systems down if opened. But when she double-clicked on the email address, it seemed legit, so she went ahead and opened it.

She still hadn't told anyone about it. Not even her husband, Gus. Although they weren't together at the time of the Ben Taggart incident, Gus had said if he ever encountered "the scumbag" that he would "subject him to waterboarding". Bee was therefore hesitant to ignite Gus's protective spirit, especially when she hadn't verified the contents of the email or the author.

Just like every other day in the last six months, she found herself reading the email once more.

Dear Bee, we've never met, however I've followed your career and think you're awesome. Which is why I feel compelled to warn you about your new chairman, Mr Max not-so Magnifico. He's a complete and utter psychopath. If you don't believe me, look up Dr Robert Hare then look out for all the signs. And definitely watch your back. Yours, Vanessa Rudgens.

She then searched for Vanessa Rudgens online *again* (and couldn't find any trace of her) then prayed (even though she most certainly wasn't religious) that it wasn't true because there was no way she could ever face another bully after Ben bloody Taggart. She closed the email and forced herself to carry on with her day.

Next task—today's calendar. Looking at all her meetings made her head spin, not to mention all the pop-up reminders that had started pinging from 6am. Stuart colour-coded all diary entries meticulously—blue for internal meetings, green for client meetings, purple for events or lunches. No white space, like today, meant she had to be *on* non-stop. No slacking off for even five minutes to indulge in her secret, feel-good pastime of watching dog videos on Instagram or something more useful like checking the daily avalanche of messages in her sons' school WhatsApp group chats. Nope, today it was back-to-backs, starting with the board meeting at 8am right through to 10pm. She wouldn't see her two boys, 11-year-old Otis and 13-year-old Ollie, before bed so she was determined to leave the office at a reasonable hour tomorrow. Her goal was to bookend at least two days per week with seeing their faces and she always *tried* to work from home on Fridays so she could drop them at school. She considered this 'flexible' working good role modelling for her employees, especially the young women. After all, *you can't be what you can't see.*

She drummed her fingers on her desk while staring at the calendar. "This is ridiculous, Stuart. Can you please start leaving some free space in the diary so I can at least go for a wee!" she called out loud enough that he could hear her, but not so loud that the other employees on the floor would.

Stuart ignored her. Having known Bee for 20 years, he always knew when it was best to just stay quiet.

They met in London in their early twenties and had both, coincidentally, moved to Australia in 2017, Bee to take on her new role at Curban Capital and Stuart with his Australian boyfriend, who promptly dumped him on arrival. Heartbroken and broke, Stuart had contemplated returning to London until Bee offered him a job as her assistant. She had realised that she needed someone she could trust implicitly in this new big role of hers. That's what optimist and author Simon Sinek, whom she followed avidly on LinkedIn, recommended. *"You wouldn't go scuba diving by yourself—it's dangerous and stupid—leadership is the same. You need someone right by your side."* For Bee it didn't matter that Stuart's background was in fashion PR and that he'd never stepped foot inside an investment bank. Trust was Bee's number 1 hiring requirement, the other stuff he could learn on the job. And for Stuart it was the money that enticed him. Double his fashion salary, which made up for the lack of designer freebies that he was used to.

"You need to get ready. It starts soon," Stuart called out.

"All right, all right, I know. I mean, it's the board meeting, of course I know it starts soon."

Stuart must have picked up on her fretful tone, because he immediately got up from his desk and strolled into her office. "What's wrong?" he asked in a slow, drawn-out way as if he were addressing a toddler on the verge of a meltdown.

"I told you, I'm fine. Absolutely fine." She wasn't fine. Her nerves were getting the better of her. She reached for her huge cream leather Saint Laurent tote from under the desk and began rummaging around for her calm pastilles. She loved that bag because it was so roomy that she could effortlessly toss everything into it. However, she hated it for the same reason because it made finding things quickly a challenge.

"Ah, there they are. Thank fuck for that." Bee swore a lot around Stuart but tried desperately to keep a lid on it around the employees. Not exactly befitting of a CEO to have a potty mouth. She pushed two of the mixed-berry-flavour pastilles out of the packet and popped them into her mouth.

"Yeah, right. C'mon, what's wrong?" Stuart repeated. He slid his perky, squatastic bottom onto the edge of her desk, crossing one of his polished black Prada loafers over the other, admiring them in the process. He raised his perfectly tweezered eyebrows, tilted his head and folded his arms. Bee knew she couldn't just palm him off, he obviously knew something was up.

"I don't know. I guess I'm just nervous. You know I always get nervous before board meetings but today's different. It's a biggie," she said. "I've probably read too much about *Him* and now I've made this persona up in my head. I mean, his reputation precedes him."

Him. Max Magnifico, their new chairman.

Max was a celebrity of sorts in investment banking circles and known as 'The Gladiator', a name bestowed on him by a client after Max "fought to the death" to get a major merger across the line. Everything about him was so nauseatingly perfect. He and his Indian heiress wife were your typical alpha couple, adhering to all society's aspirational norms by attending prestigious private schools, gaining MBAs from Harvard (where they met), enjoying early career success, having kids in the mid-twenties, and owning multiple residences, including a chateau on the French Riviera, a newly renovated fifty-million-dollar waterfront mansion in Sydney's Mosman, a forty-five-acre stud farm in Bowral next to Nicole Kidman and Keith Urban and a 'beach shack' on the NSW South Coast which, from the pictures, looked anything but shacky.

This stuff was all too fairy tale-like for Bee. Her path to investment banking was nothing like his. *It* found her; she didn't seek *it* out. After finishing with average grades in English literature from an average London university, she was clueless about what to do with her life until a fast-talking Irish recruiter talked her into an executive assistant job at an investment bank (*whatever that was*, she thought at the time). And because money was a major motivating factor, she jumped at the eighteen-thousand-pounds-per-year salary, generous perks and annual bonus. Money meant independence and nice things.

Max liked very *nice* things judging by his jet-setting lifestyle and penchant for fast cars. But among everything Bee had read about him, and she had read *a lot*, there wasn't so much as one chink in his gladiator armour. No scathing news articles, no Twitter take-downs, no personal fuck-ups, not one flaw to suggest that this Vanessa Rudgens, whomever she was, was right.

"I'd hide *that* if I were you," suggested Stuart with his eyes fixed on a glossy magazine sitting on Bee's desk. It was a copy of *Forbes* from earlier in the year with Max gracing the front cover. The headline 'win at all costs' had made Bee jolt when she first saw it. She tossed it into the paper bin under her desk then let out a loud groan. "God, I wish I didn't feel so nervous."

"How many coffees have you had?" asked Stuart. He stood up and began rearranging the generous bunch of blush-pink peonies in a glass vase on Bee's desk. Pink peonies were Bee's flower of choice between the months of October and December, and a fresh bunch was delivered to her office every Monday morning.

"Just the one flat white." She paused before adding "Large", almost apologetically. A regular was usually fine but a large could sometimes bring the jitters on, and Stuart knew that.

"And the podcast didn't help?"

Bee caught Stuart checking out his reflection in the window. He turned his head to the side, fiddled with his coiffed quiff then pulled a duck face. She wondered if he was paying full attention to what she was saying.

"No. Bloody useless. That guy's voice winds me up. Nobody speaks like that." She picked up her AirPods and returned them to their white charging case. "While I remember, can you order me dinner from that healthy place, Office Fresh, or whatever it's called. A nice salad. Make sure it's the crunchy kind. None of that soggy quinoa crap."

"Got it," Stuart said as he returned to perfecting the peony arrangement. "I still don't get why he's coming to work here. He's got more money than God and—"

Bee cut him off. "I told you, Curban Capital is entering a new growth phase." She caught herself doing that thing where she suddenly switches from 'friend Bee' to 'boss Bee' and her language becomes more professional, and her North London accent takes on a more refined tone. "Max brings client relationships and that means more business which means more money. And more money means—"

"Happy shareholders." Stuart cut Bee off this time.

"Exactly."

Although she defended it, Bee knew that Stuart was right to question why it was necessary to appoint a new chairman and grow the business. After all, the company was knocking it out of the park. Profits were solid. Clients were happy, so were employees—they had just been named one of *The Financial Report*'s 'Best Places to Work'.

Culture was important to Bee, but she knew that bumper profits and juicy dividends were what shareholders cared about most. They made that glaringly obvious by the way they hurried through to the financials part of the agenda at their quarterly shareholder meetings. It was *always* about the revenue, not the people making the revenue. She had to really grit her teeth through some meetings which was precisely why she needed Stuart by her side. He was her confidant in all work-related matters, an ear to bend when the shareholders, or the board, for that matter, were doing her head in.

And that was precisely why he was going to be massively aggrieved when she finally revealed her six-month-long secret.

Chapter 2

Rosie Reid was running late for her regular Monday meeting. Her morning had been derailed, as it often was, by one of her high-maintenance clients calling at the crack of dawn to demand she fix an article they considered "egregious". Client complaints were more often than not unfounded, but after fifteen years heading up her own PR firm Rosie knew her job was half crisis management and half ego management. When welcoming a new intern at Reid & Co Counsel the number one lesson she shared was *"While our clients have incredibly thick skins when it comes to business, they have seriously thin skins when it comes to their image and the press."*

The day started at 5am. No snoozing because every minute counts in getting across the day's press coverage! She scooped up her MacBook from the floor next to her bed. She had tossed it aside at midnight, swearing to change her bad bedtime habits.

"You must start leaving technology outside the bedroom," her $300/hour counsellor had told her, *again,* at their last session. Easier said than done when you're running your own business and clients call at all hours.

First up, an espresso. Like a true addict, she couldn't switch into work mode until she felt the coffee shooting through her veins. She had recently tried to go without her three long blacks a day because of her sleeplessness and heightened levels of anxiety, but only managed five days. She decided instead to stick with the coffee and medicate with temazepam instead.

"I will prescribe you something, but keep in mind this is just a Band-Aid solution to a much deeper problem," the same counsellor had claimed.

Her workday began with a scroll through the day's media coverage that had been conveniently packaged into a report by the journalism students working the nightshift. The aim was to finish reading all coverage by 6am then start her laps. But an interruption to that plan came by way of a call at 5:59am from Bill Sykes, one of her long-standing clients.

"These quotes are bullshit, Rosie. Jenny got the wrong end of the stick. You need to call her up and sort this out."

Bill was referring to Jenny Wallis, the well-regarded, award-winning editor of *The Financial Report*'s companies' section who never got the wrong end of the stick. Rosie had known Jenny for as long as she had been working in PR and despite the banter and occasional eye rolls, there was a mutual respect between them. They understood each other's roles in the dance-of-information exchange. Jenny was armed with a pencil and a thirst for a good scoop while Rosie was always armed with a bag of carefully crafted messages like a magician trying to weave her client's narrative into the spotlight.

"Well, *good morning,* Bill." Rosie said good morning emphatically, hoping that Bill would realise he had rudely forgotten to greet her. "I've read it all and you know what, I think Jenny's done a pretty decent job."

"But this quote about the business having a terrible year, it's not what I actually said," barked Bill.

Rosie had to lower the volume on her phone because he was shouting. He always shouted when he was panicking.

"I've recorded the interview so I can check exactly what you said, but what do you think you said?" Rosie asked, knowing full well he'd said word for word what had been reported.

"I definitely didn't use the word terrible."

He did. Rosie knew it. And now seeing it in black and white, he regretted it. It was a common mistake made by her clients.

"And then there's the bit about having to clear out the dead wood. I clearly said that bit was off the record—"

Rosie interrupted. "And how many times have I explained that there *is* no off the record?" It was seriously like talking to a child. In one ear and out the other. Despite being the CEO of a global consulting business and gifted at giving speeches, Bill's media skills were dire. He always put his foot in his mouth, especially when he was being interviewed by Jenny. Maybe it was her deep, sexy newsreader voice or her ample cleavage that made him drop his guard. Or maybe it was just how fucking brilliant she was at extracting information. Like a clever detective putting the suspect at ease with simple questions before going in for the gotcha moment.

"Look, leave it with me and I'll see what I can do," said Rosie. "Maybe the online version can be tidied up but the print is done. It can't be changed."

Rosie knew Bill's biggest concern was the online version, because that was what his big bosses offshore would be reading. And she also knew that his bollocks would be on the line if she didn't smooth over his clumsy words.

"Fine, just see what you can do. I'm in meetings this morning. Text me." And he hung up. No goodbye, of course.

"Goodbye, Bill. And fuck you."

Knowing Jenny wouldn't answer a call before 8am, Rosie decided to crack on with her morning routine—thirty laps in the fifty-metre outdoor pool of her apartment complex. As a bronze medallist in one hundred metre freestyle at the 1998 Commonwealth Games, she now used swimming as her meditation.

The pool was her sanctuary. It was the only part of her day when her phone wasn't in her hand or within grabbing distance. The rest of the day she was always on call, like a doctor. She often received panicked calls late into the evening or early in the morning when clients had just read an article that they were unhappy with. But if they *were* happy with what they read, she never heard a peep. That was lesson number two for the interns—*"A client rarely calls to say how pleased they are or that you've done an excellent job. Nope, they only call to complain!"*

A quick shower to dechlorinate with a good face and body scrub. It was a particularly angry scrub this morning. With every stroke of the exfoliating glove against her thigh, she cursed Bill.

After a brief dab with the towel, she wiped the steam from the mirror and saw her tired, puffy eyes staring back at her. Could she keep working at this pace for much longer? Such long days at her clients' beck and call.

She entered her walk-in wardrobe, leaving a trail of wet footprints on the plush grey carpet. The news said it was going to reach thirty-five degrees Celsius and there were bushfire warnings in place across New South Wales. She selected a brand-new Prada white cotton rib tank that highlighted her broad, muscly swimmer's shoulders and a pair of relaxed wide-leg linen trousers in beige, completing her ensemble with black Balenciaga platform flip flops. Knowing she was behind schedule she quickly applied a tinted moisturiser, a few strokes of pink blush and a couple of brushes of black mascara and headed out the door, leaving her damp, golden-brown bob to dry in the warm air.

After ordering an Uber, she decided it was time to call Jenny and clean up Bill's mess. *Ugh.*

"Please. It's really important you take that sentence out." God, she hated how pathetic she sounded when grovelling for edits.

"Rosie, this is insane. He said it. And anyway, the print is done so I'm not sure what the point is," Jenny said snootily.

"I know, I know. But he'll get in trouble from management offshore and they'll probably tell him never to speak to the press again. And that means no more interviews for you." Rosie held her breath, waiting for Jenny's reply.

"Well, I'll do it this once, but give the guy some bloody media training. It's such a waste of my time."

A quick text to Bill to tell him *"It's being sorted",* to which he replied with the praying hands emoji. *Idiot.*

The traffic was building as the Uber made its way towards Circular Quay. "I'll just get out here," she said, rushing out at a red light. She shot a quick text to Jazzy at the office—*2 mins away*—while sprinting across the light rail track on George Street with the oncoming train not too far in the distance. She started zigzagging her way up Martin Place past all the casual strollers, coffees in hand, loudly chatting through their AirPods.

Stopping for the red light at Castlereagh Street, she took a moment to breathe in the smell of summer in the city. Sure, there was the waft of diesel as commuter-filled buses passed, but beyond that were the different scents of generously applied perfume and freshly washed hair from passers-by. She loved observing the women in their summer attire, sun-kissed limbs, form-fitting tops and perfectly pedicured toes peeking out from stylish strappy sandals. And she loved the energy in the air; the possibilities that the sunshine and warm weather bring, like an après-work swim at the beach or an Aperol Spritz on a rooftop bar overlooking the harbour. Well, for all the passers-by, at least, because *she* would most likely be working late again.

Her mind came back to the red lights, which were starting to irritate her now. She decided to bolt. A courier van came out of nowhere, screeching to a halt, stopping her dead in her tracks. The dreadlocked driver leaned out of his window and shouted, "Oi! What the fuck do you think you're doing, you crazy bitch?"

Rosie shouted back, "Well you need to slow down, you fucking hippy."

He flipped her the bird and sped off while the bystanders shot her looks of disapproval and eye rolls. She made her way past the crowd hanging around the counter at the cafe in the lobby of her office building and grabbed her pre-ordered long black. She loved any app that allowed her to beat the queue. Racing into the lift she pressed the level twenty button repeatedly then saw someone making a dash towards the doors.

Forget it. "Sorry!" she called out insincerely while pressing the 'close door' button. She didn't want anyone from the lower levels slowing her down nor was she in the mood for awkward lift chat about the hot weather.

She exited the elevator and pushed her way through the double glass doors of Reid & Co Counsel with her back. Paula, the receptionist, rose from her seat and walked towards her.

"Morning, Rosie, how are you?" she asked.

"Great, thanks, Paula," she replied while doing a double take of Paula's black vagina-skimming skirt. Paula's outfits had become more risqué of late, and Rosie wondered why. New squeeze, perhaps? Regardless, today's skirt wasn't long enough for someone whose job was to greet clients. This was Rosie's least favourite part of running her own business—the managing people and handling sensitive situations. And Paula was a sensitive snowflake.

"Please can you ask one of the interns to get me a media download on Hugo Hamilton, you know, that bar and restaurant guy. I want any clips from the last ten years, please, and they need to be emailed to me in the next thirty minutes before I head out to meet him. Thank you so much."

"No problem, will do," replied Paula.

Rosie watched as Paula returned to a seated position behind reception where, thankfully, her tiny skirt was out of sight.

Mondays always started with a thirty-minute meeting where the three senior account managers—Rosie, Jazzy Jeffries and Simon Pincombe—discussed what they each had on for the week ahead. COVID had brought a downturn in client business and while things had started to improve in the last few months, Rosie was focused on bringing in new business and acquiring new clients. That was the thing about being the boss, you had to be laser-focused on revenue. But she would never go back to working for someone else. Been there, done that.

When she was a junior PR assistant at a large Sydney agency, she was astounded by how much clients were invoiced for her services—$275/hour—versus how much she pocketed—$52/hour, and that was before tax. Her boss at the time was a fiery red-haired Scot called Jean who looked and behaved like she'd had a hard night on the whiskies, consistently red-faced, dour and so bloody lazy. She was one of those 'you do all the work and I'll take all the glory' types.

So, Rosie thought, *fuck it, I can do this myself.* She worked from the dining room table in her one-bedroom apartment for twelve months, slowly building her own client base. Within two years, she began renting a small studio office in Surry Hills and hired three staff. Thirteen years later, she had a team of twenty, which she decided was the perfect size. Not too small that you need to do the grunt work yourself and not too big that you're panicking about having too many mouths to feed.

Rosie hurried over to the small, round meeting table where Jazzy and Simon were seated, patiently waiting for her arrival. "Hi, guys. So sorry I'm late. I'll explain everything in a moment," Rosie said, taking a big swig of coffee. A few drops leaked from the lid, staining her crisp white singlet.

"Great, I'm seeing a new client today." She grabbed a tissue from the nearby bench and began dabbing the stain. "Fuck it," she said, noticing it spreading.

Sighing, she turned her attention back to the meeting.

"Let's start with you. What have you got going on this week, Simon?"

Simon Pincombe was a plump, rosy-cheeked thirty-something ex-political staffer who had worked in a former prime minister's office, something he would always drop into conversation. "When I was working for the PM ... we used to ..." But putting that to one side, Rosie loved having him for financial reasons because his client business was reliable and lucrative—*very* lucrative.

"I'm working with the Department of Education on their summer maths campaign," he said, bursting with excitement. "A press release will go out this week, followed up with several TV and print interviews. It's going to be quite a splash."

Poor Simon. He really did cream his pants over the most mundane projects. There was nothing remotely 'splashy' about a maths campaign.

He added, "We're launching an innovative maths hub where—"

"That's fine. We don't need all the details," interrupted Rosie, waving her right hand in the air. "Jazzy, how about you?"

Jazzy Jeffries was the antithesis of Simon. Her client business was less reliable and much less profitable, but she made up for that by being gorgeous. British and in her early thirties, she exuded effortless cool vibes and made anything look good, even Crocs with socks! She had previously worked for London's PR queen and party planner to the stars, Phoebe Beardsworth.

"I'm taking TechNo to lunch this week," Jazzy answered in her clipped London private school accent. "They've gone a bit quiet and I've heard someone at Lawson PR is sniffing around and trying to steal them away. So, I'm going to have to work my charm." She smiled at Rosie.

"And who could resist your charm?" said Rosie. Realising that her comment was borderline creepy, she cringed. "Er, yeah, good luck, keep us posted on how it goes," she continued with her head looking down to hide her blushing face.

After taking a few seconds to regain her composure, she added, "Okay, so over to me. Well, this is an interesting one. I took a call last night from Hugo Hamilton. He's the bar and restaurant guy, wealthy, married, man about town."

Simon chimed in with, "He's a sleazy prick."

Rosie's eyebrows rose. "Thank you for not beating around the bush, Simon," she said as she set her iPad down on the table and Googled *Daily Life* Hugo Hamilton.

Daily Life, *Monday, December 1, 2022*

Hugo Hamilton exposes himself to young female employee

Bar and restaurant owner Hugo Hamilton has been accused of harassing a former female employee. Twenty-one-year-old Ms Indie Thomas from

Cronulla claims he slapped her on the bottom at a work event, then unzipped his pants and waved his "shrivelled chipolata penis" around.

"I read this one on the way into work. Blimey. Doesn't look good, does it?" said Jazzy while lifting Rosie's iPad to take a closer look. "And the chipolata reference. That's a bit mortifying." She grimaced.

Everyone knew Hugo Hamilton. He opened his first bar with family money at the ripe old age of twenty-two and had grown his empire to twenty venues across Sydney. He regularly appeared in the *Daily Life*'s side bar of celebrity gossip, but today's gossip wasn't the usual glowing puff piece about one of his new venue openings. It was scathing.

"Anyway, he calls around 7pm on my mobile. I'm not even sure how he got my number," explained Rosie. "He's ranting and it's hard to keep up with him. He tells me he was called by Cecilia Meadows at the *Daily Life* saying she's running a story about him harassing a former employee."

"I agree with Simon. He *does* look like a sleazy prick," Jazzy said, zooming in on a photo of Hugo at one of his infamous venue-opening parties, flanked by a group of ten women in Moulin Rouge-esque suspenders and bustiers. "I mean, just going off this photo, who's gonna think the guy's innocent?" She turned the iPad around to show Simon the photo.

"You're one hundred per cent right," he said. "He's looking guilty from where I'm sitting. How about you, Rosie, do you think he did it?"

"The jury's out for me until I meet him today. I need to look him right in the eye." She looked down at her watch and was overcome with panic, again. She felt like the day was already getting away from her. "Shit, I've got to leave in two minutes actually. Then after that I'm sitting in on an interview with Bee Bloom and the new chairman at Curban Capital, Max Magnifico."

"Is that his real name? It sounds like something out of Luxe Listings," laughed Simon.

"Yes, of course," Rosie said curtly. She rarely found Simon funny. If Jazzy had said the same thing, she probably would have laughed, which wasn't fair, but she couldn't help it. Simon always irritated her when she was tired. "So, Max *Magnifico* is back in Australia after two decades overseas. The main message is that he's come out of retirement to help the business grow and pull in new clients. They're both really attractive—I'd go as far as to say they're the Sienna Miller and Eric Bana of investment banking—so I'm thinking a photo of them sitting together on a lounge, side by side. Fingers crossed we get the front cover tomorrow."

Curban Capital had been a client of Rosie's since Bee Bloom's appointment as CEO five years ago. After years of providing advice to white middle-aged men, Rosie cold-called Bee and practically begged her to use Reid & Co Counsel while she navigated her new role as one of the few female CEOs in Australia. She admired Bee's 'battler' story of rising to the top in a male-dominated industry and felt they would be a good match. And she was right. Five years later, their working relationship had never been better. Bee was all class. Max was all class too, judging by everything she'd read on him. She wasn't going to admit it to anyone, but she felt slightly nervous about meeting him. After all, he was an industry legend. So powerful. The Gladiator!

"Right, I've gotta get going to the Northern Beaches for my Hugo Hamilton meeting," Rosie said, grabbing her Gucci handbag, iPad, more tissues and a bottle of San Pellegrino from the office fridge to tackle that pesky coffee stain. She made her way down to the street where she ordered an Uber Premier. There was no way she could cope with that ninety-minute journey in an Uber X, which, knowing her luck, would be a Toyota Corolla with inadequate air conditioning. When the black BMW SUV pulled up, she breathed a sigh of relief and jumped in. Before the driver could even greet her, she barked, "I have work to do so I'd appreciate no chit-chat. Thanks so much."

Head down, she began her deep dive into Hugo Hamilton.

Chapter 3

"It's time to play the music, it's time to light the lights ..." sang Stuart. He always sang the theme tune of *The Muppet Show*, his favourite kids' program from the 1980s, before board meetings. He told Bee the board members reminded him of the show's stale, bumbling characters.

Bee stood up from behind her desk, looked over her Mac monitor and mouthed "stop", trying not to laugh. She straightened her Totême navy silk pencil skirt and tugged down the matching jacket that cinched her size ten waist.

"It's not too booby, is it?" she asked Stuart while continuing to adjust the jacket. She hated anything that was chesty because double Ds like hers had the potential to invite unwanted stares. That was why she usually opted for pussy bows, high collars or round necks. All her work outfits were impeccable, thanks to Stuart's fashion expertise and lust for shopping. He had, without any instruction from her, made the curation of her weekly outfits his top priority. The frequent cardboard box deliveries from Net-A-Porter and Matches embarrassed Bee, but excited him. Like a child on Christmas Day, he frothed at the mouth while unwrapping the tissue to uncover the new items which were mostly dresses, skirts and blouses. There were never any trousers—she didn't 'do' trousers, and only wore more conservative suits for the quarterly board meetings, like today.

The corporate wardrobe sure had come a long way since she started out in investment banking. Her first employment contract had stipulated "female employees must wear skirts, not trousers, preferably knee length or just below the knee, no longer". The Gen Zers at Curban Capital would be appalled if they knew what Bee tolerated back in those days. For client meetings she had always been told by the same senior male colleague to "go and put a bit of lippy on". It had pissed her off enormously, but she'd bitten her lip. She'd bitten her lip about a lot of things while she climbed the corporate ladder. But not now. Now that she was a CEO, she was determined to lead by example and weed out any bad apples along the way.

Right on cue came an incoming call from Gus. He always called before a board meeting or important client pitch to wish her luck. She assumed he set a timed reminder on his phone because he was prompt to the second. He had recently taken a step back from running his own successful construction business to help with their boys while they were in between nannies. Bee was initially worried how it might work out, especially how Gus would cope with some of the more mundane domestic duties, like picking up her dry cleaning. Fortunately, he had embraced the change and even said he was enjoying being more involved in the boys' lives. Damn, she felt lucky to have him.

"How's my favourite CEO doing?" he asked

"You know. Okay, I suppose." She hesitated. "How are the boys this morning?"

"They're good. Ollie's already on the bus and I'm just about to drop Otis."

Bee heard Otis's little voice calling out in the background but couldn't make out the words.

"He says good luck," said Gus.

"Thanks, Otis. Tell him good luck at school. I better go. I'm due downstairs in five."

"Remember, you're awesome. They're lucky to have you."

"Love you," called out Otis.

"Love you too." She smiled to herself while glancing at the two photo frames on her desk. The first frame held a photo of the family on a rollercoaster at Disneyland Paris. It was a photo the boys had insisted on buying, wanting to remember Bee's look of sheer terror. The second frame held a shot from a family holiday in Bali, taken at a beach bar during a breathtaking sunset. She had contemplated whether to include a third photo in the mix, one of just her and Gus. However, she quickly changed her mind, deeming it a bit cringeworthy.

After hearing Bee's phone hit her glass desk, Stuart shouted, "Give your hair another brush, it's still messy. Or tie it back."

She gestured "okay" and began combing her shoulder-length, freshly highlighted blonde locks with her fingers, then tied them up into a loose ponytail with a black velvet scrunchie. *How weird that these have come back into fashion after all these years,* she thought. A quick brush of red lip gloss to match her red fingernails and she was almost ready.

Exiting her office, Stuart proceeded to rattle off all the necessary items for the meeting.

"Fully charged laptop, notebook, pen, phone, smile."

"Tick, tick, tick, tick and ha ha," replied Bee. She straightened her skirt and jacket again.

"You look fab, darling," said Stuart, marvelling at the suit which he had picked out online for her.

"Come on then. You're joining today to take notes, remember. And you better not embarrass yourself by doing a crap job. All the board members will be reading them."

As they made their way down the staircase, they passed a group of chatty employees from the technology team who were returning from their morning coffee run.

"Morning, Sarah, good weekend?"

"Amazing, thanks, Bee, yours?"

"Fabulous, thanks."

"Jake, how was your trip to Europe?"

"Brilliant, thanks, Bee. It's good to be back here though. Missed the place."

"Well, welcome back."

Bee's heart expanded when she saw happy employees enjoying their place of work. It wasn't always easy to keep them happy—there were deadlines, long hours and demanding clients—but she did what she could.

"Good morning, Bee. My, my, my, you look *magnifique* today," said Davide, the receptionist. He was seated behind the sleek, timber front desk, smiling widely at Bee as she approached him. "That colour is so chic and Parisienne on you," he added.

Bee cringed at how complimentary Davide could be. He always sucked up to her. And Stuart always rolled his eyes and tutted under his breath.

"*Merci*, Davide," Bee replied.

Being French, Davide asked that people pronounce his name the French way, Dah-veed. And Bee liked to exchange a few French words with him now and again, just for fun.

"And you look incredible as always. Is this a new one?" She pointed at a navy-and-white polka dot pocket square tucked neatly into his suit jacket.

"It's, how do you say, an oldie but a goodie," he giggled.

Stuart appeared to be squirming in his Pradas.

"This isn't an oldie but it was on sale which makes it a goodie," Bee said, patting her waist.

"Well, it's ..." and instead of using words Davide pouted his lips, winked and gave a thumbs up.

Davide took his job very seriously, which pleased Bee. Stuart on the other hand called him *nez marron*—a literal translation of brown nose in French.

Bee tilted her head in the direction of the boardroom and asked, "Is everyone here?"

"Yes, they've been in there for about ten minutes. Everyone has a coffee, and I'll send the morning tea in around nine thirty," replied Davide earnestly. "I met the new chairman. Mr Magnificent." His eyes sparkled.

"It's Magnifico," Stuart said in a tired voice.

"I know," Davide snapped. "It was a joke."

"Well, it wasn't funny, *David*." When he really wanted to annoy Davide, Stuart would address him the Anglo way.

"*Merci, Davide*," Bee said, kicking Stuart's ankle.

"You're most welcome," he replied while looking over at Stuart with a screwed-up face.

Bee let out a deep breath as if to prepare herself one last time, turned on her heel and walked towards the boardroom.

"You don't need to do that, you know," Stuart whispered to her as they walked side by side.

"Do what?"

"Say your outfit was on sale. I don't know why you feel the need to do that."

"All right, Stuart. Thank you. I just don't want people thinking I'm some pompous, out-of-touch boss lady."

Bee worked hard at being relatable, which was why she hated the cardboard boxes full of clothes arriving at the office. She didn't want to look extravagant when she knew some staff were budgeting amidst a cost-of-living crisis.

"And stop tutting at *Davide*. It's childish. I thought you two would get on."

"Why? Because we're both gay? Or because we dare to be different by not wearing the same navy suit or chinos as all the other blokes?"

"That's not what I meant. Anyway, now's not the time for this chat. I need to focus," she said as they headed towards the double doors of the Curban boardroom.

The boardroom had been a terrifying place for Bee when she was a young female banker climbing the ranks of a global investment bank in

London. The uncomfortable silences and intimidating stares had made her voice tremble as she presented to the suited and booted men (and it was always men) around the table. To manage her stage fright, she enrolled in a series of boardroom impact courses and over the years, with coaching and practice, she had transformed into a confident, persuasive presenter. But one thing had stayed the same in the boardroom—the lack of gender diversity. It was still very much a boys' club where openings for positions were advertised in small circles of mates from similar backgrounds or former schools.

There were seven men and one woman, not including herself, on the Curban Board. And there they were now, all standing in a circle to the side of the large twenty-seater oval-shaped board table with coffee cups in hand. Arthur Andrews, the board's chairman, was holding court as usual. Amazing gravitas for someone so hobbit-like. He stood at five foot five inches with a small frame and the beginnings of a hunchback from all those years of curling over a desk. His grey hair was perfectly combed and neatly parted to the side. He wore John Lennon-like round spectacles resting on a bulbous nose peppered with large juicy blackheads that Bee had the urge to squeeze. He always wore a grey suit, blue shirt and red silk tie. Although he was from a different generation, and although she sometimes disagreed with his antiquated views, Bee had a soft spot for Arthur. He had a teddy-bear vibe that was endearing.

"Ah, there you are," he said, glancing down at his watch.

That, however, was one habit that irritated her. Arthur always looked at his watch when she arrived for a meeting. It made her feel like she was late, when it was him that was early.

All board members turned to Bee and chorused, "Good morning, Bee."

"Good morning, everyone," she replied assertively. *"It's all about projecting your voice and commanding attention as soon as you enter these board meetings,"* her voice and body language coach had taught her.

"Bee, let me introduce you to our new chairman, Max Magnifico," Arthur announced. "And Max, this is Bee, our wonderful CEO."

"It's an absolute pleasure, Bee. I've heard so much about you," said Max.

She was immediately struck by how much more handsome and taller he was in person, around six foot two. His dark brown wavy hair was slicked back neatly around his tanned, freshly shaved face. His navy suit with slim-fit tapered trousers hung on him so perfectly that it just *had* to be custom-made. He wore a crisp white shirt, opened at the top, no tie and scuff-free brown lace-up brogues. He quite simply oozed 'rich'.

She held out her hand. "Pleasure to meet you too. It's great to have you on board finally."

He stepped forward, moving a bit too much into her personal space. She had the urge to step back but didn't give in to it. She got a waft of his cologne. It smelt familiar, maybe Terre D'Hermès.

"We're all really looking forward to working with you," she added.

He stared at her intensely with large dark brown eyes while performing a bone crusher handshake. Despite the painful squeeze, she felt the softness of his hand. *No washing up or gardening for this gladiator,* she thought.

When he released her hand and stepped back his eyes tightened. He examined her with a lingering stare that surprised her because it felt deliberately pervy. Usually, men tried to be more discreet when ogling. He then fixed his eyes on her pink Gucci slingbacks, tilted his head and narrowed his eyes further before giving a weird nod, as if he approved. Maybe he was expecting her to be a frump and was surprised by her eye for fashion. She mimicked his movements and stared down at his shoes then stepped back. "Great brogues," she said.

"Ah, a fellow shoeaholic." He laughed. Then he quickly ran his eyes over Stuart, who was standing next to Bee, before turning his back on them both.

"This is Stuart. My assistant," Bee said to the back of his head.

Max turned around and flashed an insincere smile, before saying, "Sorry, I didn't see you there." But Bee and Stuart knew he *had* seen him, of course he had.

"And these are Pradas," Stuart piped up.

Bee felt a blush coming on. *What an odd first exchange.* Her head was telling her, "*Here's the legendary investment banker we've all been hearing about for the last six months,*" but her gut was saying, "*Something's off.*" It was just an involuntary feeling she got.

She looked over at Arthur who had a puzzled look on his face. "Great, shall we begin?" he asked, a little uncertainly.

As they made their way to their seats, Stuart brushed past Bee and under his breath whispered into her ear, "He's a perve."

Exactly what she was thinking!

Chapter 4

One hour and twenty minutes into her Uber ride and Rosie was starting to feel nauseous. She had been intent on using the time wisely and spent most of it looking down at the iPad in her lap reading coverage about Hugo Hamilton. She opened the window for some fresh air. It felt warm and smelt salty.

While stationary at a red light, she took a moment to take in the beachside suburban vibe. A trio of tanned shirtless surfers with shaggy wet hair sat together on low stools at a cafe, drinking juices with their bikes and boards parked next to them. A couple of young mothers were chatting away in matching active wear, pushing their toddlers in matching buggies. A white van was delivering trays of fruit to the IGA store and two men who looked like real estate agents, only because they were wearing suits, stood on the corner talking. It intrigued Rosie how people enjoyed this kind of village life, so far from the city, with too much sand between their toes, everyone knowing each other's business. You wouldn't catch her living in suburbia. She was a city chick through and through.

As they pulled off at the green light Rosie asked the driver, "How much further is it?"

He didn't respond, not even when she asked again. Was he actually ignoring her? "Are you mad because I said no chit-chat when I got in? I'm just really busy with work right now and have a new client I'm about to meet."

She was rattling on now. So, when the driver didn't respond again she decided to tap him on the shoulder.

"Yes?" He appeared startled. "Please look at the sign," he replied in a throaty, monotone voice, pointing to a sign hanging off the back of his headrest.

It read *Dear Passenger, my name is Alex and I'm deaf. That means I can't hear you, but I'm a great lip reader so if you need to speak to me tap me on the shoulder once and wait until we've stopped. And don't bother shouting, because that doesn't work! Smiley face. Thank you.*

Rosie was embarrassed. The sign was there right in front of her face, and she hadn't noticed it. There were a lot of things she didn't notice as she multi-tasked and rushed from one client meeting to the next. It was starting to annoy her, just like how Bill and most of her needy clients were annoying her. In fact, she blamed work for almost everything right now, including her single status.

The driver slowed and turned right down a one-way street that opened up to a crescent-shaped bay of golden sands and turquoise ocean. There were Norfolk Pine trees to the right and high fences concealing the multi-million-dollar properties on the left. Coming to a stop, the driver turned to Rosie and said, "We're here. One hundred and twenty-five Ocean Road."

"Okay, thank you very much," she shouted, then remembered the 'don't shout' message on the headrest. She quickly gave a thumbs up instead. The driver smiled back appreciatively.

Stepping out onto the sandy street, she straightened her trousers and tried to brush out the stubborn creases with her hands. She retucked her singlet into the waistband of her trousers, shook her tousled bob and made her way up the crazy paved pathway to two big white gates. She pressed on the video buzzer next to the words *Big Daddy's House. Bit of a strange name for a home, but whatever.*

"Hello?" greeted a stern voice.

"Oh, hi, there. I'm Rosie Reid from Reid & Co Counsel," she called, leaning into the video intercom. She could see her reflection in the camera and noticed that she was frizzing from the humidity. There was no reply from the other end, just the sound of the intercom disconnecting and a long buzz followed by a click. Knowing she was no longer on camera, she did something she hated people doing—she licked her hand and slicked down the wayward strands of hair with her saliva.

The two white gates opened slowly to reveal a lush and meticulously manicured garden. Giant Strelitzias and palm trees created a canopy of shade over two landscapers standing on ladders trimming high bushes. Rosie felt like she was in a tropical retreat. If only she was heading for a massage instead of a meeting. The pathway led to a three-storey Hamptons-style house with white weatherboard cladding, large windows with white shutters and a pitched roof. As Rosie counted the windows, guessing how many bedrooms the house boasted, she saw a tiny grey-haired lady in casual chino trousers, a white t-shirt and apron coming towards her.

"Hi, Rosie. I'm Jocelyn, the Hamiltons' housekeeper. Let me take you through. Hugo is on the terrace."

Rosie followed Jocelyn and her squeaky plastic housekeeper shoes up large sandstone steps at the side of the house to a vast entertainment terrace that oozed 'wow' factor. *Now this could definitely be on Luxe Listings.* It easily measured one hundred square metres, larger than her apartment, and boasted sweeping views up and down Pittwater and the Ku-ring-gai Chase National Park.

She removed her Celine sunglasses from her bag and slipped them on. The bright sun was making her squint, or was it the lack of sleep?

She saw Hugo on the phone, so she quietly hooked her bag over the back of a rattan dining chair and continued to admire the view. A seaplane was taking off and another was coming in. Probably guests of the nearby Jonah's boutique hotel and restaurant. Her tired self fantasised about being on that seaplane for a split second.

Hugo looked over and silently mouthed "one second". Rosie gave a thumbs up. He was older and much fatter than his photo in last week's *Sydney Times* profile piece. His thinning hair was clown-like with fuzz on top and wispy bits on the sides and back of his head. His blue-and-white-striped linen shirt was a few sizes too small, the buttons at full stretch, struggling to contain the large stomach which hung over his navy chino shorts. Rosie was surprised how dishevelled and angry he looked. He sounded angry too. Maybe he thought he was talking quietly but she could hear every word of his conversation.

"I'm haemorrhaging money here. It needs to be open for business in two weeks or someone's gonna get it. Call the builder right now and tell him we're not gonna pay him unless he gets the job finished on time. I've got to go. I've got a PR fixer here to help shut down that slut that went to the papers. I'll call you back later."

Rosie tried not to look like she'd overheard the conversation. She hated being called a fixer. It was so demeaning to her profession. And slut? Wow. Things were not getting off to a good start.

"Sorry about that," Hugo said, making his way towards her. He wiped his sweaty hand on his shorts then held it out. "Good to meet you, Rosie." He removed his black Ray-Ban Wayfarers to reveal tired, bloodshot eyes with dark puffy circles. She got a waft of stale alcohol breath which reminded her of her ex after one of his big benders. She shivered.

"Great to meet you," she said, but what she really wanted to say was *"Hi, I'm the fixer. Now tell me about this young employee who you're calling a slut."* Through gritted teeth she added, "What an amazing home you have. You know I don't think I've actually ever been this far out of Sydney before. Now I'm here I can definitely see the appeal." It was a lie, of course. The only appeal of living so far out of the city was the killer view which she could never afford.

"Well, this is the family home. I have a penthouse in the city where I stay a lot of the time. You know, working strange hours isn't always that compatible with family life."

Rosie nodded, thinking *I bet. More like you want your wife at home and your mistress in the city.* If she had a dollar for every time a male client said that she would be a retired *fixer* living on a sprawling estate up in Byron Bay.

"Tea, coffee?" asked Jocelyn. She had been standing there the whole time but was so mouse-like that Rosie had forgotten about her.

"A still water is fine, thanks."

"Take a seat," Hugo said once Jocelyn had left, motioning to the chair where Rosie's bag hung. "Looks like you've already had your coffee," he smirked, moving his eyes to the coffee stain on her top.

His tone was dripping with sarcasm. And she found his smirk a little unkind. There was no need to make her feel self-conscious and sloppy.

"I want to start by saying this is a pack of lies; it never happened." He pointed at the papers that were strewn across the large teak dining table. "I want to go on the record and say it's all rubbish. And I want *you*"—he was now pointing at Rosie—"to run a smear campaign on that grubby tart and say she's just after my money."

Wow. It was straight down to business. No pleasantries or questions about how her morning had been so far. Fine. She was dying to get on with hearing his side of the story anyway. One of her strengths was her ability to allow the client to vent before making any comment on the situation at hand. Lesson number three for her interns: *"Let the client rant away and only when they have finished do you jump in and start providing counsel."*

Rosie also had an excellent radar for liars after covering up hundreds of lies over the years for her clients. She would make a brilliant juror if she was ever called for duty. *He did it,* she thought. He was already acting defensively, his neck was red and blotchy, and he was sweating, a lot.

"Okay, Hugo, let's just take a step back," she began calmly. "As you probably know, there's always the truth and then there's public opinion. I need to know what the truth is, so I can help manage the public opinion."

She wasn't sure by the look on Hugo's fat, sweaty face that she was calming him down, but she continued anyway.

"I don't like surprises. I need it all out in the open before we can start working together. So naturally, I've got to ask you if any small detail of what's been said is true."

Hugo's neck became redder; beads of sweat rolled down his forehead and dripped onto his shelf of a stomach. He grabbed a napkin from the fancy rattan holder on the table and patted his forehead. "Rosie, if you don't believe me then why did you come here? I need people around me that are going to do as I say, not question me." He banged his fist on the table.

She *had* annoyed him. That was now obvious. Perhaps he was used to having sycophants around that never dared question him—'yes' people— but that wasn't how she worked.

"I just don't like surprises, Hugo. And it doesn't matter whether *I* believe you or not; it's what the public thinks. I saw that you were the first contestant to be kicked out of *I'm a Celebrity Get Me Out of Here* in 2017. Why do you think that was?" she asked, knowing she might be skating on thin ice.

"Tall poppy syndrome. Jealousy," he replied with a narky tone. His brows furrowed and a scowl formed on his face. He crossed his arms, appearing irritated that Rosie had brought this subject up. "I just had a lot going on with the business at the time and to be honest I just wanted to get the fuck out of there, no pun intended. They were all lowbrow celebs, dumb arses that didn't hold my attention. Nobody of any real intellect."

Geez, no wonder he was kicked out. He reeked of arrogance and superiority. Rosie had read that his fellow contestants included a politician and author, a neuroscientist-turned-TV presenter and a former Olympic decathlete. Not exactly what you would call dumb arses.

"Now, the other thing that you're going to do"—he pointed his stubby fingers at Rosie again, and she didn't like it—"is get some photos out there of me with a huge packet on show."

"Sorry, I'm not following," she said. She did follow but couldn't believe that he was shifting the conversation to his "chipolata", as *it* had been described by his victim. This meeting was going from bad to worse.

He abruptly leapt out of his chair and angrily grabbed his crotch. "Packet, cock, dick."

Jesus. She was taken aback by the demonstration. She wanted him to stop. It was *way* too much for her sore, tired eyes. She glanced down at her fingers and wondered if *it* was as small as her pinkie, then looked back up. "I still don't understand what you're asking."

"For fuck's sake. I thought you were meant to be good at this stuff." He rolled his eyes, sat back down, then leaned across the table. "I assume you have Photoshop, so pad me up a bit down there and send the photos out to the press covering the story."

At that moment, Rosie heard footsteps and looked over to see a tall, slender woman striding towards them.

"Ah, here comes the wifey," said Hugo. *Wifey!* Rosie hated that word. It was so patronising.

As she approached, Rosie noticed how striking the woman was. She looked like a model from a P.E Nation Instagram campaign dressed in leopard-print cycling shorts, matching crop top, white ankle socks and black trainers. Her glossy caramel-coloured hair was scraped back into a tight bun and her features were hidden behind oversized black Dior sunglasses.

"Hi, there, I'm Lucy," she said in a high-pitched bubbly voice then removed her sunglasses to reveal the most dazzling sea foam green eyes and perfectly symmetrical face.

"Lovely to meet you," said Rosie. As she put her hand out to shake Lucy's, Lucy leaned in and kissed Rosie softly on the cheek.

"I prefer kisses to shakes," she giggled. "So what have I missed?"

As she slinked over to Hugo and bent down to peck him on the cheek, Rosie couldn't take her eyes off her perky butt and thigh gap.

"A crop top, darling! That's a bit young for you," he sniggered, while eyeing Lucy up and down. "And you've been ages. I thought you were just going to the gym?"

Lucy blushed, seemingly embarrassed by his snide comments in front of a stranger. "I had a trainer today, darling, so the session was longer."

"Well, I needed you here, goddamn it," he hissed, visibly cross.

To Rosie, their exchange felt strange—more like a father who was cross with a teenager daughter than a wife and husband.

"Well, I'm here now," said Lucy, while taking a seat at the head of the table to create a triangle between her, Rosie and Hugo.

They sat silently for a few moments. Rosie was surprised how relaxed Lucy appeared. If *she* was married to someone who had just been accused of sexual harassment, even if they were innocent, she would be tearing their eyeballs out, not casually strolling back in from the gym and pecking him on his chubby, sweaty cheek.

Maybe her calmness was spaciness from some kind of medication, like Zoloft or Xanax. That could be the only explanation. And why didn't she stick up for herself? She was rocking that crop top with washboard abs. Hugo was punching well above his weight.

"Okay, so this is what we're going to do." Rosie decided to cut through the silence. "We're going to put out a very bland statement. Something about how the allegations are unfounded and ..."

Come on, think, Rosie. She racked her brain over how on earth she could polish this turd. "And that if it comes to it, you will vigorously defend any claims. No TV or interviews for now. We just need to see how this all unfolds over the next few days."

There were *never* going to be any TV interviews for Hugo, certainly none that Rosie would organise. Because once the public saw what *she* saw, he would be done, cancelled. Thankfully, Hugo didn't challenge her on this decision.

Another long, awkward silence followed. Lucy stared into space while

Hugo looked like he had irritable bowel syndrome, shifting his weight from one fat sweaty cheek to the other.

"And then we will draft up some what we in the PR business call key messages that will help with conversations and questions you get from those around you," added Rosie.

"Key messages?" questioned Lucy. "Don't we just say to friends and family that it's all rubbish?"

"They're not really for talking to friends, it's more for randoms that might put you on the spot," Rosie clarified. "You're a high-profile couple and whether you like it or not you *will* get ambushed."

Another long silence. Hugo patted his head again with the napkin. Though it was thirty-five degrees in the city today, it felt like fifty degrees on this terrace. Rosie's throat was closing in the humidity and from the panic she was starting to feel about the work ahead of her. She gulped her iced water that had appeared without her noticing.

"Okay, okay, I think that sounds okay," said Hugo, scratching his bald head.

"Great. I'm going to get out of your way. I'll send a statement over shortly. And I'll need you to sign our terms of business and arrange a deposit for the estimated work. The usual stuff," Rosie explained.

"Of course," nodded Hugo as he pressed a button underneath the table. Like a modern-day servant's bell, it must have set off a sound in the house, because Jocelyn reported for duty in thirty seconds flat.

"Jocelyn will show you out," he said as he stood up, mopping his sweat beads once again with the soaked napkin he pulled from his pocket. Lucy moved over to stand alongside Hugo, perhaps to create the impression of a supportive wife. She smiled at Rosie, but behind those dazzling eyes something was definitely up. Rosie just didn't know what.

Chapter 5

Lucy left Hugo on the terrace shouting at a builder on the phone. She needed to escape from him until she got her head straight. Despite pretending everything was fine, she was in shock and still processing everything that had unfolded in the last twelve hours.

The call came in at around 7pm the previous night from Cecilia Meadows at the *Daily Life*. It was just her and Hugo at home. Their eldest daughter, Fleur, was at university and rarely came home these days. Their youngest, Maya, had gone back to high school that Sunday afternoon, ready to start her school week. As a weekly boarder at one of Sydney's elite private schools, she only came home at weekends.

Hugo was sitting on a bar stool at the long marble kitchen bench watching Lucy pour them both a glass of their favourite Shiraz.

She tutted when his phone rang. "Who's calling now?" she muttered, turning to the stove.

"Dunno. I don't recognise the number," Hugo said. He answered the call on speaker mode and Lucy could just about make out the faint female voice over the bubbling Bolognese sauce she was heating up for dinner.

"Hugo, this is Cecilia Meadows from the *Daily Life*. I'm sorry to disturb you on a Sunday evening. I won't take up too much of your time."

Lucy assumed the journalist was calling about another puff piece on Hugo's new bar in Surry Hills. Hugo appeared to be thinking the same because he cockily looked over at her. He rolled his eyes, and she laughed before ducking into the pantry to fetch some pasta.

"I'll cut right to the chase, Hugo. I'm writing a piece on a sexual harassment claim by one of your former employees," announced Cecilia.

Lucy overheard the full sentence, but it was the words "sexual harassment" that had pricked her ears up. She instantly stopped the rustling of pasta packets, quietly shifted on her toes and turned her head towards the pantry's entrance to hear more clearly.

"We've been advised that a staff member who left your employment about six months ago is alleging you acted inappropriately towards her. Her name is Indie Thomas, if that helps jog your memory."

Frozen and silent, Lucy didn't dare to take a breath.

"Hello, are you still there?" asked Cecilia.

It was rare for Hugo to be lost for words, so Lucy knew he was rattled. He cleared his throat. "Yes."

"We're gonna run the story in tomorrow's paper. This is a courtesy call to let you know and to ask if you'd like to make any comment?" Cecilia offered.

It was a bit late for Hugo to rustle up any decent comment and Cecilia would have known this, which was precisely why she had left the call to a Sunday evening. Knowing how impulsive and rude Hugo could be, Lucy wanted to dive out of the pantry and grab the phone to ensure he didn't say anything stupid. She knew from her pre-kids' career as a TV presenter not to get sucked in by a reporter's ambush strategy. Even the most media-savvy politicians could be caught out by a good old-fashioned ambush.

"You've caught me in a meeting," lied Hugo. "This is clearly very serious, so I'm going to have to get back to you. Give me thirty minutes, please."

Phew. A sensible reply. Lucy knew Cecilia would be sitting on the other end of the phone either recording or typing any words uttered. The journalists she worked with in the past took enormous pride in trapping their subject.

"It can't be any longer than thirty minutes, Hugo," Cecilia said firmly. "We're on deadline."

"Thank you. Thirty minutes. I'll call back."

Lucy detected panic in his voice but hoped Cecilia hadn't.

After the call ended, she remained frozen like a statue. Could she just hide in the pantry and pretend this situation wasn't actually happening?

Hugo called out, "Lucy. Lucy, come out here."

She quickly grabbed two bags of pasta from the shelf and shuffled tentatively out of the pantry and towards the kitchen bench. She set both packets down in front of Hugo and asked, "Which one do you fancy? Penne or spirals?" She didn't know why she asked. It was a stupid question.

"I don't fucking care about the pasta," shouted Hugo. "Didn't you hear any of that conversation?" He stood up from the bar stool and his eyes tightened under the brightness of the rattan pendant light hanging inches from his head. His stance was gorilla-like with fists clenched and he hunched over, nostrils flaring, pot belly at full puff.

He didn't scare Lucy. She was used to this angry behaviour. He spent most of his life shouting, whether at her, the kids, his staff, the builders or someone else. The only person he didn't shout at was his *mummy*. Such a mummy's boy.

"Wait. Are you sure you hung up? Check before you say anything else," Lucy asked, panicked. She'd had one of those *'think you've hung up, but you haven't'* experiences with a friend and been paranoid ever since.

Hugo grabbed the phone, checked it by pressing the screen multiple times with his index finger and tossed it back on the kitchen bench. "It's fine."

Lucy looked at him. He was starting to sweat, which was standard for him in summer. Actually, it was standard for him in winter too since he'd packed on the weight.

"Why are you staring at me like that?" Hugo asked sharply.

"I'm not staring at you like anything." She looked down at the bag of spiral pasta to break the stare.

"This is bloody outrageous. Someone's out to get me. Who is this Indie Thomas? I can't even remember us hiring anyone with that name." His face had turned red and blotchy, and two large veins throbbed in his neck.

Lucy walked over to the utensils drawer and pulled out a pair of scissors. She came back to the bench and cut open the bag of penne. "I think we'll have this one." Another dumb thing to say, but she was actually lost for words.

"You know it's bullshit, right, Lucy? Jesus. You don't believe her, do you? You've gone all quiet and weird. Lucy. Look at me."

Of course she had gone quiet. What did he expect? It's a bit hard to act normally after a call like that. Did she believe him? How did she know? She had no context, no story, just those words "sexual harassment" ringing in her head. Just five minutes ago she was only interested in what she was having for dinner. Now her heart was pounding. It was an unusual feeling because, since she began taking anti-depressants three years ago, her heart rarely pounded. The drugs numbed her, which was precisely the effect she was going for after years of feeling panicky and treading on eggshells around Hugo.

But there was no numbing this situation. It was what they call an out-of-body experience, where a person no longer feels part of their surroundings. Her own kitchen felt foreign, the lights seemed brighter, and the floor moved like she was out at sea. She gripped hold of the kitchen bench and steadied herself, looking across at Hugo. He suddenly felt like a stranger. Of course she wanted to believe him, she really did, but there was something in the way he looked at her that only a wife of twenty years can see in a partner's eyes. He was really, really, angry. And possibly guilty. No, *very* possibly. She reached for her glass of Shiraz and downed it in one then topped herself up and downed the second glass. She exhaled all the air in her body, audibly, and wiped the red wine residue from the sides of her lips.

"Lucy. Come on, Lucy. We need clear heads. Not pissed ones," he boomed, taking the glass from her hand and placing it on the bench. She hated the way he did things like that—treating her like a child, deciding when she'd had enough to drink. He controlled every aspect of her life from what she drank to where she lived, her weekly allowance and what she wore—when he was actually around, that was.

She'd been fiercely independent when she had met him and, at the time, that was what he loved about her. But it all changed when the girls were born and he, coming from a very 1950s' upbringing, decided she should be at home.

She went back over to the cooktop and turned the gas knob off, leaving the Bolognese in the saucepan to cool down. She had, naturally, completely lost her appetite.

"What are we going to do? What do we do in a bullshit situation like this?" he shouted. He started pacing around the kitchen with his hands clasped behind his head, revealing large sweat patches under his armpits. He was breathing more heavily, almost out of breath now.

Yes, what are we going to do? Lucy thought. The reality of this PR disaster was setting in. Who believes a middle-aged white guy accused of harassing a young female employee these days even if they *are* innocent? Er, maybe only another middle-aged white guy. With her TV head on she knew that this Cecilia Meadows *Daily Life* article would be great fodder for the entertainment news or the morning news programs. Then there was social media and all the comments that come with that. What will people say? Their friends, the office, her parents? Oh God, the kids, the kids, the kids!

"Babe, we need to tell the kids. Like *now*," she panicked. Her heart pounded faster.

"Not yet," said Hugo, tersely. "I'll call Max. He'll know what to do. Yeah, that's what I'll do. Wait here."

With that, he went outside to the terrace to make the call. She noticed how he had deliberately closed the doors behind him so she couldn't hear. It was a move that made him appear guilty because those bi-fold doors *always* stayed open on a balmy summer's night.

She watched intently as he leaned over the white wooden balustrade, holding the phone tightly to his ear. A long trail of sweat running the length of his shirt was growing by the second as he became more animated, throwing his left arm in the air emphatically. He glanced back over his shoulder to check where she was, appearing concerned that she might have edged closer to within hearing distance.

The call lasted ten minutes. When he came back into the kitchen, his breathing was still heavy, and he was even sweatier. He reinstalled himself at the kitchen bench and began frantically scrolling on his phone.

"What did Max say?" asked Lucy softly, trying to restore some calm.

"He's given me the number of this spin doctor. Everyone calls her 'the fixer', apparently."

"What kind of fixer? I don't think this is something that can just be fixed," Lucy said meekly, knowing full well it would get right up Hugo's nose.

Sure enough, Hugo's eyes widened and he tutted loudly. "Well, she bloody well better be able to fix this one otherwise I'm fucked. Anyway, why don't you just have another wine while I deal with this. You're obviously already drunk and of no use to me."

He pushed her wine glass across the kitchen bench. So now she *was* allowed it!

I'm fucked, he'd said. How about *we're* fucked! He was just thinking about himself, as usual. All Lucy could think about was Maya and how she would be teased at school. Teenage girls could be such bitches. Fleur would probably be fine because girls had usually outgrown their bitchiness by the time they got to university.

One thing was for sure—Lucy's friends would have a field day because they had always detested Hugo. Now they had good reason to say, "I told you so." Between worrying about their reactions, her girls and Googling Indie Thomas, she didn't get a wink of sleep.

At 5am she decided to head out to the dog park in her black Range Rover with blacked-out windows, wearing her biggest black sunglasses, with Beano, their cavoodle, in the front seat.

It was still dark when she arrived and plonked herself down on the green park bench overlooking the ocean. Usually so upright and aware of her posture, she sat hunched over with her hands tucked under her legs, staring out at the dark, eerie water. While Beano darted around chasing wild rabbits, she cried and cried and cried. She had given herself permission to cry until sunrise. Once the sun was up, she was going to put her game face on, meet with this PR fixer that Hugo had hired, then drive to Maya's school and explain everything. But right then, in that moment, she wanted to disappear.

She was abruptly pulled out of that dark thought when she felt a tap on her shoulder. Instantly, she jumped to her feet. "Oh my God."

"I'm so sorry. Are you okay? I didn't mean to startle you," the stranger said. Lucy began frantically rubbing the tears away, snapping back to reality and aware of the fact that she was a complete mess.

"You're shaking. You poor thing. Sit back down, please, sit back down," she said with her hand on Lucy's shoulder. "I don't have any tissues but I've got a napkin here in this dog bag. Here, take it." She pulled out a light brown napkin from the small bag that hung across her body, handed it to Lucy, then knelt beside the bench and smiled at her. It was a kind smile.

"Thank you," Lucy sniffed.

"Excuse me, excuse me. Are you going to do anything about this mess over here?" shouted a voice in the background.

"Stay there, I'll be right back," said the stranger to Lucy.

Lucy could hear the two voices in some kind of disagreement and turned around to see what was happening. "I know the dog has done a poo. I was just about to pick it up so there's no need to take that tone," said the kind stranger.

"People like you give this dog park a bad name. Come on, Fergus," the other woman said as she stormed off with her black miniature schnauzer trailing behind.

Lucy watched the stranger as she deposited the dog poo into the bin at the corner of the park. She was dressed in black active wear and black Stüssy cap.

"Sorry about that. What a bitch. I was about to get that poo. I think it was your dog, not that it matters," she huffed.

"Oh gosh, sorry. I'm so sorry. I was a million miles away," Lucy said.

"Honestly, don't worry about it." She waved her hand then took a seat next to Lucy on the bench. "Now that nutter's gone, are you okay? Is there anything I can do?"

"I'm fine, thanks," Lucy lied. "I just haven't slept at all." She lifted her sunglasses up, resting them on top of her head. Obviously this stranger would never believe her eyes were puffed from lack of sleep because she had heard her crying. "I need some cucumbers to get rid of these bags," she joked.

"Or teaspoons."

"Teaspoons?"

"Yeah. Haven't you heard of that hack before? Put two teaspoons in the freezer overnight and in the morning, you press them against your eyes for a few minutes," she said demonstrating with her two hands placed under her own eyes. "It's genius. My mum taught me. Try it out."

"I will. Thanks for that." Lucy felt her spirits lighten just a little. "I'm Lucy. Lucy Love."

"Bee. Bee Bloom," she mimicked, which made Lucy chuckle.

"That's a gorgeous name."

"Thank you. Yours too. And who's this?" asked Bee as she patted Lucy's cavoodle.

"That's Beano. I bought him for some company at home." Lucy didn't know why she had blurted out to this complete stranger that she needed company. She immediately felt embarrassed.

Fortunately, Bee didn't pick up on it and just said, "Well, he is totally gorgeous."

"And yours?" asked Lucy.

"Ah, that's Garry. Gazza or Gaz. He's our boxer, cross lab, cross something else, we think. The kids kept asking for a dog, but I just felt bad getting one because we're out of the house so much with work and sport on weekends. Anyway, we've made it work."

Lucy watched as Bee affectionately grabbed Garry's face in her hands and shook it around, making the dog release drops of white foam-like dribble onto her black leggings. "Er, yuck," she said trying to wipe it off. "Ugh, I'll worry about this later. Do you drink coffee, Lucy?"

"Yes."

"What can I get you?" Bee asked, pointing in the direction of a yellow van parked twenty metres away with Mug Shot in black squiggly writing on the side.

"I'd love an oat flat white, please. Let me give you some cash." Lucy reached into the side pockets of her cycling shorts, quickly realising she didn't have any cash because she had left the house in such a rush.

But she needn't have worried because Bee was already striding towards the coffee van. Lucy liked this Bee woman. She had a manner that was completely disarming. And she was kind.

Garry and Beano had struck up their own doggie friendship and were happily playing chase, Garry running off with a stick between big dribbling jaws and Beano chasing behind.

Lucy looked at her phone. There was no message from Hugo. He was probably still fast asleep on the sofa. And she assumed that her family and friends hadn't seen the *Daily Life* article yet, but in two hours it would be everywhere, and she would be inundated with calls. The thought filled her with dread. She felt the tingle of panic in her hands and her eyes fill up again with tears.

"Here you go," said Bee, handing Lucy her coffee.

"Thank you so much. I need this," Lucy sniffed, wiping her nose with the napkin.

Bee sat back down next to Lucy and leaned forward with her hands on her knees so she could see Lucy's face fully.

"Is there anything I can help you with? I mean, I know I'm just a random at a dog park, but I'm a good listener if you'd like to talk. No pressure." Bee smiled softly, her round eyes fixed on Lucy.

Lucy lifted her shaking right hand up to her mouth to take a sip of coffee.

"You're still shaking. Wait here. I've got a hoodie in the car, let me get it for you." A couple of minutes later Bee returned with a large black Rip Curl hoodie. "It's my son's so it might be a bit smelly, sorry," Bee said, sniffing the hoodie before passing it to Lucy.

Lucy put her sunglasses and coffee cup down on the bench and pulled the hoodie over her head.

"It suits you," joked Bee. Lucy laughed and took another sip of her coffee. As they sat on the bench drinking their coffees, Lucy looked back out to the horizon while Bee threw the stick for the dogs.

Lucy didn't feel the need to speak. It was a comfortable silence.

After about five minutes Bee said, "Look, Lucy. I'm so sorry but I have to get going. I have an 8am meeting in the city and obviously still need to get dressed," pointing at her active wear.

"Of course. Thank you so much for the coffee and for …"—Lucy paused—"for listening and caring. I don't think anyone's asked how I feel for a long time." Lucy surprised herself again how easily she divulged this intimate detail. This time, Bee picked up on the comment.

"Listen, Lucy." Bee crouched down in front of Lucy, resting her hands on Lucy's knees. She looked up at her face. "I hate seeing people cry. I just get this compulsion to help in some way. I'm not sure why." She looked up to the sky, reflecting on that thought. "Maybe I'll ask my therapist about that one." She laughed. "But like I said, I'm a good listener so I'm going to put my number in your phone and I implore you to call me if you need to talk."

This act of kindness was too much for Lucy and she immediately burst into tears. "I'm sorry, so silly of me ... I just ... I just ..." she blubbered, not able to finish her sentence.

"No, don't be. Please." This time Bee went in for a hug and Lucy hugged her back. They held the embrace for at least thirty seconds while Lucy cried into Bee's shoulder. When Lucy felt strong enough to peel her head off Bee's shoulder, she thanked her and brushed away the tears with her napkin, which was now soaked and rapidly disintegrating.

Bee entered her details into Lucy's phone then said, "Take a deep breath, do a lap of the park, maybe even stop by the water fountain and splash some water on that gorgeous face of yours. Okay?" She held Lucy by the elbows, gently shook her and stared deep into her eyes.

"Okay, yes, okay," Lucy agreed.

Bee gave her one last hug then walked away, beckoning Garry. Lucy watched as she started her car and noticed the window go down. She could see Bee was yelling something but couldn't quite make it out.

"Pardon?" Lucy called out and Bee shouted back, "Teaspoons."

Lucy gave a thumbs up and smiled as Bee drove off. *Could this be a new friend*, she wondered? She didn't want to come across as a stalker, but she was definitely going to call Bee. After all, she *had* offered. A bright orange sun was now beating down on her. She suddenly felt hot and realised she was still wearing Bee's hoodie. A warm smile crossed her face when she considered how she now had a perfect excuse to see

Bee again. Then, in an instant, her smile turned to a grimace when she thought about going home. Oh, how she would love an excuse to hide from Hugo all day. *Maybe one more coffee before facing the music*, she thought.

As Lucy walked into the kitchen after Rosie left, she could still hear Hugo shouting on the phone. God, even the neighbours could probably hear him. Everything was exactly as she had left it last night after the call—the hardened Bolognese sauce in the saucepan, the penne and spiral pasta packets on the kitchen bench, and two empty wine glasses next to them. It was a small mess really, but she knew Hugo would complain that she hadn't cleaned it up yet.

She would do it later. First, a shower. She went upstairs into her en-suite, locking the door so Hugo couldn't try and have sex with her. It was *her* en-suite, not *theirs*. He had a bathroom all of his own where he displayed his expensive beauty creams and serums. They had to be lined up perfectly, all facing forward. For someone who didn't care what he ate, drank or shoved up his nose it amused Lucy how he cared disproportionately about his skin care regime. And his exceptionally high standards for tidiness around the house were a stark contrast to his scruffy personal appearance.

Lucy looked at herself in the large mirror hanging over the double vanity. Her bloodshot eyes didn't look like her own. She felt hungover, despite only drinking two glasses of wine last night. Normally, when Hugo wasn't around, she would easily polish off two bottles by herself. She considered whether it was actually exhaustion rather than a hangover that was affecting her today. After all, she hadn't managed to get a wink of sleep.

She popped one of her anti-depressants out from the packet and knocked it back with a handful of tap water. *Maybe another to get through today?* She looked back down at the packet and decided that increasing her dosage probably wasn't the best idea without her therapist's approval. Her clinical depression was a secret between her and her therapist. Hugo couldn't know because he lacked understanding and empathy towards mental health issues, often saying people struggling just need to "snap out of it". And her friends didn't know because having the condition was at odds with her former bubbly self. *"What, you? No way?"* they would say for sure. *"What do you have to be depressed about?"* They assumed she was living her best life, in her fancy house on the Northern Beaches, not needing to work with all the money in the world. But maybe if they actually asked her how she was doing, she might give them the *real* version of her life.

She tossed her gym outfit into the wicker basket under the vanity, not that it needed washing because, despite telling Hugo she'd been to the gym, she hadn't been anywhere near it. After reading the horrendous *Daily Life* article, how could she show her face at the gym? Or anywhere, for that matter. She wondered how others would perceive her, whether they would cast sympathetic glances her way as 'the poor wife', or if they would instead label her a fool, assuming she had been aware of her husband's actions all along. Either way, she couldn't step foot outside. She was a prisoner in her own home.

Turning to the side, she gazed at the silhouette of her naked body in the mirror. As she ran her hands over her stomach, a wave of self-consciousness washed over her, triggered by Hugo's hurtful comments about her crop top. They were particularly hurtful given they were made in front of a stranger. And what did he know? The sales assistant at P.E Nation had said with a body like hers she could get away with anything from the new collection. *And* who the fuck was he to talk, sitting there like Jabba the Hutt. Frustration welled up inside her as she tightly clenched her fists, questioning why she had been so silent lately. The woman she used to be would never have allowed herself to remain voiceless, and she yearned to resurrect that resilient and empowered version of herself.

Chapter 6

Bee clicked to the next page of the presentation displayed on the large screen at the end of the boardroom table. She was over halfway through the section on 'outlook for the next quarter' and, so far, Max had not made one single comment. Pretty odd, given his whole *raison d'être* was future business opportunities. She was starting to think he wasn't paying attention.

He had nipped out once to take a call, and he'd checked his phone more than three times. On the occasion when he did look Bee's way, he drummed his fingers slowly and audibly on the table, giving her a sense of impatience. And his expression wasn't one of interest; it was a puzzled stare that made her feel like she had something stuck between her teeth. She moved her tongue around her teeth to check, just in case.

When Max put his head down to check his phone for the fourth time Bee had had enough.

"I think I'll just pause there for a moment and see if Max has any questions." That presentation had taken her and four of her staff a week to pull together, so he better start showing some respect.

Max lifted his eyes, looked at Bee, paused, then looked at the screen. "I don't really have any questions as such, but I do have more general comments. It's just a matter of whether you would like them now or at the end?" he asked as he tossed his iPhone down in front of him.

After all those years working overseas, Max's accent was only faintly Australian. His pitch was low and his tone silky smooth. You could say it was a voice made for radio.

Bee's voice coach once told her that a lower voice adds credibility to leadership, which is why some women with high-pitched voices are told to go low. *"I'm not saying become Elizabeth Holmes, but just take it down a notch,"* she had coached her.

"I think we'd be happy to hear them now, wouldn't we, Arthur?" suggested Bee as she glanced over at the older man.

"Yes, go ahead," Arthur agreed.

Max stood up from his chair and turned his back on the table. He stared out of the floor-to-ceiling glass windows overlooking the harbour and put his hands in his slim-fit trouser pockets. This was his infamous gladiator stance that Bee had seen in photos online—feet wide apart, butt tightly clenched, biceps flexed and chest puffed. He then turned back to face the table and, not looking at anyone in particular, said, "I have two words— tougher and expand. Let me explain."

"Please do," interjected Bee.

"We're not aggressive enough." He paused for a moment. "I think we're losing out on business simply because we're not tough enough." His gaze turned to Bee. "We need to be tougher."

He unfolded his arms and ran his fingers through his thick hair to brush back the strands that had strayed onto his forehead. He certainly fancied himself. Bee shifted on her seat. *He finally speaks and it's a jibe.* She would never start with a negative. It's just bad manners.

"Would you like to expand on that?" she asked, shooting a steely stare his way.

"I've just had some early feedback. From old friends. Contacts. You know. People in the market telling me that we're too soft."

Bee sat forward and tucked her chair in tightly under the table. She didn't like where this was going. She placed one hand over the other, sat so upright she could feel her spine stretch and pulled her shoulders back. It was a *commanding* position taught by her body language coach.

"Do you want to share some of the names? I might know them." She had an inkling he was bluffing. Why even say that if you're not going to share your source?

"I doubt it. Anyway, let's stick to the point I'm making," Max said, returning to his seat opposite Bee. "We. Need. To. Be. Tougher."

Bee felt her heart begin to beat a little faster and a slight dryness in her throat. It reminded her of how she used to feel in the early days of her career. She swished the remaining drops of saliva around in her mouth and swallowed. She didn't want Max to think she was nervous or that she was irked by his comments, but it was hard not to take the "we're too soft" personally.

"This is 2022, Max. And organisations need to be more considered." Bee took a breath. She didn't want to sound defensive either, even if she was feeling that way. "We've built Curban Capital on the values of kindness, respect and integrity. We, frankly, don't want to be seen as tough."

She glanced around the board table, hoping for back-up. Rudy Chalmers, one of the longer-serving members, began flicking awkwardly through his ring-bound papers. Sandra Saunders, in her bobbly faux Chanel jacket, was scribbling notes, presumably to avoid eye contact. Arthur was twisting his silver ballpoint pen around in his hands, looking vacant, probably wondering when morning tea would be served. Stuart sat with his mouth open, staring blankly at Bee.

They were saved by a knock at the door. Davide entered followed by two of his wait staff dressed in a uniform of black trousers, grey shirt, black waistcoat and black tie.

"Is it that time already?" Arthur said, seemingly breathing a sigh of relief.

Bee sat back in her chair and folded her arms, watching Davide as he walked towards the table with a tray full of pastries.

"Oh yum, Davide, I see you brought my favourite. Chocolate croissants." Arthur beamed, licking his lips.

"But of course. We aim to please," said Davide with a wide grin.

Stuart groaned audibly from the end of the table.

Arthur called out from the opposite end of the table, "Are we boring you, Stuart?"

"Nope, all good, just taking a breath."

Davide made a 'ha ha' face at Stuart then continued placing the tray in front of Arthur while the two waiters began taking coffee orders.

Bee knew it was best to order a chamomile tea, given how edgy she was feeling, but couldn't resist another flat white. Tiredness was creeping in. She was up late last night putting the finishing touches to a different strategy presentation for Max. Now she wished she hadn't bothered. "Flat white. Large. Please."

Stuart looked over at Bee with a concerned look on his face knowing that she was now well and truly over her daily caffeine quota.

Bee listened for Max's order. *Bet it's European style, no milk.*

"Double shot espresso, please."

She was right.

"And do you have any almonds?" he asked the waiter without looking at him. "If not, can you ask my assistant to bring some in, please. Ten to be exact. And they need to be activated."

The waiter crumpled his nose then moved on.

Bee had read about Max's extreme dieting in his memoir, *Whatever It Takes*. If he wasn't fasting for sixteen hours a day, he was off dairy, meat and sugar. His daily exercise regime was just as extreme. A cardio workout followed by a thirty-minute weights session with a well-known personal trainer to the stars. Even his holidays were extreme: heli-skiing in Aspen, grand prix driving in Monaco, diving with great whites in South Africa, sky diving in New Zealand. No beach holidays for this high-flyer.

"Let's keep going," Arthur mumbled through puffed-up hamster cheeks, filled to the brim with chocolate croissant. Bee hated people talking with their mouths full. She shot Arthur her best disgusted look, which he either didn't understand or chose to ignore.

"I think Max needs to talk us through his second word—expand," scoffed Bee.

This better not be another dig.

"Max, five minutes only, please," said Arthur. "We must keep going after that otherwise we're going to run over time."

There was no way Arthur would let the agenda run behind. He ran a very tight ship and always had important networking lunches to get to.

"Sure," said Max, scanning each board member to ensure their eyes were on him. "Expand. What do I mean by expand?"

As she watched Max, Bee had to admit that it was more than his silky radio voice that captured people's attention. It was his presence, the way he sat, so comfortable in his skin and confidently talked off the cuff.

"We need to set Curban Capital up for the future. We need to broaden our client base. Our current focus is way too narrow. We're missing out on great opportunities in oil, gas, casinos. You know?"

"And there's a reason for that," Bee quickly interrupted. "We focus on clients that run environmentally or socially responsible companies. So, unless we're changing the whole premise of what we do then I don't see how, or why, for that matter, we would *expand*." Bee made air quotes as she said the word.

There wasn't a peep. All Bee could hear was deep breathing, croissant munching, coffee sipping, paper shuffling, pen tapping and sniffing from around the table.

"Arthur, is there something I'm missing?" she demanded. She didn't care that she was starting to sound cross because the very core of the company she oversaw was being questioned.

"Bee." Arthur gave one ahem and then another. "Max is here to build on our successes. And that means grow the business and bring in new clients."

"I understand that, Arthur. But I was led to believe that 'grow business'"—she repeated the air quotes—"meant build on what we already have, not completely change ...”

It was Arthur's turn to interrupt now. “Bee, let's take this one offline.”

'Take offline' was a term used in meetings, meaning the matter should be discussed later and privately in a smaller group. Bee hated it, along with a whole raft of other meeting lingo, like 'run it up the flagpole'.

“And make it soon, please, Arthur.”

“Yes, Bee,” Arthur said in a lowered, almost patronising tone. “Next item: people and culture,” he continued.

Suddenly Bee got the feeling that Max and Arthur might have been having side meetings without her, because Arthur didn't seem that surprised by Max's out-of-the-box comments. Had they been chatting strategy, without her, prior to him arriving in Australia? Something wasn't right. The words from the email played in her mind—“watch your back”.

She studied Arthur and noticed he had a big chocolate smudge at the side of his mouth. She dabbed the side of her own mouth to drop him a hint, but he was oblivious. He did tend to lack self-awareness.

“I have some comments I would like to make, please. On people, that is,” said Max.

Bee resumed her commanding position. “About them needing to be tough?”

“That can wait. I want to talk about the man on reception.”

“Who, Davide? He's fantastic, isn't he?” said Arthur.

“He might be that, Arthur, but I don't think the reception is the best place for him. He needs to be redistributed, immediately.”

“And why's that?” retorted Arthur.

“Face doesn't fit. Clients should be greeted by a woman, simple. And it shouldn't be too hard to fix. You know, I've always found ex-trolley dollies make excellent receptionists and there's surely still some out of work after COVID.”

Bee was astounded. Had he really just said that? She glanced over at Stuart who was catching flies with his mouth wide open and fingers frozen, unable to type the words into the minutes. There was another knock at the boardroom door. Davide reentered with a small glass jar. He handed it to Max. "Your almonds."

Max looked at the jar, checked the contents, and nodded. "Thank you, Daniel," he said, without looking at Davide.

The room fell silent as the two waiters went around the table serving everyone with their coffees. Nobody dared look at Davide, except Bee. She watched as he stood at the door supervising his wait staff. He was a true perfectionist and prided himself on having exceptionally high standards. If those waiters got just one coffee order wrong, he would berate them in the kitchen galley afterwards. Once coffees were served, the waiters left the room followed by Davide, who closed the double doors behind him.

"They're referred to as cabin crew, Max. Have been for a very long time," Bee said through frowning brows. "And the lovely, super-efficient, extremely well-regarded employee that just delivered your almonds is Davide, not Daniel. Isn't that right, Arthur?" She moved her eyes to Arthur.

"Yes, yes, it is. However, I think it's best we take that one offline too, please, Max," said Arthur, obviously not wanting to take Max on in public.

But Bee thought Max's comment should be discussed now, by everyone. After all, it was discriminatory, and the board members had a responsibility to govern a workplace free of discrimination. Bee eyeballed each board member around the table. Didn't anyone, even Sandra Saunders in her bobbly jacket, want to make a comment?

It seemed not. Everyone was happy brushing the comment under the carpet where lots of difficult topics went. Were they afraid to question Max? Were they too in awe of this powerful enigma they'd all heard so much about and who now sat across the board table from them?

Bee couldn't allow herself to fear him, not for one moment. She had made a promise to herself never to be scared again after enduring Ben Taggart. Now he had been a complete and utter psychopath. And much to her disappointment, it was starting to look like Max was one too. *Sigh.*

Chapter 7

Lucy: Hi Bee, it's Lucy from this morning. I just wanted to say thank you again. So kind of you. I owe you!

Bee: Hi Lucy. All good. You don't owe me. Hope you're ok, or at least feeling a bit better. ☺

Lucy: I owe you a coffee at the very least.

Bee: Maybe a wine instead? 😏

Lucy: Done! ☺

Bee: I'll send some dates & times later. Busy week I'm afraid. 😬

Lucy: 🥂

Lucy was over-caffeinated. She could tell from the way she was acting. A bit hyper and a bit twitchy. Just like alcohol can make you do things you wouldn't normally do, she felt like the caffeine and her temporary hyper mood had urged her on to text Bee. Reading Bee's emoji-rich, light-hearted texts, she liked her even more. She knew she should be making her way over to Maya's school right now for the dreaded conversation about Hugo and his harassment drama but couldn't resist a quick Google search on Bee. Another fifteen minutes wouldn't hurt. She set her laptop down on the kitchen bench, pulled up a bar stool and began.

Wow, wow, wow. Right away multiple pictures of Bee appeared. Oh, where to start?

Wikipedia: Bee Bloom (born 1978) is a British banking executive and the chief executive officer (CEO) of Curban Capital, a position she has held since 2017. Children: 2. Partner: Gus Bloom (m-2008).

She scrolled through the photos which were mostly of Bee in corporate shots—at the office, outside the office, arms folded, arms by her side, looking at the camera, looking to the side, sitting next to a bunch of men on a stage with a Madonna microphone hanging off her ear. Lucy zoomed in on some of the photos hoping to find imperfections—a terrible pair of shoes, a spot on the chin, a stain on the dress—but there were none. Bee looked bloomin' incredible in every single photo. Great style, great skin, good teeth and *so* beautiful. She had noticed how naturally pretty she was this morning, with a make-up free face and hair tied back in a scruffy low ponytail, but in some of these photos, all dressed up with make-up on, she looked like a movie star.

Wow, wow, wow, she thought again. *Kind* and *a power bitch*.

Next, Lucy Googled *Bee Bloom Family* and found an old *Financial Report* interview from 2019. *Bee Bloom: Women lead differently to men. Bee Bloom is often cited as one of the most powerful women in banking. She tells* The Financial Report's *Jenny Wallis how women lead differently from their male counterparts.*

Lucy zoomed in on a quote that caught her eye.

"Women are generally much more empathetic and focused on creating supportive cultures. They bring a certain level of emotional intelligence and lead with kindness."

Hugo could do with taking a leaf out of Bee's book. He most definitely lacked emotional intelligence, choosing to lead like a dictator. Despite Lucy's attempts to persuade him on multiple occasions to be more considerate towards his staff, his dismissive response was always, "What would you know?"

At that moment, Lucy was startled by a tap on the shoulder. "Shit." It was him.

"What you up to?" he asked, looking over her shoulder towards her screen.

"Nothing." She snapped the laptop closed.

"Oh yeah? I don't believe you." He nudged her out of the way and reopened the laptop. "Who's this you're looking up? Bee Bloom? Let me guess, one of those token corporate females," he sniggered.

"Why would you even say that?" God, she hated the way he was always so quick to diminish successful women. He couldn't just say something positive.

Hugo inched closer towards the laptop. "Curban Capital. That's where Max has just landed." He stepped back and walked around the bench to the sink, ran the tap, pumped the Aesop hand wash twice and began washing his hands.

"Who, Max Magnifico?" asked Lucy.

Hugo exhaled loudly. "Yes, darling." His tone was condescending. It was a familiar tone of late and she was getting sick and tired of it. She couldn't remember how long ago it started, but he seemed to huff and puff at most of her questions these days. And he was always making snide remarks like, *"Blimey, Lucy, this room is so messy it's like we've been robbed"* or *"What on earth have you been doing all day?"* It was *always* about slighting her. He *could* ask some of his questions in a less demeaning way but that wouldn't achieve the desired impact. He wanted to make her feel useless. She *did* fill her days with general *stuff,* but it was a lonely existence so far out of the city. It was *his* idea to buy a family home in suburbia and it was *his* idea to pack the girls off to boarding school from the age of five. If only the girls had gone to a local public school, then she would have met local mums and enjoyed mums' nights out at the local Thai instead of ordering takeaway for one. She ate breakfast, lunch and dinner alone from Monday to Thursday. Sure, she had Jocelyn, her little wiry super-efficient housekeeper, but Jocelyn was intent on keeping their relationship strictly professional, never wanting to sit at the kitchen bench and chat over coffee.

Hugo ripped the last two sheets of kitchen roll from the holder, dried his hands and tossed the soiled sheets into the bin under the sink.

"I've gotta run."

"Hang on. When will I see you next?" She spotted his 'week' hold-all duffle bag on the floor. That usually meant he would be staying at the penthouse until Friday. "We're in the middle of a crisis and I have no idea what's going on." She was panicky, maybe from the coffee or the prospect of being left alone all week.

"Lucy. Lucy, precious Lucy." He cupped her face into his puffy hands and in a child-like voice said, "Don't you worry your pretty little head about this today, okay?"

His face just inches from hers, she spotted a white speck on one of his nostrils and it certainly wasn't his *Crème De La Mer* face cream. What was he playing at having a line this early?

"Rosie is going to fix everything. You heard her this morning. And plus, that's what we're paying for," he added.

Hugo's idea of fixing things was to throw money at the problem. If the kids came home upset, give them some cash. If Lucy felt lonely, buy her something designer. If he'd harassed an employee, pay a PR person to make it go away.

He kissed her forehead, then walked towards the door, picked up his bag, looked back over his shoulder and shouted, "We need more kitchen roll," then closed the door behind him.

Lucy reached across the kitchen bench, grabbed the kitchen roll holder and angrily threw it to the ground. "Get it yourself," she shouted at the door. Then, as the room fell silent, her heart sank. Nobody was coming today. Jocelyn had a day off. The gardeners didn't come on Mondays. No pool guy to chat to. It was just her and Beano and it was the loneliest she'd ever felt.

In that moment, she realised she had an important decision to make. Either sit there in her active wear, wallowing in her loneliness, *or* put on one of her nice dresses that had been gathering dust and go out.

I refuse to mope around. She used her new kickass doggie park friend, Bee Bloom, as her inspiration and picked out a Zimmerman tiered midi dress with billowing sleeves and high strappy sandals. She was surprised how much the dress instantly lifted her mood. Maybe she should do this dressing up more often.

"Hi, I called earlier to let you know I was coming to see my daughter, Maya Hamilton," Lucy said to the bespectacled lady with mousey hair and a resting bitch face behind the desk. With the glasses resting on her nose, the lady looked up at Lucy and then back down to a notepad sitting next to her computer.

"Oh yes, yes, of course. I wrote it down here. Come this way," she said, her face transforming into a welcoming smile. "I've booked this room for you and your daughter. Please, you first."

She directed Lucy into a small room with a round table and four chairs. "There's some water there in the corner, help yourself. I'll let Maya know you're here." She smiled softly. "And Lucy, I probably shouldn't be saying this ..." she whispered, "but I saw the papers and I do hope you're okay." She smiled softly again and closed the door.

Lucy steeled herself so she didn't cry at this act of kindness. She didn't want to look upset in front of Maya.

Keep it together. Be strong. Be ... Bee!

She poured two glasses of water and stood at the window overlooking the vast school grounds. It was more like Downton Abbey than a school. A gated entrance with gravel drive that went on forever. It wasn't an ideal surface to navigate in strappy sandals. She was grateful classes were in session so that the pupils hadn't seen her hobbling from her parked car to the reception. She hoped Maya's class wouldn't give her grief or pry into why she was being taken out of class. A parent was only allowed to visit their child under 'urgent' circumstances. Clearly, the kind reception lady approved Lucy's visit because she felt sorry for her. The door opened and in came Maya with a worried expression on her face. "Is everything okay? Is it Dad? Is it Beano? What's happened?"

Lucy hugged Maya tightly and said, "No, darling, everything's fine. I've just come for a chat."

Maya freed herself and took a step back. "But I know you can only come and visit if someone dies. And why are you all dressed up like that?" she said, looking her up and down with confused eyes.

"That's not entirely true, Maya. And look, maybe I made out it was urgent because I wanted to see you. Come on, let's sit down for a minute."

Lucy wasn't going to explain how she had ended up in her Zimmerman dress. That was a story for another time. She pulled out one of the wooden chairs for Maya and then one for herself. They sat next to each other with Lucy resting her left hand on Maya's right hand.

"Maya, we need to talk about your father."

"See, I knew it. Something's happened." Maya's eyes widened.

"Hang on. Please, let me finish." Lucy gulped. "There are some false accusations about him—"

"What accusations?" Maya interrupted.

"Please, Maya. Let me finish. I know you want to ask questions, honey, but just let me finish."

Lucy paused. This was harder than she thought it was going to be. "Your father has been accused of harassing an employee. Now, it's not true. He says it's not true. And we have to support him while we deal with … while we deal with the accusations." She spoke carefully to ensure she used the right words.

"What kind of harassing? Do you mean sexually?" demanded Maya in a loud voice.

"Just speak a bit quieter, honey." Lucy could immediately see Maya's body stiffen and rage bloom in her eyes. She started biting her nails, not that she had anything left to bite. She looked past Lucy towards the window and continued nibbling at her nails until Lucy grabbed her hands. "Maya, please, say something."

Maya crossed her arms and slumped into the chair. "What do you want me to say? I mean, I don't for one second believe him."

Lucy sat up in shock.

"I bet he did it. I bet he's fucking guilty."

"Maya, don't use language like that about your father."

"Mum, just stop. It's my turn to finish what I'm saying now." She sat back up in the chair and threw her sinewy arms, just like her mother's, above her head. "I've seen the way he is around my friends. He's a perve. They're fucking fifteen years old and he eyes them off. It's disgusting. You know some of them call him the lurcher, after my party last year."

Lucy had pretended she hadn't noticed Hugo's wandering eyes at Maya's fifteenth birthday. It had been a pool party at their home and all the girls had sashayed around in high-waisted bikinis with cheeky bum bottoms and matching teeny tiny bandeau tops. They danced to the latest hits, quite provocatively, Lucy thought, waving their acrylic nails in the air and tossing their long ringlet curls from side to side. Hugo and Lucy had sat on the terrace sipping Dom Perignon, when she'd noticed him watching the girls a bit too intently. He thought she couldn't see his eyes darting around behind those Ray-Ban sunglasses, following the girls as they went in and out of the pool. His eyes had lingered on one friend in particular who was lying in the pool on a watermelon-shaped float with her arms behind her head. A couple of hours later, after polishing off a second bottle of Dom, she had seen him dad-dance his way over to where the girl was dancing and grab her around the waist.

Maya had stormed over and shoved him out of the way. "Dad, go to bed. You're embarrassing."

Hugo had jolted, giving Maya a filthy look, before staggering back to the terrace where he'd sat until midnight drinking whisky and chain smoking.

"Maya, listen to me," said Lucy. "It's not true. We *have* to believe him. I would believe you if you told me that you hadn't done something you were accused of." Lucy wasn't sure her words were convincing; after all, she didn't believe them herself.

Maya leaned back in her chair and fiddled with the coiled hairband around her wrist. She looked contemplative.

"He's your dad, Maya. He loves you. I love you. Trust me," begged Lucy.

And just when Lucy felt she might be getting through to her, Maya blurted, "No. I'm sorry, Mum. I don't believe him." She stood up, walked towards the door then turned back and added, "I'm not coming home this weekend if he'll be there. I'll ask if I can stay at school."

Before Lucy could beg further, Maya had already walked out of the room and closed the door. Now it was her turn to slump into the chair. She couldn't blame Maya for how she felt. Maybe she would have felt the same if she were in her shoes. But Lucy knew Maya's anger would be short-lived because despite living quite independently and maturely as a weekly boarder, she still loved her home comforts on weekends. Fleur, on the other hand, was a different kettle of fish and Lucy was dreading calling her.

Chapter 8

"Well, that was one of the most uncomfortable board meetings I've been to in a *long* time," Bee said to Stuart as they climbed the staircase to the forty-first floor. As soon as Arthur had officially closed the meeting, Bee excused herself and quickly made her way out of the boardroom with Stuart hot on her heels. She would usually hang around and exchange pleasantries with the board members before they scurried off to their networking lunches. But the whole Max charade had pissed her off, big time.

"Tell me about it. I wasn't sure if I should be noting all those off-the-cuff comments by our new chairman," Stuart added, trying to keep up with Bee's pace.

"Quickly. There's something I've got to tell you before this bloody press interview," Bee whispered as they traversed the open-plan floor past rows of employees.

They arrived at her office and hurried inside.

"Close the door," she motioned as she sat down at her desk. She hit the keyboard and started searching for the email from Vanessa Rudgens. She had copied the contents and saved it down in a file on a private drive before deleting it from her email.

"Oh God! You're not pregnant, are you?" asked Stuart.

"No! Of course not. Ah, there it is." She opened the file and before she began reading the contents, she explained how it had arrived in her inbox.

"You've sat on this for six months," exclaimed Stuart. "Why?" She could see that he was shocked *and* upset because she *never* kept secrets from him. It wasn't that she didn't want to share it, it was more that by sharing it, it became real.

"Don't get your knickers in a knot. I didn't even tell Gus. I kind of assumed that it was just some crazy person, like a *Fatal Attraction* bunny boiler who was out for revenge. Think about it, Stuart. We did all that Googling, read all those articles, and I'm even reading his stupid memoir and there is zero dirt on the guy. Well, except for that one tantrum with *The Financial Times*."

Bee quickly glanced through her glass windows to check nobody was coming or watching. Glass offices were such a giveaway these days. She had learned, from being in one for five years, that the people outside pick up on a lot more than you would think.

"Well, are you going to contact her?"

"Oh shit. Change the subject." Bee panicked. She quickly moved her hand over her mouse. File. Close. File. Open. Quick. Quick. Find another file to open. Press Interview, *Financial Report*, December 1, 2022.

"Knock knock," said Max as he entered Bee's office.

Shouldn't you knock knock then wait wait to be called in? thought Bee. Even for a chairman, it was a tad impolite to just enter. She disliked how some senior colleagues assumed their presence trumped the more junior employee in the room and that what they needed to say couldn't wait. Chief Financial Officer Garth Hughes was consistently guilty of this hierarchical behaviour. He often charged into Bee's meetings declaring there was an urgent matter needing her attention. But nothing Garth had to communicate was *ever* urgent.

"Max, we're just going over the prep for *The Financial Report* interview," said Bee, checking on her screen that she had successfully transitioned to the right file. "Have you gone over everything? It was sent through last week by Rosie Reid from our PR firm."

Max ran his fingers through this hair. As he did, he glanced down at his bicep and appeared to flex. "Oh, I never look at those briefing documents," he said, waving his hand around. "Wing it, I say. It's more natural. That's what the journalists want." He laughed brashly to reveal perfectly aligned, brilliant white teeth. They had to be veneers.

"I always read them. Thoroughly," scoffed Bee. "Rosie put it together so we would be on the same page in our messaging. After all, it's our first joint interview."

"I know what I need to say, Bee. I'm a big boy," he said arrogantly. "Anyway, it's not a two-way exchange. We tell these hacks what we want them to write, and they print it. Simple. And if they don't, then they need to know there are repercussions."

Bee assumed *repercussions* meant the actions he took against the one journalist at *The Financial Times* who wasn't willing to play by his rules. Billy Bridges, who regularly roasted the corporate elite in his extremely well-read weekly column, had dared to call Max a *"grossly overrated and overpaid banker who would be better suited to a car dealership in Blackpool"*. Max was said to have flown off the handle, screaming obscenities at the editor and threatening to rough up Bridges down a dark alley. He'd then withdrawn the advertising contract, valued at ten million pounds per year, between the investment bank where he had been working at the time and the paper. Bridges had kept his job, but he never mentioned Max *ever* again in his future columns.

"Did you want something, Max? It's just I *do* have this prep to do. The interview is in one hour."

Max stepped towards Bee and as he did, she noticed his eyes land on the paper bin under her desk and his eyebrows raise at the sight of his own face staring up at him. *Oh crap,* she had forgotten to put the *Forbes* magazine in the shredding bin. Thankfully, he didn't say anything. His gaze then shifted towards the floor-to-ceiling windows and out across Sydney Harbour in the direction of the Opera House. "I wanted to see what kind of view you have. It's not bad."

"Not bad? It's bloody awesome," countered Bee.

Max's eyes scanned the city skyline and the company names sitting atop the skyscrapers. He lifted one hand to his chin and began caressing it pensively with his thumb and index finger. "Why don't we have our name on this building?" he asked.

Bee rose from her chair, positioned herself next to Max and gazed outwards in the same direction. "We don't want or need our name up in lights. We're fine just the way we are. Plus, it's expensive."

Max turned to Bee, wagged his index finger, then tapped the end of her nose. "You see, Bee. That's entirely the wrong attitude *and* why it's time for you to put your big girl pants on."

Bee gulped with shock. Was he really telling her to grow up? He'd used the word *tougher* in the board meeting but now, without an audience, he was choosing insulting language to make his point.

"It's time to play with the big boys. That's why we *do* need naming rights. We need presence, we need power, and we need to tell this lot we're here," he continued in a shouty voice while pointing at the buildings in the distance. Then, as quickly as he entered her office, he turned on his shiny brogues and exited. Bee heard him faintly say, "Power. Presence," as he disappeared around the corner and out of sight. Bee and Stuart looked at each other, their mouths agape with incredulity.

"What a cunt," blurted Stuart. "No wonder his heiress stayed in France."

Bee sat back down in her chair, eyes still gazing towards the corner that Max disappeared around. She agreed with Stuart, but hated the C word and wasn't about to repeat it.

"He seriously has a problem." Stuart's anger was flaring up. His frown deepened to the point where even a faint wrinkle became noticeable on his typically smooth forehead. "I mean, is he actually for real?" He then deepened his voice to mimic Max's "power and presence".

It had been so long since Bee had come face to face with a bully that she had forgotten how to cope with her emotions in the moment. She should have dealt with him right there and then, not let him speak to her in that way, but his insults made her freeze.

"You have to get hold of this Vanessa Rudgens person," said Stuart.

"Yes?"

"I don't know yet," answered Bee.

"And who the hell's this Dr Robert Hare when he's at home? What's that got to do with Mr Gladiator?"

"I already looked *him* up. He's legit. A highly regarded Canadian psychologist specialising in psychopathy. He says psychopaths aren't just behind bars, they're in boardrooms."

"No, you don't say!" Stuart joked. It was his feeble attempt to lighten the mood.

Bee rolled her eyes, turned her chair and set her gaze on the harbour while Stuart returned to his desk. She remembered what she'd read last night about psychopathic traits: glibness and superficial charm, grandiose sense of self, need for stimulation, cunning and manipulativeness, lack of remorse or guilt, lack of empathy, shallow affect. She retrieved the *Forbes* magazine from the paper bin and began rereading Max's interview. She wanted to check for any of these traits. However, she only managed to reach the end of the first paragraph where he boasted about how he "single-handedly shook a company up and changed it forever". Annoyed, she abruptly closed the magazine and marched it over to the shredding bin, which was five metres away from Stuart's desk, and forcefully pushed it through the narrow opening. As she marched back to her office, Stuart peered over his screen with quizzical eyes.

Stuart was waiting to meet Max's assistant, Suzy Scott. He was sat at one of the cafe-style tables in the open-plan meeting space adjacent to reception. A few other tables were occupied by teams having their Monday morning catch-ups over coffee and toast.

Now, Stuart wasn't the type to get stressed; he was usually as cool as a cucumber—a trait Bee adored in him. But he had to admit that Max's little performance and this Vanessa Rudgens revelation had got his pulse up a little. He could tell Bee was ruffled by it, so, being protective of Bee, it ruffled him too. He wanted to take the bull by the horns and track Vanessa down and find out what she knew about Max. These investment bankers could be slippery fuckers, he knew that much, but a psychopath? That was a whole other layer he hadn't considered.

He looked down at the time on his laptop. Suzy was running three minutes late. Prompt as always, he tutted and tapped his fingers on the table. His new yellow gold Cartier Love Bracelet caught his eye and distracted him temporarily. He twisted it around to get a better look under the pendant lamp hanging over the table. It was a treat to himself after he received his annual bonus. He didn't believe in saving. Spending on beautiful pieces fulfilled him.

He knew that his splurging worried Bee, however. She often asked him when he was finally going to start saving for a deposit and get on the property ladder. Sydney's property prices kept rising and she was worried that the market was getting away from him. *Plus, renting is dead money*, she would say. To get her off his back he would do a quick scroll of properties for sale in his desired area. When he realised what he could afford he promptly closed that browser and reopened the one with a shopping basket full of designer clothes.

At that moment, he caught Davide glancing over at him and forced a fake smile. It annoyed him how everyone in the office commented on how immaculately dressed Davide was. After all, *Stuart* wanted to be the office gay that everyone came to for fashion advice. Stuart assumed his colleagues just didn't get his style as it was too high end. Davide was much more high street. Sure, he was super smart and polished, but he really only changed the colour of his shirt and pocket scarf; everything else looked the same. He often saw Davide and his partner Frederik out at the gay bars on the weekend, but Stuart and Davide never spoke to each other. They just acknowledged one another with a quick head tilt. It was as if there were an unspoken acceptance of their mutual dislike. In the office, they did their best to act professionally but couldn't resist the odd dig from time to time. Every Thursday they bickered over the Friday night drinks order. Davide was a stickler for keeping within the assigned budget, while Stuart advocated for more expensive wines that were to his liking.

"Would you please stop with being such a tight arse now, Davide? No more of this sav blanc crap," Stuart had said at their last meeting. "It gives me a headache. It's Riesling or Pinot Grigio from now on, please."

Suzy was now seven minutes late and Stuart was getting impatient. He was about to instant message her when he heard the sound of heels clacking on the polished concrete floor. He turned around to see a tall woman strutting towards him like she was on the Victoria's Secret catwalk. She tossed her long blonde blow-dried locks while talking loudly on the phone. "Please get back to me today. Thank you, got to run now," she said.

Stuart stood up. Even at five foot ten he felt towered over. How tall was she? Maybe six foot?

"Suzy Scott, pleased to meet you."

"Stuart Sanderson. Welcome to Curban," he said, jovially.

His welcoming smile was met with a frosty glare and limp handshake. Suzy pulled out a chair and sat down at the table. She had an impeccable, ballerina posture with shoulder blades sloped down and head and neck straight as a pole. Stuart felt hunched in comparison and immediately pulled his chair in, forcing his spine to straighten. She crossed her long, model-like legs and pointed one foot up in the air to reveal shiny petal-pink Valentino Rockstud shoes. She was dressed in a grey Hervé Légere-style bandage dress and wore Hermès jewellery—a yellow gold and white Clic H bracelet and gold earrings. Being an expert in luxury items, Stuart was able to quickly tally the cost of her complete outfit—over three thousand dollars, for sure.

She placed a green leather notepad on the table with the initials SS embossed in gold and caught Stuart glancing at it. "It's lovely, isn't it?" she boasted. "Max bought it for me. As a welcome-to-Curban gift. He's got the best taste." She stroked the grained calf leather with her long pianist fingers.

"Wow, that's kind. So how long have you worked for him?" But what he really wanted to ask was, *How much is Max paying you?*

"I managed his affairs in London for eight years and New York for five. Then I was employed elsewhere while he was living in France. And of course, he reached out as soon as he accepted the role here."

Stuart was puzzled by Suzy's unplaceable accent, which was a blend of Australian, English and American. To clarify, he asked, "So you're Australian but worked in London for eight years?"

"Correct."

"But you sound kind of British."

"I'll take that as a compliment," she replied. "Anyway, let's get started, please. I have another meeting right after this one."

Uptight and up herself, thought Stuart. He got the impression she was incapable of chit-chatting, unlike him.

"First, I'd like to discuss Max's needs."

"His needs? You make him sound like a patient," laughed Stuart.

Suzy shot back a glacial glance, her eyes cold with heavy lids. "Yes, his needs in terms of what makes his life comfortable in the office given how much time he spends here. And he has *extremely* high standards. As do I." She blinked her long, fake eyelashes.

Stuart's curiosity piqued as he wondered about Suzy's age. It was hard to tell with the heavy make-up. Her forehead, creaseless, was surely Botoxed. And her cheeks were chipmunk-like and presumably plumped with filler, her lips pouty and glossy. Her face told one story—smooth, tight and porcelain—while her neck, chest and arms were dotted with freckles. Or were they sunspots? She wore a signet ring on her right pinkie but there was no wedding band. Her hands were also freckled. *"If you want to know a woman's age, just look at her hands,"* Stuart's dermatologist told him when he was getting his own sunspots zapped.

He was annoyed how the harsh Australian sun had changed his complexion. He didn't even sunbathe here and always wore SPF 50 on his face. Not like when he lived in London and lathered himself in olive oil on his annual trip to Mykonos.

"Can we please start with facilities?" asked Suzy.

"Sure, fire away," replied Stuart.

"Is there a gym on site?"

"Yes, it's in the basement and it's for the whole building."

"I'll need that blocked out between 5am to 6am on Monday, Wednesday and Friday for Max's personal training sessions."

Stuart burst out laughing. "You're kidding."

Suzy's face was expressionless.

"You *are* kidding, right?"

"Of course not," she tutted. "Are *you* kidding? Max can't exercise with staff present and he certainly can't be exercising at the same time as random people from this building."

Stuart's eyes widened in astonishment. Max the Gladiator clearly wasn't a man of the people. He was a greedy bastard who wanted the arena all to himself.

"Please email me the details of the building manager and I'll take care of that myself."

"Okay, good luck," Stuart said jokingly. "Her name's Barbara and she runs the building with an iron fist. No special treatment for *anyone*." He shook his head.

"We'll see about that." Suzy tapped her extra-long false talons on her iPad causing Stuart to shudder in discomfort. He hated that noise. For a split second, he wondered how she managed to perform everyday tasks like picking her nose or wiping her bum with them.

"What about the chef? I'll need to meet with them to discuss Max's diet."

"You're definitely kidding this time."

"Do I look like I'm kidding, Stuart? Could you please take this meeting seriously?"

"We don't have a chef here, Suzy. We have two baristas that help Davide on reception, and we use the cafe downstairs for food," Stuart huffed.

"Oh my God. That's so underwhelming and cheap," Suzy snorted. "I now see why Max said things need shaking up here."

Stuart was offended. *Who does she think she is?* Shaking up indeed! Maybe he should share his fashion CV with her and list all the chic events he'd hosted *and* drop some big celebrity names. That would shut her up.

"Nothing needs shaking up, Suzy, everything works really well here, including using the cafe downstairs for our catering," he said, deciding to rise above it.

"That won't work for Max. He's used to having a chef on site. He hosts lunches all the time. We'll need that sorted asap," she exhaled, irritated. "When we worked in New York we hired the most amazing chef from Balthazar in SoHo. It was incredible. All the clients wanted to lunch in our office rather than go to a restaurant, it was *that* good." Her eyes lit up as she boasted.

"Well, I wouldn't get your hopes up here. We're much lower key." Stuart was dying to change the subject. He wanted to know more about *her*. Everything about Suzy screamed perfection and he wanted to find a crack. "I love your hair. Did you do it yourself this morning or did you go to a blow bar?"

"Excuse me?"

"It's so perfect. I'm just intrigued if you styled it yourself."

"Yes, I styled it myself. Okay. Can we keep going with my list now, please?" She pretended to be annoyed, but Stuart suspected she secretly liked the compliment. *I mean, why would you style your hair so perfectly and not want anyone to comment on it?*

"Now, this is an immediate priority. 'The chairman's lounge'." She gestured with her hands as if she were announcing a new Broadway show.

"Yessss?" Stuart asked, not having a clue what she was talking about.

"Max doesn't do office. He does lounge. I have a Pinterest board of what we want it to look like and we have our own contacts to get working on it."

"Okay," said Stuart, while thinking *What the hell is a chairman's lounge?*

"Max and I can't be roughing it with the plebs," Suzy said before letting out a high-pitched screech that startled Stuart. *Was that actually her laugh?*

"That's it for now." And with that she snapped her iPad cover closed, picked up her filo and clip-clopped her way in the direction of her temporary office behind reception.

Bitch. And he knew a thing or two about bitches from his time in fashion. *Wait until Bee hears about this!*

Chapter 9

I strenuously deny any allegations of sexual harassment against me. These claims are completely untrue and distressing. Staff safety has always been my top priority across all my venues.

"What do you think? Rosie asked Jazzy. They both sat forward in their chairs, chins cupped in their hands, staring at the words on the screen. It was amazing how three sentences could consume the brainpower of two experienced PR pros, but Rosie knew the first rebuttal in crisis management was the most important. If she was honest, the words had taken a bit too long to craft and she knew why. She didn't believe them. But she would *have* to start believing them before she picked up the phone to her list of journalists and got to work defending Hugo. Two or three years ago she would have had no problem concocting a story to fit the crime committed, but lately she felt less capable of lying. She had, after all those years of not giving a toss, acquired a moral compass.

Work was work and she was able to compartmentalise before. She was a gun for hire, able to do anything for a client in exchange for a handsome cash reward. She had built her business on the premise that there is the court of law and the court of public opinion. Her job was to use her contacts in the media to influence the court of public opinion. And she was excellent at it. She had become known as 'the fixer' in corporate Australia ever since the emcee at a conference in Melbourne had compared her to Jon Voigt from the same-named 1998 movie. *"Ladies and Gentlemen, please welcome our next guest speaker. She's the fixer—the cleaner who takes care of all her clients' mistakes. Please welcome, Rosie Reid."* Rosie had laughed along with it as she made her way to the stage to take her seat, but inside she'd been cringing.

"I think it looks good," replied Jazzy. "I mean, it's really all we can say for now." She stretched back into her chair and raised her arms above her head, letting out a loud yawn. Rosie watched as Jazzy's lemon-coloured short-sleeved buttoned shirt rose up to reveal her toned and tanned stomach.

"Oh, sorry about that. I think I need another coffee," Jazzy said.

Embarrassed that she'd been rumbled eyeing her off, Rosie turned back to the screen and said, "Agree. Right, let's get this to Hugo for his approval and I'll get started on the key messages." She started typing furiously away on her keyboard.

"Would you like a coffee?" Jazzy asked.

"No. All good, thanks."

Rosie watched as Jazzy made her way to the small kitchen area at the centre of the office. She wasn't usually attracted to girls—she had only kissed two in her drunken university days—but she knew she had a crush on Jazzy. She excited her. She was intoxicating. And Rosie knew she wasn't the only one intoxicated by her. People gazed at Jazzy with puppy-dog eyes, they fake laughed at things she said, things that really were *not* funny at all, and they always over-talked like people do when they're nervous around staggeringly good-looking people. But Jazzy's most awesome characteristic, beyond her toned tummy, was that she didn't know just how bloody gorgeous she was.

Rosie became aware of her feelings for her when a group of colleagues from the office decided to kick on after a long boozy day at the Melbourne Cup races at Royal Randwick. They were all dressed up to the nines to meet the strict dress code requirements for the Australian Turf Club Member's stand where they were guests of a client. Jazzy wore a floaty purple dress, strappy sandals and a Gucci silk-twill headband that only *she* could pull off. After catching the light rail to Oxford Street, they decided to go to Stonewall Bar where the DJ was playing greatest hits from the eighties. While everyone rushed to the flashing dance floor, Rosie bought a round of vodkas and a sparkling water for herself then stood leaning against the bar, transfixed by Jazzy. She was particularly mesmerising that night with her smoky eyes and loose hips that swayed in time to the Human League's 'Don't You Want Me'. Rosie blushed when Jazzy turned and caught her staring. She pointed at her eyes with two fingers making a V sign then pointed the fingers at Rosie, before dancing towards her. Rosie felt her heart skip a beat. As Jazzy leaned in, Rosie smelt her musky perfume and felt the softness of her long blonde locks against her face. She tingled.

"Not a dancer then?" Jazzy shouted in Rosie's ear.

Her breath was hot, and Rosie felt it all over her body. "I don't feel like it right now," she shouted in response.

"Well, can I ask you something then?"

"Sure."

"It's kinda personal," slurred Jazzy while taking Rosie's hands in hers.

"Okay, I feel pressure now." She held her breath in anticipation. Had Jazzy noticed her lingering stares, and did she feel the same?

"Are you happy?"

"Am I happy?" Rosie repeated. What kind of a question was that? She immediately started worrying about what was coming next.

"Yes. Are you happy? You're always working. I worry about you. *We* worry about you. You need to have more fun." Jazzy stood back, swaying to the music again while she waited for Rosie to reply.

Rosie didn't know where Jazzy was going with this, but it certainly wasn't a conversation for now—not in a gay bar where she could hardly hear herself. Plus, she had just noticed Simon's beady eyes on them. He didn't miss a trick.

"I'm so sorry. I hope I didn't offend you," said Jazzy, appearing to notice, despite her drunkenness, that Rosie looked uncomfortable.

"It's fine. Just another time, not now."

Whitney Houston's 'I Wanna Dance with Somebody' came on and Jazzy let out the loudest "woo-hoo". She pulled Rosie close and twisted her under her arm. Rosie cringed. She felt as stiff as a board, unable to feel the beat.

"Come on. Come and dance," Jazzy pleaded.

"Maybe the next song," Rosie lied. She had no intention of dancing. In fact, she had decided everyone's (except Jazzy's) annoyance level had reached its peaked and it was time to slip out the back door.

The next day everyone arrived at the office hungover with extra-large coffees and bacon and egg rolls in hand. Jazzy didn't bring up their conversation, nor did Rosie.

That was about one month ago now, so she assumed it was deep and buried like a lot of drunken conversations. In that month, Rosie had thought more and more about Jazzy and her question—"Are you happy?" Jazzy had used the words "we" so had the team been talking about her and if so, what had they been saying? They obviously thought she was miserable and worked too much. And they were right.

Rosie returned to finalising Hugo's draft statement. She opened a new email and started drafting.

Hi Hugo, please find below our suggested statement. We have until 4pm to get this out. Any comments, please send them through, or you can call my mobile. Could you also please sign the attached terms of business? The details for payment of the deposit are also attached. Kind regards, Rosie.

She then began reviewing the briefing materials for her interview with Bee Bloom and Max Magnifico but was stopped in her tracks when Hugo's reply came through within one minute. *Wow, so fast.* She was impressed.

"Is that it?"

Actually, no, she wasn't impressed. No greeting, no please, no thank you. Just like Bill Sykes.

"Yes, that's it," she replied. She couldn't help herself.

"Fine, just get it out then."

"Done."

Oh, how she would have loved to add, *You're welcome, chipolata.*

There was no time to dwell on his rudeness. She had to get to the Curban offices for her interview with Bee and Max. She was feeling a tad anxious about meeting Max after all she'd heard about him. He cared deeply about his reputation, that was clear from the interviews she had read about him, so she was hoping this one with Jenny would go smoothly because her own reputation depended on it.

When Bee arrived at the Bennelong meeting room, she found Rosie standing in the corner fiddling with the pens in their stainless-steel holder.

"You can have one of those if you really want," Bee called out.

Rosie turned around and laughed. "Thank you. I think I will take one."

After they kissed each other on the cheek, Bee took a seat at the table. She wasn't in the mood for chit-chat today. She didn't want Rosie to know, but she was dreading this interview and not because she was worried what *she* might say. She was worried how Max would behave. "I've let Max know where we are so he should be here any minute," she said.

Rosie took a seat next to Bee. "So, what's he like?" she asked softly.

Bee looked back at the door like she was checking no one was coming then replied "Confident and …" She searched for another word to describe what she had witnessed so far. "And surprising." She knew her words didn't sound convincing. She wasn't a great liar. And she kept her eyes on the door because she also couldn't lie while looking at someone. Thankfully Rosie didn't ask her to explain what she meant by *surprising*, because fast footsteps could be heard coming towards the meeting room. They could only belong to Jenny Wallis. Always rushing around from one interview to the next, Jenny always gave an impression of *Don't you know how goddamn busy I am?*

"What a morning. Gosh. Welcome to Monday!" Jenny said speedily. True to form, she entered the room appearing frazzled, brushing her bushy TV presenter hair from her round face. "Am I sitting here?" And without waiting for the answer, she plonked herself down in the chair opposite Bee. She began gulping water from the glass like she'd just finished a marathon. "Oh, this one *is* mine, isn't it?"

Rosie and Bee nodded then watched Jenny lift the technology box at the centre of the table and begin frantically searching through the cables.

"So, this is all on the record, right? And there's no time for quote checking, right. Right?"

"Hi, Jenny," Rosie said, looking over at Bee with big eyes. "Let's just wait for Max to arrive and then we can discuss the format for the interview."

Jenny waved her hand in the air then continued to fiddle around with the cables until she found the correct one for her laptop. "Ah, there we go."

The three women knew each other well. Rosie spoke to Jenny daily about whatever client she was trying to either get into or keep out of the papers. Bee had been interviewed at least ten times by Jenny over the course of her five-year tenure at Curban Capital and Jenny would often call on Bee for insights into what deals they were working on. After exchanging a few pleasantries about what they each had planned for the Christmas break, Bee decided to call Max's assistant Suzy to check on his whereabouts.

"Suzy, we're all in the Bennelong room for the interview. Can you send Max in please, thank you."

Rosie and Jenny had resumed their discussion about holidays.

"I can totally recommend Callala Beach for you, Rosie. It's heaven. Nothing to do but just hang out at the beach, swim, have lunch, take a nap, eat dinner and repeat."

"I'm more of an activity-holiday kind of person, but thanks for the recommendation," Rosie said.

"C'mon, Rosie. You're telling me you don't need to just chill now and again?" Jenny guffawed. "I can't survive these days without our beach getaways. Everyone gets so tired and cranky by the end of each school term, especially me."

Oh, here we go, thought Bee. This is where Jenny goes on about how tired she is, like it's some competition, and how Rosie could *never* be as tired as her because she doesn't have kids. She'd witnessed it every time they'd conducted interviews.

"Yes, maybe I do need to chill out but I can't just lie around on a beach. I get, well, I get bored."

Rosie sounded like she was getting fed up with Jenny's emphasis on the beach point. Bee found it boring too. She looked down at her watch, growing increasingly irritated by Max's tardiness. Timeliness was important to her, really important. Max might be the new chairman, but right now he was being disrespectful to the three women sitting around this table. Bee huffed. "Let's get started, Jenny. You can ask me questions and then let's loop Max in once he gets here."

It was a whole fifteen minutes later when there was a knock at the door. Max entered with a takeaway espresso cup in one hand and his iPhone in the other.

"Apologies, ladies. I was held up on a client call," said Max.

Lie, thought Bee.

He made his way over to Rosie first. She stood up and they shook hands. "I'm Max, good to meet you." Then he turned and walked over to Jenny. "Jenny Wallis, how the devil are you?" He opened his arms up affectionately and kissed her on her left and right cheeks, French style.

"I think it's been about ten years, hasn't it?" gushed Jenny. Her cheeks flushed.

"So you two know each other then?" Bee asked through a feigned smile.

They both looked at Bee and started to reply at the same time, causing them to talk over each other.

Max laughed. "You go, Jenny." He took the seat next to Bee and placed his coffee and his iPhone down on the table in front of him.

"We do. My father was one of Max's clients back in the day before he sold his business," said Jenny, looking across the table at Max with goo-goo eyes.

"How are Ray and Janice?" asked Max.

"They're in Stellenbosch outside Cape Town at the moment for a friend's seventieth. Always travelling. Making up for all those cancelled trips because of COVID. But they'll be back in Sydney for Christmas, which will be lovely," she gushed again. "We'll all have to catch up."

This exchange was making Bee uncomfortable. She just wanted to get on with this interview.

"So, Max let me get you up to speed with where we're at and perhaps you can fill in any blanks."

"All on background, right, Jenny? And if you need to quote me, you'll send them through to Suzy and I'll check them. That work for you?" Max said, flashing a wide smile at Jenny.

Bee glanced over at Jenny, knowing that she had only fifteen minutes ago said that she wasn't going to allow any quote checking. Jenny hesitated and fidgeted in her seat for a couple of seconds before saying, "Yes, of course, Max. For you, that's totally fine."

She was like putty in his hands. *Groan.*

Bee couldn't help noticing that there was a different dynamic in the room with Max present. Jenny played with her hair and asked her questions faster, like she was nervous. Rosie was quieter than normal. She observed how Max dominated the conversation and how Jenny was only too happy to indulge him.

"Why Curban? What a great question." Max was now indulging Jenny. "Well, I love a challenge. I think I can expand the business in a way that delivers better results for our shareholders. And I have that fierce, competitive, winning spirit that's needed right now."

"The Gladiator is back," Jenny giggled childishly.

"You betcha."

The rest of the interview was a car crash as far as Bee was concerned. Max went completely off script. He barely came up for air which meant Bee couldn't get a word in and the two moments where she tried, Max mansplained then redirected the conversation back to him. *I, I, I* was all Bee heard. *There's no I in team!* She was elated when Davide knocked on the meeting room door to let her know *The Financial Report* photographer had arrived. She would rather stick pins in her eyes than sit through any more of this interview. "Let's wrap things up there then, shall we?" she said. "You should have enough for your piece, Jenny, but please give any of us a call if you need to check anything. Or to check quotes," she added with a knowing smile.

They made their way to the reception; Bee trailed Max and Jenny, listening to them compare their favourite ski locations. Whistler was great last year but Japan was incredible this year. Something to do with La Niña making the snow better in Japan. Rosie was ahead of everyone, fussing with the photographer about the best location for the photo.

"Louis the photographer wants to do it here," Rosie called out while pointing at a black leather couch. "With this artwork in the background it's going to look amazing."

She rearranged the scatter cushions and stood back, looking pensively at the sofa. "Perfect!"

The photographer shifted his umbrella-like equipment around then clicked away, taking several test shots while Max and Jenny continued to chat. They were now talking about the Australian Open in January and what games they had tickets to.

"Oh, we always go to the men's final," boasted Max. "This year we're going with Russell Crowe. He always rustles up great tickets." He nudged Jenny.

It was a terrible joke, but that didn't stop Jenny from cracking a loud laugh.

"Okay, if we can get Bee and Max sitting down now, please," Louis said, beckoning the pair over to the sofa.

"Wait a minute. Are you using this background?" asked Max, pointing to the black-and-white Aboriginal artwork hanging on the wall. Before anyone could answer, he added, "We need the company logo in the background so people can see who we are. I mean, people know who *I* am, but it's good for them to see that I've arrived at Curban so they know where they can find me." He laughed, but there was a seriousness to his tone.

Bee, already seated on the edge of the sofa, looked up at Max. "It's slightly tacky to have logos in the background. We're not EPL players coming off the pitch after a match." She chuckled, but stopped as soon as she saw his stern-looking face. "And it doesn't work well for the photo, right?" She looked over at Louis, knowing he would agree because they'd had the same conversation a few months ago.

"Yep, Bee's right. It's not a great look for this kind of photo and it can blur," Louis shouted over the clicking, with his camera held up to his eyes.

"All right, let's do it *your* way this time," Max said stiffly. As he sat down, he slid his hand across the sofa and tapped Bee on the knee. She turned around and with his head tilted downwards he said under his breath, "Don't *ever* disagree with anything I say, *especially* in front of people. It's only day one so I'll cut you some slack, but you need to know that it's *always* got to be my way, Bee Bloom."

His words stung. They felt unnecessarily spikey for such a trivial disagreement. But she realised in an instant that wasn't the point. It was his power play.

Max leaned back, looked towards Louis, opened his legs as wide apart as he could stretch them, pulled down the cuffs of his white shirt from beneath the arms of his suit jacket, twisted his gold Hermès cufflinks so the H was facing upwards, then ran his hand through his hair, tucking loose strands behind his ears. Then, without checking if Bee was ready, he ordered, "Okay, now shoot."

Chapter 10

After leaving Maya's school, Lucy decided to take herself off for a bit of retail therapy in Double Bay. She liked how good it felt to be out of active wear for once. Dressing up had lifted her mood and she figured she deserved another little lift.

As she walked into the first boutique on Cross Street, she was immediately greeted by two eager sales assistants. They knew a VIP customer when they saw one! Lucy often received invites to their special VIP events, but always declined to attend because of her crippling social anxiety. She asked the assistants if they could help her pick out some nice dresses, shoes and bags for the summer and they were only too happy to oblige. In fact, it was like they sniffed out her buying mood because they practically ran around the store gathering up items for her to try. Meanwhile, three other customers were being completely ignored.

Lucy gulped when she was asked if she were paying the twenty-thousand-dollar bill by cash or card. *No, don't feel bad. I deserve it*, she told herself.

With her shopping bags nestled in the crooks of both elbows, she floated down the cafe-lined streets without a care in the world. She popped the boot of her Range Rover and began lining up all the bags neatly. As she did, she heard a "Get that shot, quick, quick", and when she turned around, she caught sight of two photographers across the street, one with a camera around his neck and the other with a huge, long lens pointing at her. Had they been following her? And for how long? In a state of panic, she frantically pressed the 'close boot' button on her keys, only for them to slip out of her trembling hand. As she spotted the keys land under the car, she quickly bent down to retrieve them. However, a sudden gust of wind lifted her dress up, revealing her underwear—the kind of underwear you don't want anybody to see, the chewing-gum-grey Bonds period undies. She had worn them for extra protection in case her period leaked onto her light-coloured dress. Mortified, she mustered all her energy to retrieve the keys, stood up, swiftly closed the boot, and ducked into the safety of her front seat. She hurriedly started the engine and screeched out of her parking space, driving at fifty kilometres down the twenty-kilometre-per-hour street, causing all the cappuccino-sipping grannies to turn their grey up-dos in her direction. Her heart was in her mouth.

Five minutes up the road and safely out of sight, she pulled over, slid down in the front seat and sobbed uncontrollably. Before she knew it, she was gasping for air and experiencing a sharp chest pain. A panic attack! She spotted a shopping bag on the floor in front of the passenger's seat and reached for it with her trembling left hand. She placed the bag over her mouth and nose and started breathing in and out slowly. *Inhale, exhale, inhale, exhale.* While her breathing eventually normalised, her anxiety remained. Could her life get any worse? She was a laughing stock. And now her own humiliating moment was likely to become a meme.

Two hours later, Lucy arrived home to an enormous bunch of flowers lying on the mat at the front door. They were her favourite—red roses. She guessed there were at least three dozen, and they would have been absolutely stunning had they not been left in the direct sunlight. All the flowers and leaves had wilted. What an extravagant waste.

She was welcomed by an ecstatic Beano as she walked through the front door. *At least someone was pleased to see her.* She threw her shopping bags on the floor, slipped out of her pinching high-heeled sandals (which she was out of practice wearing these days), set the roses down on the kitchen bench and lay on the floor, allowing Beano to jump all over her.

"Who's a good boy? Are you a good boy? Yes, you are! Yes, you are!" She struggled to get the words out as he licked all over her face. "C'mon then, let's get you a doggie treat."

He followed her to the pantry, wagging his tail excitedly, and watched as she removed a pig's ear from the white porcelain jar with the words *Treat Me Good* across one side. "Sit. Paw. Good boy," she said before handing him the ear, which he snatched and ran off to devour in his dog bed.

She stared at the shopping bags fanned across the floor and felt pangs of buyer's remorse. She had been excessive and greedy.

She plopped herself down on the wooden floor beside her shopping, slumping over with legs spread apart, shoulders hunched and black panda eyes caused by smudged mascara. She felt like her bunch of roses—wilted. She remembered when she and Hugo first got married, she was a rosebud full of promise with a blossoming TV career, then in full bloom she became a mother of two healthy girls, and then she slowly began to droop mentally and physically.

A text alert sounded on her phone, and she let out a weary sigh. She had that feeling of dread again and desire to disappear. Would anyone notice? Would anyone even care? She mustered up the small bit of energy she had left and peeled herself off the floor before checking her phone. Fifteen messages were waiting for her reply.

Babe. What an arsehole.

WTF Lucy. Can't say I'm surprised. I've always said he was a monster.

I hope you're going to kick him out, that bloody bastard.

The comments didn't surprise her. Vindication for those who had always hated Hugo. She'd always heard stories of people who broke up with their partner only to find out their friends had hated them the whole time. But Lucy had the opposite problem—most of her friends had made their dislike for Hugo known from the outset. They claimed he was a player and that she could do better.

When Lucy first met him in one of his bars, she didn't know who he was. That was what Hugo loved about her. And Lucy was different to his previous girlfriends because she didn't make it easy for him and she didn't care about his money. Hugo actively pursued her and was the epitome of the perfect gentleman, at least initially. However, this was the side of him that her friends never had the chance to witness.

Lucy considered if *those* friends had been right all along. Maybe love *is* blind and maybe Hugo was a player and she hadn't seen it. She looked at the wilted roses on the kitchen bench and wondered if she could revive them. She Googled *tips to revive wilted roses* then began unwrapping their brown paper packaging.

A small greeting card fell out from between the droopy stems. *Dear Wifey, we'll get through this BS. Insieme per sempre. Hugo xxxx.*

Insieme per sempre was their special couple's phrase meaning *together forever* in Italian. Hugo had the words engraved into an antique gold heart-shaped locket that he presented in a small black velvet box while they were on their honeymoon in Puglia, Italy. He had said the hand chased ivy leaves symbolised everlasting love and fidelity.

"I'll never take it off," Lucy had said while looking down lovingly at the locket hanging on her chest. Inside was a photo frame where, when they returned to Sydney, she had placed a photo of them from that night, dining at the Grotta Palazzesse overlooking the Adriatic Sea. It was the most romantic, loved-up night of her life.

As Lucy looked down at the locket hanging around her neck, she was reminded how thoughtful a gift it was at the time. It wasn't lavish, it wasn't designer; it was perfect. *He* used to be perfect but had morphed into a big, fat, balding, shouty, angry, fifty something who perved on fifteen-year-olds and harassed his staff. And who was she? The depressed, binge-drinking wife who spent her days sipping oat flat whites in the burbs.

"Fuck him," she screamed out. "FUCK HIM." Her voice was louder and angrier. "FUCK HIM, FUCK HIM. FUCK HIM." With a swift motion, she yanked the chain off her neck and tossed it aside. Then she reached for the greeting card, tore it apart and scattered the shredded pieces onto the kitchen bench. Consumed by anger, she flung open the fridge, grabbed the first bottle of alcohol she could find, which was a French Rosé, and began gulping it down in large swigs. It slipped down so quickly and easily that the bottle was gone in just six gulps. She didn't even taste it, but she did feel it. It gave her an instant sense of sedation and she wanted more. It was 3pm and probably a bit early to be wasted but who cared, nobody was there to judge her. Like most of her weeks, it was just her and Beano. All she had to do today was crawl to bed. As she walked to the fridge another text alert sounded.

"Bugger off," she shouted. "Can't you see I just wanna have a drink in peace?" She might turn her phone on silent after checking this one last message. It was from Rosie Reid. *Please, not her. What does she want?*

Call me, it's urgent. Thanks!

Perhaps another female employee had come forward. Where there's one there are fifty; maybe he's the Harvey Weinstein of the Sydney bar scene? She stood swaying, staring blankly at the phone when another text appeared. *Like ... really urgent.*

Rosie wasn't someone she wanted to speak to while she was feeling tipsy, because she worked for Hugo, and everything would get back to him like it always did. She couldn't understand how, because she only drank heavily when he wasn't around, but he appeared to be aware of her increased alcohol consumption these days. Surely he wasn't counting the bottles in the cellar? He hated her drinking more than one glass. *"Wifey, I think that's enough now,"* he would say if she reached for a second glass. So bloody controlling.

Lucy: I'm a bit tied up right now, Rosie. What's urgent?

Rosie: There's an article in the Daily Life *... best we talk about it rather than text.*

Lucy: Oh ... has it got me in it?

Rosie: Yes. It's all fine. I can try and fix things up a little but need you to give me a call.

Lucy: Okay. Two minutes.

Rosie: Thanks.

Lucy made her way to the kitchen sink, turning on the tap and splashing her face with cold water. She then dried it with a tea towel that carried the lingering scent of last night's Bolognese sauce. She removed a can of ginger lemon kombucha from the fridge and took a seat at the kitchen bench, steeling herself for the inevitable embarrassment. And there it was.

Daily Life, Monday, December 1, 2022

Lucy Love gets her knickers in a twist while drowning her sorrows with retail therapy

Lucy Love was seen today in Sydney's Double Bay, drowning her sorrows in some retail therapy. Love, whose husband, Hugo Hamilton, has been accused of harassing a female employee, looked like she didn't have a care in the world as she shopped up a treat at the various high-end boutiques.

"Hi, Rosie, it's Lucy."

"Hi, thanks for calling me back. Look, there's an article running in the *Daily Life* online and I hate to tell you but it's got a photograph of you with your dress up."

"Yes, I've just seen it."

The article was much worse than she expected because there were multiple photographs of the whole ordeal: her breezing through Double Bay, her face in shock as she noticed the paps, her bending down, a zoom-in of her knickers, the bags all lined up in the boot (when some families were struggling with increased grocery bills) and her speeding off.

"Are you okay, Lucy? This must be awful for you."

These weren't the words Lucy expected to hear from the PR spinner hired by her husband. She expected to be berated; after all, it was yet another PR disaster.

"I'm here to help, you know, Lucy," Rosie said, softly.

Lucy paused, desperately trying to hold it together. *Must not cry, must not cry*, her internal voice said before she blurted out, "It's a fucking disaster. I'm a mess. It's the worst day of my life and I, I, I just want to ... KILL HIM."

"Lucy?"

"Yes," she sobbed, loudly.

"I'm coming over. Have a nice hot bath or do something relaxing until I'm there. I'll be about an hour and twenty, depending on traffic."

As Lucy started to tell Rosie she didn't need her to come over, she had already hung up.

Chapter 11

Rosie really didn't want to be trekking back up to the Northern Beaches again. She had already spent three hours or so in Ubers today, but she could tell when someone was in a dark place.

Not only was she naturally attuned to people's emotions, she was also a trained AA and Lifeline crisis support volunteer. Her training had taught her one invaluable lesson—a conversation can change a life—so she never ignored someone who needed help, even if it was a huge inconvenience.

"Rosie, I feel so bad for you coming out all this way. It's going way above and beyond what Hugo must be paying you for," Lucy said after opening the door. Lucy had obviously been bawling her eyes out because she looked like she'd gone a few rounds with Mike Tyson. *Poor thing*, thought Rosie.

"This isn't work, Lucy. I'm here because I'm genuinely concerned about you. It's a big deal what you're going through now."

Rosie followed Lucy down the hallway. It was spotless, soulless and devoid of any family vibe. There were no photos of the Hamilton family on show, no shoes at the door, or keys left on the side buffet. It was as if the house was up for sale or had been freshly styled for a magazine shoot. The brilliant white panelled walls gave way to high ceilings with three iron and glass pendant lamps hanging in perfect sequence. There was a beautiful dark wooden buffet with expensive-looking candles at one end and a glass vase filled with eucalyptus gum leaves at the other. A matching wooden bench, with two perfectly plumped cream cushions, was positioned at the end of the hallway with a striking Aboriginal bark painting hanging above it. Rosie recognised the artwork because it had caught her eye at a recent art fair, as had the fifty-thousand-dollar price tag.

She turned right into a kitchen and casual lounge area with glass doors that opened out on to another expansive terrace, not the one she had sat at earlier today. This one was higher up. She took a seat on a bar stool at the end of the long kitchen bench. "So you took my advice and had a bath then?"

Lucy's hair was wrapped in one of those quick-dry hair turbans and she wore a white waffle bathrobe and matching slippers. "I did. I don't even like baths. I get too hot in them, so I only lasted about three minutes. Now I just feel all puffy." She looked down towards her stomach and retied the robe's belt. "Anyway, have you eaten? I'm starving. I haven't eaten all day because of all this," she said, throwing her hands up in the air.

"I haven't and I'm starving too." Rosie was relieved because she was getting hangry. She'd only managed to scoff one Carmen's muesli bar all day.

"Let me see what we have." Lucy opened up the double doors of her fridge and began poking around.

Rosie glanced over Lucy's shoulder to sneak a peek of the contents. This fridge didn't scream family; it looked a lot like her own. Empty! Except for some kombucha cans and a few half-eaten dips. Lucy closed the doors and went into the pantry while Rosie looked around. There were shopping bags strewn across the floor, an enormous bunch of wilted roses sitting in the kitchen sink, a golden locket and pieces of torn-up card on the kitchen bench, and next to them one empty bottle of Rosé (no glass in sight) and another unopened.

Lucy emerged from the pantry looking defeated. "I don't know what I can make for us." She exhaled. "Do you like Thai?" Her eyes brightened at the idea.

"I *love* Thai," answered Rosie.

"Okay. Let's do takeaway. My shout." She paused with a worried expression. "But you'll have to drive my car to pick it up because I've had"—she looked over at the empty bottle of Rosé—"a bottle of wine."

"No problem," said Rosie.

Rosie heard a crunch and instantly regretted driving to the restaurant. For someone who owned a Fiat 500, Lucy's Range Rover was like driving a tank.

"Shit, Lucy. I'm so sorry," Rosie said, looking over at Lucy. "I'm not used to the reverse camera and all the beeping."

Lucy was holding her hand over her mouth, giggling. "Hilarious. Even I could have done a better job parking, and I'm drunk."

They both inspected the car behind which, from what they could see in the dark, appeared to only have suffered a slightly crumpled number plate.

"Phew," said Rosie, looking at Lucy. "I thought I'd done some serious damage."

"It's nothing, but I'll get a bit of paper and a pen from the wait staff and leave my number on the windscreen. Just in case any paps are watching us," Lucy joked.

Rosie liked Lucy's sense of humour and that she seemed to be a good sport, considering what a shit day she'd had.

The Thai Tanic restaurant was empty except for two tables. At one, an elderly couple sat hunched over, trying to pick up their fried rice with the chopsticks in their shaking hands. At the other, a group of ten women dressed in similar-patterned midi dresses sipped Rosé and munched on spring rolls. While Rosie and Lucy waited at the counter for their takeaway order and a pen and paper, Rosie noticed the women staring at them. They then all turned their attention to something on their table that Rosie couldn't make out, but they were all looking downwards. They huddled in closer like a bunch of schoolgirls on a playground and began whispering.

"Do you know those women over there?" she asked Lucy.

Lucy looked over at the table. "School mums' night out. I see them all the time. They come here every other Monday," she replied before writing her name and number on the scrap of paper she had been given. "Right, I'll just pop this outside. Back in two secs."

Rosie casually strolled over to the table where the group of mums sat, pretending to search for the bathroom. The mums didn't notice her because they were too busy scrolling through the photos of Lucy in the *Daily Life*. She knew it.

"OMG, did you see this one with all the shopping bags? Wonder what's in there. She's always in active wear when I see her."

"And what about this one with her knickers and cellulite on show. So embarrassing."

Rosie coughed over their laughter, capturing their attention. Their heads lifted in sync and their eyes widened.

"Hi, ladies, having fun, are we?" Rosie said with her hands on her hips. "Now, I'm guessing you're all mums who have kids at school. How sweet. So let me ask you this. If they were doing what you're all doing right now, would you be proud of them? And before you answer that, how about if your child was the subject?" Rosie looked around the table. One woman with pursed lips and mean eyes turned the iPad over. "None of you are game enough to reply. That's what I thought," she said and turned on her heel and walked back to the counter where the white plastic takeaway bag was sitting. "Thank you very much," she said to the waitress, picking up the bag and strutting out the door.

"Great! It's ready," Lucy said, completely oblivious to the fact that she was the subject of gossiping.

Back at the house they ate their Pad Thai and chicken Penang curry on the terrace. The view, while different from the daytime, was spectacular. The full moon illuminated the ripples of the dark ocean and little speckles of light dotted the headland in the distance. The only noises were those of the cicadas and the tiny waves rolling in on the beach below.

"Don't you get scared here all alone?" Rosie asked.

Lucy looked out into the distance and even under the dim night-time lighting, from the lanterns placed around the terrace and candles burning on the table, Rosie could tell she looked sad and pensive.

"I know I would." Rosie loved her city apartment living. The dull sound of traffic while she lay in bed at night, knowing that there were other people above, below and to the side, and her Hulk-like 24/7 security guards all made her feel safe. Plus, there was a main entrance, lift and her own front door that all needed keys.

When she had spent the weekend in the country or at a remote location, she never slept that well. Any creak or animal sound would startle her, and she would spend the night gripping her pillow with one eye open.

"Sometimes," Lucy replied before taking a generous gulp of wine. "I never wanted to move this far out of the city. It was Hugo's idea." She placed her glass back on the table, retrieved the wine bottle from the chiller then topped herself up. "I definitely drink too much. But the days can be long during the week and 3pm feels like 7pm" She looked at her glass and swirled its contents, appearing lost in contemplation. "You know?"

Rosie didn't know if the *you know* was a question. But no, she didn't know. Her day was the polar opposite with 7pm feeling like it should be 3pm There were not enough hours in her day. She didn't want to pretend to Lucy that she *did* understand because she didn't. She changed the subject instead. "Do you have any friends around this way?"

"No, none close by. Some are still in the east, and some moved interstate and overseas. Anyway, what about you, Rosie? I'm sick of talking about me. Tell me about *you.*" Lucy's voice switched into a more upbeat tone and she sat forward in her chair attentively.

"I don't like talking about myself. Can't we keep talking about you?"

Rosie laughed, while nervously tucking her bob behind her ears. Rosie was confident at leading a conversation about *anything* except herself. The minute anyone asked her anything personal she clammed up. She was sick to death of being taken down a path of enquiry that always culminated in the questions "Why are you single?" "Why do you work so much?" "Why no alcohol?" and "Did you ever want kids?", all the standard questions you would expect from married types in their forties. That's partly why Rosie liked hanging around younger people, because their world usually revolved around work and sex, not marriage and kids. And that was why she liked Jazzy's company so much.

"Do you love what you do?" Lucy asked.

"Wow, that's a tough one to start."

"Oh sorry. I didn't think it would be. I mean, isn't it amazing to be running your own business and ... well ... just working? I used to love working."

"Do you miss it?" Rosie asked, trying her best to redirect the chat back to Lucy.

"No, no, no, no," said Lucy, wagging her finger at Rosie. "I know what you're up to. Stop trying to get out of talking about yourself."

"Okay, Lucy." Rosie rolled her eyes, playfully. "It all depends on what's going on with my clients. If it's a tough day for them, then it's a tough day for me."

Lucy's eyes narrowed and she tilted her head to the side. "So today was tough then because of us—the nightmare Hamiltons?" Her tone was apologetic.

"I've had harder, don't worry." Rosie decided it was best to keep her answers short so Lucy wouldn't read into them. The last thing she wanted was to make her feel worse.

"Do you think it's true?" Lucy asked, her eyes filling up with tears. She cast her eyes downward and began fiddling with the loose strands of the straw placemat in front of her.

Rosie leaned forward, sliding her plate aside to create space for her elbows to rest on the table. "I think you know your husband best. Listen to *him*, not everything that's been said or will be said about him. And this is just the beginning, Lucy. Things are about to get messy. I mean, really messy," she warned as she reached across the table, gently grasping Lucy's hand. "So, you've got to brace yourself."

Lucy's phone rang. "Oh no, that's my other daughter. I need to speak to her."

"I need to be getting home anyway, so I'll slip out."

As Rosie picked up her bag from the kitchen counter she could hear Lucy say, "Fleur, darling, I've been trying to reach you all day."

It was almost 10pm when Rosie arrived home. She threw all her possessions down at the front door and headed straight for the sofa. She turned the TV on and scrolled through Netflix for something easy. This wasn't a time to be watching any serial killer docos. She went with a replay of *Schitt's Creek* and her favourite episode when David opens his new apothecary. As she sank deeper into the sofa, her head resting on a scatter cushion, she couldn't stop thinking about Lucy rattling around in that enormous house on her lonesome. Where the fuck was Hugo? He had taken the charade of keeping up appearances too far, neglecting his family and Lucy when they needed him the most. Rosie felt sorry for her because she knew what awaited her—more victims.

Chapter 12

The Financial Report, *Tuesday, December 2, 2022*

Max Magnifico building something bigger and better at Curban Capital

Max Magnifico says he's got what it takes to build Curban Capital into something greater than it is today. He has thrown a warning shot at his competitors too, saying he's back to rule the roost.

"Two flat whites coming right up," said Luca, the barista at Baccino cafe, when he saw Bee striding towards the counter. She loved the familiarity of her morning coffee routine. A quick chat with Luca about the weather and sport, followed by a scan of the hard copy newspapers on the bench in front of the coffee machine.

"Oh God," she groaned, staring at the front page of *The Financial Report*. She had read the article on her iPhone but seeing it in hard copy, so big and bold, made her cringe. *Oh my hair, my teeth, my posture.* Couldn't they have airbrushed it?

"Bellissima," shouted Luca as he began frothing the milk.

Luca was your typical tanned-all-year-round Italian. He was blessed with long dark curls that were usually slicked back into a tidy man bun, big brown eyes, a warm smile and irresistible dimples. He wore a black t-shirt with the words Baccino on the chest next to a small embroidered Italian flag. It was probably one or two sizes too small judging by the way the sleeves hung just over the shoulders to reveal bulging biceps, but Bee suspected that was the look he was going for. He was an exceptional barista: fast, good at conversation and always upbeat. The fact that he made exceptional coffee was just a bonus.

"Not to me," Bee shouted back over the puffs of steam, feeling a slight blush coming on.

In the photo, she appeared rigid, pressed against the armrest with her arms folded and legs crossed tightly. Meanwhile Max was manspreading with a relaxed posture, exuding charm and looking dashing. But that wasn't what irritated her most. It was obvious from the article's contents that Max had indulged in a follow-up call with Jenny to further boast about himself. It had turned into a puff piece entirely on him. A free advertisement for Max Magnifico! There were no quotes from Bee and there was nothing about how well the business was performing. It was Max is a fierce competitor, Max knows how to win, Max is the best in the business.

"Don't be so hard on yourself, Bee," Luca said in the smooth Italian accent that mirrored his smooth silky coffees. "You women are always so critical of yourselves."

He slid the two coffees (one for her and one for Stuart) across the counter and into her waiting hands. She immediately looked down at the handwritten message in red ink on the lid. It read *Take two day by day* with a love heart. That was another little bonus of Luca's coffees—he always wrote messages of encouragement on her lid, and she loved it. If she was ever going to recruit a Chief Positivity Officer, the role was his!

"You have a great day. Say hi to Stuart for me." He winked and her face flushed.

Bee arrived at the Curban reception to a lot of hustle and bustle and what looked like removal people coming out of the goods lift and heading towards the reception. One of them, who was wearing a green polo t-shirt with *Bespoke Living* on his huge right pectoral muscle, said "Excuse me, love" as he wheeled a trolley past her carrying a large cream armchair. Another brushed past carrying a tall green plant in a concrete potter. There were large plastic bags overflowing with striped linen cushions blocking the doorway to the kitchen galley.

"Oh, Bee, there you are. I've been trying to call you," said Davide, arms flapping in the air.

"What's going on?" she asked, resting the coffees on the reception counter.

"I came in at 6:50am to all of this chaos. Nobody told me anything. I still don't even really know what's happening." He couldn't get his words out quick enough. Davide wasn't good at dealing with things he didn't know about in advance or that weren't listed on his daily clipboard of activities. "I'm sorry I haven't even had a chance to get myself dressed and freshened up." He flapped his arms around again.

Bee noticed he was still in his Lycra bike shorts, matching Lycra t-shirt and bike shoes. Men in Lycra always made Bee uncomfortable. *Just don't look at the crotch area,* she said to herself, but it was so hard not to because it was … well … it was just there, screaming back, *Look at me!*

"It's fine, Davide. Let's get one of the waiters out on reception and you get yourself sorted. But what *is* all this stuff?"

"It's Max and Suzy."

Bee could hear him trying to catch his breath.

"They have builders in here knocking down walls and setting up a new room for Max."

"What builders?" Bee squawked. She could tell her high pitch alarmed Davide. He shot her a frightened look, then shrugged.

"It's fine. Don't worry." She attempted to regain her composure. "Leave this with me. Go on. Get ready."

She politely shooed Davide away and started looking for Max. The removal men were making their way through what looked like a new opening where a meeting room used to be. A small Perspex frame with the words *Private* hung to the side of the door. Pectoral man was turning the armchair sideways to make it fit through the doorway. Bee followed him.

Where a large meeting table had stood just the day before now resided two cream-coloured lounges positioned to face each other. A low wooden coffee table occupied the space between them, creating lounge vibes.

A lady in the same *Bespoke Living* polo shirt was busy plumping cushions while another rearranged plants. Two men wearing white gloves were working out where to hang a large artwork that was resting against the wall. And there in the corner of the room, seated behind a large oak desk, was Max. Facing out of the window, and talking loudly on his phone, he was oblivious to the organisation going on behind him.

As Bee approached, she heard him say, "As I was saying, there're a few loose ends I need to tidy up. Obviously, we've got that obstacle that needs to be removed first before we can crack on with our plan." With a sinister chuckle, he spun around on his chair to find Bee standing beside his desk. A surprised expression overtook his face. "Look someone's just arrived to see me so I better run. See you on Friday." He slowly placed his phone on his desk. "Here she is. Curban's answer to the Artful Dodger," he said before bursting into "Consider yourself … at home, consider yourself … one of the family!" with his hands on his hips.

"The Artful Dodger is a cockney. I am not." Surely, he knew his British accents. After all, he *had* lived in London for years.

"Whatever you say. Anyway, I didn't hear you come in."

"Well, it would be hard to with all this commotion going on." Her eyes darted around the room to emphasise her point.

"Oh yes, they've been working all night so it will be finished in no time." He stood up, moved around to the front of the desk and perched his bottom on the corner. He then folded his arms and leaned back into a casual slouch.

"You didn't want to let me know that you planned on taking walls out to create an enormous office for yourself?"

"It's a lounge, but I won't quibble over the details. And anyway, I don't need your approval, Bee. I'm the chairman and you're the CEO." He pointed to her as he said CEO in a disdainful tone. "So, last time I checked, that means I'm above you." His stare lingered, waiting for a reaction.

Be cool, Bee, she repeated to herself. "You were getting an office next to me. Work was due to begin this weekend. You know that."

"You know what they say—if you want a job done properly, do it yourself." His tone was even and controlled and he kept his eyes on her, watching for any flinch, any sign that he was unnerving her.

"I explained to you several times that the building manager said no construction could happen until next week because of the other work going on in the building. So, they're going to be really pissed off with all of this …"—she looked around the room again—"… this chaos."

Max smiled smugly. "Just so you know, as we're still getting to know each other, the rules are … well, there are no rules—for me, that is. I am *above* the rules and *above* the law, *frankly*. So I don't give a toss what the building manager said. In any case, we won't be in this building much longer. I'm talking to a few property mates about us relocating to the new skyscraper." He puffed his chest out with that last sentence.

"You're …" She was lost for words.

"I'm?"

"Ridiculous." There were other words in her head that she refrained from using. Max didn't seem perturbed. Instead, he said, "Your gay assistant, Stephen."

"It's Stuart," she snapped. "You're not good with names, are you? And there's no need to use the word *gay*."

"Yeah, anyway, Suzy told him yesterday morning that we were going ahead with a lounge. Didn't he tell you?" He smirked. "Oh he didn't, did he?" He tutted and shook his head. "That's a bit slack."

His face was smug, and she wanted to smack it. It was amazing how someone could be so handsome and yet *so* ugly all at once. She was tempted to return his Artful Dodger comment by labelling him Veruca Salt because his behaviour mirrored that of an entitled, spoiled brat.

However, she realised that stooping to his level would serve no purpose. She didn't want to become as awful as him. Instead, she said, through gritted teeth, "Okay, Max. You get your office, lounge, whatever you want to call it, finished. I've got to get ready for our 9am with the new interns. I'll see you there."

She turned and used every muscle in her body to walk in a slow, composed manner. It was just as well she was walking slowly because Suzy came flying through the doors at breakneck speed, plated poached eggs in one hand and an espresso in the other. They hadn't been formally introduced yet, but Bee had heard Max gush about this "incredible assistant" on multiple Zoom calls.

"Oh, oh, Bee, hi. Sorry, I would shake your hand but I've got mine full."

Bee moved to the side to let Suzy through the doorway. As Suzy walked past, Bee felt her eyes do a sneaky head-to-toe scan of her outfit before she raced over to Max like her life depended on it.

"You didn't tell me about Max's lounge," Bee whispered angrily on the phone as soon as Stuart answered. She was hiding in a meeting room beside reception and could hear street noise on Stuart's end of the call.

"What? Suzy mentioned a lounge yesterday morning in our meeting but that was *only* yesterday morning, and I haven't had a chance to debrief with you. She's a nightmare, by the way. Do you know she—"

"Stuart," Bee interrupted. "He's gone ahead and created this whole new area for himself without even running it past me. I can't believe he did it. And you should have heard how he spoke to me."

Stuart let out a high-pitched shriek. "What! How dare he!"

"Where are you? Just get into the office as quickly as you can. I need you."

Frustrated, she hung up and made her way to the reception to retrieve her coffees while muttering Max's *"the rules are ... well, there are no rules"* under her breath.

"I'll fill you in later," she said to Davide who was now in position behind the reception desk sans Lycra.

"Good morning, everyone, and welcome to our intern orientation."

Emily Bain, Head of Human Resources, was standing at the front of the meeting room facing a group of eager-beaver interns. On the table in front of each of them was a range of company-branded merchandise including a spiral bound notepad, a ballpoint pen and a drink bottle. A large screen with the words *Class of 2023* hung from the ceiling. Bee sat at the head of the table with an empty seat next to her for Max, when he was ready to turn up.

Emily began her presentation titled 'Life at Curban Capital', capturing the interns' attention as they listened intently.

Contrary to their young faces, they displayed an astonishing level of maturity in their commitment towards their careers. At twenty, Bee was on her gap year bumming around France. *And how could they afford to dress so impeccably*? she wondered. When she started out, she had two polyester, machine-washable suits from Marks and Spencer on rotation and one pair of chunky black suede court shoes from C&A. She remembered that her desire to dress better ignited after her first encounter in 2002 with Savannah Silva, the sole female managing director in the investment banking division.

It was September 2002, and all the executive assistants were sitting around the edge of the meeting room while the managing directors they worked for sat at a large conference table. Bee was working for David Brady, the Head of Mergers and Acquisitions, and was there to take notes. About fifteen minutes into the meeting, in walks Savannah. Impeccably dressed in a poppy red skirt suit that shouted power, matching red lipstick and nails, an elegant raven bob and sky-high black stilettos. She exuded both elegance and gravitas. A real corporate Jackie O. She casually but confidently strutted to the seat next to David Brady, placed the most magnificent cream leather bag Bee had ever seen on the table, sat down and said, "Bring me up to speed, please."

Bee studied Savannah and her incredible outfits enviously until she finally got to meet her at the Christmas client cocktail event. She had been standing shyly in the corner, sipping on her expensive champagne, watching Savannah circulate effortlessly.

"Can I get a top up, please?" a voice had said.

Bee spun around to find a young man dressed in a sleek black dinner suit. He appeared to be in his early twenties with the height of a basketball player, a lean physique and blond hair neatly parted down the middle. His face was attractive in a nerdy kind of way. A bit Matt Damon in *Good Will Hunting*.

"I'm not a waitress. I work for David Brady," she replied.

"Assistant, waitress, same thing. So, can you top me up or not?" He gazed at her intensely while holding up an empty champagne flute.

Startled by his arrogance, Bee glanced over her shoulder at the long table covered in a crisp white tablecloth where a variety of bottled beers, wines and champagne were displayed. She picked up one of the champagne bottles closest to her that was already open.

"Not that one," he tutted. He pointed at a bottle at the far end of the table. "That one, the Dom."

She didn't know why, maybe because she felt so uncomfortable, but she started walking towards where he was pointing, until she heard, "Stop right there."

She turned around to see Savannah. With one hand firmly planted on her hip and the other one holding a champagne flute, Savannah shot a frightening icy glare towards the man and asked, "What do you think you're doing?" When he didn't respond, she raised her voice and repeated her question.

"Just getting a drink." His tone changed from cocky to slightly sheepish.

"Well, get it your fucking self, okay?" she snapped in her posh English accent. "And don't ever speak to any colleague of yours like that again."

Savannah watched with a predatory intensity as he made his way towards the end of the table, refilled his glass and rejoined his colleagues. She then turned to Bee, her mouth curving into a smile. "You've got to stand up to these pricks and *never, ever* get them drinks. That's not your job. You must stick up for yourself or they'll walk all over you. Trust me, I learned the hard way."

"Okay. I'll do that. Thanks for the advice," said Bee. She was captivated by this impressive woman standing in front of her, dressed to the nines in a black satin one-shoulder cocktail dress and huge dangly diamond earrings that were probably real.

"I have an eye for good people, or should I say good women, and I've noticed how dedicated you are, Bee."

Bee was amazed she knew her name.

"You strike me as someone with potential and God knows we could use more women in this business. So, if you want to learn the ropes then come to my office tomorrow morning at 7am. And if you don't, then no hard feelings." She held her glass out and clinked Bee's. "Cheers. Now I need to keep circulating."

The next day she *did* meet Savannah and that was how her career started.

Bee's gaze swept across the table at the young female interns. It was still, some twenty or so years later, a male-dominated industry but she was determined to inspire and guide the young women in the same way that Savannah had mentored her.

As Emily handed over to Bee for her presentation on 'kindness, respect and integrity—the Curban Capital values', Max's seat remained conspicuously empty. *Rude*, she thought to herself.

"Welcome, everyone. It's fantastic to see you all here. I just want to say thank you for choosing Curban Capital for your internship. We're lucky to have you working with us for the next ten weeks," she began.

Thirty minutes later, and still no sign of Max, it was time for the Q&A session where the interns got to pose any question of their choice.

Bee: Please can you tell Suzy to send Max in here now. He's over forty-five minutes late!!!

Stuart: I just saw him in the cafe downstairs with Arthur. I'll go get him.

"Please ask anything you like. Our goal is to be as honest and open as we can be with you," said Bee.

"I'd like to know more about your background and what the key drivers were to your success," asked the pointy, elf-like intern named Mia.

"That's an interesting question, Mia. Thank you." Her train of thought was interrupted by a knock at the door. Max entered.

"Hi, there, sorry I'm late."

Bee noticed a few of the interns around the table sit up straighter and follow Max as he moved to take his seat next to her. He most certainly knew the effect he had on people and that his tardiness added to this gladiator image—him being the main event and Bee the warm-up act. He turned to Bee and flashed a wide, charming smile which caused his eyes to crinkle handsomely. It instantly annoyed Bee. One hour prior, he had been utterly repulsive, but now he emitted an air of charm. *Grr.*

"You were saying, Bee?"

Bee smiled in return. "Welcome, Max. Everyone, this is Max, our new chairman. You all have something in common with him because it's his first week at Curban Capital too. We're thrilled he's here." Bee paused and then began answering intern Mia's question by attributing her success to having a good, caring mentor throughout her career. While she did, Max enthusiastically watched, even nodding his head in parts. So, he could actually be attentive, or at least look it, when he wanted to.

"Max, would you like to have a go at answering the same question?"

asked Bee, turning to him. "The question was—what were the key drivers to your success?"

Max set his espresso cup on the table, unbuttoned the single button on his suit jacket, fanned the material out behind him, leaned back in his chair, audibly exhaled, folded his arms and looked up, scanning the ceiling. "Yup, there's so many answers to that question." He sucked in the air. "I suppose the biggest driver has been fighting spirit." He sat forward, rested his forearms on the table and formed a steeple with his hands. "It all comes down to winning. I have an inherent desire to win, at all costs, at all times."

One of the interns, Charlie, sat forward and stared attentively at Max. He appeared to be enthralled by the confidence and Hermès cufflinks, which his eyes were fixed on. "Everyone in this room needs to be the best of the best in order to win. We won't accept mediocrity and you can't afford to have one off day because if you do"—he clicked his fingers loudly while he scanned the faces around the table—"we lose. It's that simple. You need to think about this job in the same way that gladiators think about the battle arena. Always be prepared to fight, fiercely."

The room was silent, digesting Max's response. Even Bee was digesting his response. It was a tad OTT. Was anyone really buying his gladiator spiel?

"So did you always know you wanted to be an investment banker?"

Well, it seemed to be working for Charlie.

"I did. I wasn't even out of high school when I chose this as my career." And with that answer Max took the interns on a journey through his entire career for the next twenty minutes. He was on such a roll that he completely lost track of time.

Emily ineffectually attempted to interject with "Okay, that's all we have—" but she stopped when Max talked over her. And just when Bee thought he had finally finished he said, "I think we've got time for one more question. That's okay, isn't it, Emily?"

"Er, well—" Emily's voice trailed off.

"Come on. Just one more." He wasn't asking Emily, he was telling her.

"I've got one, if that's okay," said the bookish-looking intern named Ed.

"That's what I like to hear," said Max, rubbing his hands together.

"I read somewhere that one of your biggest clients is a global casino operator. I chose to intern at Curban Capital because you work with clients doing good, whether that be socially or environmentally. So, I just wanted to check that we wouldn't be expected to work with casino operators, right?"

Within a flash, Max's self-satisfied expression turned to stone. He sat motionless, staring at Ed while Ed stared back, waiting for a response. Crickets. Emily played nervously with the ring on her wedding finger while Bee stared at the presentation screen.

"Ed, is it?" said Max, finally breaking the silence.

"Yes, that's right."

"I think Emily was trying to tell us that we're running over so we don't have time for that question after all. But thanks for asking." Then he stood up, flattened out his jacket, fastened the single button, tucked his chair under the table and glanced down at his shiny Rolex. "I have a client meeting I need to get to and the most valuable lesson that you will get to learn over the coming weeks," he said, pulling on his cuffs, "is that clients come first, always. Have a great week."

And again, in gladiator fashion, he exited the arena, leaving Bee to perform the final act on her lonesome.

Chapter 13

"Okay, three more sleeps until our big night, woo-hoo!" said Stuart, jazz hands flapping and shoulders shimmying.

It was the weekly meeting about the end-of-year party with his small group of helpers, comprising Davide and four of the executive assistants from different divisions of Curban. The *woke* staff, as Stuart referred to them, had advised the group not to label it a Christmas party for fear of offending certain people.

"I've invited Suzy Scott along to today's meeting, Max's new assistant, because we are hoping he'll be able to say a few words on the night."

"Excellent idea," said Davide with large, eager eyes.

Stuart suspected Davide was champing at the bit to impress Suzy. He always made much more of an effort with the *important* assistants, that is, the ones who worked for the managing directors within the firm. The end-of-year party was when Davide annoyed Stuart the most because he used it as an opportunity to talk up his event management skills.

Stuart knew he had gone behind his back last year to try and get himself appointed as chair of the party committee, a position Stuart had held for five years. He wanted to control everything about the event from the venue selection to the theme for the night.

For this year's party, Stuart had to veto Davide's Studio 54 idea. There was no way that theme would pass the front-page test given the link back to all the drugs and sex that went on inside the infamous celebrity hangout. His own idea was much more sensible and innocuous—shimmer and shine. Stuart knew Davide was huffy about not getting his way because he pretended he was unavailable for the next two party meetings.

"Let's start. Suzy must be running a few minutes late. Davide, please, can you give an update on the final numbers for Friday?" Stuart asked, looking past Davide to check if Suzy was coming. He hated that she was late for their second meeting. As annoying as Davide was, at least he was punctual.

"Okay, thank you, Stuart. I'll give you all a quick rundown of the yeses, nos and maybes, then we can move to—"

Stuart interrupted him. "Just the yeses, please, Davide. We don't need to know who *isn't* coming, just who *is*."

"Okay, got it," Davide hissed. "Five hundred and sixty acceptances. That means we are at full capacity. Perhaps on the night we'll have a couple drop out here and there, but I estimate we'll hit five hundred, no problem."

"Thank you for that, Davide. Let's move to you now, Natalie. Is everything finalised with the venue?"

"Yes, everything is confirmed. I'll just let the venue know today what our final numbers are." Stuart heard the heels coming before he saw her. Suzy was clip-clopping towards them, almost ten minutes late. "Suzy, there you are." Stuart signalled for her to come and sit next to him.

"There is a chair here," Davide called out, pretending not to see Stuart and pointing at the chair next to him. Suzy took it and set out her monogramed filo, iPad and glitter pen on the table as if she were showing merchandise to customers at Prada.

Today's outfit was another designer showcase. A sleeveless, high-neck, bodycon bandage dress in cherry red, paired with nude stilettos. Her hair was tied in a loose chignon that gave the illusion of no fuss and her make-up was caked on.

"Thanks for joining us, Suzy. We've gone through the RSVPs and we're now talking about the venue," Stuart said. He could see Davide examining her in a giddy, star-struck kind of way. "We assume Max will be attending?"

Suzy picked up her filo from the table, unclasped the gold buckle and flicked through the pages until she found Friday the fifth of December. She tapped the page with her acrylic fingernail. Stuart was wearing his brand-new Tom Ford reading glasses and could see from across the table that the evening in question was completely free.

When Suzy caught him looking, she snapped it closed.

"He's got a window from seven thirty to eight. That's it. He's completely tied up before and after."

"Oh, well, that's just fantastic," Stuart said sarcastically.

"What's the venue?" asked Suzy.

"It's Élefante," Davide replied quickly, before Stuart could.

Stuart could tell she was unimpressed. It wasn't exactly a frown, because her Botox-smoothed forehead lacked the ability to form one. However, her mouth contorted, and her head jerked backward.

"You might not be familiar with it because you've been overseas, but it's the hottest new venue down at the Quay with killer views," explained Stuart.

"No, I've heard of it," she responded with a disapproving tone.

Where did she get off being so rude? Stuart wondered. Her and the Gladiator appeared to be a match made in heaven! "Let's move to you now, Emma; can you please update us on the catering," he said. "This, as you all know, is very important to me as I love my food *and* my drink."

Emma proceeded to hand out sheets of paper. "Oh, I'm sorry, I only printed five."

"Suzy and I will share," Davide said, briskly.

As Emma began running through the list of beverages ordered for the party, Davide butted in with, "When I worked at a previous company, we always had a summer cocktail, designed by yours truly, on arrival for guests. Everyone loved it," he gushed.

Stuart clenched his jaw. Davide made a habit of starting sentences with *"When I was at"* as a way of bringing it back to him. It somehow always came back to him. Stuart sometimes felt the need to put him in his place, like now.

"Well, when I was running the *Mulberry* spring summer fashion show after-party at *Claridges* with Kate Moss, Alexa Chung and Cara Delevingne, just to name a few, we only had French champagne on arrival. The cocktail thing was considered passé. That's French for out of fashion, right, Davide?"

Stuart's words had the desired effect because he heard Davide inhale sharply.

After Emma finished updating on catering and Kimberley, who oversaw wristbands and the DJ, ran through her part, it was back to Stuart.

"So, last but not least, speeches. Suzy, can we put Max down for around five minutes at seven thirty, please?"

Suzy was busy on her phone and hadn't heard Stuart's question. Davide tapped her arm gently and she looked up. "Sorry, I'm playing cat and mouse with a travel agent re Max's yachting trip in Greece this July," she said. Stuart repeated the question, and she replied, "For now, yes, but I'll need to confirm with him today. That window that he has might close for something else."

"Well, it's the end-of-year party, Suzy. It happens once a year, and he's the new chairman, so it would be good for staff to hear from him. And I don't think I saw anything in that diary of yours for that date and time." Stuart said it in a way that was intended to be terse, terse enough that would signal to her that she couldn't pull the wool over his eyes.

She gave an exaggerated eye roll and snapped, "I said I'll confirm today", then grabbed her belongings and strutted off like a moody teenager.

"She seems nice," said Emma, looking at Stuart.

Everyone around the table laughed quietly, except Davide.

Bee was in the middle of sending an important email to a client when Stuart burst into her office, exclaiming, "Far out. I can't decide who is worse—Davide or Suzy. Why can't people just be normal?"

She continued typing.

"Did you hear me?" huffed Stuart, standing to the side of her desk, waiting for her to respond.

"Hang on. I've got to get this off." She finished typing and looked up at Stuart. "What was that?"

"I said that Davide and Suzy are nut jobs. The end-of-year party meeting, that's where I've been."

"Oh, of course. It's this Friday, isn't it? Oh gosh, what am I going to wear?"

"I sent you some ideas last week. Have you not looked at them yet?"

"Er, hello, I have been busy with other things. Can you resend them to me, please?"

"And you wanted me to remind you about sending an email to staff re party behaviour."

Bee was pleased to have diverted Stuart's attention to something other than Davide. She didn't have time to listen to him complaining right now. She had much bigger fish to fry!

"I've got ten minutes til my next meeting. I'll just do it now," she said, shooing Stuart out of her office. She hated the annual party behaviour email. It was triggering. It took her back to her first-ever work Christmas party in December 2002 when Ben Taggart forced her to sniff cocaine then tried to get her fired.

Frozen, she stared at her screen blankly. The thought of Ben Taggart made her feel physically sick. She remembered his lingering eyes and the way he laughed at her with utmost derision. What a cruel, vindictive wanker. She wondered what happened to him: did he marry? (poor them if he did) and have kids? (poor them too if he did). With that thought, she felt her lunch in the back of her throat.

She was furious she was even sparing him a single moment of consideration. And then it dawned on her that she didn't have the stomach to write the party behaviour email after all. "Stuart," she called out. "Can you get Camilla in Corporate Comms to write this party email for me? I've run out of time."

"Sure," replied Stuart. "And don't forget to look at the choices of outfits for Friday night. That's a priority."

She rushed past him, went into the nearest disabled toilet, and vomited.

Chapter 14

Rosie: Hi, Cecilia, you know that Hugo Hamilton follow-up story you were talking about? When can we expect to hear if it's running or not?

Cecilia Meadows: Not this week. More like Monday. Will let you know.

Rosie: Okay, thanks.

Rosie breathed a huge sigh of relief and fell back into her chair. "Thank fuck for that."

Jazzy peered over the top of her Mac and when she couldn't see Rosie she got up and walked around to her desk.

"Ah, there you are, all slumped down." She perched her perfect bottom on the edge of Rosie's desk. She was looking particularly beautiful today in a copper-coloured midi dress with shoestring straps and a pair of pink Marni Fussbett sandals. "So what's the latest with Hugo Hamilton?"

"It's about to get a whole lot messier. Cecilia says she has others but won't say how many or how old, just that there are other victims."

Jazzy visibly gritted her teeth. "Geez, that's gonna be tough. What are you planning on doing to counter it all?"

It was a fantastic question, but even after all these years in the PR business, Rosie didn't have an answer. Lucy was a mess and Rosie thought it was wise not to put her in front of probing journalists, so there went the idea of doing a happy-family style spread.

"I have no idea," shrugged Rosie. "If you come up with one, let me know."

Overnight, Rosie had gone from thinking Lucy was an insipid rich bitch to one of her own husband's victims. Diminished, destroyed. Last night when they had been chatting, Lucy had revealed how nervous she felt about Hugo's work Christmas party. She suffered from social anxiety and always felt out of her depth among the young, cliquey crowd. That's when Lucy had suggested Rosie come to the party and bring a plus one. She almost pleaded with her, telling her how much fun it would be. So taking pity on her, Rosie shelved her *other* plans and agreed to go.

"I don't suppose you're free Friday night and could join me at Hugo Hamilton's Christmas party?" Rosie asked Jazzy. "I've got a plus one and would really love some company."

"Yeah!" Jazzy said loudly, then grabbed her mouth before whispering, "I'd love that."

"Really? You're not just saying that?" asked Rosie. Now she felt like she was doing what Lucy did to her, pleading. "Small catch. We have to take Lucy Love with us. She needs to be chaperoned."

"I'm an awesome chaperone. Send me the details and I'll lock it in."

Jazzy slid her bottom off Rosie's desk and went back to her own. That's what Rosie loved about Jazzy—she was so easygoing. Always up for anything and delightful to be around. She brightened up the office with her permanent sunny disposition. She would never ask Simon to be her plus one, because she knew he would bore everyone to tears with tales of what it's like to work for a prime minister.

Rosie: Hi Lucy, +1 for Friday is Jazzy Jeffries. 🎊 *Let's have drinks before so you don't have to walk in alone.*

Lucy: You're amazing. 😍 🍸.

Rosie quickly sent Jazzy an instant message just so that Simon wouldn't hear: *By the way—Friday—it's Western theme!*

Rosie nipped out of the office at lunchtime for an appointment with her therapist. Because she often found herself playing the role of therapist, as well as PR advisor, to her clients, she desperately needed her own sessions.

Dr Preethi Kumar's office was in the building next to Curban Capital so Rosie thought she could kill two birds with one stone and drop in to check if Bee and Max were happy with the front page of *The Financial Report*. Rosie hoped Bee was happy, but she *really* hoped that Max was happy. If he really was one of the most connected investment bankers, then his nod of approval would count for a lot and possibly translate into referral business for her. She was going to ask Bee if they could have lunch together with Max in the next couple of weeks. Before the idea went out of her head, she typed it into her Notes on her iPhone. She also added *hire Western costume.*

"So, Rosie, it's been about four weeks since our last session. How have you been?" Preethi asked in her melodious voice. She was dressed in a coloured collared midi dress and long dangly earrings. Unlike Rosie's penchant for monochrome, Preethi was like a walking rainbow, always wearing bright outfits that made you blink. Rosie suspected it was a way of trying to brighten her patients' moods. She always wore her shiny black hair in a tight bun and minimal make-up on her flawless caramel skin.

The set-up was always the same: Preethi sat attentively in her red armchair, clipboard resting on her legs, a glass of chilled water set on the side table next to her. Rosie sat facing Preethi on the co-ordinating red sofa, upright and tense initially, chilled water on her side table and a box of tissues next to it.

Rosie had been a patient of Preethi's for three years, but in those first few minutes of each session she felt like she was starting all over again.

"I've been good, most of the time." Rosie leaned on the armrest and glanced down at her Balenciaga platform trainers. She was dressed casually today in loose trousers and a short-sleeved shirt.

"How's your daily routine going? Are you swimming, making sure you eat at mealtimes, going to bed on time, leaving the laptop and phone outside your bedroom, all those things we talked about last time?" Preethi asked while flicking through her notes.

Rosie had the urge to lie. She was here today for a particular reason and didn't want to go over this boring routine stuff. "Yes, that's all great. Sticking to everything we talked about."

Preethi scribbled away. This always made Rosie feel uneasy. She imagined that she was writing something like *lying about her routine*. What was it about therapists that made you feel like they could read your mind? Or maybe they were trained to make you feel like that, Rosie thought.

"I wondered if we could discuss something else today?" Rosie asked, rubbing the armrest with her hand. She noticed Preethi observing her nervous movements and quickly stopped, paranoid that she was reading into it.

"Of course, Rosie. What would you like to discuss?"

"There's someone that I've developed feelings for." Rosie eyes were still on her trainers, but she noticed that Preethi had laid her clipboard down.

"Okay, tell me more. Who is the person and what are they like?" asked Preethi, clasping her hands.

Rosie relaxed a little knowing that she wasn't taking notes. She hadn't told anyone about her feelings for Jazzy, because she was the boss and some people would deem that inappropriate.

"It's someone from my office. A colleague," Rosie said tentatively.

"Okay. And what are they like? Can you tell me what it is that you like about them?" asked Preethi. Rosie liked how Preethi used *they* and *them* and not assumed that it was a *him,* especially given Preethi knew that Rosie's ex was male.

"*They,*" Rosie said emphatically, "are really fun, smart, sexy." She paused. "Okay, let's cut to the chase and stop pussyfooting around. It's a her, a she, a female, with a vagina and boobs. What the fuck, Preethi.

Am I really gay, or am I having a mid-life crisis? I mean, I've kissed two girls and touched one fanny through trousers, not fully down the trousers, on a dark dance floor in New York when I was wasted." The words fell out of her mouth. She lifted her eye line from her feet to Preethi with a panicked face.

Preethi, ever the professional, remained poised and put her clipboard on the side table, leaning forward sympathetically. "Take a breath, Rosie. That all came out so fast."

Rosie reached for her water and took a sip. "Sorry, I've been holding that in for what feels like an eternity."

"It's okay, Rosie. That's why you're here. Now, there's a lot to unpack in everything you just shared, so let's start with the one you're going to like the least. You're the boss, right?"

Rosie nodded.

"So that brings a level of complexity from the outset." Preethi picked up her clipboard.

Rosie could have bet on Preethi bringing that point up first. That was the one and only reason preventing her from taking the next step and asking Jazzy on a date.

She was well versed with the *don't shit where you eat* phrase because she had advised clients on situations where they had, in fact, shat where they ate. More often than not, Rosie was called in to fix up the corporate cliché of an older, more senior male taking advantage of a younger junior female in the workplace. One of the messiest was a CEO who had been caught on CCTV having sex with the receptionist at 2am after a Christmas party *on the reception desk.* When you have CCTV evidence it's pretty hard to shift the narrative, but Rosie did her best, working around the clock to spin all kinds of stories about how it was consensual sex and that the CEO was separated from his wife at the time. It was hideous and Rosie felt dirty after it was all over.

"Yes, Preethi, I know you shouldn't shit where you eat," Rosie said.

"Well, yes, I wouldn't use that phrase but it's the right sentiment. Let's change tack. Do you think your feelings are reciprocated?"

"I don't know. Sometimes I think so and then I wonder if she's like that with everyone. She's just so goddamn nice and loveable. Everyone loves her." Rosie sighed, realising how confused she was.

Maybe if Jazzy was a *he,* she would be able to read the situation better. Dating men in her twenties and thirties had always come so naturally to her, but this was new territory. "There's an event this Friday and I've invited her as my plus one. It's a client's event so she'll think it's work, but actually I invited her because I like her, obviously."

Preethi's eyebrows rose. They did that when she was getting serious. "I'm not going to labour the *you're the boss* point, but you need to seriously consider that if something were to happen that this Jazzy would have to leave your employment."

Forty-five minutes and three hundred dollars later, Rosie emerged from Preethi's offices exhausted and even more confused than before she went in. She felt like Preethi was trying to talk her out of making her feelings known to Jazzy. She laboured the power imbalance point. *Sigh.* Rosie realised that sometimes she just wanted to pay Preethi to listen, not give advice. She decided she was going to take her own advice and reveal her feelings to Jazzy on Friday at the party.

Rosie stood at the Curban reception chatting to Davide while she waited for Bee. He was always good for a bit of office gossip and today he spilled the beans on a morning 'kerfuffle'.

"It was so crazy. Max has gone and given himself and Suzy the grandest office space. And Bee was not happy. Please keep that to yourself."

Rosie zipped her lips as Davide reached across the desk to answer the phone.

"Yes, of course. I will send her right up. Bee will see you in her office."

When Rosie arrived upstairs and took a seat in Bee's office, she noticed right away that Bee didn't look like her usual radiant self. A bit pale and distant. She was always so switched on and engaged, all the time. In fact, Rosie was quite pleased to see her more subdued. It normalised her.

"How are you, Bee? I hope you don't mind me popping by. I just wanted to see if everything was okay with *The Financial Report* article."

"I'm sorry, I should have called you back this morning. I know how you like feedback. I've just been so busy. Our new interns started today. God, they're young," said Bee.

Rosie subtly admired Bee's outfit. She wore a Prada organza dress with a collared top and loose-fitting knee-length skirt belted at the waist, and a pair of Prada slingback pumps in nude. While it wasn't something Rosie would wear, she was impressed with how powerful yet feminine it made Bee look. Rosie often felt dishevelled in Bee's company because her outfits were always so structured and well fitted compared to her own. And she always appeared to be wearing shoulder pads—either that or she had naturally square shoulders.

"So, I thought the article turned out well," Rosie said, fishing for feedback.

"Yes, me too. It was all about Max, but I suppose that's to be expected given he's the big news around here." Bee gave a half-smile.

"Did he, I mean, Max, say anything? Hopefully he was happy with the coverage."

Bee's eyes wandered across the room and out to the harbour in the distance. She let out a sigh, looking uncharacteristically downbeat. "To be honest, Rosie, I'm not sure what to say about Max. He is completely …"—she paused and looked up in the air as if she were searching for the appropriate word, then added—"unreadable. Yes, that's the best word for him." She turned back to Rosie. "But it is only day two, so I'm sure things will improve." Her tone lifted as if she were convincing herself of something. But there was no fooling Rosie, because to her, Bee was visibly and audibly deflated.

After Rosie left, Bee decided to Google Dr Robert Hare again. She wanted to remind herself of psychopathic traits and analyse which ones were presenting in Max.

Corporate psychopaths are chameleons able to disguise their ruthlessness and antisocial behaviour under the veneer of charm and eloquence—tick.

They thrive in chaos and know that others don't, so they will often create chaos at work for this reason—tick.

They lack empathy and don't care about the consequences of his or her actions—tick.

Boldness, meanness and impulsivity are common traits—tick.

And the article concluded with a quote from a contributing doctor—*There is no dealing with a corporate psychopath. You need to get out.*

But she didn't want to *get out*. She loved her job. She knew it was too soon to address Max's behaviour with Arthur. Therefore, she made the decision to set it aside for the time being, focus on the week ahead, embrace the Christmas party and reassess the situation by the following week.

Chapter 15

It was pitch black when Bee wheeled her black Rimowa suitcase out of her front door and across the pathway towards the front gate. She fearfully scanned the bushes for possums. While some might consider them cuddly and cute, she found them to be unpredictable and aggressive. She was generally uncomfortable with a lot of native Australian animals and insects, but the spiders were her biggest fear. When she read that Sydney was home to the most poisonous spider in the world—the funnel web— she seriously considered turning down the Curban job. Now, she also had the unpredictable, aggressive and poisonous Max to contend with.

She watched on her iPhone as the Uber made its way towards her house. *Three minutes away.* She looked up at the moon. It was a full circular disc illuminating the sky. Hmm, didn't a full moon mark a build-up of negative energy? When everything becomes tense, people act weirdly and there is friction in the air. How apt for her week so far—there was certainly friction in the air at Curban Capital since Monday, from 8am to be precise, and there was only one person causing it.

Two minutes away. Please don't let me have the seat next to Max on the plane. She did *not* want to spend those ninety minutes of flying time with him. The car ride from Melbourne Tullamarine airport to their first client meeting in the central business district would be more than enough time to talk about the day ahead.

One minute away. She would need a large flat white as soon as she got through the security check. She ran through the schedule for her whirlwind trip in her head. Client meeting, client lunch, more client meetings and client dinner. It was 4am now and she estimated that she wouldn't get to her hotel until eleven.

Arrived.

When her silver Toyota Corolla Uber pulled up at the pavement outside the domestic departures drop-off, she saw Max exiting his Uber in front. A Tesla with falcon wing doors. Grrr. What was he playing at? It was company policy to take a standard UberX, not the Premier. It was a childish move, but she ducked down in the backseat so he wouldn't see her.

"Do you mind if we just wait a couple of minutes?" she asked the driver.

The driver, who was dressed in head-to-toe leopard print with matching car accessories (steering wheel, handbrake and gear shift covers), glanced over her shoulder. "Hiding from an ex-boyfriend, are we? Fair enough." She chuckled.

"No! He's not an ex-boyfriend. He's someone I work with. It's just a bit early to see him, that's all." She peeked out of the car window to check Max was gone.

"Yeah, yeah, whatever you say." She strummed her diamond acrylic nails on the faux fur steering wheel cover while smacking her gum repeatedly. Another smack of that gum and she was out of the Uber and into the airport terminal.

Once inside and ordering her much-needed large flat white, she caught sight of Max in her peripheral vision. He most definitely saw her too. She was about to call out, but it appeared that he wasn't in the mood for chatting either because he noticeably picked up his pace and scurried away in the direction of the lounges.

The terminal was busy for 5am on a Wednesday and the three baristas at Quickshots cafe were run off their feet, pumping out coffees to the bleary-eyed business folk. Business travel had well and truly returned after its COVID hiatus, but Bee avoided it, preferring to hold

Zoom conferences when possible. She remembered how ecstatic she was when she was asked to go on her first business trip in business class. She travelled to Europe, Asia and the USA with her work and that was fine because it was pre-kids. Now, she was all about routine and maximising her time at home.

She removed her iPad from her tote and opened *The Financial Report* app. Today's headlines were all a bit gloomy as she scrolled on and on.

Bumper bank earnings to flatline in 2024. TechTwo shares slip on $4.4m impairment. Sydney accounting software start-up costs 10pc of staff. China's annual growth falls to almost worst on record. Max Magnifico set to make changes at Curban Capital.

"WHAT?"

It's only his first week in his new role as chairman of Curban Capital, but Gladiator Max Magnifico is said to be mulling serious changes to the firm and its staff. We understand Magnifico, who is known for shaking things up, will be looking to restructure and we hear that nobody is safe.

Bee almost spat her coffee out. *Mulling serious changes?* What the actual fuck? Did he really say this or was it just speculation? She couldn't tell from the way the article was written, but usually *The Financial Report* was spot on. Their reputation was predicated on running extremely well-sourced information.

Her employees were going to read this article and start worrying about their jobs. Clients would be asking questions too. What a pain in the butt with such a busy day ahead of her. Where the hell is he? She swiftly made her way towards gate fifty-two where she waited with her arms crossed. *Rosie! She'll know.*

Bee: Rosie, do you know anything about this wretched article in today's Financial Report? *Am at the airport. It's way too busy to chat freely. Text me.*

Rosie: Hey, I've seen it. 😕 *Let me see what I can find out.*

Bee: Thanks. Can you find out who talked to them, please?

Rosie: Yep. On it. Can't be Max. Has to be a competitor trying to put you down?

Bee: Don't know. Appreciate you making some calls. Thanks.

Bee scanned the area for Max, then paused in shock when she saw someone else. Oh no, that was all she needed. Penny bloody Pryor.

Penny was a managing director at a Melbourne-based funds management company. Her vibe was Cruella de Vil in how she wore her hair with a distinctive streak of blonde among black locks, how she barged around in an abrupt manner and how she adored high fashion. And she was striking in an unconventional way, with a large, hooked nose that was always poked into everyone's business.

"Bee Bloom. How are you?!" Penny shouted at the top of her lungs.

"I'm good, Penny. You?"

Penny did her usual up and down assessment of Bee's outfit. You could say that they were professional rivals *and* fashion rivals, although Bee considered herself much more *on trend* than Penny. Penny's signature look was a power pant suit. An expensive designer suit, but a suit, nevertheless.

"I wouldn't be surprised if she had a pair of balls under that suit of hers," said a junior female who had jumped ship from Penny's firm to Curban. At Friday night work drinks with about five Rieslings under her belt, she had told Stuart and a couple of others that Penny was "a power-hungry, morally bankrupt, outright bitch who just wants to be one of the boys", and naturally Stuart had repeated the story to Bee, but it didn't make her laugh, it made her sad—sad that Penny couldn't be herself and felt like she needed to be one of the boys.

Surprise, surprise, today Penny was wearing a striking, stand-out-from-the-crowd, royal-blue satin trouser suit. Poking out from the palazzo trousers were black sky-high sandals and perfectly shellacked orange toenails. An aquamarine necklace, hanging around her sun-damaged neck, was paired with matching stud earrings.

"I'm excellent for this ungodly time of the day," she said, tossing her voluminous locks to one side before caressing them with manicured fingers. She had great hair, and she knew it. Either she was up at the crack of dawn to coif that bouffant or she had slept in a hair net on a silk pillow.

"Were you up in Sydney visiting clients?" asked Bee, feigning interest in Penny's affairs.

"Yes. A few in-person meetings here and there, you know. Thank God we don't have to do all that Zoom crap, we can see human beings in the flesh." She leaned close to Bee's ear and said quietly, "So, I just read in *The Financial Report* that there might be some changes for you guys. Anything you can share?"

"Nope. Nothing happening." *And even if there was you would be the last person to know.* "Shall we board?" she suggested before heading towards the departure gate.

Penny appeared to be struggling to maintain the pace in her red-carpet footwear. What was she thinking, travelling in those heels?

"Well, I just ran into Max in the chairman's lounge and he confirmed that things do need a little shaking up." She smirked snootily like the cat that got the cream. Bee's expression quickly hardened, and Penny noticed, instantly. "That's all he said. Don't worry. He didn't spill the beans."

"I didn't know you knew Max," said Bee as they continued towards the ticketing attendant.

"Oh God, yes, we go wayyyyyyy back," gloated Penny.

Penny's drawl bugged Bee big time, but her most irritating flaw was the way she revelled in one-upmanship. For her, information and influential connections were her most powerful tools.

"Anyway, why didn't you come into the chairman's lounge? You have membership, don't you?"

The Qantas chairman's lounge was the crème de la crème of airport lounges. Sitting atop the lounge hierarchy, membership was invitation only. It was intentionally hard to find with *Private* labelled on its discreet frosted doors. For people like Max and Penny it was a necessary membership that elevated their social standing. For Bee it was a stuffy room where high-flyers went to swing their dicks and eat and drink for free. Bee heard that Curban's chief operating officer, John Shadforth, had been sucking up to the person in charge of their travel budget for two years hoping he might get thrown a bone. But it was a running joke that he was never, *ever* going to make the cut.

"Actually I *do* have a membership, Penny, but I prefer to sit out in the terminal. The coffee is better."

When they both reached the ticketing attendant, Bee held out her phone and scanned her boarding pass.

"Welcome back, Ms. Bloom. You look fabulous as always. What a gorgeous dress," the attendant said. "Welcome back, Ms. Pryor."

Ha! No compliment for Penny. Touché! That was just the ticket to make Bee smile. She practically skipped into her row eight window seat. But her smile turned to a frown when she saw Penny in row one and Max taking a seat next to her. 1A—the best seat on the plane, of course. Tesla to the airport, the chairman's lounge and now 1A. *What will be waiting for us at Melbourne airport*, she thought—a helicopter?

Once they had reached their cruising altitude, Bee peered over the headrests to study Max and Penny. They were talking closely, and Bee could hear Penny cackling loudly over the sound of the engine. Penny looked miffed when a stunning flight attendant interrupted their chat and handed something to Max, possibly a pre-ordered pack of activated almonds. He must have said something funny to her because she let out a loud laugh then covered her mouth and made an *oops* face. The Gladiator could certainly turn the charm on for the ladies.

There was no sign of Max when Bee disembarked so she made her way to the luggage carousel. Although it was just an overnight business trip, she had packed a small suitcase with wardrobe options because Melbourne was famously known for having four seasons in one day. With no sign of him there either, she texted him.

Bee: Just getting case. Where are you?

Max: A case!!!! I'm in the car.

Bee: Won't be long.

Max: I don't have time to wait. Get another car.

Bee: It will be five minutes, tops.

Max: No can do. Penny and I will take this one. You can get an Uber.

Bee: You can't wait just five minutes ... DELETE.

Why bother? He clearly wasn't going to wait for her. She wasn't surprised Penny had secured herself a comfy ride into town with her friend from *wayyyyyy back*, but she *was* surprised that she had managed to exit the terminal so fast in those stupid heels.

Bee went straight to the location of their first client meeting and found Max in the office building's lobby café, sitting in a leather armchair, sipping on an espresso.

"Hi, Max. Hope your car ride in was smooth and quick. I'm sure I was just five minutes behind you," Bee hissed. She wanted to throw her suitcase at his head but settled for bumping his elbow with it as she pulled it to a stop, right next to him.

She pushed her anger down. It wasn't the time *or* the place for a stand-off. "Would you like another coffee before we go up to the meeting? We've got fifteen minutes." She took a seat in the chair opposite him.

"No. I'm good," he replied without looking up, continuing to tap on his phone. A copy of *The Financial Report* was on his lap.

"I read the article on changes at Curban," Bee remarked, pointing at the paper. "You wouldn't know where they got the information from, would you?" Her tone was deliberately accusatory.

He exhaled loudly, and a look of irritation crossed his face. "Nope."

"Could you do me the courtesy of looking at me when we're talking, please?" Bee stiffened.

Max placed his espresso cup down on the round coffee table in front of him and lifted his eyes to meet Bee's. He glared at her with narrow, angry eyes and a deadpan face. "I'd keep your voice down if I were you, Bee. And I would change your tone, too. You sound like you're losing your cool."

"I'm not losing my cool, Max. I'm asking you to show me some respect. You've been nothing but disdainful towards me since we met. It's unacceptable."

"Well, now you're imagining things. And anyway, in relation to today's article, you know how the press works. Surely I don't have to explain it to you."

He picked up his espresso cup, downed the dregs, then placed it back down.

"It's just very unusual for an article like that to run without some kind of background sourcing, wouldn't you agree?"

"Zip it," he jabbed. He flashed his left palm at her face, stood up, let out a groan, threw his laptop bag over his shoulder and strutted towards the lifts.

She felt his jab in her gut. *In for four, hold for four, out for four, hold for four.* Because she was a consummate professional, she parked the humiliation she was feeling. He was mistaken if he had intended to ruffle her before an important client meeting. And since he thought she had 'lost her cool', she was going to show him just how cool she could be.

She made herself as tall as she could, stretching her spine with every step towards him, and pulled her suitcase to a stop in front of the mirrored lift doors. As they both faced into the mirror, Max ran his fingers through his hair, while Bee stood motionless and poker-faced.

They stepped into the lift and two young attractive women in tight pencil dresses filed in behind them. When the lift arrived and the doors opened, Max said, "After you, ladies," while holding out his left arm. He smiled widely and the pair smiled, bashfully, in return. "I love your shoes," he said to the taller of the two. She batted her false eyelashes and replied, "Oh, thanks so much," and walked off with an exaggerated bum wiggle.

Bee: Did you find out anything about that article?

Rosie: Jenny won't disclose her sources...

Bee: Okay, thanks for trying.

Rosie: Will keep trying.

For the remainder of the day, as Bee and Max went from one client meeting to the next, it was like being with a completely different human being to the one who had snarled at her in the lobby that morning. His charming twin had returned. He was visionary, passionate, compelling, likeable and funny with the clients. Bee even found herself laughing at one of his jokes. But ultimately, she knew it was temporary and the charm tap would be turned off later when it was just her and him.

Chapter 16

"Morning, Miss Bee. Big day today?" asked Luca while immediately getting to work on her flat white order. Today, he was rocking a top knot and looked particularly handsome. She had never asked him, but she did wonder if he had a partner.

"Yep, sure is," Bee replied loudly over the hum from the milk frother. "Are Chelsea playing this weekend?"

"We're playing Arsenal at home. I know who you'll be supporting." He laughed, knowing she supported Spurs, Arsenal's London rivals. Bee didn't watch too many English Premier League matches these days, but she still liked talking about the game.

"Of course, Luca. Go, Chelsea!" she cheered.

"And you have your big party tonight?"

"We do. I'm the boss though so I need to be well behaved." She smiled with a twinkle in her eye.

"You let your hair down, Bee. You deserve it. You work so hard." He slid her two flat whites across the counter. "How's Stuart. Is he going tonight?"

"He's good. Actually, I just remembered he's got his trainer this morning and won't be in until later. Damn, I'll have to drink his coffee too." She pulled a cheeky face.

"Please, Bee, before you go, try some of this homemade focaccia bread with olives and rosemary." He pointed to a platter of bite-sized samples set out on the counter.

Bee picked up one of the smaller pieces and popped it into her mouth. "Wow. Send my compliments to the chef. Better dash."

"Enjoy the party," Luca called out.

Bee looked down at today's messages on her lid—*Dance like nobody's watching* and a love heart.

The Curban office was buzzing with a pre-party atmosphere. Groups of people were crossing the floor, chatting, with big smiles on their faces. Bee knew the staff wouldn't be doing much real work today, but she was fine with that. She knew how hard they had worked all year. This was their time to celebrate and let *their* hair down. And it was almost time for the summer break where the office officially closed for ten days. What a wonderful time of the year. She inhaled that exciting thought and brightened at the idea of spending time with Gus and the boys.

"Good morning, Bee," said Davide who also seemed to be soaking up the pre-party buzz. He shook his hands as if shaking maracas. "It's party time."

"Someone's excited!" Bee exclaimed.

"Well, you know, we've put a lot of work into it."

"I know, and thank you so much for making it all happen. We're lucky to have your creative eye pulling it all together."

Davide smiled proudly, lapping up Bee's praise. "It's an absolute pleasure. And do you have anything shimmery or shiny in that bag of yours?" His eyes moved to the white clothes bag hanging over Bee's elbow. The dress Stuart ordered for her had arrived in a clothes bag with the words *Carolina Herrera* in large, bold, capital letters. Bee had swapped it for a brand-less white bag before leaving home.

"*Bien sur*! I have stuck to the theme. But you'll have to wait until later to see it. On that note, I better dash. Full day of work first."

Davide gave her a small wave.

Bee was sampling a new patch remedy for hangovers. The marketing had sucked her in—*Big night ahead? We've got you covered. Our hangover*

patch contains glutathione and milk thistle to help reduce the headache and nausea from drinking. See you on the dance floor. She didn't have time to read the *how to use* section, so she wasn't entirely sure if she should wear a patch before, during or after consuming the alcohol, so she decided she would do all three. Knowing how freely the champagne flowed at these parties, she had asked Stuart to monitor her intake. She *did* want to let her hair down, like Luca suggested, but not *too* much. She'd been to enough Christmas parties in her time to know that the women, especially the senior ones, were judged more than men for getting drunk or staying out late.

She hated how, back in London, men would clap each other as they arrived the morning after with their McDonald's breakfasts tucked under their arms. The loudest claps went to those who pulled all-nighters. They even ran wagers on who could stay out the longest. Fortunately, nobody behaved like that at Curban. And if they did, they'd be out the door.

On Fridays, Stuart arrived later than usual because he had his weekly personal training session with an Alexander Skarsgård *Tarzan* lookalike. Stuart made no secret that he only selected the trainer because of his looks. And on Fridays, Bee liked to walk the floor for thirty minutes and have impromptu chats with staff. She began by checking in with the new interns. It was the end of their first week and she was keen to hear their thoughts. They all quickly assembled in the meeting room, which pleased her. She liked how this bunch seemed eager to please because there had been years when some interns thought *she* should be pleasing *them*.

"Okay, so is everyone here?" She looked around the table and counted. "Hang on, there's one of you missing. Ed, yes, Ed, where is he?"

Charlie piped up. "He hasn't been in since Tuesday."

"Is he okay? Is he sick?" she asked, concerned.

"We haven't heard from him. I've texted him but didn't hear back. Kinda weird."

The others stared back at her blankly.

"Okay, I might check with Emily in HR."

Bee tried not to look disappointed. It was odd that a diligent intern like Ed was absent in his first week. She wondered if he had jumped ship to a big global firm like Goldman Sachs. The interns did sometimes receive multiple offers from competitors which explained some of their cocky attitudes. But Bee had interviewed Ed herself and thought she'd pegged him correctly as honest, hard-working and loyal.

"How's everyone's first week been? Shall we just go around the table, starting with you, Mia?" she said.

Twenty minutes later, she breathed a sigh of relief. The feedback was nothing but positive. She assumed they were telling the truth because if there was one thing she knew about this generation it was that they liked to speak their minds! With Ed on *her* mind, and a few minutes to spare before her next meeting, she decided to stop by the HR department and the office of Emily Bain. Emily was sitting at her desk on a Zoom call with her headset tucked into her bob. A bouncy personality with a bouncy bob. That was bouncy Emily.

Bee stood at the door and mouthed *"One minute"* to Emily while holding up one finger, to which Emily responded by putting her call on mute and dropping her headset down to her shoulders.

"Sorry, just on a call about our new employee assistance program."

"It's fine. Sorry to disturb you, but I wanted to know if you've heard what's happened to Ed Turner, the intern. He was here Tuesday but none of his team have seen him since then."

Emily's bouncy smile quickly turned to a grimace. She put her headset back on, told the participants she was jumping off the call, then hooked the headrest on its charging station.

"Why the panicked face, Emily? What's happened?"

"Come in and close the door." She motioned for Bee to take the seat opposite her. "He's gone."

"What do you mean, gone?!" Bee exclaimed.

"He's not coming back." Her voice was quiet and her expression pained.

"Okay, Emily, please stop talking in half sentences. Just tell me. I know you think I take it personally when staff leave us for rival firms, but you can't exactly hide it from me."

Emily's eyes anxiously darted beyond the walls of her glass office. Genuine terror consumed her features, as if she half expected a deranged axe murderer to appear.

"I've known you for five years, Emily, and I've never seen you like this. What's going on?" Bee's tone was a mix of impatience and concern.

"Max told me to let him go. No, in fact, he used the words *get rid of him and do it quickly.*"

"Did he say why?"

Emily looked to be fighting back tears because her lips quivered and her eyes shimmered. As she took a deep breath, her inhalation sounded shaky too.

"He said his face doesn't fit and told me to get him out by the end of the day. And then he told me not to tell you. I'm so sorry, Bee. I've never been in a position like this before. I didn't know what to do." She looked heavenward.

"It's fine, Emily." Bee knelt down beside her. Looking up into her wet eyes, she rested her hands on Emily's knees and felt them trembling. "Emily." She paused, her expression changing from concern to anger. "Did you feel threatened?"

"It's fine, Bee."

"Emily, you need to be honest," Bee interrupted in a firm tone.

"Yes ... yes, I suppose I did." Her voice trembled like her knees and her face was full of fear. "He basically said if I didn't do exactly as he said that I would be following Ed out the door."

"Jesus fucking Christ. What's wrong with this man?" Bee stood up and started pacing around Emily's office. Then, it came to her. "I think I know why he wanted Ed gone. It was that casino question. Max went weird after Ed asked that. And you know why Ed asked it. Remember? His interview."

Emily nodded.

"I'm going to handle this right now." Bee took a deep breath and stomped off to find Max. He wasn't going to get away with this. She had to nip his bad behaviour in the bud before he caused more damage. It was only his fifth day, for God's sake, and he was trampling over people without any regard.

He wasn't in his *lounge* and snappy Suzy (as Stuart had now labelled her) didn't know where he was. *What a great executive assistant—not knowing where her boss is.*

She needed Stuart!

Bee: Have you finished at the gym? Hurry. Need help!

Stuart: Not far. What's happening????

Bee: Meet me downstairs by Baccino. Hurry. NTV.

NTV (Need To Vent) was code for urgent. And Bee knew those three letters would get his Prada loafers moving a bit quicker. At times like this, she didn't lean on Stuart for advice; she just wanted to vent and get her thoughts out.

She checked his whereabouts on the *Life360* app, marvelling at how she was able to know exactly how far away he was. She had initially downloaded the location-sharing app on her phone to track her boys' movements but added Stuart for those moments when she needed to find him, like now.

While she waited on the street, she saw Max walking towards her with a man she didn't recognise. She ran into the clothes store on the corner and found a position where she could watch. She pretended to be browsing the rack of silk blouses in front of her. Max was smiling, animated, seemingly telling a good joke, because the other man's head was tilted back in laughter. The man was tall and lean with distinctive white Santa-Claus hair, a handsome tanned face and a good suit. They shook hands and Max walked back towards the office, leaving Santa Claus hailing a taxi.

There was something going on. You didn't need to be a super-sleuth to work that out. Who was this man and why was he meeting with Max?

Two minutes later when it was all clear, Bee exited the shop.

"What were you doing in *that* shop?" Stuart shouted as he approached her. "Their clothes are hideous. Tell me you didn't buy anything?"

"No. I was just looking. Let's do a quick lap."

On their quick lap around the block, Bee relayed to Stuart how Max had fired Ed over his casino question, how Emily was a quivering mess and how she had just spotted Max looking like he was up to something with a mystery man.

Stuart stopped Bee and grabbed her arm. "It's time you got hold of the mystery emailer. You have to know what she means by psychopath," he pleaded. "This mystery person might be a hit man for all we know."

Bee's head jolted. "Not funny."

"I'm kidding," said Stuart. "Well ... you never know. Stranger things *have* happened."

Chapter 17

Rosie: Yee-Haw! Confirming we'll see you at 6pm Rainbow Bar.

Lucy: Sure will! Thanks again for chaperoning me.

Rosie: Did you decide what to wear?

Lucy: Yup. Madonna Don't Tell Me video vibes. Not sure I can pull it off.

Rosie: You can definitely pull that off.

Lucy did her best to sound excited about Hugo's Wild West party, when in reality she was anything but. It couldn't have come at a worse time. The thought of turning up, with all his staff watching her, had her quaking in her cowgirl boots. She wished she were more like Hugo, able to put on a show no matter what was going down. She knew how busy he was—he started every conversation these days with a snappy "I'm so busy, darling"—but it was a tad cruel not to spend a couple of nights at home with her this week.

The only conversation they'd had that was longer than two minutes was when he ranted about *her Daily Life* article. How dare he! What about *his* article? He suggested that she lay low to avoid embarrassing herself further and even suggested that she miss the party, but it was Rosie that changed his mind. She said that Lucy's absence might be conspicuous. It was better that they presented a united front, otherwise divorce rumours would start to swirl around.

And what about him laying low? Fat chance. He was still allowed to stuff his face every day at his favourite lunch spot down at Woolloomooloo Wharf while she ate a salad alone at her kitchen bench.

As she sat at the kitchen bench sipping her morning coffee, she began reading the article in today's *Sydney Times,* which Rosie had organised as part of Hugo's reputation recovery plan.

Sydney Times, *Friday, December 5, 2022*

Hugo Hamilton adds new secret phrase to help patrons in danger

Restaurant and bar operator, Hugo Hamilton, will open the doors to his new bar in Surry Hills in just under two months. Inside the female bathrooms, patrons will find posters with a secret phrase that they can use if they feel unsafe at any time. Hamilton says the posters are necessary due to the increase in reported cases of women feeling in danger in bars across Sydney.

It was ironic. The harasser claiming to help the harassed. A bit like Rolf Harris being a child protection advocate. Plus, other bars had been doing this for years with phrases like *Ask for Angela.* Lucy knew it was Rosie doing her best PR work, but she was still surprised how Rosie was able to spin such garbage. It struck her as a disingenuous vocation for such a genuine person.

Lucy always checked the *Most Viewed Today* section of the paper online because she was curious what other people were reading. Hugo's article was the number two trending story after one about a mysterious giant egg that had washed ashore in Japan.

She began reading some of the comments.

"What about if it's your own staff that feel unsafe, Hugo????"

"No point putting a poster up when you're the one making the women feel unsafe."

"How's your wife, Hugo? She left you yet?"

Yikes, that one made Lucy sit up. A random person commenting on her marriage, her life, like they knew her. Standing on the sidelines judging. Who were these faceless busybodies that took the time to write comments on people's personal lives?

But it wasn't just randoms giving their two cents' worth. During the week Hugo's mother, Pamela, had called from her farm in Kiama with hers.

Pamela was Australian born and bred with no English heritage whatsoever but that didn't stop her from faking Received Pronunciation—the accent regarded as the most prestigious form of spoken British English. "Just wanted to check how you are doing after that appalling article where your undergarments were on show. What on earth were you thinking, my dear?" she had asked.

At eighty years of age, Pamela was showing signs of losing her marbles. Her judgement had always been poor, and she had always been incredibly right wing, but lately she was prone to coming out with completely inappropriate comments.

"I mean, how mortifying to be standing there in Double Bay like that. You must get yourself some new undergarments right away. You can't possibly keep Hugo interested in you by wearing items like that."

As someone who never left the house without backcombing her thinning hair, planting two circles of pink blusher on her sagging cheeks and applying a stroke of pink lippy on her disappearing lips, Pamela was always impressing on Lucy how important it was to look your best, for the sake of her marriage.

"Actually, Pamela, I'm more mortified by the *other* article. You know, the one about Hugo harassing someone at work."

"Oh dear, that's just a load of cowpat. My Hugo would never do anything of the sort. And anyway, these young girls are asking for trouble with the way they dress. You make sure ... erm ... Flora ... and ..."

"It's Fleur and Maya."

"Yes, you make sure Fleur and Maya always dress in a way that is becoming of them. None of these tarty dresses with holes in all the wrong places."

"Women should be able to wear what they want, Pamela," huffed

Lucy. "A bit of flesh shouldn't be an invitation to sexual advances."

And just like that, because she never liked Lucy disagreeing with her, Pamela pivoted the conversation back to the farm. "The cows are causing us so much stress at the moment."

Lucy wondered how *she* would react if Maya or Fleur had been accused of something terrible. Would she defend them? Are you blind to your children's faults? The girls had never put her in an impossible situation like that, thank God. Of course, there had been times when they acted like terrible teenagers—unappreciative, moody, bitchy, vaping in their bedrooms, drinking too much—but her eyes were open to all of it. Pamela's were well and truly closed shut! She often got on her soapbox about drugs. "Anyone caught with any form of narcotic should be hung or shot by firing squad," Pamela had said. No clue that her own son couldn't function without at least one gram of coke a day. But Hugo had his mummy wrapped around his little finger. And he had Jocelyn wrapped around his little finger too. During the week he had couriered two Hermès boxes to the house—one for Jocelyn and one for Lucy. He always bought Jocelyn a scarf; she must have at least twenty by now. But that didn't stop her from squealing with childlike excitement when she opened the box. "Oh wow, it's beautiful. Look at the colours in it." She tied it on right away while standing in front of the full-length mirror.

Lucy's gift was a pair of lacquered Pop H earrings in red. She held them in her hand for a few seconds then repacked them into the black velvet drawstring bag that sat inside the orange Hermès box. They were lovely and expensive, obviously, but they weren't her. She didn't like anything overtly designer like a H for Hermès or G for Gucci. How had Hugo not worked this out after all these years? She looked down at her locket and sighed.

"You're not going to try them on, Lucy?" Jocelyn had asked, looking surprised.

"I'll try them on later. I need to sort my outfit out for tonight first."

The scarves were a way of Hugo reminding Jocelyn that she worked for *him*; *he* paid for her services and therefore she was required to keep an eye on Lucy. Or at least that was how it felt to Lucy.

To 'lay low' and not get photographed shopping again, Lucy had ordered several different party outfits online. She had created a Pinterest board of ideas before she decided to emulate Madonna in her 'Don't Tell Me' video. Her hairdresser and make-up artist were booked in for the afternoon to help her achieve the desired look. She was going all out!

In her walk-in wardrobe, she laid out her outfit on the rectangular chaise longue. She had a leather puffed-sleeve cowgirl shirt, leather boot cut trousers with chaps, a bedazzled chunky belt and a black cowgirl hat. She took out a pair of black steel toe-cap cowgirl boots from her shoe rack and set them down next to the chaise. Then, she opened her glass jewellery drawer, selected a pair of turquoise feathery earrings and held them up against her ear, checking how they worked in the mirror. Perfect! Maybe it wasn't so bad to be going to the party after all and maybe, just maybe, she would actually have some fun.

In the same glass drawer, she had hidden a bottle of CBD oil which arrived earlier in the week for her to trial. The pharmacist who ordered it for her made her swear she wouldn't tell anyone where it came from. "Only take it before bed because it might interfere with your Lexapro. And don't drink on it," she had warned her. "Make sure you come back next week and tell me if you experienced any side effects."

A small trial now won't hurt, thought Lucy. She squeezed a dropper full of the oil under her tongue, leaving it there, as instructed, for one minute, before swallowing. It tasted of weed. *Not bad*, she thought, licking her lips.

Rosie sat at her desk, preparing for a call with Hugo. In front of her was a report of the media coverage from the week. Her job was to analyse it all so she could give Hugo an update on how their PR plan was tracking.

It wasn't that technical a task—she just had to categorise each article as favourable or unfavourable—but it was tedious. And she would bet money on the outcome—ninety-nine per cent unfavourable, for sure. The public had turned on Hugo, just like they had when he was in the jungle.

Better be prepared for the inevitable question that clients always asked when coverage was unfavourable—*Well, what am I paying you for then?* In her inbox she had seen an email from the perennially whinging client, Bill, with the subject 'Urgent'—it was always urgent. He'd apparently had a ticking off from the big bosses in London for cocking up his *Financial Report* interview. He wanted to have a call with Rosie to discuss *how to fix the problem.* He just needed to get better at doing bloody interviews and stop sucking up to Jenny and her big boobs!

Rosie wondered what Jazzy would be wearing tonight. They hadn't discussed costumes, but she was in no doubt that Jazzy's would be cowgirl cool. Hers, on the other hand, was a quick fix one-hundred-and-fifty-dollar rental from a costume shop close to the office. Probably stained and stinking of BO, highly flammable and scratchy. Luckily, she did own some old Isabel Marant cowgirl boots which were hiding in her tote under her desk, away from Simon's prying eyes.

Rosie was beginning to wonder if Simon also had the hots for Jazzy. He did this annoying swallowing thing when he was around her and, because he lacked self-awareness, he probably thought he was in with a chance.

Jazzy always used the word 'partner' when she talked about exes, making it hard for Rosie to confirm her sexual preferences. She desperately wanted to know but didn't want to ask her to clarify. An idea sprung to mind—maybe she could ask Lucy to pose the question tonight.

Rosie spent the next hour reviewing Hugo's coverage and it confirmed her thoughts—ninety-nine per cent horrible. The comments were furious and vitriolic. And although they were mostly from women, men were commenting too.

"Would you want your daughter working at your office?? I bet the answer is no!"

"You sleazy prick. I hope your bars burn down."

"Suck on your chipolata dick, you sex pest."

They went on and on and on ... She was surprised he hadn't been lynched, but there was still plenty of time for that to happen. The thought of addressing the negative commentary *and* the Cecilia Meadows follow-up article with possibly more victims caused her hands to tingle, her right eye to twitch and a pulse-like throbbing in her forehead.

Stress, panic. Preethi had taught her techniques for responding to stress, like mindful walking. It was boring but she decided to give it a go and took herself around the block for ten minutes while listening to *bells and chimes for calming meditation.*

She passed the regular handful of shameful smokers on the corner of the office tower, hidden away, not for public consumption. They were a live puffing advert of why not to smoke with gaunt, grey-tinged faces and skinny frames. The vapers were an entirely different bunch. They strutted around the CBD proudly puffing on their little e-cigarettes like it was the coolest pastime on the planet.

Feeling no benefit at all from the bells and chimes, Rosie returned to the office where it was time for the Zoom call with Hugo. Postponing it wasn't going to work because, as Preethi also taught her, it gives more time for the anxiety to build and take on a life of its own. She clicked on the link to open the call and waited for Hugo to join.

Like Rafael Nadal before every serve, she had a nervous process that she ran through to settle her nerves before handling tricky clients. She rubbed her sweaty palms on her knees, shifted around on her chair, tucked then retucked her bob behind her ears, checked her freshly applied red lip stain, and waited and waited. At the seven-minute mark, a face appeared on the screen, a young, female face.

"Hi, Rosie. I'm Erin, Hugo's assistant," she said with an upward inflection. High-rising terminals were a pet hate of Rosie's. Erin appeared to be eighteen years old, with sparkly, dewy skin, too much make-up, ringleted blonde hair. She wore a black halter neck top that scooped around her ample perky breasts. "I'm afraid Hugo is caught up, erm, with something, erm, urgent. It's literally just come up, erm. So, can we do this call later? Like maybe this afternoon?"

Erm, no. I've literally just worked myself up for this call, thought Rosie. Typical.

"Of course. No problem." She clenched her jaw. "I'll see him tonight anyway. I'm a guest at the party."

"Yeah, but it's a *party,* so he *literally* won't have any time to *erm,* discuss work," she said, again with an inflection as if it was a question, not a statement. Erin began looking beyond her camera, lifting her hand and signalling with her talons for nails that she would be one minute.

Erm, you literally need to go back to an English class, literally.

"Got it. In that case, I'll just see him tonight," scoffed Rosie.

"Amazing. See you there."

Rosie sat back in her chair, cross that she got all worked up for nothing. Paula came rushing over, juggling a white costume bag and poke bowl.

"Here you go, Rosie. One cowgirl costume."

"Thanks for picking it up. But not everyone in here knows where I'm going. I'm trying, well, I *was* trying, to keep it low key. Can you just hang it up in the cupboard behind reception, please?"

Paula looked offended. That was her most annoying trait; she always took things the wrong way. There were certain tasks that she was responsible for, like making sure the coffee pods didn't run out, replenishing the bar fridges, keeping the printer stocked with paper—but if Rosie reminded her, Paula would huff and puff and make up excuses for why she hadn't had time.

Since she was already offended, Rosie decided to seize the opportunity and address the wardrobe issue. She followed Paula to the reception desk and when they both came to a stop she said, in a quiet voice, "Look, I'm really cool with most outfits in this office. It's relaxed, casual but it still has to be professional. So if you're wearing a skirt"—her eyes moved to Paula's skirt—"it needs to be a certain length."

Paula's face contorted with rage. She tossed the costume bag and poke bowl on the reception desk, freeing up her hands, then yanked her skirt down and scowled. "Ta da."

"Very funny. You need to do a bit more than that." Rosie pointed at her skirt this time. "C'mon, Paula, we can all see your knickers when you're sitting down. It's not a good look in an office, with clients. Please don't wear that one again. I've seen you wear some lovely stuff before."

In typical snowflake fashion, Paula grabbed her poke bowl and said, "Fine. I'll wear a maxi skirt on Monday then," and strutted off towards the kitchen.

FFS.

Chapter 18

Lucy walked into Rainbow Bar just after six o'clock. She had arrived early but wanted to make sure that Rosie was there before her because she was too self-conscious to sit at the bar alone dressed as a cowgirl. She hadn't been into a bar, other than one of Hugo's, in at least ten years. To kill time, she asked the Uber Premier driver to go around the block not once, but twice, and when the driver made a fuss, Lucy pulled out a one-hundred-dollar note. "That's more than enough to circle for ten minutes," she said, and the driver gladly accepted. She topped herself up with another squirt of CBD oil, just to take the edge off before going into the bar.

The bar was packed to the rafters with a young advertising and media crowd. They were casually dressed, drunk and shouty. She felt old and hot, temperature hot. After the luxury of an air-conditioned ride, the humid Sydney city air hit her like a truck. She felt trickles of sweat running down her back inside her leather shirt, her bum was sweaty and expanding under the leather chaps, while beads of sweat were forming on her upper lip. She removed her cowgirl hat and used it to fan herself. As she moved through the crowd, she heard herself squeaking. Suddenly the Madonna-inspired outfit didn't seem like such a good idea in the summer heat.

"Lucy! Lucy! Over here."

Lucy turned around to see Rosie sitting on a stool towards the rear of the bar next to an attractive young woman.

"You look bloody awesome," Rosie yelped excitedly as Lucy approached her.

"Thanks, but I'm a bit on fire inside all this leather. And you two look incredible!"

"You say you're on fire? Well, I'm scratching like a monkey with fleas in this." Rosie readjusted the red and white bandana around her neck. They all burst out laughing.

"Let's get you a cold drink and sit under the fan then, shall we? Oh, and sorry, this is Jazzy from my office. We work together."

Lucy leaned across Rosie and kissed Jazzy on the cheek. "Lovely to meet you. Thank you so much for coming. You two have saved me from the embarrassment of walking in alone," she said in a raised voice, trying to make herself heard over the loud crowd.

"Are you kidding? We've been pumped for this party all week," replied Jazzy while rolling her hands and shimmying her shoulders. "Go and grab those seats; I'll get us a round of *cold* drinks." She winked at Lucy.

Lucy wasn't sure if it was the CBD oil or the relief of seeing Rosie and Jazzy as dressed up as her, but her nerves had melted away. Rosie was wearing something that looked rented—a black mini dress with short sleeves and a silver trim, a silver sequin fabric belt with a matching black and sequin-trimmed cowgirl hat, and black cowgirl boots. Jazzy could be wearing her own clothes—copper-coloured flares, a gold belt, a denim cowgirl shirt, a straw cream hat with a gold chain. They both looked sexy and fun. And it looked like it wasn't just Lucy who thought that—they were getting stared at from nearly every table of men in the bar.

Jazzy returned with a tray holding two tequilas and two margaritas. "And one non-alcoholic cocktail for you." She handed a cocktail glass to Rosie.

"To a fun night." Jazzy held out her shot glass and Lucy raised hers. They both downed the contents simultaneously and Lucy shivered as she bit down on the lime segment.

"You're not having one?" Lucy asked Rosie.

"I don't drink. I used to, but not anymore."

Lucy noticed how Rosie, usually confident, was avoiding eye contact. She gazed down at her glass and pushed the ice around with the straw. "It's a long story and pretty boring."

"Oh, I'm sorry. I didn't mean to make you feel uncomfortable."

"You're not. I guess I'm just not used to talking about it." Rosie inhaled. "I was engaged to this guy called Orlando." She exhaled. "He was an alcoholic; took him a while to admit it, and it was just one relapse after the other. I became sober too, to support him, you know. It's amazing how it changes the dynamic in not just your own relationship but in *all* your friendships too. In the end, I just wasn't strong enough to keep propping him up, but I *did* stay sober."

"Rosie, I'm so sorry."

Rosie lifted her head. "It's fine. I've made my peace with it now. Anyway, let's move on from one heavy subject to another. Are you okay, Lucy? I know you were anxious about tonight. I think you're really brave."

"Me too," added Jazzy.

"Thank you. That's really sweet. I'm still cringing about being photographed in my horrible granny pants, because nobody wants to see that. And I need a bum lift apparently. Did you see that comment?"

"They can all get fucked. You're hot and I can already tell you're smart and funny," said Jazzy.

Lucy gave herself a little internal fist pump. She liked this work colleague of Rosie's. She knew how to make a woman feel good!

Bee used the ladies' shower room at the office to dress for the big party. She slipped on her Carolina Herrera shimmering gold gown, with long sleeves and side split, paired with gold metallic Gianvito Rossi shoes. It wasn't an outfit she would have chosen herself, a tad glitzy and shiny, but Stuart convinced her. He said the dress was a "timeless key piece" that could be worn again and again, therefore she would get her money's worth, and the shoes were the same—"able to go with any outfit". He was a brilliant salesman because Bee had no idea where or when she would wear either again.

Earlier in the day she had popped out to Mecca for a professional make-up application to match her sparkly outfit, followed by a visit to the Glow Blow Bar for some bouncy waves. She felt like she was on her way to the Oscars!

"Well, what do you think?" she called out to Stuart as she twirled in front of his desk.

When he looked up, his whole face lit up. "Oh my fucking God, Bee Bloom. This ... is your best look *ever*!" He walked over to where she was standing and spun her around again to get another look.

"You don't look too bad yourself," Bee said.

It felt like Stuart had gone through fifty different outfit ideas during the week and landed right back at the beginning, with his first choice—a Celine sequin-embellished woven shirt with black tailored trousers and Dior loafers.

"Is it all right? It's not too much, is it?" he asked Bee. "I'll look better than Davide, won't I? I mean, he's probably just wearing a boring suit with a sequin pocket square."

"Don't start." Bee frowned. "It's not a competition. Anyway, sit tight, I've got to finish my speech for tonight and knock off a few emails then we'll get a taxi. There's no way I'm walking through town in this gown and shoes."

"No siree!" agreed Stuart.

Bee sat at her desk and quickly scanned through her emails. There was one from Max with the subject 'Important!'

I need you to take a client meeting for me next week. I'm going to be away. Suzy will send the details, it read.

Bee often reminded her teams about email etiquette and how it only takes a couple of seconds to include a salutation. Max's email proved he was above this basic courtesy.

Hi Max, I'll also need details about the client please—company and executive information—assuming it's a new one of yours? See you at the party. Bee.

Where was he? What was the point of having that fancy lounge when he was never in it? After seeing him with the mystery Santa Claus, she hadn't managed to track him down. She was still fuming about the whole intern Ed thing and really didn't want to address the matter at the party. And his behaviour towards *her* was also top of mind. He made her feel like the very sight of her made his eyes roll.

She turned her attention to her speech. It wasn't going to be long; she had timed it and it was coming in at two minutes and thirty seconds, which was perfect. She opened the draft, which was a series of spaced bullet points in a large font. From all the public speaking and speeches she did these days, she found it was always better to have bullet points that prompted her rather than a full script. It was boring if you just read word for word from a piece of paper. She hated that.

When she arrived at the part where she was to introduce Max, she went blank. What could she say about him? A week ago, she would have said *We're thrilled he's finally here and so excited about what the future holds—the new era of growth.* If she was being truly authentic, she would say *It's been a tough week; he seems like a complete dick and he speaks to me like I'm shit on his shoe. But don't worry, because he's the Gladiator and he's going to fight to the death at Curban.*

And what was *he* going to say? He'd already shown how he marched to the beat of his own drum. *No point sitting here sweating on it*, thought Bee.

"Okay, let's go," she shouted to Stuart, then grabbed her coordinating gold clutch bag from her desk. "I've decided I'm going to go off the cuff for some of my speech. It's just not coming to me right now, and I don't want to be late."

"God, you sure about that? You *never* do that!" exclaimed Stuart, grabbing his own clutch bag.

'Welcome to the Wild West' read the large wooden sign hanging at the front door of Hugo's new bar. The three women made their way across the straw carpet that led to two giant cacti made from green balloons. At the door, two self-important door bitches were busy ticking people's names off the guest list. Lucy had seen photos of partygoers at the Burning Man festival on Pinterest while she was searching for outfit ideas, and these two looked like they would be right at home there. Lots of flesh and Oopma Loompa fake tan. They were dressed in matching pink metallic bikini-style bras covered in rhinestone fringes, denim cut-offs that were more underpants than shorts and pink cowgirl hats with more rhinestone fringes. The sole distinction in their attire was their boots: one sported a pair of gold over-the-knee stiletto ones, while the other wore a vibrant pink cowgirl boot.

"Name, please?" blurted out the one in the gold boots.

"Lucy Love. I've got Rosie Reid and Jazzy Jeffries with me."

She scanned the list with her heavily glittered eyes and when it appeared like she was struggling to find the names, Lucy whispered, "It might be under Hamilton. I'm Hugo's wife."

That caught Gold Boots' attention. She immediately looked up, raised her thick, slug-like eyebrows and gave the three women a quick once-over. Up close and under the entrance lights, Lucy noticed the thick layer of foundation on the young girl's face. Why did young girls with beautiful skin do that to themselves? She also noticed she was wearing a pair of Hermès earrings, the same ones Hugo had given her but in white. She suspected they were fakes; after all, how could she afford real? However, she couldn't get a good enough look to confirm because her vision was slightly blurry. *It must be the oil kicking in*, she thought.

"Lucy, hi. I'm Erin. Hugo's assistant. We've spoken on the phone before. Come in."

She unclipped the red rope and ushered the three of them inside. Lucy felt Erin size her up as she walked past. Hugo's staff often did that.

Erin began fussing around with her phone. "If you could just wait here a sec. Hugo asked me to call him when you arrived. He said you need a photo together."

The photo was probably another desperate PR stunt. Maybe it was Rosie's idea to get a couple shot out to a few journalists and on Hugo's socials. That was just how this whole keeping-up-appearances thing worked these days. But jeez, it was all so shallow.

Hugo suddenly appeared from behind a plush velvet curtain like a magician. He approached Lucy with an awkward, clumsy hug and equally awkward kiss. After giving him a quick once-over, she realised his costume was easily two sizes too small. He wore a white shirt that was bursting at the buttons, a black suede waistcoat that couldn't be fastened and black leather trousers that could pass as leggings. And to finish things off he sported a black and white bandana and a black leather cowboy hat labelled Big Daddy. But the most disturbing part of his costume was the bulging crotch. He had obviously stuffed something down there.

"Wifey, what's this outfit?" he shouted loudly, standing back, looking Lucy up and down. "And who's here with you?"

"I brought Rosie and her colleague Jazzy."

"Rosie. I didn't recognise you."

Hugo hugged Rosie in an overly familiar and affectionate way. He then yelled, "Oh, who have we got here then?" while leering at Jazzy.

Obviously sensing he was going in for a hug, Jazzy stepped back, causing Hugo to stumble. When he steadied himself he shot Jazzy a death stare. Lucy heard him mutter "frigid bitch" under his breath. She could tell he was already coked up to his eyeballs because he was always overly affectionate with people he didn't really know and his voice sounded different. It became squeaky and loud, really loud. His pupils were dilated and he was pale and sweaty. He looked ugly. At that moment, she was suddenly aware of a shift in her feelings for him. She wanted to get as far away from him as possible.

"Let's get a quick photo, wifey, then you get yourself into the party."

Hugo pushed Lucy, a bit too forcefully for her liking, towards a 'wanted' sign where people were queuing to have their photos taken. He yelled at the photographer that he was the boss and that she better take his shot first if she knew what was good for her.

As they stood on the straw carpet posing for photos, Lucy felt the ogling eyes and judging whispers of onlookers. She smiled timidly, hating every moment of it. Meanwhile, Hugo lapped up the attention, striking different poses with every click of the camera. He grabbed his bulging crotch and shouted over at Rosie, "Make sure you get this shot out to the vultures." The photographer appeared to be appalled by his behaviour. When the charade was finally over, Lucy turned to walk away, only to be startled by a heavy slap on her backside from Hugo. She immediately stiffened, feeling desperate for another soother to loosen her back up. Making sure nobody was watching, she reached into her bag, removed her oil and quickly gave herself a few more drops.

Rosie was standing behind Lucy as they waited to enter the venue. She recognised the door bitch from the Zoom call earlier in the day. Her perky breasts were on full display in her rhinestone bra. There was something very unlikeable about her on the screen and even more so now in person, and she was unimpressed with the way she looked Lucy up and down, checking her out. Rosie was glad she had agreed to accompany Lucy, because she could see how daunting it would be for her to attend like this alone, surrounded by Hugo's entourage.

The venue had been completely transformed into a western saloon with hay bales and wooden carts throughout. One cart with a ripped cream sheet for a roof and wooden wheels held large glass jars full of

Wild West-inspired cocktails—a Western Sling, a Midnight Cowboy and a John Wayne. Another displayed pork sliders on wooden trays and another offered cupcakes with chocolate butter icing and Pringles for cowboy hats with red liquorice as the trim. There was an apple bobbing competition with Reward bags sitting to the side of a wooden barrel, a fortune teller's wagon, a tacky bucking bull and a DJ playing 'Rhinestone Cowboy' while dancing behind his decks on a straw-covered stage.

"This is amazing!" Jazzy screeched. "You stay here. I'll get the cocktails."

As Jazzy headed in the direction of the Watering Hole, Rosie turned to Lucy. "You okay?"

"Yeah, I'm good, thanks. That whole photo thing was a bit awkward, that's all. I hate having my photo taken. Your friend seems fun."

"Yeah, she's pretty cool."

Rosie thought Lucy seemed drunk already. Her speech was a little slurred and she was swaying ever so slightly. She instinctively wanted to keep an eye on her and make sure she was okay, because it didn't look like Hugo was going to.

The crowd was mostly staff from his twenty venues in Sydney, over three hundred people, Rosie estimated. The rest she assumed were his bankers or lawyers because they looked out of place with their suits. It was going to be a helluva long night with this lot.

Bee's sandals with stiletto heels kept getting caught on the uneven pebbled forecourt of Circular Quay. With her arm securely looped through Stuart's for balance, she carefully watched her feet take each step forward. When she lifted her head to check her direction she was overcome with emotion. Before her, the Opera House in all its splendour with the Harbour Bridge in the distance, the sun peeking over its arch. On a cloudless summer's evening, Sydney always took her breath away. She was on her way to join several hundred staff from the company she led as CEO. Wow! She wanted to pinch herself with pride. She tugged on Stuart's arm. "Let's get a quick selfie. I want to remember this moment."

While Stuart reached inside his clutch for his iPhone, her eyes filled with tears. "How lucky are we to live here?" she sniffed. "It's incredible, isn't it? All those miserable summers in London, desperate for some sun. And working together, you and me, after all those years. I love seeing your gorgeous face every day." She affectionately squeezed one of his cheeks, just as she would do with Otis and Ollie.

Stuart noticed Bee's eyes were shimmering. "Are you crying, Bee Bloom?" he teased.

"Maybe," she replied shyly.

"Oh come here, you silly sausage." He hugged her tightly and whispered into her ear, "Love you, my BFF."

As he said it, Bee hugged him tighter. In that moment, she felt they were the closest they had ever been in their twenty years of friendship.

"I couldn't do all this without you, you know that," she spluttered.

"Oi, get off now, you're going to crease my expensive shirt," he joked, pushing her away before stroking his shirt. He held up his iPhone and pushed Bee to his left side. "This is my better side. And I've got it set on the Clarendon filter. That should give us a lift."

She rolled her eyes. God, he was vain.

Once inside Élefante's foyer, they made their way up the stairs towards the Sunset Room, where the party was being held. Davide was standing at the door greeting guests and checking wristbands, along with his helpers, Nat, Emma and Snappy Suzy. As Bee and Stuart approached, Stuart leaned into Bee. "I knew it. So predictable. Just a plain black suit and sequin pocket square after all. He could have made more of an effort."

"Satisfied now then, are you?" Bee muttered under her breath.

Nat and Emma were dressed in similar silver sequin midi dresses and silver strappy peep toes while Suzy wore a boned bodice gold lamé mini dress with platform gold sandals. Her boobs were pushed up so far that they were practically touching her chin.

"Well, aren't you lot a sight for sore eyes. You all look incredible," Bee said.

"But the award for best dressed goes to you, Bee, no question," gushed Davide as he looked Bee up and down. Nat and Emma glanced at other and gave a small eye roll.

Bee cringed and felt compelled to play down her extravagant outfit. "It's one of my eighty per cent off specials."

Snappy Suzy was silent, which Bee presumed was because she was one of those people who welcomed compliments but didn't dish them out herself. Davide held out a silver tray of filled champagne flutes and Stuart took two, one for him and one for Bee.

"I *do* think we should have gone with a summer cocktail on arrival but there's always next year, I suppose," huffed Davide, clearly still miffed with Stuart's veto against the idea.

"Thank you, guys, for organising this wonderful party. The venue is absolutely stunning. Best ever, honestly." Bee looked at Nat, Emma, Davide then Suzy. "Now get inside and enjoy yourselves. Let the paid wait staff do this champagne and wristband stuff."

She moved across to Davide and quietly leant in and asked, "Has Max arrived yet?"

"Not yet. I can let you know when he does."

"Yes, please, *merci beaucoup*."

As Bee and Stuart walked away arm in arm, Stuart glanced over his shoulder and, with his lips pursed, smirked at Davide.

The Sunset Room was a crescent-shaped space with concrete and pink granite terrazzo flooring and white birch panelled ceilings, but its most striking feature was the windows stretching the full length of the room, providing an unobstructed view of the harbour.

A five-piece band, dressed in black-and-white ensembles, was tuning their instruments while guests huddled around high cocktail tables. Waiters in bow ties circulated offering drinks and fancy canapés, with some of the hungry staff hot on their heels. While Bee was taken aback by the spectacular views, something else appeared to be on Stuart's mind.

"Bee, darling, you *have* to *stop* going on about how much of a bargain your clothes are. You're cheapening yourself and to be frank, it's unnecessary and embarrassing. Everyone knows you get paid the big bucks. You're the CEO!"

Her smile slipped into annoyance. She didn't like Stuart's tone or that he was popping at her now. "I'll stop doing *that* when you stop your childish bickering with Davide."

"Fine," snapped Stuart.

"Fine," Bee snapped in return.

They then walked off in opposite directions. This was their relationship to a tee—one minute hugging and laughing, the next sniping at each other. More like brother and sister than boss and employee.

"I'm just going to the toilet," shouted Rosie to Lucy and Jazzy over Shania Twain's 'Man I Feel Like a Woman'. She followed partygoers down the poorly lit stairs and into the toilets. Girls and guys were heading into cubicles with retro-louvered saloon doors. As the doors swung shut, she heard giggles followed by sniffing. There was *a lot* of coke at this party, that was for sure. She worked her way up the row of doors, checking for feet at the bottom. Sticking out from underneath one of the doors was a pair of boots and, as she moved closer, she noticed they were gold, and from their position, with soles and heels facing upwards, it appeared like the owner was kneeling on the floor. Her eyes moved up the door to a man's head tilted backwards. He was moaning with pleasure. *Is this guy getting a blowjob?*

"Hey, what are you doing in the blokes' toilets?" shouted a loud voice in the distance. The words jolted her *and* the people behind the saloon doors. Rosie saw the gold boots disappear and the man's head jolt forward. Shock overtook her face. It was Hugo.

"Shit, I thought they were unisex," she shouted, then ran out, pushing past the cowboy standing in the doorway.

Shit, shit, shit, that was Hugo and those gold boots were Erin's. She ran into the adjacent female toilets and hid inside one of the cubicles, standing on the toilet lid to hide her feet. As she listened to the girls in the neighbouring cubicles sniffing coke and laughing, she panicked. What would Preethi say in times of panic—breathe deeply, inhale and exhale. But the smell of urine and poo was too pungent.

"Rosie, I know you're in here," she heard a man's voice call out. It must be Hugo. She held her breath and nose.

"I'm just going to wait until you come out," he taunted.

There was no way of pretending. She had seen *him,* and he had seen *her.* She unlocked the door and saw his silhouette, with a distinct pot belly, standing next to the sinks.

"Listen, I know you think you saw something, but you didn't."

Rosie walked towards the closest sink and began washing her hands. She kept her eyes down under the ultraviolet lights that hung overhead. Hugo inched closer and stood behind her. She felt him watching her in the mirror.

"It was just a bit of coke. That's all you saw, right, Rosie?"

She could feel his breath on the back of her neck. She continued washing her hands until he leaned over and turned the tap off. She glared at him in the mirror. His mouth set in a hard line, nostrils flared and veins popping in his neck. He was disgusting. She turned around; their faces were only inches apart. She smelt the alcohol seeping from his pores and his stale, heavy breath.

"Right, just a bit of coke," she said firmly. She turned her head, reached for a paper towel and proceeded to dry her hands, then tossed the damp towel in the bin, all the time keeping her eyes on him.

As she walked off, Hugo yelled, "Just remember, it's Big Daddy who pays your bills, not Lucy; that's where your allegiance should be. Did you hear me?" And when she didn't reply he repeated, "I said, did you fucking hear me?"

She kept walking and didn't look back.

It was almost ten o'clock and the dance floor was heaving to the sound of Taylor Swift's 'Bad Blood'. Jazzy and Lucy danced seductively, singing along to the lyrics while the bankers in suits encircled them. Rosie made her way to the bar and took a seat close enough to the dance floor so she could keep an eye on them both. Lucy was more than tipsy now; she was drunk. Shaky on her feet, she kept banging into the suits, who were only too happy to steady her in a groping way. Poor Lucy. Oblivious to the fact that Erin, the golden boot floozy, was giving her husband a blowjob right under her nose. What the fuck was he playing at? So careless. Anyone could have walked in on them.

Now Rosie had the conundrum of what to do with this information. If Lucy was a long-term friend, of course she would tell her, right now! But she had only known her for one week and, while she liked her a lot, she didn't want to be the one to break up her marriage.

Bee was busy circulating among her staff. She was like Savannah Silva all those years ago, moving effortlessly from one group to the next. It had taken time and a lot of practice to become such a pro and she wished Savannah could see her now. As one of her early mentees, Bee thought she would be really proud of her. All the staff were vying for her attention. That was one of the perks of being the CEO—you never ran out of people to speak to. She was on her second champagne and deep in conversation with the finance team when Davide came rushing over.

"Sorry to disturb you, can I please have a word?" His voice was trembly and his face panicked.

Bee excused herself from the group. "What's going on, Davide?"

"Max has arrived. But Nat didn't recognise him, so she asked him for his wristband. And he said he didn't have one and got pretty angry about it." The words spilled out rapidly.

"Why didn't he just say who he was? Not everyone has met him yet, that's why I asked him to speak tonight."

"Yes, but he was really cross; I mean, *really* cross."

"Did he say something?"

"He just said 'Don't you know who I am?'" Davide faked a deep, angry voice for effect. "And then he charged past Nat."

"Thanks for letting me know. I'll smooth it over. Don't worry about it."

And just like that, Bee's bubble burst and her mood switched from excitement to disappointment.

On the terrace, she caught sight of Max, dressed in a timeless dinner suit, his hair slicked back in a sleek, wet-look style, and a whisky glass in hand. Although he might have resembled a James Bond advert, she had discovered within just one week that his personality mirrored that of Lyutsifer Safin. Standing at least a foot shorter and looking up at him was Arthur in his standard suit and red tie.

Right. She strutted over to their table, convinced that Max had noticed her approach and read his lips as he said, "Leave it there, she's coming."

"Bee, I thought it was a gold Oscar walking towards us," joked Max. But Bee didn't laugh. Couldn't he just pay her a normal compliment like a normal human being?

"Thanks, Max. You two look as thick as thieves. What were you talking about?" She looked at Arthur then back at Max.

"Just what a great job Suzy's done with the party," Max lied.

Suzy! Bee exclaimed internally. She hadn't lifted a finger. That was a lie too!

"I'm delighted you could spare a moment from your busy schedule to join us." Her tone was deliberately laced with sarcasm. What she really wanted to say was I wish you hadn't bothered coming because you've ruined my high. She asked Arthur if he would mind chatting to a few staff so she could get Max to herself. Arthur agreed and promptly walked to the neighbouring table. Now, which gear would Max be operating in tonight—charming or charmless? A waiter stopped by to refresh drinks. Bee accepted a champagne top-up while Max declined another whisky.

"Max," she said, earnestly.

"Bee."

Max had his back to the Harbour Bridge. The sun was setting behind him, creating a weird aura-like field of light above his head. Bee squinted, regretting that she hadn't packed sunglasses.

"What happened with the intern Ed Turner? You asked him to leave on Tuesday."

Max swirled his whisky while maintaining his gaze on her. She heard the ice cubes clinking against the side of the glass. It was a good old-fashioned stare-off and he was doing his best to intimidate her with his dark eyes.

"You know who I'm talking about, right?"

"Yes, that Harry Potter do-gooder," he bristled, putting his glass down on the table. He straightened his posture and pushed his shoulders back like a boxer sizing up their opponent.

"Not Harry Potter. Ed Turner. And I wouldn't call him a do-gooder, just a good human."

"Well, you know what. If he wants to *do good,* he should have joined Greenpeace. We don't get paid to have a conscience; we get paid for doing deals for clients, whether they're in casinos, mining or alcohol."

A waiter made an ill-timed interruption with a tray of smoked salmon blinis, her favourite canapé. She was starving but declined; she didn't want to be worrying about dill sticking in her teeth during this tête-à-tête. Max declined too, presumably because it was one of his carb-free days. She set her champagne flute and clutch down on the cocktail table. A serious conversation required a serious stance of her own.

"Listen, you don't know this because you weren't involved in the interviews, but Ed had a very good reason for asking that question. And had you spoken to me before you asked Emily to let him go, I would have told you this." Bee scanned the tables closest to them to ensure no one else would hear what she was about to say next. "His father was a gambler who racked up huge debts and then killed himself. Ed was just ten at the time. There you go."

She searched Max's face for an emotional reaction but there was nothing. He didn't seem to care, not one bit. In fact, his face was like stone.

"My God, you're naive. Everyone has something personal going on, but you have to leave it at the door when you go to work. We don't have time for people's sob stories."

Bee felt a rush of anger creep up inside her and she suspected it showed. Max, on the other hand, was so devoid of emotion that she could have been talking about the weather.

"I could tell Ed was going to make things difficult, so he had to go. And we, or should I say *I*, need to do these things to make a statement—to send a message to the other minions that anyone who challenges me is *out*."

There was another ill-timed interruption, this time from Stuart.

"We're ready for speeches, you two."

Max reached to the inside pocket of his tuxedo jacket and pulled out a folded sheet of paper with handwritten notes.

Bee picked up her clutch and champagne flute and turned to Stuart. "Can you give me five? I just need to visit the ladies'."

Stuart nodded. Usually so perceptive, she realised that he hadn't noticed the tension between her and Max.

A handsome young man dressed in a suit with blond surfer-like locks took a seat at the bar stool next to Rosie. "Can I get you a drink?" he asked.

"How old are you?" Rosie guffawed, shocked by his speedy advance. He was at least fifteen years her junior.

"Old enough to buy you a drink," he joked. As he smiled at her she noticed his cute dimples and nice teeth.

"But they're free."

"True. So can I get you a *free* drink then?"

She thought to herself that this banker was not only young but also quick-witted. "Sure. A sparkling water, please."

"Big night for you then." He laughed while trying to catch the waiter's eye.

"Massive, you have no idea."

"I'm Joe."

"Rosie."

They shook hands and waited for the topless male bartender in ultra-low-cut jeans to come and take their drinks order.

"Do you think that's baby oil or coconut oil?" Joe asked as he looked in the direction of the bartender whose washboard abs were glistening with lashings of oil.

"Coconut. Definitely. I got a waft of it when I sat down."

"You with them?" Joe looked over at Jazzy and Lucy.

"Yep."

"They seem fun. Is one of them your girlfriend? You haven't taken your eyes off them."

"No." She was aware she reacted hastily and defensively so she quickly explained. "One of them is a client's wife, Hugo Hamilton's wife, so I'm kind of working."

"Oh yes, the infamous Hugo Hamilton. Smug fucker. We had a meeting with him during the week to discuss his debt refinancing package. He might be good with bars, but he ain't good with money." Joe shook his head and Rosie's ears pricked up. She remembered that her invoice still hadn't been paid despite Paula chasing it up, twice.

"So he's got some financing issues, has he?" Rosie prodded, taking advantage of the fact that Joe might be ten beers in and a bit loose-lipped.

"I probably shouldn't be saying this but it's not looking great. He's got stacks of debt. Interest rates are going up so it's costing him a fortune to borrow. He's completely overstretched himself and I wouldn't be surprised if he goes bankrupt."

"What!" Rosie's shriek startled the young banker. He almost jumped off his bar stool and the regret of his loose lips was obvious on his face.

"Oops, there I go with my big mouth. I've had too much to drink. Don't know what I'm talking about. Forget what I said."

And before he could put his foot further down his mouth, he lifted his bottle of beer off the bar and strolled back to his group of friends. Now, for Rosie being sober could be boring and hard work, especially at parties, but it was the best way to be for extracting useful information from unsuspecting drunk people. It wasn't inconceivable for Hugo to be in huge amounts of debt; after all, COVID had been a disaster for the bar and restaurant industry. And she could easily verify the information with Bee because she might have heard something in her banking circles. Sydney was a small city that way. What with the blowjob and now the bankruptcy gossip, Rosie felt like she was holding a ticking timebomb.

Bee breathed a sigh of relief when her speech was over. With her 'game face' on, she had thankfully managed to find some completely inauthentic comments about Max. Stuart, who was standing at the front of the crowd, appeared relieved too. He gave two thumbs up and a wide smile, while the rest of the crowd applauded her. She stepped off the makeshift stage and handed the microphone to Max. In exchange, he handed her his empty whisky glass and phone even though there was a cocktail table right next to him. *Prick*. It was a deliberate move to make her feel subservient and it reminded her of when Ben Taggart asked her to top up his glass.

She watched as Max paced up and down on the stage, purposefully and confidently. His commanding radio voice was so easy on the ear. Unfortunately, his words were not as much to Bee's liking—he used aggressive language like "here to win, best of the best, fight hard, beat the competition, no points for second place", which Bee worried might not strike the right chord with the audience.

Curban had its own 'tone of voice', most firms did these days, to express its character and personality and you certainly wouldn't find any of Max's phrases in there. Instead, you'd find words like "approachable, trustworthy, humble, honest, open, collaborative". It was yet another example of how Max's character and personality were misaligned with hers and the company's. He might as well have come dressed in a gorilla suit and beat his chest on stage.

His phone, in her right hand, vibrated. She was tempted to take a sneaky peek. It's not like he would notice because he was too busy enjoying the sound of his own voice. It vibrated a second time. Just a quick look? She had to.

Penfold: Remove the obstacle!

Penfold: Get rid of her.

The phone vibrated again.

Penfold: Then you've got a deal! 🔫

She glanced up at the stage, then slowly returned the phone to a face-down position. She shuddered. The penny dropped and this was the cold, hard proof that *he* was up to something. Her gut instinct was right—*she* was the 'obstacle' that they wanted to remove.

Who was Penfold? The white-haired man from earlier? And what was the deal he was referring to? She snarled, stiffened and fumed all at the same time.

Max had underestimated her; he had mistaken her kindness, respect and integrity for weakness. You don't spend twenty years of your life in investment banking to be pushed aside by some has-been trying to make a comeback. She watched him pace the stage, repeating his phrases "best of the best, win, competition", then in a split second, he fell, lost his footing on the stage or went too close to the edge, but he was now on the ground.

Suddenly, she found herself bursting into loud, uncontrollable laughter. She laughed so hard she felt a gush of pee and immediately clenched her lower muscles. When she noticed Stuart looking over at her, she put her hand up to her mouth. It could have been a nervous laugh, a way of releasing all the pent-up anxiety, or it could just be the funniest thing she had seen in years.

Stuart rushed over. "Get a grip. I think he's hurt himself," he said.

"Shit, sorry." She composed herself and walked over to the small crowd huddled around Max. Davide, the dependable first aider, carefully examined Max's ankle while Max writhed in pain. When Max let out a yelp, Bee burst into laughter once more, prompting Max to scowl at her. "What's so bloody funny?" he shouted.

"Nothing. Are you okay? Shall we get a stretcher?" She suggested the stretcher, knowing how humiliating it would be for him to leave his first Christmas party that way. It was uncharacteristically mean of her, but he deserved it.

"It's bloody painful. Be careful," he yelled at Davide. "Can you ask my driver to come and get me? Now!"

Suzy rushed off while Davide and Stuart helped Max get to his feet. His face was a mix of anger, pain and embarrassment. Bee desperately tried to hold it together as Max hopped away on his left foot, leaning on the shoulders of Stuart and Davide.

Noticing the party had come to a complete standstill, and in an effort to jump-start the atmosphere, the band began playing the Black Eyed Peas' 'I Gotta Feeling'. It had the desired outcome and the dance floor filled immediately with waving arms and jumping bodies.

When Stuart returned from escorting Max to his driver, he came over to Bee with two champagne flutes. It was a forgiveness gesture for their mini tiff on arrival. He smiled and she smiled back and when they both heard the band start to play one of their old favourites, Chaka Kahn's 'Ain't Nobody', they grapevined in unison onto the dance floor, joining the hordes of dancers.

They sang and danced in perfect sync, reminiscent of their nightclubbing days in London, with their hands swaying above their heads. Bee might not have danced so freely if Max were still present. Even if he hadn't hurt his ankle, she suspected he wouldn't have danced. He belonged to that category of people who stood on the periphery, watching and judging, never allowing himself to be part of the fun in the way that old school leaders did, and always ensuring there was a line of separation between him and the 'minions'.

Davide and Suzy then raced onto the dance floor to Beyonce's 'Single Ladies'. Suzy had suddenly come to life after a few drinks and was uncharacteristically jolly. Maybe she was also relieved that Max had gone home.

Suzy and Davide danced out the steps from the music video and Suzy held her left hand out, pointing at her wedding finger, singing "If you liked it then you should have put a ring on it." She then slut-dropped, repeating this move another five times, and each time Davide screeched with excitement. The party was in full swing and Bee was finally letting her hair down. She would deal with the 'obstacle' revelation tomorrow.

It was close to eleven o'clock and Rosie was running out of steam. She'd just managed to extract herself from the most boring conversation with two insipid blondes who chewed her ear off about what a great boss Hugo was. On the dance floor, Lucy was struggling with the increase in tempo. The DJ had moved into the doof doof part of the evening, much to the delight of the young ravers. However, poor Lucy, softly swaying side to side, looked like she was at her own silent disco dancing to Fleetwood Mac.

Hugo, who had been missing in action since his blowjob, now danced his way through the crowd. He enthusiastically pumped his arms to the beat, much to the crowd's delight. As he passed by, some ravers even gave him appreciative backslaps. When he saw Lucy he stopped, visibly unimpressed. He leaned in and said something in her ear, which she didn't like because she pushed him away. He then grabbed her arm and said something again in her ear. Rosie decided to go over, sensing things might escalate.

"Take her home. She's a bloody mess," he shouted at Rosie.

The circle of bankers that had been dancing with her all night suddenly dispersed, possibly fearful of being punched by an angry-looking Hugo.

"What the fuck is going on here, Lucy? Rosie, get her home," he barked again.

Rosie quickly signalled to Jazzy to take Lucy's right arm while she held the left and they walked off slowly through the doof doof dancing crowd. When Rosie turned back, she caught sight of Hugo immediately diving back into dancing among a crowd of cowgirls. Who does that to their wife? Asks someone who barely knows her to take her home in that state. There was zero love, zero care factor.

On the way out they passed Erin shamelessly riding the bucking bull. Rosie had an urge to crank that control up as high as it would go and send her flying. Once outside, she told Jazzy to take the silver taxi that was waiting at the pavement while she leaned Lucy up against the wall and ordered her an Uber. Hugo was right, she *was* a mess, and she really shouldn't be going home by herself. Rosie would *have* to accompany her in yet another bloody Uber all the way up to the Northern Beaches. A Friday night, two weeks out from Christmas, and the fare surged by a multiple of four. A four hundred-and-fifty-dollar ride. She had option but to accept the fare. Once she saw a Hyundai Getz would be collecting them, she groaned loudly then turned around to find Lucy slumped in a dishevelled heap on the floor.

Chapter 19

Bee felt surprisingly hangover-free for the morning after a party. Maybe those detox patches did work after all. She sat up in bed, reached for her phone and saw fifteen missed calls from Stuart and Rosie. Stuart would be calling to run through his list of the party's worst and best dressed, as he always did. He really had missed his calling as one of those bitchy writers who pulls celebrities apart after a red-carpet *faux pas*. While it was always entertaining to listen to, Bee didn't have time for it right now. Today, her focus was firmly on the three smiling assassins—Max, Arthur and this Penfold guy.

She drew the curtains and began making the bed, ensuring all the decorative cushions were plumped and in place. No matter how much of a rush she was in, she had a weird superstition about always having to draw the curtains and make the bed. To her, it felt like the day wouldn't get off to the right start otherwise.

Gus appeared, carrying a brown paper bag and two coffees on a cardboard tray.

"Did you get me a chocolate croissant from Staple Bakery?" Weekdays her staple was chia pudding, not because *she* liked it, but because her waistline did. However, *pain au chocolat* was her indulgent weekend pastry of choice.

"I sure did," replied Gus, handing over her coffee and croissant.

"OMG, Gus Bloom. What did I do to deserve this?" She ripped open the brown paper bag, pulled out the croissant and took a huge bite, causing the pastry to flake all over her chest. "It's still warm too." She moaned with pleasure and a full mouth.

"Well, that's the good news, but I'm afraid I've got some bad news too." He gave her a concerned look, like something serious had happened. "You better take a look at this." He handed her his phone.

Sydney Times, *December 6, 2022*

Banker behaving badly—Leaked videos show CEO Bee Bloom partying

Curban Capital CEO Bee Bloom is facing more than a hangover this morning after she was captured in leaked videos dancing drunkenly. One source went as far as to claim that Bloom was on drugs. Another source said it was tone deaf to be holding a lavish party when Australia is facing a cost-of-living crisis.

She looked at Gus in disbelief. "It's bullshit. I had four champagnes, tops. And am I not allowed to dance with my staff at a bloody Christmas party?"

"Of course you are, honey."

She sat on the chaise at the end of their bed. Gus took a seat next to her and put his arm around her back. She pressed play and held her breath as she watched a five-minute video of herself dancing.

"If people think that's wildly partying, they need to get a life," she scowled. The footage showed Bee dancing with her hands above her head, singing along to the music. There was no slut dropping, unlike Suzy, or team pogoing like the HR team.

"Someone has to be setting me up. This is so tame it's not even funny." She pointed at the phone screen. "And drugs? Who would even say that about me?" She wasn't just embarrassed that this material had found its way into the public domain, she was hurt. Someone at that party, a staff member, was responsible. She had never been the kind of CEO who mistrusted her staff, she had never felt the need to ask them to leave their phones in their bags, because she knew she had earned their respect and trust. But today that trust had been broken for the first time. And she was gutted.

But why now? In the last five years, Curban had hosted three Christmas parties—they skipped two years due to COVID. There had also been end-of-financial-year celebrations when they hit higher-than-expected profits. Considering 'why now', she stood up, placed her hands on her hips and exhaled loudly through gritted teeth. She felt like Garry at the dog park when he felt cornered—heckles up and snarling, teeth on show. "Someone is setting me up and I think I know who it is."

"Hang on, Bee, let's not rush to any conclusions. I know you're mad—I would be too. But think about it. Maybe it wasn't leaked. Maybe someone sent it to a friend who has a friend at the paper. It's just ended up in the wrong hands. You know how these things work."

Gus was doing that *Ted Lasso* thing that he always did, trying to see the positive, thinking that nobody could be capable of acting so vindictively. His positivity was sweet at times, but right now it was annoying. Bee snapped, "No, Gus! It was that slippery fucker, Max."

"The chairman! Why would he do this? I thought you were excited about him joining and he's only been there one week." A look of confusion crossed Gus's face.

"You have no idea." It had been such a busy week that she hadn't found a moment to explain how dreadful Max's first week had been. She stormed into their walk-in-wardrobe and Gus followed. "Max the Magnificent. Pah! More like Max the Manipulator, Max the Manoeuverer, Max the Malevolent, Max the Maleficent, Max the Menacer."

She pulled out the drawer with such force it nearly came off its hinges, rummaged through the piles of underwear before throwing one black bra and one pair of flesh-coloured underpants on the floor. She was also usually superstitious about wearing a matching set of underwear but was willing to let that one slide today. Then, she frantically grabbed at a dress, causing the hanger to flip into the air and hit Gus on the head.

"Slow down. Where are you going?"

As she began dressing herself at speed, she mumbled, "Gus, this entire week has felt like a year. So much has happened but I don't have time right now to explain, I need to speak to Rosie Reid and manage this situation before it catches on fire."

"Who's Rosie Reid?"

"You know—the woman who does the PR for Curban. She knows all the journalists."

She tipped her head upside down and tied her hair into a tight top knot. As she searched for her trusty shearling Birkenstocks, she began texting Rosie.

Bee: Rosie, Sydney Times *article. What the hell? We need an emergency meeting. Where can we meet?*

Rosie: Hey, Bee, yup, we def do. Seen it all. So sorry. Hideous. Am at a client's house—long story ... can you come here? It's Avalon.

Bee: Send me the address. On my way!

Rosie had been awake for a couple of hours but hadn't been able to face Lucy yet. She'd had a horrible night's sleep in Lucy's spare room, wrestling with the substantial collection of pillows, fluffing them and refluffing them over and over until she finally fell asleep at around three o'clock. Should she tell Lucy everything, just a little, or nothing at all? Far out. Why did she walk into the wrong toilets last night and see those gold boots under the door? And why did the young banker want to tell her all about Hugo's money problems? Ignorance was definitely bliss.

It was *supposed* to have been the night where she would confess her interest in Jazzy. Well, that plan had been completely blown out of the water because, just before Hugo burst onto the dance floor with his terrible dad dance moves, she had noticed Jazzy getting close to Joe, the young banker with cute dimples. Grrr. Had she missed her chance?

Lucy woke to the scorching bright sun streaming through her bedroom window. She was face down, fully dressed and roasting hot. Squinting, not quite ready to open her eyes fully, she patted around the surface of the bedside table for the air conditioning remote control. The hangxiety kicked in immediately. How did she get home? The last thing she remembered was dancing with that lovely friend of Rosie's whose name she'd forgotten. Then tiny snippets came back to her—Hugo dancing, Hugo grabbing her, Hugo yelling at her. She slowly turned around, expecting to see him in an equally sweaty and hungover state, but he wasn't there. *Typical*, she thought. Through her squinted eyes, she spotted her handbag on the floor at the end of the bed, contents spilled out: phone, lipstick and one empty bottle of CBD oil. She winced, remembering that the bottle was supposed to last her one month.

When she checked her phone, she saw a one-liner message from Hugo at 4am saying she was "a mess" and that he was staying in the city. *Fuck him*. He was the goddamn reason she was a mess. She tossed her phone back on the floor and trudged into the bathroom, cradling her throbbing head in her hand.

Her reflection in the mirror made her shriek internally—big black Alice Cooper eyes, false eyelashes hanging off, lipstick smudged up her cheeks and bird's nest hair. After setting the water temperature to cold, she crawled into the shower and sat on the cold tiles, letting the cold water wash over her. With her legs tucked up, she noticed a bruise the size of a cantaloupe melon on her right thigh. How did she get it? She winced again, realising *this* was a low point. Beyond the pounding headache and nausea from her Wild West cocktail hangover, she was ashamed and disappointed in herself. Her relationship with alcohol had turned toxic, just like her marriage. Once again, she was overwhelmed by that all-too-familiar sensation of wanting to just disappear.

Wrapped in a bath towel, she took dolly steps to the kitchen with her eyes squinting, unable to take in the bright sunlight that filled the room. She stretched to reach the medicine cupboard, now in desperate need of some Panadol.

"Morning," said a loud voice behind her. She screamed, dropping her towel and the basket of painkiller medications on the floor. She turned around to find Rosie sitting at the kitchen counter in a white fluffy bathrobe. "I hope you don't mind. I found this in the wardrobe in your spare room. I didn't fancy putting that stinky cowgirl outfit back on."

"How did *you* get here?" Lucy asked, picking up her towel and rewrapping herself, embarrassed that Rosie had seen her full frontal. "Ouch," she groaned from the sudden movement.

"I brought you home," said Rosie. "Listen, I hope this is okay, but I've got a client popping by quickly. She's in a terrible crisis and I said to meet me here and we'd go for coffee and then she'll drive me home."

"Okay," Lucy said sheepishly. "Want a coffee now?"

"Love one."

Lucy fumbled around for at least five minutes, struggling to make the coffees. Eventually, Rosie kindly told her to sit down and offered to make them. Lucy smiled feebly and shuffled over to a stool, taking a seat. She then washed down two Panadol with a big glass of chilled water.

Gus nervously watched from the door connecting the garage to the house as Bee reversed her Tesla. He was most likely worried that she was going to hastily crash into his souped-up work Ute. As the garage door rolled down, she waved at him until it closed. She knew he would be thinking how crazy it was for her to be racing off to a stranger's house to hold an emergency meeting. She also knew that he wouldn't ever say that to her. No matter how crazy she got about work, whether it was working late or torturing herself over the annual bonuses for staff, he wouldn't intervene because he knew how much it mattered to her.

She also knew that he wished she would switch off now and again, especially when they were on holidays, but never went on about it. Case in point was last year when they were in Fiji.

Bee had been very conscious that their family time had repeatedly been interrupted by work calls, so for one call that she knew would drag on for two hours, she had pretended she was going for a massage. Instead, she had camped out in a straw cabin by the adults-only pool, knowing that Gus wouldn't be allowed in there with the boys. That day, however, he must have left them in the bure on their iPads while he ventured to the pool for a solo swim. She had spotted him and quickly hid in the gardens until he was gone and, although she was certain he saw her, he never said anything. That was one of the reasons why she loved him, because he understood her so well.

According to her GPS navigation system, the drive to Rosie's client's house would take approximately twenty minutes. She searched for music to play—should it be angry to match her mood? Or something tranquil to calm herself down? She opted for *Harry's House*. Harry always made her smile. She sang 'As it Was' at the top of her voice while cruising at sixty kilometres per hour towards Avalon. On the car's display screen, she saw Stuart calling incessantly. He would have certainly read the *Sydney Times* article by now, or someone would have sent it to him. And there were other callers too—Camilla in Corporate Communications, she would want to know what they were going to say to staff, other media and shareholders about the leaked videos. CFO Garth, he would be concerned about the excessive spending reference in the article. And Emily in HR would just want to see how she was feeling and if she needed to use that new employee assistance program for some counselling. Bee sent all callers to voicemail. This wasn't her usual style, because she always answered calls, but this wasn't a usual day.

This must be the house. She arrived at one hundred and twenty-five Ocean Road and pressed the intercom. After being buzzed through and finding a parking spot, she strolled towards the front door of the house. As she did, she recognised the person waiting for her and it wasn't Rosie.

"You!"

"You!"

"Bee?"

"Lucy?"

Rosie appeared from behind Lucy. "Do you two know each other?"

Lucy and Bee burst out laughing. "Oh, we've been friends for ages," Lucy said.

"Small bloody world," remarked Rosie.

"So, you're Rosie's client too then?" Bee asked.

"Not quite," Lucy responded coyly. "Come inside and we'll fill you in."

Bee and Rosie took their seats across from each other at the outdoor dining table on the terrace, enjoying the breathtaking ocean view. Meanwhile, Lucy ordered Uber Eats. They had agreed that it would be best to hold their urgent meeting at Lucy's house, away from any prying eyes. Lucy, being alone for the weekend, gladly offered to host, saying she would love the company.

It was a hot, sunny summer's day and certainly not conducive to wearing a black cowgirl outfit, so Rosie had asked Lucy if she could borrow something. When Lucy had showed Rosie into her walk-in-wardrobe, Rosie let out a loud gasp. "Wow," she had exclaimed. "You're the Marie Kondo of the Northern Beaches."

"Not me," Lucy had replied, rolling her eyes. "Hugo paid for a wardrobe stylist to come and fix it all up a couple of weeks ago. He hates mess. Help yourself to anything," she had said, as she stepped over her last night's outfit, which lay in a pile on the floor.

"I want their number," Rosie had exclaimed, her eyes wide with excitement as she scanned the shelves, racks and drawers.

Everything was perfectly organised—clothes grouped by garment type, colour-coded and hung on neutral velvet hangers only. Not one rogue dry cleaner's wire hanger to be seen anywhere. The shoes were neatly arranged by style, the collection dominated by the stiletto variety. Stacked hat boxes and handbags were lined up next to cashmere sweaters on tidy shelves. Zimmerman dresses aplenty; *they must be her favourite designers*, Rosie thought. A plain white peasant style caught her eye and she slipped it on, checking the fit in the full-length mirror. It suited her. Maybe Lucy wouldn't miss it if she kept hold of it, she had cheekily giggled to herself.

"You should see this one's wardrobe," Rosie whispered to Bee.

"I bet. Has Lucy been a client of yours for long?" she asked, patting Beano, who sat in her lap.

"Technically she's not the client, her husband is—Hugo Hamilton."

Bee's jaw dropped open and her eyes widened. Rosie knew that look. It was clear she had read the headlines and shared the same sense of disgust as every woman in Sydney regarding the accusations.

"The one who has been accused ..." Bee's words trailed off, possibly because she didn't want to say the words "sexual harassment" out loud.

Rosie nodded.

Bee glanced into the kitchen at Lucy who was still placing the Uber Eats order. She exhaled loudly, shaking her head. "Poor her. And kids?"

"Two girls. One at uni, the other in high school." Rosie hadn't given much consideration to Lucy's girls given she wasn't a mother herself. However, she could discern from Bee's expression that the involvement of children in this messy situation was a cause for concern.

"Jesus, how hideous. And what *exactly* are you doing for him?" Bee asked.

Rosie sensed a tinge of judgement from Bee. Maybe Bee was wondering how she could manage the image of someone accused of harassing a female employee.

"I said yes because ... because ... oh, for the money, I suppose," she stuttered, suddenly aware of how this statement made her sound completely devoid of ethical principles.

"I'm not judging you, Rosie. I just wondered how you go about helping him. Do you set up interviews? Or tell him to stay quiet for now? I'm genuinely interested in how you manage it all. It's a huge responsibility."

Rosie quickly realised that Bee wasn't judging her. Of course she wasn't because that wasn't her style. She knew Bee better than that. Her own thoughts revealed more about her personal feelings towards the situation. "Sorry, Bee. If I'm honest, it's been a fucking nightmare and I just want to tell him to get stuffed." She closed her eyes then bowed her head into her hands, shamefully. "It's so much worse than that one allegation."

Lifting her head, she peered over her shoulder to check Lucy's whereabouts. She was now fiddling about with the coffee machine, so Rosie took the opportunity to unburden herself.

In a soft voice, leaning across the table, she asked, "Have you heard, you know, in your banking circles, if Hugo might be going bankrupt?"

Bee looked shocked. Her jaw almost hit the floor. Rosie warned her, "Can you try to look normal while we're having this conversation, please. So, we don't draw attention to the situation, if you know what I mean." She gestured in Lucy's direction.

Bee closed her mouth and nodded. "I haven't, but that's not to say it's not true. I would need to ask around with the bankers that lend money to businesses like his. I can make some confidential calls, if you like?"

"Yes, please. That would be amazing. Next thing"—she peered over her shoulder again—"I caught Hugo getting a blowjob off his assistant last night at his Christmas party." As soon as she finished the sentence, she reminded Bee not to look shocked. "And then, the final thing ..."

"There's more?" Bee's eyes were now well and truly bulging out of her head.

"The final thing, this Cecilia Meadows from the *Daily Life* says there are more women claiming they've been harassed by him. Like I said, it's a fucking nightmare."

"You *have* to tell Lucy, Rosie. She *has t*o know. You would want to know if it was you, right?"

They both sat silently contemplating the situation. Rosie caressed her chin, while Bee looked down to the floor, her eyes closed.

"Well, I'm sorry, I've given up with the coffee machine and ordered in," Lucy said, taking a seat at the table next to Bee. A look of confusion crossed her face. "Oh sorry, you two are discussing crisis stuff. Shall I make myself scarce for a bit?"

Rosie and Bee looked at each other, then Rosie looked at Lucy. "No, Lucy, I think you'd better sit down. There's something I need to tell you."

Chapter 20

Bee sat silently with a reassuring hand on Lucy's knee while Rosie recounted all of Hugo's wrongdoings. Bee's big, concerned eyes darted back and forth between Lucy and Rosie, like she was umpiring a game of tennis.

Fifteen minutes later, Rosie leaned back in her chair and exhaled loudly. She appeared to be relieved, but she also looked upset because tears shimmered in her eyes. "I'm so sorry, Lucy," she said.

"That fucking bastard," muttered Lucy under her breath. Receiving this dump of information in such a short space of time made it hard for Lucy to think of anything else to say that would convey how disgusted, hurt and embarrassed she felt. A workplace affair, bankruptcy and *more* victims. It was a trifecta of horror. But if she were to rank them according to which one was most horrifying, the serial employee harassment was hands down the worst. That was scum-of-the-earth stuff. To think that her own husband was capable of harassing *multiple* young women made her stomach turn. She could live with bankruptcy. After all, entrepreneurs went bankrupt all the time. Failure was even applauded in places like Silicon Valley. And extra-marital affairs weren't such a surprise in Hugo's industry.

"Clearly I'm going to tell Hugo that I won't be working for him, effective immediately," Rosie said firmly.

Lucy acknowledged this but didn't immediately respond. The cogs were turning inside her head while she tried to make sense of everything. "Those earrings," she blurted out.

"Earrings. What earrings?" asked Rosie.

"Of course that little bitch couldn't afford Hermès earrings. He bought them for her. At the same bloody time that he bought mine." Lucy shook her head. "Such a cliché."

It seemed so obvious now in the cold light of day. What else had been happening under her nose that she was too medicated to notice? One thing was certain—she wasn't going to stand by and continue being one of his victims any longer. This was her wake-up call to finally initiate the long-overdue changes she needed to make!

"I know you might look at me and feel sorry for me, but don't. I've put myself in this position by ignoring all the red flags. I should have mustered the courage to confront it earlier. Yes, I wasn't aware of the harassment, of course I wasn't, but I had a sense that something was amiss."

As she contemplated the duration of this feeling, she couldn't help but reflect on how long she had allowed it to persist. Was it five years? Perhaps even longer? Anger boiled inside her as she ruminated on her own gullibility and weakness. Hugo had reduced her to a medicated, binge-drinking mess. Now, she was determined to find her way back to her former self.

Looking heavenward, she said, "Last night it felt liberating to be out on the town, dancing with men who were actually paying me some attention. I was being offered drinks, told I looked hot. I felt the most attractive I've felt in ..."—she paused—"in years."

She sat up in her chair, alert. "Do you know what? I think I'm relieved. I needed something this hideous to force me into action and get me out of this existence, because I have been *existing*. I haven't been living, that's for sure." She turned to Rosie. "So, Rosie, you do what you need to with Hugo. It's fine with me. I need to focus on my girls and our financial dilemma, that's if *those* rumours are also true."

The financial situation worried her, given she hadn't needed to think about money for fifteen years because Hugo controlled everything from his command centre in Surry Hills. Jocelyn was their household CFO, managing all the domestic bills and accounts for the girls, paying their school and university fees. Lucy was clueless. "What makes me so cross is that I gave up my career. And for what? Who is going to employ me now? I'm just some washed-up old has-been TV presenter who'll be shopping at Aldi."

"I hear Aldi's pretty great these days," said Bee.

"As if *you* shop at Aldi," joked Rosie." I suppose you go there on Wednesdays, hunting through the buckets too for their weekly specials, do you?"

Bee scrunched her face up in jest. "And stop this old has-been crap, Lucy. You would be an asset to any company," added Bee.

At that moment, the door intercom buzzed, and they all jumped.

"It's just Uber Eats," laughed Lucy. "Coffee and food, yippee!" She clapped her hands, excitedly.

Over the next hour, the trio drank coffee, ate bacon and egg rolls, and chatted about everything except Max Magnifico and Hugo Hamilton. They intentionally kept the conversation topics light and covered all the latest pop culture gossip, including who would be the next James Bond (Bee said Henry Cavill, Lucy said Idris Elba and Rosie said Taron Edgerton); who Harry Styles would date next (Bee said *her* in her dreams, Lucy said Taylor Swift (again) and Rosie said Dua Lipa); and Meghan and Harry's royal rift. Then, Rosie decided it was time to get serious.

"Okay, ladies, sorry to spoil the fun, but that's enough chit-chatting, it's time to face the music." She sat forward, downed the dregs of her coffee and set her empty cup down on the table. "Lucy, we'll need a laptop so I can take notes. And a pen and some Post-it Notes if you have any, please, the coloured ones. We'll use my phone to record some of our work—just letting you know so you don't freak out." She eyeballed Lucy and Bee. "And let's go inside, shall we? It's getting too hot out here to work. And we need a big table."

"The dining room," suggested Lucy.

"I agree," added Bee, fanning herself with her hand.

Lucy showed Rosie and Bee to the dining room then went looking for their meeting supplies in Hugo's home office. She returned five minutes later with a laptop, a pen holder full of pens and a book of yellow Post-it Notes. "Will these do?" She handed the notes to Rosie. "It's all I could find."

"Yes, I can work with those."

Lucy was excited to show off her formal dining room. It was styled off a beach house in the Hamptons that she had found on Pinterest. A circular dark wooden table sat at the centre of the room on a rattan-style rug. Six wing-back dining chairs upholstered in a cream fabric were equally spaced around the table, while another two sat either side of a dark wooden buffet holding a glass jar full of shells. The three women sat at the table in a semi-circle with Rosie positioned in the middle.

"You can tell you have girls," said Bee. "Lots of cream. I definitely couldn't do cream in my house." She laughed. "It's very tasteful. I love it."

"It's never used, that's why it looks so good," declared Lucy with a tone of sadness as she glanced around the room.

For Rosie it was time to switch into crisis PR mode. "This, ladies, is our war room."

Lucy was instantly impressed and sat to attention in her wing-back chair.

Rosie's fingers flew across the keyboard as she typed with urgency. "First let's establish your goal. What is it that you want to achieve? Second, how do we go about achieving it?"

"What if we've got more than one?" asked Lucy. "I mean, I can think of at least five."

"Okay. But let's prioritise. Number one should be to establish if the rumours are true. Because if the rumours *are* true and Hugo *is* going bankrupt, you will need to one, find somewhere else to live and two, get a job. And if there are more victims you will need to one, immediately announce your intention to divorce him if you want to save any face at all and two, keep a low profile while he gets ripped apart by the press."

The reality of what lay ahead suddenly dawned on Lucy. They weren't just any couple that could quietly go their separate ways. Hugo had a profile. And if there *were* more victims, a lawsuit could follow, dragging on for years. She groaned loudly.

"I know it sounds harsh and it's going to be tough. But this bit"—Rosie pointed down at the laptop—"this bit is the hardest. Once you have a plan, and with our support, you're going to get through this. I promise."

Lucy thought Rosie was trivialising the situation by expecting 'a plan' to be the hardest part of the nightmare that lay ahead of her. Now in full 'PR' mode, she was coming at the situation with her work hat on. Lucy squeezed her eyes shut to fight back the tears.

Bee must have noticed because she sat forward and said, "I'm going to find out what I can about these bankruptcy rumours. And don't worry, I'll only ask people I trust."

"Thank you," said Lucy.

"And I'll keep speaking to Cecilia about the victims. She's got a rubber arm after a few wines, that one. I'll make a note now to take her out to lunch on Monday," added Rosie.

Rosie looked down at her watch then quickly turned the conversation to Bee's dilemma. "And Bee, you need to issue a statement slamming this Christmas party bullshit and find out who leaked the damn video. Then, get Stuart on the case, get him sniffing around the office to see what he can come up with. We need to know asap who is setting you up."

Rosie peered over at Bee. A look of worry clouded Bee's pretty features.

"There's something I should tell you first." Bee drummed her fingers on the table nervously. "A few months ago I was sent an email warning me that Max was a psychopath."

"Who from?" Rosie boomed. "Why don't I know this?"

"That's exactly what Stuart said. God, you two are alike sometimes. It was from a stranger. Her name is Vanessa Rudgens. I thought she was a crazy jilted lover of Max's. But then ..." Bee drummed her fingers faster now. "I saw it for myself this week. It's true. He *is* a bloody psychopath and he *definitely* wants me out. And I *read* it for myself last night." Her expression hardened and her tone became angry as she explained how she had read the text message from someone called Penfold. Then she shared how Max had taken pot shots at her all week. As she did, tears filled her eyes. "Honestly, I thought we were done with behaviour like that."

Lucy leaned across the table and placed her hand on top of Bee's.

"I knew it. I knew something was up," Rosie boomed again. "You weren't yourself in the interview last week. We need to look into this Vanessa Rudgens, immediately. I'll do that." She typed frantically. "You focus on the video. And what those schemers are up to. We need to find out what they're planning to do with the business and when."

Two hours and twenty-three minutes later, Rosie announced, "That's a wrap."

She threw her pen down on the table and started taking photos of the Post-it Notes with scribbles on them. During that time, Rosie had expertly crafted a crisis plan for both Lucy and Bee, outlining everything they needed to do. "It's time to come out swinging," she said.

While they had been workshopping, Bee's *Sydney Times* article had climbed its way to the most read article of the day. The comments were in the hundreds, mostly supportive and some even sympathetic of Bee's partying. And then there were the ones calling for her to be sacked immediately.

"Wow, that's brutal," Bee said, visibly deflated. "Why do they want me sacked? Nothing's even been proven yet."

"Because you're a banker. The general public love to hate a banker. *And* because you're female. Do you honestly think a bloke would be getting this much stick?" remarked Rosie. "We need to get your statement out immediately."

Bee nodded.

Rosie typed away as Bee watched nervously.

"I am really disappointed to see videos of me dancing at a private event leaked to the public. I was celebrating the end of a very successful year for our company with my staff who have worked incredibly hard and deserved a celebration of this kind. I drank four champagnes, danced to a few songs and had a great evening. Beyond that, there is nothing else to say."

"Okay, that's been sent to fifteen journalists. Let's wait and see what the response is."

"Yes, you go, girls!" After sitting silently for a little while because she was on the verge of a hangover vomit, Lucy finally got her energy back. "I just want to say how amazed I am by both of you. You're both such power bitches." She reached out to fist bump them both.

"I'm not really a fist bumper, but just for you." Bee held her fist out.

As it was now late afternoon, Lucy suggested, "How about I order some Thai?"

"Can't, sorry. I need to be getting back home," Rosie said, closing the laptop and handing it to Lucy.

"Me too," added Bee.

Lucy's heart sank at the prospect of being left alone with all those thoughts swirling around in her head. She was worried how much Rosé she would get through. The expression 'drown your sorrows' came to mind. *Sigh.*

"You're welcome to come to my place for dinner. I mean, if you're just going to be here by yourself," suggested Bee. She presumably picked up Lucy's downcast face. "It won't be anything fancy. We usually just do takeaway on Saturdays, it's very low-key," she added.

"Are you sure?" Lucy asked, trying to mask her eagerness.

"Of course. I'd love you to come and meet the crew."

"I'm paying though. I insist."

Chapter 21

Rosie woke early after yet another restless sleep. When would she ever get to sleep through the night again? Now, she found herself experiencing anxiety about her inability to sleep, which was only exacerbating her sleeplessness. She had taken four temazepam, which was double the recommended dose, yet she still couldn't manage to sleep through the night. *FFS.*

Her bedroom was dark. Outside the thunder rumbled loudly and heavy drops of rain fell on the window. Saturday's sun and heat had turned into one of those late afternoon storms which raged on all through the night, bringing cooler temperatures and less humidity. *Yes! Goodbye frizzy hair, for now at least.*

Rosie wasn't the spiritual kind, never had the urge to do the ashram-in-India thing, but she *did* consider heavy rain a sign that it was time for her to cleanse herself. The last cleanse she did was of the juice variety and it lasted three days. She still remembered the hunger pangs and how the marketing spiel sucked her in—*This juice cleanse is a unique detox experience that exposes your habits and shadows. It has everything you'll need to achieve your healthiest self. Great shifts occur when we dedicate time and space for deep healing.* The cleanse she had planned now was going to be a similar detoxification experience, she hoped.

After spending a day helping Bee and Lucy extract themselves from their toxic situations, it was time for her to take a long, hard look at herself and make some big decisions of her own. Profit had always been her motivating factor, but seeing the dollars roll in each month no longer fulfilled her in the way it used to. Like Lucy, she had ignored the red flags for too long. What was her goal? Simplify, consolidate, realign, rightsize—different words, same meaning, she used them all interchangeably for her corporate clients to explain why they were 'downsizing' and letting staff go. In non-corporate lingo, her goal was to delete the dicks by undertaking a client cleanse.

And how? She intended to hold each of her clients up against a principles rather than profit-based sniff test and if they didn't pass, they were out, gonski! This sniff test would comprise two simple questions. The first—is the client a good human? The second—are their sins forgivable? Yes, that would do for now. Hugo Hamilton was already on the cutting room floor, but who would be next? Motivated by the challenge, she jumped out of bed and went about her daily routine. She even snuck in her laps while the rain pelted down on the pool.

"Cleanse. Wash away. Detoxify." She repeated the three words to herself as she followed the black line up and down the pool.

As it was Sunday, the Reid & Co Counsel offices would be empty. If anyone *did* work on weekends, they did so from home, so she knew she wouldn't be disturbed. When she arrived, she made herself a coffee then ambled around the office, sipping as she went. She passed the desks of her twenty employees, studying how they each had personalised their areas with photo frames, snacks, coloured highlighters and toiletry collections. She then sat on the large brown leather sofa in the reception area and gazed out of the window to the dark clouds hanging over Sydney Harbour. A fancy office with harbour views used to mean success. Now, it didn't feel so important. She would have to say goodbye to this amazing view and return to a studio in Surry Hills.

And she was ready for the change. *Surry Hills is way cooler and more fun than the CBD. Goodbye suits!*

She sat down at her desk, purposefully, and set her two Rolodexes full of client business cards in front of her. A modern woman in many ways, she still used this old-fashioned rotating business card filing device that was invented in 1956. They were her two babies—her crown jewels—that never left the office. Paula had tried to introduce her to a new online filing system called RoloNext but she refused to use it.

Where to start? Reid & Co Counsel managed forty-three clients in total and she knew how much revenue every single one of them was worth. But that didn't matter now. She also knew their deepest, darkest secrets. The secrets that she had buried and had made a note of on the back of their business card. Begin with A: Igor Abashin—bullied three female colleagues, called them "fat and stupid" to their faces. Tim Butterworth—history of making pregnant women redundant and rehiring men in their positions. Nathan Collins—caught using his corporate credit card at strip clubs. She ripped the three cards from the plastic ring and tossed them on the floor dramatically, for her own satisfaction, and then kept going, letter by letter, client by client, secret by secret until she was back at A.

She looked down at the pile of cards on the floor. Twenty-five in total. Just eighteen clients remained. Had she been too ruthless? Maybe she needed to put some back in just to make sure she could actually keep her business alive.

Nope! No going back now. She gathered the pile of cards and threw them into her tote. She might have a burning ceremony later to make sure they were properly gone, because if they ended up in the wrong hands, well, that would be professional suicide. She saw the name Max Magnifico appear on her phone screen. What did he want?

Max: I have something we need your help with. It's board level stuff so all hush hush right now, please keep to yourself. That means Bee doesn't know yet. Can you please be on standby early next week?

Rosie: Of course. I'll be here and ready.

What she didn't add was, *here and ready to tell you to get stuffed.*

She had to play along for now so she didn't raise any suspicions. Max had underestimated her *and* Bee. It was naive and transactional of him to assume that her retainer meant she was *retained* for any kind of work and to dismiss the relationship she had with Bee.

Poor Bee. Max had just come along and in an instant decided that he was going to remove her from the job that she was bloody awesome at. That thought motivated her to Google this mystery Vanessa Rudgens. Who was she? And what exactly happened to her? It sounded like she had been screwed over by Max too.

The search results were all of Vanessa Hudgens the American actress and singer; nothing came up for Rudgens. She tried Googling Vanessa Rudgens and Max Magnifico. Some very distracting photos of Vanessa Hudgens with Austin Butler and Zac Efron came up, but that was it. She checked every social media platform and nothing. Now she was confused. Did Vanessa Rudgens even exist? Was it a nom de plume?

Fortunately, Rosie knew a brilliant Polish female hacker with an uncanny ability to uncover hidden information about people. Cipher, as she was known, called herself a digital vigilante driven by a thirst for justice in an unjust world. Not knowing what Cipher looked like, Rosie imagined her as Lisbeth Salander from Stieg Larsson's Millennium series with a striking punk appearance, piercings and dark clothing. Her English wasn't great, and her social skills were worse, but Cipher always delivered. The phone rang just once.

"Speak," barked Cipher.

"It's Rosie Reid. I need you to try and find someone for me, please."

"Uh huh."

"Can you run a search on someone called Vanessa Rudgens. Anything you can find. Who she is, where she's worked. The usual stuff."

"One thousand dollars. Transfer now or no work."

"Hang on. It was half that last time."

"Shit has gone up."

"Fine. I need it done today though for that price."

"You're pushy today. Fine." And she hung up.

Lucy was woken by an unknown number calling on her mobile. She let it go to voicemail and when she saw that the caller had left an audio message, she listened immediately, curious to know who would be calling on a Sunday morning from a private number.

"Hi, Lucy. This is Bethany Byron. I'm your neighbour two houses down. You left your number on my windscreen last week outside Thai Tanic. But that's not why I'm calling. Could you please ring me back when you have a moment? Thank you."

If she doesn't want to talk about the car smash, then what is she calling for? Lucy got out of bed, taking the phone with her into the kitchen. She wanted to open the folding doors to peer down at number one hundred and thirty-one, but the rain was too heavy. She couldn't see beyond her own back garden.

As she made her morning coffee, she remembered the lovely evening she had spent with Bee and her gorgeous family. She realised she had only drunk two glasses of wine, not her usual two bottles, and felt surprisingly energetic this morning as a result.

She had excused herself around ten o'clock, not wanting to outstay her welcome, even though she could have easily stayed longer. The way the conversation flowed so effortlessly made it feel like they had known each other for years.

Bee's home was instantly welcoming, just like her. From the moment Lucy stepped inside she could feel the warmth and comfort of a *real* family home. The hallway walls were adorned with a salon hang arrangement of family photos and the kitchen, which was obviously the heart of the house, was cosy and lived in.

Lucy had observed the beautiful dynamic between Gus and Bee as they lovingly bounced off each other. Their laughter filled the room as they shared stories about how they met in London. She could see the deep admiration in Gus's eyes as he looked at Bee, and witnessing *real* love like theirs didn't make her feel sad. In fact, it filled her with happiness and strengthened her conviction that leaving Hugo was the right decision. Bee's boys were just as charming as their mother, with impeccable manners. And to her surprise, they were also great conversationalists. She thought boys their ages just grunted or wanked off in their bedrooms.

Lucy left feeling a lovely warm buzz from being around Bee. *That's how people* should *make you feel,* she thought, and she wanted more of that Bee buzz.

She placed her coffee on the kitchen bench, picked up her phone and pressed *call.*

"Bethany, hi, it's Lucy from down the road. You just left me a message."

"Oh, Lucy. Thank you for calling me back." Bethany had an energetic and friendly tone which surprised Lucy. "As I said in my message. I'm not calling about the car. I hate the thing anyway. Wish you would have crunched it right up, to be honest, to give me an excuse to get rid of it."

Lucy giggled.

"No, I'm calling because I read the articles and, well, I felt compelled to reach out and say that I went through a terrible divorce twenty years ago, still haunts me to this day. Malingering motherfucker tried to take half of the company I built. Anyway, the point is, if you need to get out, and need a place to stay, I can help."

Lucy was speechless. "I, I, I, sorry, I don't know what to say," she stumbled at last.

"I have a small penthouse apartment. It's three bedrooms, dog friendly, right on Manly beach. I can't rent it out because I had too many bucks' and hens' parties hire it out for weekends and got sick of the cleaners complaining about finding dildos, penis straws, G-strings and condoms."

Lucy laughed.

"So it's sitting there. Empty. I can't imagine what you must be going through. I swore to myself if I ever saw another woman being wronged by her husband that I would lend a hand. And I don't like the way some women around here like to take others down and gossip. It's so suburban."

This completely caught Lucy off guard. "Bethany, I don't know what to say. I haven't even thought about what I'm going to do yet. It's all happening so fast." She was in disbelief that a complete stranger from two doors down, whom she had never exchanged a word with, was offering her free accommodation. "I need to find a job first so I can pay you, Bethany. I don't know how long that will take."

"Lucy, you take your time. Why don't you have a think about it? And call me back during the week. I can tell I've put you on the spot."

"I will. I'll call you back. This is way too generous."

"And don't be a stranger. I have a great new DeLonghi coffee machine. Don't know how to use the bloody thing, but I can try to make you a coffee sometime."

"That would be lovely. And Bethany, thank you, so, so much."

Bethany had just proven to Lucy that sometimes friends and supporters can be found in the most unlikely of places.

Chapter 22

Stuart had called and texted Bee relentlessly all weekend.

Shade!

Fingers fallen off?

Are you dead?

You better have been run over or had a heart attack, Bee Bloom!

He had texted Gus too, obviously in the hope of trying to find out what the hell was going on, but Gus was under strict instructions not to reply. Stuart had even texted Otis and Ollie, to glean the slightest information, but there he was also met with a wall of silence. By Sunday night, Bee knew he would be completely freaking out, so she finally called him. Oh boy, was he pissed off with her.

"You're lucky I'm even answering this call," he huffed.

"Listen, I don't have much time. There's a storm brewing and I can't tell you everything right now but it's a big one."

"You sound like you're working for MI5 now, but whatever," he huffed again.

"Meet me tomorrow at Cafe Sopra at 6:30am. Wear something smart. We need to be at our most powerful. And that's all I can tell you for now." There was silence on the other end of the phone. "Stuart, please."

"All right, all right."

"Great. See you tomorrow. Six thirty," she said.

"Okay." His voice softened. He could never stay cross with Bee for long.

The next morning Bee found Stuart tucked away in a banquette at the back of Cafe Sopra. "Someone's an eager beaver," she said.

It was six twenty and she thought *she* was early. Rosie was the one who had suggested Cafe Sopra because it was hidden down a laneway, at the opposite end of the CBD to the Curban offices. A safe spot for their clandestine meeting. Only three of the twenty tables were occupied, but a steady stream of office workers were trickling into pick up takeaway coffee orders.

As Bee sat down and opened her tote to take out her laptop, Stuart grunted, "This better be good, Bee. You better have a bloody good reason to have avoided me all weekend. I was really, *really* worried. And what's with the black outfit? Hang on ..." He leaned forward, concerned. "Has someone *actually* died?"

"No. God, no."

It was unusual for her to be wearing full black in summer, but she had intentionally picked out her outfit last night. *What says 'power'?* she had asked herself, standing back, scanning the dresses hanging in her walk-in-wardrobe. *What says 'control'?* She'd cast her mind back to a branding session that was held to debate the future of the Curban brand. Spike, the well-known brand expert with a bald head and all-black ensemble, including thick-rimmed glasses and high-top trainers, educated the Curban management team about the psychology of colour. He had said that black was the colour of authority, power, sophistication and strength. She remembered because she had a lot of black in her wardrobe. And black was perfect for today's occasion.

She decided on a Gucci black roll-neck dress with capped sleeves and a chunky belt, paired with Gucci GG logo block-heel loafers and simple gold jewellery.

"I told you we needed to dress powerful. This is what I came up with." She pointed at her dress.

"I approve." Stuart nodded. "And this is what I came up with." Stuart was wearing black tapered pants, his Prada loafers and a short-sleeve cream knitted cotton-blend polo shirt. "These are the ones I wore to the party, they're my best," he said, pointing at his trousers. "You didn't give me enough time to dry clean them, so I've had them airing on my balcony all night."

"And I approve too," she said, looking him up and down. "Coffee first, explanation second."

They ordered flat whites and, while they sipped, Bee told Stuart how she had seen the message on Max's phone, how she suspected Max had a mole who filmed her at the party, and how Rosie had put together a plan for them. Stuart usually had a habit of interjecting, but he sat patiently and listened.

"Fuck me," he said when Bee finally finished her monologue.

"I really need to know if Arthur is involved because if he is ..." She exhaled. "If he is, well, I don't know what I'm capable of doing to him."

"Maybe someone *will* die after all," sniggered Stuart.

"Which brings me to your priority. You need to find out who did the filming. Just don't do anything illegal. Speak to Angela in Tech and find out if we can do a search on devices for any texts or emails that went to this mobile number or email address on Friday night." She slid Stuart a piece of paper across the table.

"I can't actually believe it, Bee. Hang on, you don't reckon it's Davide, do you? That *nez marron*. I wouldn't put anything past him."

"I know what you're doing and of course it's not him. You know how much he loves his job. And me, for that matter."

The cafe was filling up now and Bee became conscious that their chatter might be overheard.

"Start with this person." She slid him another piece of paper with the initials SS. She took it back once he'd glanced at it.

"Oh yes, *her*. Good thinking."

"Right, let's get cracking."

Bee and Stuart arrived at the office at the usual time of eight o'clock, again not to draw any attention. She didn't need another coffee, but she couldn't walk past Luca without ordering one from him. Stuart paraded off to the lift without her, prattling on about how she cared too much about what other people thought.

"Miss Bee, I saw that article. How dare someone do that to you?" Luca shook his head and Bee noticed how his usual upbeat, smiley face had been replaced with a frown. It was the Sicilian coming out in him. All Godfather like. She was confident that if she wanted Max roughed up a bit, Luca would certainly oblige.

"This one is on the house, Miss Bee," he said, sliding one flat white her way. Today's message—*don't let anyone cast a shadow on your awesomeness* and a star.

At reception, Davide wasn't himself. In fact, he *did* look like someone had died.

"*C'est vraiment terrible*, truly terrible," he said when Bee approached him. "This dancing video business. I'm so sorry for you, Bee."

"I know, it's terrible. But this is the world we live in." She didn't even know what she meant by that. It was just words to avoid saying anything else.

She stopped by the kitchen, tipped her coffee out, worried that the extra caffeine would send her into a frenzy, and hastily walked into Max's lounge. She was disappointed not to find him sipping on his morning espresso or tucking into his perfect egg whites.

Suzy was there though, and she stood up quickly from her desk. "Bee, how are you?"

Bee noticed that Suzy appeared a bit worse for wear. Not just in the way she was dressed, but in her face. *I suppose everyone has an off day now and again*, she thought.

"Hi, Suzy. Where's Max?" asked Bee in an uncharacteristically firm tone. She scanned his lounge, expecting him to pounce up from a plank position behind his desk.

"Oh, didn't he tell you?" Her voice was soft and sheepish.

Bee shook her head.

"He had to make an urgent trip to New York. He'll be back on Wednesday morning."

"Which flight?"

"QF12. It arrives at 8:35am."

"Okay, I'll go and find Arthur in that case."

"Actually, Arthur went with him." Her voice was even softer and a tad apologetic.

Bee stepped forward, towards her. She wanted to look right into her eyes. "Thanks, Suzy. Did you have a good time Friday night?"

"Yes, it was great fun," she replied, then immediately cast her eyes downwards to her feet.

"Good. I'm glad." Bee let her eyes linger, not long enough to make Suzy uncomfortable, but long enough to pick up on how twitchy she appeared. She nervously twisted her hair around her fingers.

"Good to hear. See you later," said Bee, before walking towards the door. She felt a tinge of panic, as the plan was already scuppered by Max and Arthur disappearing with no warning to New York. Surely this was to finalise their plans with Penfold.

Bee: Max and Arthur in NY. FFS. Back Wednesday.

Rosie: That's okay. Stay cool. We move to Plan B.

Bee: Okay.

Rosie: Can't find any trace of this Vanessa Rudgens by the way. I've had to outsource. Stay tuned.

At her desk Bee opened her email to find sixty-three new messages from clients, peers and staff.

For what it's worth, I think what they wrote is out of order.

Who gets to tell you that you can't dance at a party?

You're the best CEO ever, don't let this stuff get to you.

As she worked her way through all the heartfelt messages, she sensed tears welling up inside her. Strangely, all the support and love were overshadowed by the cruelty of one conniving individual. How would everyone react when they found out that she was gone? Sacked. Hung out to dry. The prospect of being gone and waking up on Thursday morning with nowhere to be filled her with dread.

Chapter 23

Daily Life, *Wednesday, December 10, 2022*
Is Hugo Hamilton on the verge of bankruptcy?

Sources say that Hugo Hamilton is facing bankruptcy as the debts for his twenty bar and restaurant venues pile up. Hamilton has multiple outstanding loans with banks and with interest rates rising, he's on the hook for higher repayments, just like the rest of us with mortgages. Hamilton didn't respond to our calls yesterday.

Lucy read the article while lying in bed and chuckled to herself. Happy Monday, Hugo! The plan was in full swing—Rosie had successfully leaked the bankruptcy rumours to Cecilia Meadows. This information was in exchange for an update on the supposed other victims that had come forward against Hugo. That and an expensive lunch in the city.

Hugo would be fuming, no doubt, blaming everyone except himself. The bankers would be first, then his lawyers, then his staff, then last, but not least, Lucy. And all those people whom he owed money to, like the multiple building contractors, would be calling him to find out if it was true. Lucy had asked Rosie on Saturday how much Hugo's outstanding PR bill was, so she could pay it now before accounts were frozen. Rosie declined, but Lucy insisted.

Lucy started her day as normal by taking Beano for a walk. It would be good to clear her head for the big day ahead. She figured that Hugo would be blindsided. He was so self-absorbed he would never in a million years imagine that *she* could be capable of leaving *him*. Maybe he would have a heart attack and drop dead, taking all his debts with him. *That wouldn't be such a bad thing*, she thought. Then immediately felt guilty for thinking it.

Rosie had counselled Lucy on what to wear for the showdown on Saturday before she left. "Nothing floral. It's too mumsy. We're going for smart and sexy." They picked out a Zimmerman red-and-white-polka-dot crop top (because Hugo hated her in crop tops) with gold sailboat buttons, a coordinating skirt with matching belt, and Jimmy Choo white sandals with a gold ankle strap.

"Fierce," said Rosie when Lucy twirled around in front of the full-length mirror. Lucy also decided to get her hair blow dried because it always made her feel like the finished product. It was her 'thing' from working in TV. It was always about having good hair. Good hair could lift any outfit, not the other way around. She took an Uber into the city. She might feel too shaky afterwards to drive herself home, and she would *definitely* need a drink. It hadn't surprised her that Hugo decided to stay in the penthouse all weekend.

Hugo: Lots on in the city this weekend, wifey. Need to be here to supervise the kids.

Lucy: Of course, darling. I understand. She played along.

His next message wasn't so polite. After Lucy had avoided all his calls late last night and this morning, he was pissed off.

Hugo: Where the fuck are you? I'm in deep shit.

She doubted Gus ever took that tone with Bee. All the more reason to leave him.

Rosie grabbed her *beat the queue* coffee and jumped in the lift, doing her usual press the 'close door' button to avoid speaking to others. It was the same old start to a Monday morning. Bill texted at six o'clock. He was *still* on *her* case about organising a fixer interview because his bosses offshore were on *his* case. She had decided to keep Bill in her Rolodex for now because, despite being hugely irritating and demanding, he hadn't misbehaved like others.

Hugo had left her a voicemail at eight o'clock screaming *"call me now"*. Little did he know that *she* was the one who leaked the bankruptcy information. She just had to hang in there until Lucy had met with him before she could tell him to get stuffed.

When she stepped out of the lift, she immediately caught sight of Paula's resting bitch face peering over the reception desk. *Sigh.* Rosie really didn't have time for any people management today. When Paula got up and moved around to adjust the pink lilies sitting atop the reception counter, Rosie noticed she was wearing a maxi skirt. A protest obviously. And she was still frosty, answering with single-word answers to Rosie's questions.

"Boo," came a voice from behind Rosie as she filled her water bottle. She jumped.

"Sorry. I didn't mean to startle you," said Jazzy.

Jazzy looked tired. Still beautiful with her flawless English Rose skin however, her eyes were sunken with dark rings. "Sooooo, how was your weekend," she asked cheerfully.

"Busy with Lucy. After that whole Friday night debacle, I had to stay the night and look after her, blah blah blah." She really couldn't be bothered to get into the detail.

"I hope she's okay. It was a fun night. I had a lot, I mean, *a lot*, of fun."

Her water bottle now full, Rosie turned to face Jazzy and noticed how smug and beaming she was.

"I spent the weekend with Joe." She nudged Rosie. "You know, Joe the banker, not such a wanker." Her eyes widened, suggestively.

"Yes, I know who you mean." Rosie tried not to let the instant rush of jealousy show on her face and in her tone of voice. "Well, that's awesome, Jazzy. He seemed cool, for a banker." She picked up her water bottle and coffee cup. "More details later. I've got to keep moving. Busy day."

It was a diversion tactic, to allow her time to gather her thoughts until she was able to say something more convincing. After all, she remembered how after one-night stands she loved dissecting the event with someone, because it was like reliving the whole experience. She sat at her desk and typed a whole load of nothing to pretend she was working. Type, type, type, nothing, nothing, nothing, look busy, look busy. How did she really feel? Was she gutted? Or maybe it was just the idea of Jazzy that she loved, in the way that you confuse your feelings for someone when you're around them too much. And she wasn't one hundred per cent sure it was lust; she didn't have urges to go down on her. She just really liked her values, her personality, her style, her face and the way that she always uplifted the mood in the office. It made total sense that Jazzy would be a banker's type and he would be hers. And Rosie had to admit that Joe was hot. She might have liked him too if she were ten years younger.

She sent Jazzy and Simon an updated invitation for their usual ten o'clock Monday meeting. The location was changed from the office to the lobby cafe. "Just fancy a change and a real coffee," she said in the attached note so they didn't suspect anything.

"We're changing focus. We're ditching the clients that we have to lie for. Simple. It leaves us with eighteen," Rosie announced as soon as Jazzy and Simon took their seats. She decided to be direct and package it all up quickly. No point dragging the news out.

Simon and Jazzy simultaneously gasped.

"But ..." Simon began.

"Hang on, Simon. I've made an appointment with the accountant today. Both of you need to come. We're going to take our latest accounts and talk about those eighteen clients and how much we make from them."

"Why?" asked Simon. "I mean, why do we need to do this?"

"I'll explain that part in a minute. With eighteen clients we'll need to cut back to three juniors for each of you and one office manager. That leaves ten of us running the new streamlined business. You need to think about which team members are in and which are out and I need your list of names by tomorrow, close of business."

"This is all so sudden, Rosie. Where's this coming from?" Simon asked. "Are you sure? I mean, business is going great guns."

Trust Simon to lack awareness. He was ex-government, after all, and had lived and breathed spinning stories in his previous life.

"You know what green hushing is, right? The deliberate suppression of negative environmental information by companies. Well, what we're doing"—she pointed to the three of them—"could be considered blue hushing. We're concealing the sins of our clients."

Simon's face twisted. Jesus, did she really have to spell it out to him?

"Covering men's arses, because when I did my spring clean yesterday I was reminded of all the lies we've spun to protect their public images. And it made me feel sick."

"I love the phrase blue hushing. So fitting," Jazzy smiled.

"We might even need a brand refresh. To align with our new direction," added Rosie.

"This actually sounds really exciting, Rosie. I'm behind you all the way," said Jazzy.

Rosie could always count on Jazzy to play along nicely. But Simon, with his lucrative clients, could easily use this opportunity to go it alone. Maybe take a couple of the juniors with him and continue blue hushing.

"Thoughts, Simon?" asked Rosie.

"Well, seeing as you raised the subject of brand refresh, it might be a good time to review the name. I'm thinking something more acknowledging of others."

His face lit up and Rosie knew what he was getting at. He wanted *his* name up in lights. He had been angling for this promotion for a while.

"Fair point and it will definitely be considered. Anything else?"

Simon and Jazzy both shook their heads.

"Okay, this week is going to be really busy. I've got stuff going on with Bee Bloom that's going to take priority. So I need you both around to take care of the office. First, here are the client names that are in and the ones that are out." She pushed a list across the table to Jazzy and Simon and asked for the bill.

Chapter 24

When Lucy arrived at Hugo's office, she was surprised how quiet it was. Either his staff started their day really late, or they had gone on strike, fearing his speculated bankruptcy would mean no more pay cheques. Occupying the ground and first floors of an old industrial building, the office boasted soaring high ceilings, exposed brick walls, polished concrete floors and an abundance of natural light, thanks to huge windows. The designer furniture gave it an edgy, contemporary feel, as did the open-plan meeting rooms that were sectioned off by curtains hanging from poles in the ceiling. She had to hand it to Hugo, he was talented at creating amazing spaces.

His office was situated at the back of the building and, thankfully, had its own door. Her conversation wouldn't be one to have behind a curtain. As she approached, she heard his voice. Angry and shouty, it made her shiver.

"Hey, Lucy," said a familiar voice. It was Rupert, Hugo's Venue Manager. "You here to see Hugo?"

"Oh, hi, Rupert. Yes. Is he in his office?"

"Yup, on the phone to builders. Go straight in."

"Thanks."

No going back now; she grabbed the handle. *C'mon, get your shit together. Do not capitulate. You can do this.* She closed her eyes and burst in, immediately overcome with a pins-and-needles sensation all over her body. She was losing her cool—this was *definitely* not part of the plan.

Hugo stood up from behind his desk—the awful mahogany antique desk with a green leather surface that Pamela had given to him from his childhood home. It came with matching swivel chairs and was completely out of place in this trendy office space, but Hugo, the mummy's boy, was too chicken to refuse when Pamela offered it.

"What the fuck, Lucy?" He held the phone away from his ear, eyes popping out of his head.

"Don't you what the fuck me. What the fuck you!" She couldn't believe she actually gave back to him. Startled, he stood staring at her. A faint voice could be heard coming from the phone in his hand—"Hugo, Hugo, are you still there?"

"Yeah, mate. I'll call you back." The voice was still talking when Hugo hung up.

"Sit down. We need to talk," she demanded.

Her legs felt like they might give way, but she mustered a façade of confidence as she stepped towards the desk. She sat down on the awful swivel chair and gripped the frame. It felt like gripping a roller coaster tightly, with knuckles turning white, while anxiously awaiting the inevitable thrashing. Everything in her body was stiff, from her fists to her jaw to her stomach.

"All right. But if I sit down, you better explain to me where you've been," he spat.

"No." She had the urge to slap his fat, sweaty face. He really had let himself go in the last few years, while she was never allowed to. "I won't explain where I've been until you explain where *you've* been?"

"Duh, here at work, of course," he replied, condescendingly. He was pulling that face that was so familiar to her: the stroppy teenager-like one where the goal was to make her feel dumb.

"Oh yes, and you've been *so* busy. Haven't you? Busy bonking your assistant. That's why you haven't had time to come home."

"What! Are you on drugs? Are you drunk again?" His fat face flushed with indignation.

"Typical you. Pointing the finger at me. Stop lying. You've been rumbled."

"Oh yeah, by whom? Have you been spying on me?" He swivelled, insolently, side to side in his chair.

"That doesn't matter. You've been rumbled. The jig is up." She loved that phrase. It summed up his position so succinctly.

"That Rosie chick. It was her, wasn't it?" His tone became defensive.

"It doesn't matter, Hugo. That's irrelevant. The point is that you're a cheating liar. And what about Indie Thomas? Is that all bullshit too?" Lucy used his victim's name because she wanted him to know that it was etched in her brain.

"Of course it's bullshit. It never happened. You've got to stop reading the bloody news and listen to *me*," he protested, flapping his arms in the air. "People have always tried to take me down, you know that. This is no different."

As she observed him closely, the final shred of belief she clung to, that he was innocent, vanished into thin air. She pictured him forcefully ushering the young woman into his office on a Friday evening, following their boozy team drinks. Did he push her onto his mummy's desk and whip out his penis? Was she afraid? Would this traumatic experience scar her for life? What disgusted her to the core was the realisation that he had subjected someone's daughter to this horrifying experience, when he was a father of two girls himself. The anger she felt towards him was now creeping up inside her, ready to erupt like a volcano.

"This is *very* different, you fucking piece of shit," she screamed. "You're delusional. You need help." In that moment, she felt a surge of rage so intense that she imagined herself attacking him with a blunt instrument. She stood up from the chair, deliberately turning her back on his smackable face. Taking two deep breaths, she focused on regaining her composure, reminding herself that she had more to say.

"I'm moving out," she announced as she turned back around. "I can't live in that house. I need a fresh start and anyway, I've always hated living that far out from the city."

"And where do you think you're going to go?" he mocked.

"I've found a beachfront apartment in Manly for three months. Then I suppose I'll figure out the rest later."

He laughed with such force that one of his shirt buttons popped open. "And how on earth are you going to pay for that? Didn't you read the news today—I'm going bankrupt."

"Actually, it's free for the first three months." *Yes,* she thought. He wouldn't have seen that coming.

"Ah, so there's another man. Shacking up with him, are you? That's the real reason why you're leaving me and why it's free." He sat forward in his chair, resting his clenched fists on the table.

"Hugo, for fuck's sake, I've just told you I'm leaving you because you're a cheating liar. You preyed on a young woman who trusted you. And for the record, you preyed on me, too." She stared down at him sitting in his chair. "I'm a shadow of my former self and *you* did that. I don't even know who I am anymore. And I don't know who you are. You're *certainly* not the man I married." She cast a filthy look to express her disgust.

"Stop playing the victim, making out your life is so miserable. You have everything you ever wanted. I gave you everything you asked for." He didn't appear remorseful, not one little bit.

"No. You gave me what *you* wanted to give me. There's a big difference. I don't want to get nasty, but I'll be filing for divorce. You've left me no other option."

Hugo stood up. "This is nuts, Lucy. Stop. Think about this, for the sake of the girls, our family."

The tables were *finally* starting to turn in this argument, in their dynamic. Lucy was in control for the first time in ten years. *You got this,* she thought to herself.

"That's exactly who I *am* thinking about. How would they look at their mother if I were to stay with their cheating father? In case you didn't know—they're old enough to know exactly what's going on. What kind of relationships would they have later in life if they thought cheating, preying, controlling behaviour was all okay?"

And suddenly, the realisation hit him like a ton of bricks. He wasn't the untouchable and immensely successful impresario he had always believed himself to be. He was a failure—failed businessman, failed father and failed husband.

The colour drained from his face, and he collapsed into his swivel chair, before letting out a loud wail. His body began to shake and he started bawling uncontrollably.

Lucy's eyes widened in disbelief. She resisted the urge to console him. *Stay put. Do not capitulate.* It wasn't easy for her to stand there and watch him cry like a big fat baby, because she was a decent human being. But she had to admit there was a small part of her that felt satisfied. Satisfied that he was capable of an emotion other than anger. She reached for her handbag and removed her gold heart-shaped locket, set it down on the desk and stepped back.

"I've got to go now, Hugo. I'll be in touch once I've spoken to the girls."

He glanced at the locket then continued bawling.

"Oh, and by the way, the Manly apartment is our neighbour's. There are some people in this world who don't do things for money, they just do it to be kind. Fancy that." She hoped he'd heard what she'd said over his blubbering. It was the final 'stick it to him'.

She opened the door and Erin almost fell into her. Had she been listening at the door the whole time? They were inches apart, so close Lucy could smell her tacky perfume. Probably Tommy Girl.

"I've got something for you," Lucy said, walking towards Erin's desk. She removed a small orange box with brown ribbon from her bag and placed it on the desk. "These Hermès earrings aren't my style. You have them. Oh, and Hugo might need some tissues."

Then, she turned on her heel and walked towards the exit, as fast as her Jimmy Choos would carry her. Outside on the street, she hailed the first taxi she saw, jumped in, told the driver where she was headed, then sank into the back seat. It was a hot summer's day and yet she was shivering. Was it adrenalin? It must be. Had she said everything she wanted to? It all seemed like a blur now. She tried to type a text to Rosie, but her hands were shaking.

Lucy: I've done it, Rosie. My hands are shaking I can barely type this text.

Rosie: Breathe. Well done. I'm meeting Cecilia in fifteen minutes. Suggest you join us. You might want to hear it first-hand?

Lucy. All right. I suppose I do. Send me the restaurant details.

Lucy asked the taxi to stop at Martin Place, outside her old office, which was only two blocks away from the restaurant. Everything looked the same from the outside. She could see the TV presenters through the glass windows, sitting at the U-shaped news desk, with all the screens and ticker tapes broadcasting around the office. She loved that job. Her girls had never seen her on the TV and she wished they had. Why did she allow Hugo to follow his dreams and quash her own? Him and his bloody 1950s upbringing.

Good luck with that, Erin. He'd be asking her to exchange those gold boots for an apron and iron in a matter of weeks. Ha!

In the Broadway Brasserie, Rosie was seated in a curved velvet banquette around a white-clothed oval table. When she spotted Lucy, she immediately stood up and went over to hug over.

"Hey, you've done it. I'm really proud of you." Rosie looked her in the eye and rubbed her arms. "Lucy, this is Cecilia Meadows. Cecilia, this is Lucy Love."

"Lovely to meet you," said Cecilia, shaking Lucy's hand.

"You too."

Lucy took a seat in the middle of the banquette with Rosie and Cecilia either side. Cecilia was dressed formally, more office worker than journalist, in a black shift dress, white jacket and sensible black court shoes. In her late forties, she had one of those asymmetrical bobs where the front is longer than the back and the owner feels the need to tilt their head. The red lipstick, painted on her thin lips, was running into the fine lines around her mouth and her crinkled eyes were decorated with lashings of black mascara. After exchanging a few pleasantries about the brasserie's magnificent art deco features, Rosie steered the conversation to the reason they were there—Hugo.

"Listen, thanks for running the piece on Hugo today and these bankruptcy rumours."

"They better be well sourced, otherwise I'm in for it," Cecilia said, buttering a thick slice of baguette while trying to catch the waiter's attention. "I need a wine."

"Let me get that." Rosie caught the waiter's eye and ushered him over. "Please bring us a bottle of something red, French, not your best, not your worst either. Middle of the road. That okay with you?" She looked over at Cecilia, who was stuffing the baguette into her mouth. She nodded.

"As I said, we're grateful you ran that piece and you'll find out it is true. That's right, yes, Lucy?"

"Yes. But you can't quote me in any of this, right?" Lucy panicked. She never really had trusted the whole 'off the record' and 'on the record' stuff when talking to media. It seemed to her that *nothing* was ever 'off the record'.

"No, Lucy, this is all on what we call background; that means nothing will be quoted," said Rosie, as she patted Lucy's hand.

"Okay." She felt a bit stupid, like the stay-at-home mum in the middle of a professional woman's sandwich.

The waiter arrived and poured a small drop of wine in Rosie's glass for her to taste.

"Just pour, I'm sure it's fine," Rosie said quickly, gesturing at the waiter to fill Cecilia's glass.

"We need to know about these other victims. We don't need names. We just need confirmation that you *do* have others," said Rosie.

Cecilia took a big swig of wine, glanced over at Lucy then set her glass down. "Are you sure you want to know this?"

Lucy leaned in. "I'm absolutely sure."

Cecilia took another big swig from her glass. "Okay. There are three others. One is nineteen …"

Lucy gasped loudly in shock. "That's the same age as my daughter, Fleur." She reached across for the bottle of wine and filled her glass to the brim, then inhaled it.

Rosie's eyes widened; so did Cecilia's.

"Are you sure you want me to go on?" asked Cecilia.

Lucy nodded.

"The other two victims are twenty-two and twenty-four. The first incident occurred four years ago. It seems Indie was the one who spurred the others on to come forward. A bit 'me too' of them."

Lucy leaned further in across the table towards Cecilia and asked in a soft voice, "What kind of harassing are we talking about? Sexual?"

"Yes," Cecilia said firmly.

"Oh my God." Lucy clutched at her chest. Was that sharp pain she felt a heart attack or a broken heart? She wanted to ask how far he went with each of the young women. Did it start with unwanted sexual comments then move into unwelcome advances before dialling up into full-blown touching and groping. Was his signature move flinging his chipolata around after a few lines? And if so, why? Why would he do that? Did he want to make the young women feel powerless? There were so many questions she wanted to ask, more detail she wanted to know, but at the same time she didn't want to know any of it. *Oh no, is that a panic attack coming on?* She couldn't catch her breath. She reached for her water, but it slipped out of her shaking hand causing the glass to smash into pieces on the tiled floor.

Rosie quickly moved closer and whispered, "Close your eyes and breathe, just breathe," in her ear. When her palpitations slowed, she felt the glares from neighbouring tables. "How embarrassing. Everyone's looking," she said as the waiter swept up the shards of glass around her feet.

"Who cares about them?" Rosie replied, staring down the pair of women on the table closest to theirs. The women got the message and quickly turned their attention back to their steak frites.

"Are you ready to keep going now?" asked Cecilia.

Lucy nodded.

"I've now got permission from the three victims to go ahead and publish their stories tomorrow and Rosie said you would like to make a statement. Is that right?"

"Yes, I think so." Lucy hesitated. Indecision was always an issue for her but there was a big difference between deciding what to order for dinner versus what kind of public statement to make about sexual harassment.

"Lucy. You *have* to make a statement. You cannot sit back and let this one run with no comment. You will be destroyed."

"Okay, okay. I can't give it to you now. But I do want to say I'm divorcing him." She cast her eyes down towards her now ringless wedding finger, and with a quivering voice, she added, "And that I think the victims are brave."

"Okay, I need it by 4pm though," Cecila said. "Now, can we order? I'm starving."

Rosie gave a discreet eye roll to Lucy and Lucy managed a faint smile in return.

Everything was moving so fast now. There really was no going back.

Chapter 25

It was 7pm on the dot when Savannah Silva arrived at restaurant Balthazar in New York's SoHo district. Having flow in from London the day before, she had her sights set on some much-needed retail therapy before a week filled with client meetings. With a daily top temperature of four degrees Celsius, winter shopping in New York was always much more pleasant than the suffocating summer heat.

Her favourite waiter, Christophe, was working tonight. He was a strikingly good-looking young man with an Austin Butler-like face and pout, who always ensured her requests were attended to. In return she always left a generous tip, typically thirty per cent of the bill.

She had requested one of the side nook banquettes off the centre of the restaurant for her dinner with Walter Goldberg, her older and hard-of-hearing client. After almost three decades in investment banking, she had successfully segued into managing the personal investments of a small number of uber-wealthy clients. She didn't love it, but there was no way she was ready to retire. The thought of it filled her with dread.

"Your guest hasn't arrived yet, Ms Silva," said Christophe, taking her faux fur coat over his arm and walking it to the cloakroom. While she waited for him to return, she glanced at her reflection in the vintage mirror hanging over the host station. She patted her sleek raven bob and readjusted the double-layered Chanel CC logo pearl necklace that hung over her black cashmere turtleneck. She then scanned the crowded dining room, her eyes quickly landing on two familiar faces. The first was a former colleague, who acknowledged her with a nod. The second belonged to the daughter of a client, who was engrossed in capturing photographs of her salad. People photographing dinner plates for Instagram was a pet hate of hers.

"I've seated you back here, as requested," said Christophe, motioning towards the far end of the dining room. She had requested one of the side nook banquettes off the centre for her dinner with Walter Goldberg, her older and hard-of-hearing client. She manoeuvred her way through the crowded dining area, keeping her eyes on the black-and-white chequered floors, not wanting to catch any more eyes.

Arriving at her table, she quickly glanced at the three men sitting in the adjacent banquette before shimmying into her seat. She ordered a Scotch on the rocks and carefully placed her newly acquired treasure, a black leather Saint Laurent bag, on her lap. As she waited for Christophe to return with her order, she took the opportunity to quickly catch up on a few emails before Walter arrived.

"If Bee Bloom is as smart as you say she is, then she'll realise this is for the best," boomed one of the men carrying a subtle Australian twang.

Savannah's ears instantly pricked up. Did she just hear the name Bee Bloom?

It wasn't a common name. Intrigued, Savannah shifted just a little closer to the neighbouring banquette and tilted her head towards the man closest to her. Out of the corner of her eye, she noticed he had strikingly white hair. Sitting next to him was an older man, and across from him was a handsome man who appeared to be in his early fifties.

"You say that, Max, but I've known Bee for much longer than you and this will devastate her, and the staff, come to think of it," the older man said.

Quickly realising she might be listening in on a private meeting about her friend and former mentee, Savannah decided to record the conversation. She slipped her phone up on the wooden ledge separating the two banquettes, behind the head of the white-haired man.

"C'mon, you and I both know this isn't a popularity contest." The handsome one was talking now. "Her road at Curban has come to an end and staff, well, they will understand. And if they don't, they can follow her out the door."

"That's a bit heartless, Max," the small one chimed.

As she listened closely and heard their names, Savannah established the identities of two of the three men. One of them was Arthur Andrews, the chairman of Curban Capital. The second man was Max Magnifico, the investment banker she had never worked with but had heard so much about. But who was the one with white hair with his back to her?

"It's the truth. We don't have time for people to wallow in the past. They're either on board or they're gone." Max clicked his fingers loudly.

"You could at least show a little compassion."

Savannah continued to listen intently, determined to gather as much information as possible without drawing attention to herself. She kept her head titled downwards, her hair strategically covering her face, and her eyes fixed on the menu in her hands.

"All right. Let's talk money. We need to agree on her payout, her hush money, whatever you want to call it," said the man closest to her.

"And don't be stingy. We must do the right thing." The older man was obviously the kinder of the trio. She heard him excuse himself to go to the bathroom.

Once he was out of sight the other two carried on talking. "Listen, Arthur has a bit of a soft spot for Bee so we need to entertain that a little. He's finding this, a bit tricky, shall we say."

"Right, he doesn't have the killer instinct like us, hey?"

They both chuckled, like two evil comic villains.

"So what kind of deal can we get away with then? Let's make it as low as we can," said the white-haired one.

"Couldn't agree more. Look, don't get me wrong. It's not that I don't like this Bee Bloom. She seems perfectly nice. But nice just isn't going to cut it when we bring our two businesses together," said Max.

"So who have you got in mind to take over? You mentioned someone called Penny Pryor when I was in Sydney, but do we really want another female?"

Max began laughing. "My thoughts exactly. No, we don't. Penny is tough but she's done herself out of a job by being too needy and chasing me for an answer ever since I mentioned it to her on a flight to Melbourne. Plus, she's menopause age and we know what that means." He laughed again. "I've actually been talking to Michael Webster, he's an old Graybournian. One of us. Good stock."

"Now we're talking, Max. I like your thinking."

Savannah was boiling in her banquette. *Good stock, you dying breed of stuck-up dicks. An old Graybournian. Grrrr.* She had worked with several 'Graybourne old boys' in her former investment banking life and they were all the same. They tangentially injected stories about their boarding house days into conversations and continued to wear items like rugby shirts with the school's name and emblem well into their fifties. They also referred to each other as if they belonged to an exclusive group, almost cult-like, and as if their attendance at Graybourne defined them. This was the kind of elite shit she had been trying to put an end to for over thirty years. *If it hasn't changed by now, when will it?* She was itching to stand up and take them on. Oh, how she loved a good rumble with the relics. Did this pair have children? How would the cycle of toxicity ever break if they raised their own with the same morals? And the employees they lead? Would they inherit the culture these relics had set or change it for good?

The older man had now returned to his seat. "I've asked for the bill," he said.

"So what's the timing, Max?" asked the man closest to her.

"We arrive back in Sydney early on Wednesday morning and are setting up a board meeting for ten o'clock. She'll be gone by the afternoon."

"Gosh, Max. I heard you were ruthless, but this is something else."

"It's business, Arthur. A transaction. I think you need to take the emotion out of it."

"Mr Magnifico. Your bill," said the waiter.

Savannah slipped her phone off the wooden ledge and back into her new handbag. Those conniving bastards. *It's 2022 and they're still at it,* she thought. *Over my dead body.*

With the Cecilia Meadows lunch and accountant meeting behind her, it was finally time for Rosie's most anticipated task of the day. She sat in a meeting room behind the Reid & Co Counsel reception and dialled Hugo's number on the Polycom desk phone. It was the same excited butterfly feeling she had experienced when telling her old lazy Scottish boss, Jean, that she was leaving the agency.

The phone rang once.

"What the fuck am I paying you for if I can't get hold of you?" Hugo screamed.

"Hi, Hugo." Rosie's tone was deliberately light, breezy and sunny. "How are you?"

"Awful. Horrible. Hang on. Haven't you even seen what's going down?"

She resisted the urge to laugh at his panicked voice.

"Yes, I have. I wonder where they got all that information from. Seems odd, doesn't it?" She was playing with him and loved it.

"I told you, tall poppy. There're always people trying to cut me down. Why didn't you call me back last night or this morning?"

"I've been busy with other clients, sorry about that. And since you haven't bothered to pay your first invoice, I didn't bother hurrying to get back to you." She laughed to herself as the words poured out.

"You what?" he shouted.

"But don't worry, your wife settled your bill. So I think we're done. I was just ringing to wish you luck. Because you're going to need it."

And she hung up.

"Yesssss, that's what you get!" she shouted at the Polycom phone, sticking her two middle fingers up. It was immensely satisfying; in fact, more satisfying than she had imagined. One dick down, twenty-four to go. The other twenty-four clients would be informed over the next two weeks, once she had finalised what staff were staying at the firm, and which were going. The announcement was going to be brutal for the staff, because Reid & Co Counsel was like a family business.

When she exited the office, she spotted Paula glancing over from her seat at the reception desk. "What was all that about?"

"That, my dear Paula, was me saying good riddance to someone who didn't deserve our time."

"It's beyond embarrassing, Mum. I can't even believe it," cried Maya.

Lucy had decided to have a three-way call with Maya and Fleur. Her phone was sat on the kitchen counter, on speaker mode, next to her glass of white wine. She was trying her hardest not to chug it, like normal.

Rosie had recommended she stick to two glasses maximum per night. *"Wine is not your friend right now,"* she had said when they left Broadway Brasserie earlier in the day.

"I know, darling," Lucy said to Maya.

"No, Mum, you don't. Do you know how bitchy some of the girls are here? They already teased me when that last article came out," shouted Maya. "When we were getting changed in PE the other day, Sophie Perkins kept saying, "Stop looking at us. You're a perve, just like your dad." And all week, when I walked past, she shouted out, "eew.""

"Tell her to piss off, Maya. Stand up for yourself," Fleur sniped. "And stop popping at Mum. It's not her fault. How do you think she feels?"

Fleur really hadn't said much last week. Had Lucy mistaken her silence as nonchalance, when in actual fact she was probably hurting just as much as Maya? It was likely she was telling bitches to piss off too but didn't want to let on. There was a deafening silence on all ends of the call.

"Girls, you're old enough that I'm not going to beat around the bush." She took a deep breath. "It's going to be awful. But I will do everything I can to protect you from it all," said Lucy. "And I've decided I'm going to move out of this house and ... and ... I'll be divorcing your father." She washed the words down with a big swig of wine and waited for their response.

"Well, he's dead to me, so I don't care," Maya yelled. She began sobbing and Lucy instantly regretted calling her. It dawned on her that this was too much for someone of Maya's age to handle, much more than any teenager should ever have to bear. Despite her initial desire to tell both girls in person, Lucy was racing against the clock to ensure they didn't hear the news from someone else first. She couldn't imagine how they would have felt if a friend had approached them with news that their father was now accused of harassing not one but four young women. In his debauched, disgusting mind Hugo had clearly not given any thought to his daughters. They would be scarred for life after this and maybe he would be dead to them.

"You don't mean that. You're just angry right now. He's still your dad, Maya."

"No, Mum, I do."

Lucy steeled herself; she didn't want to wobble and cry. She wanted to be strong on the phone for Fleur and Maya's sake and then allow herself to be vulnerable in person, when she could hold them close. "I'd like you both to come home tomorrow, please. I'll speak to the school and university about you having the rest of the week off. We'll talk about what's going to happen and you can ask me any questions you want."

"Okay, Mum," agreed Fleur.

"Maya, is that okay?"

"Fine. Anything to get away from the bitchfest here," sniffed Maya.

After hanging up, Lucy reached for her glass. She tried to resist the urge, but she couldn't. Not tonight. She downed it then went to the fridge and poured herself another large glass. She wanted something to snack on, but the fridge's food shelves were empty. Everything in her life felt empty right now, except for her trusty wine glass.

Chapter 26

Bethany Byron had called Lucy, asking if she would like to pop over for a coffee. She had seen today's *Daily Life* and wanted to check Lucy was okay.

Daily Life, *Friday, December 12, 2022*
Three more victims allege Hugo Hamilton harassed them
Three more victims have come forward claiming to have been sexually harassed by Hugo Hamilton. This follows allegations made last week by a former staff member of Hamilton's and rumours that he is on the verge of bankruptcy. Hamilton wasn't available for comment.

Pamela had also rung, multiple times, in fact, and Lucy kept sending her calls to voicemail. What was her soon-to-be ex-mother-in-law going to say this time? That the new victims *deserved* it? That her precious boy wasn't responsible? And how dare Lucy break up their marriage? Pamela would be whizzing around the golf club in her buggy telling all her like-minded golf buddies that it was all utter garbage.

And anyway, Rosie had explicitly told Lucy to lay low and only answer urgent or friendly calls. *"Don't speak to anyone unless they're going to make you feel better."*

Pamela was not urgent and she definitely wasn't going to make her feel better. Rosie had also told her not to read too much news or social media.

Bethany's house sat on a double block and was twice the size of Lucy's, not that she was comparing, she was just struck by its grandness. It was the very definition of a mega mansion. She had Googled Bethany before leaving the house, discovering she was the founder and CEO of Urban Style, a vegan bag and accessories company that she founded twenty-four years ago. Lucy felt overawed by her success and entrepreneurship. Had she wasted her own prime career years? There was so much regret, so much should've, could've, would've but just didn't. *Sigh.*

Bethany breezily opened the front door wearing blue and white matchy-matchy silk trousers and shirt set and kitten heel mules with her phone pressed to her ear. Her honey-coloured hair was styled with a soft kink and her make-up was perfectly minimal. She looked great for her 45 years.

"Come in. Just finishing up a call with a stockist," she said, motioning for Lucy to step inside.

As Lucy trailed behind Bethany, she couldn't help but feel as though she had stepped into a modern art gallery. In the brilliant white hallway hung a series of contemporary artworks in Tasmanian oak frames. They weren't her style, but she appreciated them, nonetheless. At the end of the hallway was a large, framed cover of *Entrepreneur Magazine* with Bethany gracing the front and the words 'Entrepreneur of the Year 2021'. Bethany led them through a brilliant white kitchen with light oak floorboards and finally to an entertaining terrace decorated with sleek, minimalist outdoor furniture.

"Sorry about that. How are you?" Bethany asked as she placed her phone on the table. "I saw your quote in the article, and I have to say, good for you, saying goodbye to that cunt of a husband."

Bethany poured them each a glass of iced water from a carafe that looked like a piece of art. Wow, the C word. Bethany might look like a lady of the manor, but she didn't sound it.

"How are your girls doing?" she asked Lucy.

The *Daily Life* article had included photos of Maya and Fleur snatched from their Instagram accounts. Rosie pleaded with Cecilia to exclude their names and photos, but that was one point that Cecilia refused to back down on. The fact that Hugo was the father of two girls, one a similar age to the victims, was too good for her story.

"They're not great, obviously, but they're coming home today and they'll spend the rest of the week with me." Lucy let out a loud sigh. "They're going to hate me." She closed her eyes and let her head fall downwards.

"They *will* be angry, because they have every right to feel that way. After all, they've just found out their father is a grade A cunt." Her wide eyes peered over the top of her blue glasses that matched her matchy-matchy set.

Oh, there goes her mouth again.

"And they might even take that anger out on you temporarily. But they *will* respect you, maybe even admire you with time." Bethany placed her hand reassuringly on Lucy's knee. Lucy couldn't help but glance down at it. Her eyes were drawn to the stunning Kate Middleton-like engagement ring on Bethany's wedding finger.

"I can't imagine them *ever a*dmiring me." Lucy kept her gaze downwards. "If only I had something they could admire me for. I bet yours admire you, being an entrepreneur and all."

"They couldn't give a toss what I do. But that's a story for another time," Bethany said, waving her left hand in the air. "And hey, this isn't the time to be beating yourself up about decisions you've made in the past. You've got a new path in front of you now. Anyway, didn't you used to be a successful TV presenter?" Bethany reassured through raised eyebrows.

"Sort of," said Lucy, holding her glass up to her mouth.

"Not sort of. I Googled you and saw all those photos of you interviewing celebrities and schmoozing at parties. A-ma-zing!" Her eyes sparkled with excitement.

"You Googled me?" Lucy laughed. "I Googled *you*."

Bethany giggled then said, "Do you know what, Lucy Love—I love that name, by the way." She strummed her fingers on the table. "I think I might know how we can put those skills of yours to use."

Stuart had his list of employees that he wanted to interrogate, and Davide was at the top, even though Bee said he could never have leaked the videos to the media. Nobody in the Curban office was safe. As far as Stuart was concerned, everyone was a possible suspect and he was going to do his damn best to find out who had double-crossed Bee.

To say he was enraged was an understatement. How bloody dare someone do that to Bee? She was the best CEO they would ever work for, and they would all come to realise it the minute someone evil like Max replaced her. It was like swapping Volodymyr Zelensky for Vladimir Putin. Stuart had witnessed time and time again how, behind closed doors, Bee agonised over decisions that impacted her staff. She always had their best interests at heart and this was how someone repaid her. With those thoughts running through his mind, he stomped towards the office of Angela Tan, Head of Technology. She was in her office on a Zoom call, with her headset sitting over her bleached pixie cut, oblivious to him flapping his arms at the glass window. He knocked on the door and Angela turned around, mouthing, "I'm on a call."

No shit you're on a call, Angela. He decided to barge in. No call could be more important than *this*. He was usually scared of Angela and her emo vibe. He imagined her as one of those individuals who participated in fake medieval battles in their spare time.

"What is it, Stuart? That was an important call!"

"This is *way* more important. I need you to run a search on devices to check if anyone from here contacted a journalist at *The Financial Report* on Friday night."

Angela nodded. She knew what he was getting at. He didn't need to spell it out to her, she had seen the leaked videos for herself.

"And keep it quiet, please. We don't need anything else leaking out."

"Of course. When do you need it by?" Angela asked, scribbling down notes on the pad in front of her.

"Today. Preferably in the next four hours."

"I'll do my best, but it all depends on how quickly the network team comes back to us."

"You can do it, Angela. Push them. You're good at being pushy." Stuart smiled.

It was a back-handed compliment but fortunately Angela smiled back appreciatively.

Next, Stuart stomped to Max's lounge to find Suzy. As he passed reception, he felt Davide eyeing him off. He really wanted to go over and tell him what a terrible dancer he was. He was as stiff as a board. And Snappy Suzy, well, who knew *that* ice queen could crack a smile, let alone slut drop. It was baffling that those two had struck up a drunken friendship. They had left the party together, linked arms, propping each other up while Stuart stayed behind to do a post-event check with the venue managers. Unlike them, he fulfilled his party committee duties right until the bitter end, because Bee counted on him.

"How are you, Davide?" Stuart asked, deciding to swing past reception after all.

"Well, Stuart. I thought the party all went perfectly on Friday, except for ... you know."

"No, I don't know." Stuart was deliberately provoking him.

Davide covered his mouth and whispered, "The videos."

"Oh yes. You wouldn't know anything about that, would you?"

"Me? No. Why would I?" Davide's eyes went round, and his mouth opened.

Stuart noticed and wondered if he was nervous.

"What about Suzy? Do you think she would know anything about it?"

"I have no idea. You should speak to her yourself. But she's out right now. I saw her leave thirty minutes ago. I suppose she is out for lunch." He pursed his lips. Stuart hated the way he did that when he was cross.

"Between you and me, Davide, Bee is on the warpath. I've never, *ever* seen her so angry," he whispered across the reception counter. He wanted to fire a warning shot at Davide to see his reaction. He didn't look panicked, but he *was* lost for words, for once.

Back at his desk, Stuart scrolled through the internal directory of staff to check if there was anyone he hadn't quizzed. As he did, it suddenly dawned on him that from tomorrow, yes, tomorrow, he would be unemployed and without a salary.

Overcome with panic, he opened the calculator in his phone and began working out his outgoings. According to the numbers, he would be out of money in just three months. *Fuck!* Bee had been right all those years; he *should* have saved, and he *should* have bought an apartment. He didn't want to admit it to her, because it was incredibly shallow and money-grabby, but he was holding out for a sizeable inheritance from his father in London. But with his father bouncing around and looking like he had a few more years in him, Stuart realised he might have to ask for a slice of his inheritance early, because if he didn't, he would run out of cash in three months, according to the calculator staring back at him. *Sigh, still asking for money at forty-five. How pathetic!*

An instant message from Angela Tan flashed up on his screen.

Angela: Found something. Want to come round?

Stuart: YES!!!

Angela was munching her way through a family-size bag of salt and vinegar crisps when Stuart arrived. Not the healthiest of eaters, her pedestal was always bulging with an assortment of crisps, biscuits and lollies.

"Sit down and look normal. These glass offices are terrible for prying eyes," said Angela, now sipping from a can of full-fat Coke. Stuart did exactly as she said, fearing she might remove a sword from under her desk if he didn't.

"I'll pretend I'm taking notes," he said, opening his notepad and starting to scribble.

Angela pulled a sheet of paper from her desk printer and set it down in front of Stuart. It showed a list of text messages sent from a phone. Angela circled with her red pen the owner's name: *Davide Dubois*.

"I fucking knew it. *Nez Marron*," he shrieked. "What is he playing at? I quizzed him about it this morning and he lied to my face."

"I have to say, I was surprised too. I've always thought of him as a real Curban brand ambassador," Angela said as she loudly crunched the crisps in her mouth.

Stuart picked up the piece of paper and tucked it into his notepad.

"Good work, Angela. Thanks for doing this."

He wanted to take Davide on himself first before he presented the information to Bee. Oh, how he would love to torture him by pulling his manicured nails out with pliers, like in the movies. Actually, come to think of it, that idea was probably a bit extreme. Maybe just tie him up for a bit without food then. He knew how Davide loved his food. Ha!

But putting his torture fantasies aside just for now, he came back to the point of why? *Why* would Davide throw Bee under the bus? He was the *Nez Marron*, after all. Why brown nose and then leak footage to publicly humiliate her? Did someone pay him to do it? Was he being blackmailed? Was there an accomplice, such as Suzy? Stuart had all these theories buzzing around in his head. It just didn't add up, but the evidence was there—three text messages sent from Davide's phone, one at 20.31, one at 20.44 and one at 20.52, to the contact number of the journalist at *The Financial Report*. Stuart couldn't just have it out with Davide on reception, so he sent him an invite with the subject 'Quick post party debrief' and booked a meeting room.

Stuart arrived at the meeting room early and waited for Davide. He brought the phone records with him and printouts of the leaked video news article and set everything out on the table. His plan was to let Davide look at the items and watch him squirm.

"Ah, Davide, there you are. Please come in and close the door behind you." As Davide took his seat, Stuart placed the evidence on the table and swiftly spun it around, ensuring that it was the right way around for Davide to read.

"I didn't get much notice for this debrief, so I only have fifteen minutes," Davide complained.

"Oh, this won't take long," Stuart said snootily.

"What's this?" Davide asked, picking up the sheet of paper.

Stuart remained silent. He wanted to see if Davide could work it out for himself.

As Davide scanned the document, his eyes tightened, his brows furrowed and he lifted his right hand to his cheek.

"I'm confused," he said. "Is this my phone record and why do you have it?"

"Yes, it is, and it proves that *you* sent three text messages Friday night." Up until this point, Stuart had maintained a steady and controlled tone. However, in an abrupt shift, his voice erupted into a shout. "TO THE BLOODY *FINANCIAL REPORT.*" Stuart's fury had boiled to the surface. "How could you? You conniving little prick."

"I don't understand." Davide's voice cracked. "*Sacré bleu.* This wasn't me. It wasn't me." The paper shook in his hand as he stared at it. His eyes were full of panic.

"It's your phone, so it *was* you." Stuart snatched the paper out of his hands and pointed at Davide's name and number circled in red. "Look. *Your* number, *your* name, three messages, all on Friday night."

Davide's eyes darted around, and he fiddled nervously with his pocket square.

"That's it! I knew it wasn't me." He sat forward, holding on to the edge of the table. "I gave my phone to Suzy to look after. I couldn't keep it in my pockets." He patted his pockets to demonstrate. "My trouser pockets were too tight to hold the phone, so Suzy put it in her clutch bag."

"Wow. You really are a sneaky little prick. Trying to put the blame on someone else," tutted Stuart with a tone of incredulity.

Davide's tone, on the other hand, was escalating in pitch and panic. "It's true. It is. It is. Ask her. Let's ask her."

Stuart sat back in his chair, considering this alternative theory. Maybe the little prick *was* telling the truth. It kind of made more sense that Suzy would do something like this. Davide was really only on the suspect list because Stuart disliked him so much. He *wanted* it to be him. But he didn't have motive. Suzy, on the other hand, did, by virtue of working for Max.

"All right. Let's go and find Suzy then." Stuart stood up, collected the papers from the table and left the meeting room with Davide trailing behind.

After leaving the office at lunchtime, Suzy never returned. She wasn't answering her phone or responding to texts either. It was slightly unethical, but Stuart asked Philippa, the unsuspecting junior in HR, for Suzy's address, saying Bee needed it urgently. By this point, Davide was growing impatient, even labelling Suzy a double-crossing bitch. Could he actually be telling the truth? There was only one way to find out.

Suzy answered the video intercom of her Elizabeth Bay apartment and with wide, surprised eyes, asked, "What are you two doing here?"

"Let us up. We need to talk to you urgently," Stuart said.

"What about? I'll be back at work tomorrow. We can chat then."

Davide shoved Stuart out of the way and shouted into the intercom, "Let us up now or we're going to the police." His face flushed red and his eyes popped out of his head, like a toddler during a breath-holding spell.

The door buzzed and clicked open.

"Jesus, Davide. You're actually quite scary when you're angry."

Davide didn't respond, disregarding Stuart as he barged past him and made his way through the front door.

Suzy's apartment was situated within a modern resort-style complex with manicured gardens and a communal outdoor pool. As they went up to level four in the lift, Stuart wondered how *she* could afford an apartment in this sought-after area, and he couldn't. He suspected Davide was thinking the same.

Suzy was standing at the door of her apartment when the lift doors opened. She wore a floaty Camilla silk kaftan and, most surprisingly, no make-up. Stuart had taken her for one of those never-be-seen-dead-without-a-full-face-of-make-up types. He was surprised how naturally pretty she was.

"This way," she said, walking into a lounge area drenched in sunlight. The room was femininely decorated in shabby chic decor and accents of pink—pink lampshades, pink cushions and pink throw blankets. It was small, but through the floor-to-ceiling balcony doors, Stuart could just make out harbour views. An apartment with views in Elizabeth Bay would be over three million dollars, Stuart guessed. And how on earth could she afford it? Did she get paid for leaking videos?

"Have a seat." She pointed at a two-seater white lounge. Stuart wriggled to the edge, not wanting his legs to touch Davide's. Suzy sat facing them in a matching white armchair. She offered them a tea and Davide snapped "no" before Stuart could say yes. Clearly, he was keen to get the interrogation underway!

With a look of confusion on her face, Suzy asked what all the commotion was about and why they threatened to go to the police if she didn't open the door.

"Shall you start or shall I?" Davide spluttered through his rapid breath.

"I will." Stuart eyeballed Suzy, who was sitting with her legs tucked up on the chair. "You leaked the footage of Bee to the papers. We've got proof. We don't want to hear excuses, we just want to know why."

Davide, still donning an angry and flushed expression, chipped in with, "Yes, it's time for you to start explaining yourself." Then he pursed his lips and let out an audible huff through his nostrils.

Chapter 27

Trying to keep her mind on anything Walter Goldberg was saying about his investments was proving impossible for Savannah. All she could think about was the alarming conversation she had just overheard. She had finished her salad niçoise over twenty minutes ago, but Walter was still slurping his way through escargots in garlic butter at the pace of an escargot. He was down to his last two and she had the urge to reach across and feed them to him herself.

The coup was planned for 10am. Sydney time on Wednesday which meant she still had time to organise a flight. She would just have to postpone all her client meetings *and* find some summer clothes to replace the faux furs and wool bouclé jackets that she had brought to New York.

"Don't you think?" Walter asked.

"Don't I think what? Sorry, Walter, jet lag is kicking in." She faked a yawn.

"Am I keeping you up, dear? Why don't we just get the bill?"

Hallelujah! Savannah shouted "bill" to the first waitperson she saw. Time to get this escargot into his chauffeur-driven limousine waiting outside. Dezzy (short for Desmond) had been driving Walter for as long as Savannah had known him, which was twenty years. He kindly offered to drop her at her Midtown hotel before they went on to Walter's Upper East Side penthouse, but she politely declined. Dezzy was as slow a driver as Arthur was an eater so a yellow cab would be much faster and she needed to get hold of Bee, fast.

Stuart: You're not going to believe who leaked the footage. Meet us at Cafe Sopra 8am.

Bee: Meet us? So the person will be there?

Stuart: Yes!

Bee: Finishing up a client conference call. Will be thirty minutes tops.

Bee wanted to know who leaked the footage, but didn't at the same time. What if it was one of her most trusted employees? Could she ever trust again? She wrapped up her client call as quickly as she could so she could hotfoot it down to Cafe Sopra. She dashed past reception to tell Davide to take her calls while she and Stuart were out, but he wasn't there.

Downstairs in the lobby, she saw Emily talking on the phone and waved at her. Emily didn't do her usual animated wave back. Bee was aware that Emily really hadn't been back to her best bouncy self since the whole intern Ed affair. Hearing through the intern grapevine that Ed had been fired, the remaining nine Curban interns had gathered outside Emily's office demanding, yes, demanding, because that's what Gen Zers do, an explanation. As far as they could tell, there was no valid reason for his firing. And they were right, but poor Emily had to toe the party line and say, *"We can't talk about confidential matters relating to staff."*

It wouldn't be long before an activist intern, a friend of Ed's or even Ed himself, posted something on social media. Using social media was another Gen Z tactic, to draw attention to wrongdoings and get justice. The story had all the ingredients of a post that would go viral, and Bee suspected Curban's reputation in the intern community would be mud.

Sigh. All their hard work in raising their profile among the university students gone to waste in a flash. Considering wrongdoings, Bee wondered what her strategy would be. How could she get justice? It would take a lot more than a social media post.

Hordes of coffee-sipping office workers were gathered on the pavement outside Cafe Sopra when Bee arrived. She made her way past them and inside. Every table was occupied, and she couldn't immediately see Stuart among the crowd, then she caught sight of his trademark quiff right at the back. Who was with him, with their back to her?

"It was *you*?" she exclaimed. "But why?" Her mouth fell open and her heart sank with disappointment.

Stuart stood up and moved over to another chair, offering his to Bee. "You better sit down."

"Please let me explain, Bee," pleaded Suzy. "There're things you don't know about me. And about Max."

Bee was overcome with emotions, feeling angry, confused and disappointed all at once, while Suzy had a look of desperation.

"Let her explain, Bee," said Stuart.

"Okay. I'm listening." She folded her arms and glared at Suzy.

There was a long silence while Suzy fiddled with a long strand of hair.

"Suzy, I can't sit here all day. You need to start talking," said Bee impatiently. "Let's start with why."

"I had no choice."

"Keep going."

"Come on, Suzy, just tell Bee everything that you told me," Stuart said.

"First, you need to know something about me so you can understand why," Suzy spluttered, taking a small, shallow breath. "I'm a girl from a broken home in the western suburbs of Sydney. I left school at sixteen with no qualifications, and had every job under the sun, I mean, *every* job, some really awful, before I met Max. He gave me an opportunity and pulled me out of a hole. I could have ended up the madam of some shitty brothel if I hadn't met him."

Bee could hear the shortness in her breath as she spoke and feel her anxiety from across the table. Suzy kept her gaze down and only occasionally glanced up. When their eyes locked, Suzy's filled with tears.

"All I saw were the dollars. He paid me three times what I was making in my previous role; there were bonuses, gifts, bags, dresses. *Never* anything sexual." She emphasised the sexual part because naturally that would be everyone's assumption. The old boss and assistant cliché.

"So what did Max get in return, if you were getting all those things?" asked Bee.

"I had to do his dirty work. Smear campaign stuff, like leaking your video."

Suzy twisted the signet ring on her pinkie finger, then went back to twisting a strand of hair.

"What other dirty work?"

"Covering up for him, lying for him, setting people up who he wanted to get rid of. I've lost count how many times it's happened. I feel so ashamed," she cried, causing thick blobs of mascara to run.

"Oh Suzy." Bee closed her eyes. Her body slumped lower in the chair like someone was letting the air out of her. She was torn between feeling sorry for Suzy and being furious.

Stuart reached across the table to Suzy. "Tell her the next bit."

Opening her eyes, Bee said loudly, "What, there's more? Hang on, let me order a coffee, or is it wine o'clock yet?"

As soon as the waiter had served their coffees and was safely out of earshot, Suzy blurted out, "I'm Vanessa Rudgens. It was me."

Bee blinked in an exaggerated manner, disbelieving Suzy's revelation. She looked at Stuart, who was nodding repeatedly like a dashboard cat.

"I'm the one who sent you that email six months ago. I thought you'd read it and take some action or just do something, anything, to bring him down. I had no idea, until last week, that Max was trying to bring *you* down."

"But Vanessa, I mean, Suzy, blimey I'm confused; how could I bring him down with no evidence? All you said was he's a psychopath."

"I came across that Dr Robert Hare article and thought, ta da. Max shows every single characteristic of a corporate psychopath. He should be locked up. I hate him. I really fucking hate him now," Suzy rambled, shaking her head. She cupped her face in her hands and cried, "Once he finds out I've told you, he'll make sure I never get a job anywhere again. I'm fucked," she cried louder. Her cheeks became so wet with tears that her long Amazonian hair stuck to the sides of her face.

"I'm speechless. It's all too much. I need a minute." Bee excused herself and went to the bathroom.

She closed the door to the dimly lit cubicle and stood with her hands on the small white porcelain sink, staring at her reflection in the round backlit mirror. Despite liberally applying her best under-eye concealer this morning, she had failed to cover the dark circles. She didn't just feel exhausted, she looked it. She took that same concealer stick from her handbag and began touching the circles up. After applying two dots underneath each eye, she furiously threw the stick to the floor, stamped her feet and shook her head furiously.

"No, no, no, no, no," she let out a silent scream. "This isn't fair. This isn't right. Why?" There were no tears, just pure anger. She could rip that sink off the wall, she was so enraged. Why do humans let you down like this? All she wanted in life was to be treated the way she treated others. Shouldn't kindness foster kindness? How did people like Max go through life causing all that collateral damage on others, yet remain unscathed himself? It was bullshit.

When she'd been upset with schoolyard bullies growing up, her father always used to say, "*Some people are just born mean. You can't change them. And once you realise that you'll stop getting so upset when people aren't kind to you.*"

Deciding that wasn't good enough, Bee had advocated for the introduction of morality monitors at her high school. She wanted young leaders to have the power to patrol the schoolyard and stamp out bullying. If there were morality monitors in organisations, Max would be expelled from Curban, not her.

She reached down and picked her concealer stick off the floor, washed it, and tucked it back into her bag. Gripping the sink, she attempted the square breathing technique from her meditation podcast. Breathe in for four seconds, hold for four seconds, breathe out for four seconds, then hold for four seconds. Repeat. Repeat. She opened her eyes, stood up straighter, mentally prepared herself and returned to her seat in the cafe. It was time for Max to get a taste of his own medicine. She needed cold, hard proof that he was as toxic as she knew he was. And Suzy was going to give it to her!

"Right, Suzy. Listen to me. I'm gutted about the video leaking, but I can see you're trying to do the right thing now. So what you need to do is give me some hard evidence that Max made you do this," she said firmly. "So, what have you got?"

Suzy immediately reached for her phone and began scrolling. "Here, start with this." She handed Bee her phone. It was a text from Max to Suzy on the morning of the party.

Max: Get some footage of Bee tonight. I don't care what it is, just get me something that shows her in a bad light.

Suzy: Please, not this again, Max. I can't do it this time.

Max: Don't forget I put you where you are now and I can easily put you back where you came from. Do it. No complaints. And once you've done it delete evidence. No trail. Got it?

Suzy: Yes.

This text exchange between Suzy and Max was confronting for Bee, but she also felt vindicated. It summed up just how evil he was. But what didn't make sense was why? Why was he so desperate to get her out?

She pulled herself into action mode and began telling Suzy what she needed to do. There was no time to waste. Suzy was to go home, put her out-of-office message on saying that she was unwell and not answer the phone to anyone except her and Stuart. Suzy agreed.

In that moment, Bee's initial disappointment in Suzy transformed into sympathy and understanding. It dawned on her that Suzy had been a victim of Max's for years, living in fear and desperately searching for a way to speak up, even if the only way of doing it was by sending an anonymous email.

"You're strong for doing this, Suzy. You know that, right?" Bee said.

Suzy shrugged.

"We'll get through this together." Bee placed a reassuring hand on Suzy's shoulder. Stuart placed his hand on her other shoulder and said, "Suzy, can I just ask something really quickly. Why did you come up with the name Vanessa Rudgens?"

Bee rolled her eyes. As if that mattered!

"I'm a die-hard *High School Musical* fan and have always loved Vanessa Hudgens so I just changed the name slightly." And with that, Suzy burst into tears again.

Back at her hotel, Savannah poured herself a neat scotch from the mini bar, some Dutch courage. The message she was about to deliver was brutal. She wondered how you can delicately tell someone they're being shafted. Should she even try to sugarcoat it or just cut right to the chase?

She cast her mind back to moments in her career when she had been stabbed in the back, when the political snake pit was so unbearable that she had considered throwing the towel in. But she kept going, genuinely believing that she could use her position and influence to change things for the better. There was a common thread to each of those low moments—ego. That was always the issue when the most senior men of the organisation jostled for position.

Savannah decided in the moment that she was going to put all her business affairs on hold and see this one through with Bee. She had coached her through her first crushing and she would be by her side for her last. Well, it had better be her last. She felt responsible for Bee in the same way a parent might for their child. After all, it was *her* who had introduced Bee to investment banking as a career. Would Bee blame her, the way a child blames their pushy parent later in life for forcing them into a job they ended up having an awful time in? *Please let her bounce back from this one*, Savannah thought.

She took a sip of scotch, inhaled and exhaled deeply, then hit 'call'. *Here goes.*

"Hello, Bee, my favourite Sydneysider." She immediately realised how overly chirpy she sounded.

"Savannah. I'm so glad you called. There's something going on over here and I could really use some help." Bee's tone was anything but chirpy.

"Where are you, darling? It sounds noisy."

"I'm outside a cafe. Hang on, let me find a quieter spot."

Savannah heard the tap-tap of Bee's heels on the pavement as she moved away from the crowd. From there, the call didn't exactly go as Savannah had anticipated. Because as it turned out, Bee was already aware that Max was trying to remove her. It was freakishly coincidental, like their worlds were colliding. After Bee recounted her dreadful first week of working with Max, Savannah shared the conversation she had overheard at Balthazar.

"What!" shrieked Bee.

"I've recorded it all. I'll send it to you. But listen to me, Bee, this is going to be hard, possibly even harder than Ben Taggart. And I'm going to be right there by your side. I'm looking at flights as we speak."

"You don't need to do that," objected Bee.

"Oh yes, I bloody well do."

When the call was over, Savannah poured herself another scotch then booked a first-class flight from New York to Sydney.

Chapter 28

Bee was working in her study after dinner when a calendar invite popped up on her screen. The subject read 'Ad-Hoc Board Meeting, tomorrow 10am, please make yourself available'. And there it was—the time and place had been set for her removal, exactly as Savannah had explained.

The Curban shareholders were always able to voice their opinion and agitate, but it was the Directors of the Board, i.e. Arthur and his cronies, and Max, of course, that were the ones responsible for hiring and firing the CEO. Arthur would most likely lead the discussion, which wasn't going to make for a pleasant experience. Bee wasn't sure she would be able to look him in the eye. What a traitor. She felt foolish for trusting him, for thinking that he had a higher EQ than his contemporaries. Feeling butterflies in her stomach, she reached for her phone and texted Rosie.

Bee: It's happening tomorrow, Rosie. 10am.

Rosie: Okay. Remember. You're prepared. You know what to say. Stick to the plan. Here if you need me. Good luck!

Bee: Thank you! You're amazing. 🩶

Bee held the mouse in her hand and hovered over the invite. She hit accept, then sat back in her chair, arms behind her head, and stretched. She opened the document that had been drafted with Rosie. She prayed she wouldn't go blank and panic, or worse, get emotional in the moment. That was her biggest fear—that she would start screaming like a banshee and lunge across the table with a pencil to stab Max, followed by Arthur. Then Dr Robert Hare would label *her* a corporate psychopath.

She was running on pure adrenaline now, no appetite since Sunday, just picking at unhealthy snacks here and there, which wasn't her at all. She was a regular breakfast, lunch and dinner person. And it had been tough putting on a game face at the office around her staff.

She went into the family room where Gus was lying on the lounge. He was munching on a bag of Doritos while watching *I'm a Celebrity ... Get Me Out of Here* with Otis and Ollie either side of him. He watched it every year with the boys because they relished the bush tucker challenges and watching people vomit.

"Hey, honey, I've got the invite. It's definitely happening tomorrow."

Gus turned the TV to mute.

"Dad, this is the best bit," complained Ollie. "They're about to eat kangaroo testicles."

"Go and watch it upstairs. If you're quick, you won't miss it," said Gus. The boys sprinted off, their energetic footsteps reverberating on the wooden staircase as they hurried towards the TV room.

Bee removed a partially consumed bottle of Sancerre from the fridge. Should she have a third glass tonight? Probably not. She needed to be sharp, focused, on her game. She put the bottle back in the fridge and flicked the kettle on instead. As she waited for the water to boil, she glanced over at Gus polishing off his Doritos. These next few days weren't going to be easy on him either. She remembered how he said he wanted to waterboard Ben Taggart all those years ago and, at the time, she'd believed him.

She made her peppermint tea and sat down next to him.

"I'm worried about the boys. It's going to be all over the papers. You know how cruel kids can be. First the videos and now this." She clasped her hands tightly and closed her eyes.

"Listen, Bee." Gus turned to face her. "They will be fine. And you know what, they might have one bad day of being teased and then kids, especially boys, move on to something else."

He was right. The boys had only really been teased about the video on Monday. After that they were back to fighting over who was allowed to play rugby league or basketball at lunchtime. Such a simple existence.

"It's time to worry about *you*."

"Do you think I wasn't cut out for this business and that I've just been lucky to get where I am?" This thought had consumed her thinking for the last twenty-four hours.

"Stop that right now, Bee," Gus said firmly. He took her hands in his. "You are incredible at what you do. You can't let one big bad wolf bring you down."

"Well, technically it's two bad wolves now."

Gus's eyes flickered with anger at the thought of the other bad wolf. "I know. But without people like you and Savannah, people trying to change things and call the wolves out, nothing will change."

Again, Gus was right. He was hitting all the right points tonight. He was all reason while she was full of emotions. That was because she had put her heart and soul into her work. "That job has been everything to me," she said. Then, realising that statement might have come across the wrong way, she rephrased with, "Well, not *everything*, obviously. You know what I mean."

"Yes, I know what you mean, Bee. It's been a *big* part of you, but it isn't *all* of you. I promise you, when the dust settles, you'll know your worth is much more than all of this. What's that saying—some things fall apart so better things can fall together? You'll be incredible at whatever you do next. People will be falling over themselves to get a piece of you." He clicked his fingers.

Would they really snap her up? Or would she be damaged goods? It was hard to tell in this calm-before-the-storm moment. One thing she was certain of was that in life there are those who try to bring you down, like Max and Arthur, and then there are those who uplift you, like Savannah.

It was 2am and Bee was still awake. She had left the curtains open to watch the black outline of the gum trees swaying in the breeze, thinking it would make her sleepy. But instead, she felt like a nocturnal animal with a heightened sense of sight, hearing *and* smell. She was fixated on Gus's light snoring and the smell of Garry's farts wafting her way from his dog bed. She decided to move to the sofa downstairs and watch something on Netflix.

Savannah had texted to say her flight was on time and would be arriving just after 6am Sydney time. Bee was both amazed and flattered that she was coming to support her. Even after all these years, she had never stopped caring about Bee, checking in every six months or so, asking how she was coping, did she need any advice? She treated all her mentees, past and present, like daughters. It was sad Savannah had never had children of her own, because she was one of the most loving and giving individuals in Bee's life.

To take her mind off things, Bee opened Instagram and began scrolling through her feed of dog videos. They *always* made her feel warm and fuzzy. First, one of a German Shepherd having their toenails painted by a toddler, then an abused mutt being rehabilitated by a new, loving family and finally, dogs catching the bus to doggy daycare. She watched that one at least ten times, smiling every single time. *Everyone needs a dog in their life*, she thought.

"Mum. Mum. Mum! Wake up. It's six o'clock!"

Bee could hear the words but couldn't quite open her eyes. She patted around her and felt the soft fabric of the sofa and realised she'd fallen asleep there. Ollie pulled both her eyelids up with his fingers and she caught the blurred vision of him in his school sports uniform.

"Oi, get off," she said, brushing his hands away.

"Ugh, your breath," he complained. "And you've got chocolate around your mouth too."

"Let your mum wake up, Ollie," said Gus softly, muscling Ollie out of the way. "Here. Get this down you." He bent over and handed her a glass of fizzing orange Berroca, which she downed straight away.

"Thanks," she exhaled. "Big day."

"Yes, and we're all rooting for you," said Gus.

"Go, Mum! You've got this!" shouted Ollie from the kitchen.

Bee was meeting Savannah, Rosie and Stuart at the Crown Towers Hotel for breakfast at 7am. She had one hour to get dressed and into Barangaroo. Despite her usual rule of never repeating an outfit in the same month, let alone the same week, the time constraint forced her to make an exception. She found herself wearing Monday's outfit once again, donning the black Gucci dress and matching shoes.

Stuart had reserved one of Epicurian's semi-private dining rooms with waterfront views. As Bee arrived, she noticed him meticulously draping garment bags over a plush velvet dining chair.

"Morning. What're all the bags for?" she asked.

"Oh, morning. These are all for Savannah. She asked me to pick out a few pieces for her," Stuart replied, flattening out the bags to ensure the contents remained pristine.

"How did you sleep?"

"Terrible. You?" asked Stuart, patting his own under-eye bags.

"Terrible."

Bee walked over to the floor-to-ceiling windows. Arms folded, gazing pensively towards the city, she said, "God, I love Sydney. Gus loves it. My boys love it. It was a dream come true when I got called about the job here. CEO of Curban Capital. And you know what, Stuart?" She turned to face him. "I felt like I was just getting started. We had so much more to do there, together."

Stuart approached her. He, too, had repeated Monday's outfit and looked weary under that Chanel foundation of his. "They were lucky to have you—actually to have *us,* come to think of it—for those five years. You watch, there will be a staff revolt when they hear you've been shoved out."

Bee smirked and nudged Stuart gently with her elbow.

"Did someone say coffee?" boomed a voice behind them.

"Oh my god, Savannah." Bee ran around the table and dived into her open arms. "I can't believe you came all this way."

"You know me. I love a big dick showdown." She roared with laughter.

"Did you want these here or in your room, Ms Silva?" asked the porter standing behind her. Next to him was a trolley carrying three large Louis Vuitton suitcases.

"My room, please," she replied, handing him a fifty-dollar note. "And please make sure there's enough hangers, thank you."

Despite enduring a twenty-four-hour flight, Savannah remained the epitome of elegance and sophistication. She donned a crisp white shirt with the collar popped up, smart dark-blue jeans with a black Hermès belt and huge dangly diamond earrings (most likely real). Her signature raven bob framed her beautiful face, and her vibrant red lipstick accentuated her captivating blue eyes. Bee had forgotten just how mesmerising Savannah was, with her feline-like allure.

Stuart went in for a hug and Savannah affectionately messed up his slicked quiff, knowing it would irritate him.

"Travelling light are we, Joan Collins?" joked Stuart. "I've picked out five summer dresses for you, as requested," he added, proudly pointing at the garment bags.

"Thank you, darling. I knew I could rely on you to fix me up."

As they all took a seat at the table, Bee suggested they order coffees and breakfast while waiting for Rosie. She explained that they didn't have much time because she needed to arrive at the Curban offices by 9am.

They were tucking into their chia puddings when Rosie arrived, apologising for being late. She had been held up putting a fire out for a client. Bee admired the way Rosie juggled her clients so effectively. She was continually moving from one crisis to another, while maintaining a calm exterior. A true pro!

When Bee had told her Savannah would be flying in, Rosie had almost exploded with excitement. Savannah, one of the most senior female business leaders in the world, would be their secret weapon, unleashed in an exclusive tell-all interview with *The Financial Report*. A glowing endorsement from a power-player like her, someone that Bee had worked with and been mentored by all these years, well, it would surely leave Max and Arthur scrambling.

One hour later, Bee and Stuart arrived at the office. As they ascended to level forty-one in the lift, Bee glanced at her reflection in the mirror and noticed her clenched fists with fingers tightly curled into her palms. This image, coupled with her shallow breathing, served as a clear indication that tension was building within her. Recognising this, she shook her hands free, mimicking the movements of a boxer preparing for their next round. It was a conscious effort to release the built-up tension and again regain composure for what awaited her in just one more hour.

From her office, she called Arthur's assistant to check his flight was on time and that the board meeting would also be on time. Yes, they were both running on time. Suzy was out of the way, with her out-of-office message on, pretending to be ill. Rosie was on standby at her office. Savannah stayed back at her hotel, using its business centre to hold conference calls with her clients in New York. And Lucy was at home, eagerly awaiting confirmation that the grenade's pin had been pulled. Her support crew were all in place. It was almost time.

Chapter 29

"No more muppet shows," said Stuart. "That has to be a silver lining, right?"

Bee chuckled and nodded. "I suppose so."

"You *know* so. Go on then, you better get going. I'll be waiting for you when you come out."

Knowing she would be frog-marched out of the building—a cruel reality of being fired in investment banking—she had already cleared out her personal items on Monday night. There was now nothing to suggest Bee Bloom ever existed.

She closed the door to her office for the last time, descended the staircase and walked past reception. As she did, her neck cranked when she saw a face she recognised. It was the young female flight attendant who flirted with Max on their flight to Melbourne. Where was Davide? Was he another casualty of Max's?

Feeling nauseous, her heart racing and body tense, she walked towards the closed boardroom doors and as she reached for the handle, she heard *his* voice. "Let me get that." Max touched her hand, and she quickly drew hers away. He opened the door and motioned for her to enter first. As she walked past him, she cast the meanest, dirtiest, most disgusted glare she could muster up. If only looks could kill.

All board members were seated in their usual seats, with Arthur at the head of the table. Bee took her usual seat, while Max positioned himself across from her. For today's special meeting, there were two additional faces around the table—Emily from HR and Sally Bishop, Curban's Head of Legal.

"Thank you everyone for joining this meeting at such short notice. As you know, we only ever hold ad-hoc board meetings under exceptional circumstances," said Arthur. "So I appreciate your attendance."

While Arthur ran through his usual official meeting protocols, Bee stared Max down. She felt like a bull waiting to charge. Would Max try to side-step?

"This meeting is to discuss the immediate future of Curban Capital," announced Arthur.

Finally, he's getting to the point. She was keen to get this bull fight underway.

"As you know, Bee has been our CEO for five years and, during that time, we have seen a satisfactory performance in terms of revenue and profits."

Satisfactory! she shrieked internally, glaring at Arthur while he looked at everyone else but her.

"But we, and I speak for myself and Max at this point, believe that Curban will only be able to achieve its growth ambitions under new ownership. That's why we are proposing to sell the firm to Penfold Partners in New York. We have just returned from there after several meetings with their CEO, Mr Ben Taggart."

Bee's blood ran cold. She was instantly transported back to 2002 and the London nightclub where she felt powerless while *he* stared down at her with frightening eyes. Ben was Penfold. Ben was the white-haired man. Ben had come back into her life to traumatise her all over again, and Ben and Max were two dickhead peas in a pod.

The terror must have been written all over her face because Max asked, "Are you okay, Bee? You look like you've seen a ghost." His words were followed by a sly grin.

Bee took a breath, reminding herself that she was no longer that vulnerable and voiceless young woman who was backed into the corner of a disabled toilet; she was resilient, and she certainly wasn't powerless. "And new ownership means new leadership. That's why we're here isn't it, Arthur?" Bee sat forward and scanned the faces around the table.

Except for Max, whose eyes were fixed on her, they all looked downwards to avoid eye contact. *Gutless,* she thought.

"I'm well aware of what's been going on," she declared.

"And what exactly are you aware of?" Max asked with a deadpan face.

"That you were setting me up; that you wanted me out; that you leaked the videos." She was trying so hard to maintain composure. "Shall I keep going?"

"Oh what a busy bee you've been. Great work. Good for you." Max clapped his hands arrogantly. "I guess it didn't take a genius to work it out."

"Stop that, Max. Be cordial," Arthur hissed at him.

Max stared down the table at Arthur, then back at Bee.

"Ben's offered us a very handsome price and we've agreed to certain conditions. One of them is that we change CEO. He wants to run things a little differently. I think his exact words were, *I want someone who is robust and comes with a different pedigree,*" said Max, wryly. He watched Bee like a hawk, fully aware that the words given to him by Ben would ignite her anger.

"And who's taking over. Penny Pryor?" Bee snarled, remembering back to Max and Penny's cosy in-flight conversation on the way to Melbourne.

"Don't be ridiculous." And then under his breath Bee was one hundred per cent certain she heard him add, *"not sure any woman's up to it".*

"What was that, Max? Did you just say a woman couldn't do the job?"

"Now you're hearing things," Max simpered.

"And there was the issue of your party conduct which, frankly, was not befitting of a CEO," piped up Rudy Chalmers. His head poked forward like a turtle's coming out of its shell.

"Well said, Randy," said Max.

"It's Rudy," huffed Rudy.

Bee shot Rudy a steely stare. "Oh Rudy, you're here and actually saying something, what a surprise. Speaking of unbefitting behaviour, have you forgotten about the time we had to pay someone off because of your repeated uninvited advances?"

And with that, his turtle head retreated into its shell.

"Enough. This isn't a beating-up session. We're professionals," said Arthur strongly.

"You could have fooled me," bristled Bee as she stared down the table at Arthur.

He cast his eyes downward to avoid eye contact, then said, "Emily has the paperwork for you to look over. It's a very fair and reasonable package."

Arthur motioned for Emily to bring the paperwork to Bee. As Emily placed it in front of her, Bee promptly pushed it aside, refusing to even cast a glance at it or acknowledge Emily's presence. Emily meanwhile stood still, behind Bee, clearly uncomfortable and not knowing whether to return to her seat or continue hovering.

"Here's what's going to happen," Bee said confidently. She heard Rosie's voice in her head: *Stick to the plan.* "I'm aware that this plan of yours has been in motion for some time. Thanks, Max." She glared at him. "I'm disappointed; no, actually I'm thoroughly pissed off, given how hard I've worked to line all of your pockets. Satisfactory revenue and profits, pah! Try bumper." She glared down the table again at Arthur. "And I did so while building a brilliant culture that is the envy of our competitors."

Max made a fake choking sound. Her eyes returned to him.

"I have already engaged an employment lawyer. She will be in touch with you as soon as this meeting is finished. And please don't contact Rosie Reid for her services, because her contract with Curban has been torn up and I have engaged her myself. I think that's everything." And with that, she stood up, tucked her chair in slowly, picked up the paperwork and walked towards the door, conscious that nine pairs of eyes were watching her every step.

She closed the door behind her and exhaled. Stuart sprang out of a tub chair and ran towards her. She didn't need to say anything; he knew what they needed to do.

"Come on. Let's get out of here, right now," he said, reaching out for her hand. She took his hand in hers and held it tightly. They put their heads down, afraid they might run into employees, walked past reception, into the lift, through the lobby and out of the building.

Walking out of a place she had considered her second home, and knowing she was never going back, was an odd sensation. The feeling was undeniably harsh and final. *Don't look back. Keep walking.*

As soon as they were safely inside a cab and driving away from the office, Bee collapsed into Stuart's lap, sobbing.

"Nobody should *ever* make anyone feel this low. I hate the lot of them," protested Stuart as he stroked Bee's hair gently. "Karma, I tell you, karma: what goes around comes around. They will get their comeuppance. You mark my word."

While Stuart continued venting and cussing everyone at Curban, Bee gazed at the envelope in her hand, marked *Private and Confidential.* Inside would be her official Deed of Release document outlining her severance terms. She was aware that once she ripped open the envelope, her entire five-year tenure at Curban Capital would be distilled into a single figure. "Fair and reasonable," Arthur said. She didn't trust him as far as she could throw him, which was why she was too scared to open it now.

Her head resting in Stuart's lap looking heavenward, with her eyes staring out of the taxi's window and up to the grey sky, she watched the office towers flash by and listened to the familiar noises of the bustling CBD. The world was carrying on around her while hers was standing still. From fury and vitriol, her feelings switched to embarrassment. Would people say she was incompetent, that her time was up? Her reputation was at stake, the reputation she had worked so hard to earn. She remembered a famous quote from Warren Buffett: *"It takes twenty years to build a reputation and five minutes to ruin it."*

"Are you okay?" asked Stuart, looking down at her.

"Yes, I think I'm all out of tears now." She sat up, patted her face, retied her ponytail and began rummaging through her tote. She took out her make-up bag and looked at her reflection in her pocket mirror, realising it was going to take more than her reliable eye drops to fix her bloodshot eyes. Despite the overcast sky, she put on her black Celine sunglasses.

"Oh shit, Stuart. I'm so sorry. I haven't even asked you how *you* are." She snapped the pocket mirror closed and turned to face him. "I've been so bloody selfish."

"Bee, you know I'll be fine. I don't take all of this as seriously as you. It's a job. At the end of the day, I just wanted to work for you. I don't give a shit about Curban. They can all rot as far as I'm concerned," he tutted loudly.

"Maybe don't say Curban," whispered Bee, holding her right index finger to her lips. Stuart instinctively covered his mouth, acknowledging her concern about Uber drivers potentially overhearing private conversations and even recording them.

"I hope they like the sticker I put on my screen," he smirked.

"What sticker?"

"A huge middle finger sticker." He demonstrated with his own middle finger.

"Oh, Stuart, really," she chuckled, feebly.

For the remainder of the drive to Savannah's hotel, they sat silently, staring out of the windows, holding hands. Savannah had texted to confirm a private meeting room had been booked in the name of Vanessa Rudgens. It was her way of trying to be funny and even in her emotional state, Bee managed a half-smile.

"It's over here," said Stuart, pointing at the meeting room display stand next to a set of double doors. When they entered, Bee assumed they were in the wrong room. It was a huge windowless ballroom with blue plush carpet, metallic patterned walls, mirrored ceilings and floating chandeliers. More big-Greek-wedding venue than meeting room.

"Cooee, over here," called out a voice from the far corner. It was Savannah, seated at a small round table with Rosie next to her. "It was all I could get, darling. Thankfully at a discount, because there are only four of us, not four hundred." She laughed, while squeezing Bee tightly.

Then it was Rosie's turn to hug Bee.

Adjacent to the round table was a buffet table displaying an assortment of food and drinks including sushi, a charcuterie platter, crudités and dips, pastries and a bottle of French champagne on ice. *A bit excessive for four people*, thought Bee.

"I didn't know what you would be in the mood for, so I ordered a bit of everything," said Savannah, pointing to the table. "You two sit down. What can I get you?"

"Just a coffee," said Bee. "But you might want a Scotch when I tell you who Penfold is."

When Bee revealed Penfold's true identity as Ben Taggart, Savannah's expression hardened. She stared right through Bee for what seemed like minutes, her eyes full of rage. Bee noticed her jaw clench and her lips form a straight line.

"Shall I order you a Scotch?" Bee asked, half joking.

Savannah finally broke her stare, reached across the table and took Bee's hands in hers. "How dare that despicable human come back into our lives, into *your* life. You don't deserve this, Bee Bloom." Noticing the devastation on Bee's face, Savannah's protective instinct kicked into gear. "We're going to get you through this. They will not take you down without a fight." Her eyes blazed with determination.

Bee forced a smile, grateful for Savannah's fighting spirit. She was going to need it. "I wrongly assumed Penfold was a person, not a company. And I can't believe neither of us recognised him," she said.

"Yes, well, his hair and his face might have changed, but *he* hasn't," puffed Savannah.

"So true," added Stuart while picking at the sushi tray. "Shall we toast to these arseholes with some champagne?" He lifted the bottle from the silver ice bucket and examined the label.

"I can't. I'll probably keel over," said Bee.

Stuart let out a disappointed sigh before returning the bottle to the ice bucket.

"It's time to see what's in here." Bee handed Savannah the private and confidential envelope. "I can't face opening it. You do it."

Savannah had a brief stint as a lawyer before transitioning into an investment banker, and she was capable of forensically analysing any document, no matter the length. She took the envelope, opened it and began reading. "Can you pass me a pen please, darling?" she asked Bee.

Bee handed her a pen from her bag, without looking at it.

"Curban Capital. Well, we won't be using this one," said Savannah, tossing the Curban-branded pen on the floor.

Bee watched as Savannah pensively circled parts of the document. When her pen landed on page six she paused, tapping the pen nib on the paper. Savannah's concentration face suddenly transformed into a scowl. "Those cheap bastards."

Chapter 30

The Financial Report, *December 12, 2022*

What's behind Bee Bloom's sudden exit from Curban Partners?

Bee Bloom, CEO of Curban Partners, has dramatically departed from the firm she led for five years. Sources say Bloom was asked to leave by the board due to conduct issues. More to come ...

It took just two hours from Bee leaving the Curban offices for the news of her departure to break online. All the journalists from print, TV and radio were calling Rosie for comment. She was doing her best to keep up, but it was intense. When she was on one call, she heard the beeping of another trying to get through.

Knowing Max would be charging full steam ahead with his own version of events, Rosie was racing against the clock to respond to every single journalist with their alternative narrative. Bee had been instructed not to answer any calls from journalists and unknown numbers, for fear of compromising her legal position. Rosie was instead going to provide information from a "source familiar with the situation". Sure, Max could say it was obvious who that familiar source is, but he wouldn't be able to prove it, because the journalists would never tell.

Rosie was also arranging an exclusive interview for Savannah where she would provide a glowing character reference for Bee. And Stuart, well, he had already been sent to the best boutiques in Sydney to find suitable outfits. Everyone had their part to play.

It wouldn't be all plain sailing though and Rosie warned Bee to prepare herself for some seriously disparaging comments. Max had proven he was capable of anything.

"When they go low, we go high." Rosie used her favourite Michelle Obama quote for their campaign. And it was *their* campaign. This wasn't just about Bee; it was bigger than her. It was about Rosie and Savannah, about corporate women; heck, it was about women generally. Because *all* women would be reading about Bee and asking themselves, *How can this still happen in 2022, and if it's happened to her, can it happen to me?*

"So what's the story with Bee, then?" asked Jenny Wallis in her usual hurried, bossy voice. "We're hearing she was pushed out. Can you confirm that?"

"First of all, Bee is declining to comment, so please make sure you print that. Then, I want you to say a source familiar with the situation said that Bee considers herself wrongfully dismissed and will be taking steps to review her options —"

"Legal action," Jenny cut in. There was excitement in her voice. An attention-grabbing headline must have instantly come to her mind.

"Hang on, Jenny, just let me finish. I want you to note in your article that Max was at the centre of it all. He set Bee up. He was behind the leaked videos, too—"

Jenny interrupted again. "But we received those videos from someone else, not Max."

Rosie's tone escalated. "Well, I'm telling you they came indirectly from him, under his instruction. And I want something in the article saying Bee outperformed all revenue targets and delivered solid profits for Curban shareholders over her five-year tenure."

"Uh, but—"

This time Rosie cut in on Jenny. "No buts. It's a fact. And one final point, she was much loved by her staff, and you can ask any of them yourself, any except Max, that is."

Jenny huffed and puffed. "Right, so when can I speak to her? I want the first exclusive in return for putting all this in the story."

"Listen, Jenny, we know you have cosy family history with the Magnificos. Just do the right thing and include everything I just gave you. If you don't, I'll go to your editor with a formal complaint and tell him you're conflicted."

"Are you threatening me, Rosie?" There was an edge to her voice.

"Yep," replied Rosie in the most matter-of-fact way.

Gus was standing at the front gate when Bee's Uber pulled up. He must have received a *'Bee arrived home'* alert on his Life 360 app and raced out to greet her. In true Gus style, he didn't say anything when she approached. And he didn't need to because all his words were captured in his tight hug.

"What happened, Mum?" Otis ran towards her. "Was it that awful man? Did he do something to you?" He held his fists up and narrowed his eyes. "Where does he live?"

"Mum, are you okay?" Ollie asked. Being the older child, his concern was conveyed through worried eyes.

"Hi, boys. It's *so* nice to see you," Bee cried.

The boys wrapped their skinny arms around her waist and she gently kissed their heads. This was unconditional, unadulterated love. Even Garry sensed, as dogs do, Bee's sadness because he came towards her slowly with sad eyes and his tail between his legs.

"Let's go inside, boys." Gus motioned to Ollie and Otis.

While Bee removed her shoes and put her bags away, Gus ordered her favourite chicken tikka masala with plain naan then poured a glass of her favourite Sancerre. She had wined and dined all over Sydney, all over the world, in fact, and somehow these simple pleasures always satisfied her most. You can take the girl out of North London, but you can't take North London out of the girl.

Gus sat the boys down at the kitchen table and said they were going to have a 'family talk'. Garry sat next to Bee's chair with his head on her lap, adoring eyes staring up at her.

"Now, listen, boys, the next few days are going to be tough for all of us. There might be some horrible things said about Mum, which are *not* true. We all have to stick together and stick up for each other, and especially for Mum."

The boys listened intently, their eyes wide with worry and their mouths ajar.

"What's happened? Is it that Max guy?" asked Ollie. "I knew he'd be trouble with a surname like Magnifico." He was a perceptive thirteen-year-old and now at an age where Bee couldn't just fob him off.

"I'm not going to be working at Curban anymore." Her voice wobbled.

"Why?" Otis asked with a surprised tone.

"It's a bit like the EPL." Bee thought a football analogy might make it easier for them to understand the situation. "Or Ted Lasso. You know how clubs change their coach because they think it's time for a new one, time to do things differently? Well, it's time for a change at Curban."

Confusion overtook their faces as the cogs turned in their curious young minds. All they knew was their mum loved her job; it was hard to get her full attention at times because she was on work calls, and she spent a lot of time at the office, time they would have preferred to spend with her, particularly when they were little and sick. It broke her heart closing the front door on their tears when they had cried out for her. *It will get easier,* she used to say to herself.

"Well, I don't understand why they would want to change you for another coach," said Otis. "Especially if it's that awful man who's made you sad. Who would want *him* as a coach?"

"I know, honey. But that's life." Bee patted Otis's small hand.

"Well, it's not fair. It's like when Tommy got to be student representative when he's the biggest bully in the school. You're always telling us to be kind, so why didn't I get to be one?"

It was a clever question from Otis. After all, she reminded both boys, at least weekly, that *"in a world where you can be anything, be kind"*. Their fridge was covered with school merits, recognising their kindness.

Otis Bloom awarded for always being a kind and respectful classmate.

Otis Boom awarded for demonstrating the lights of friendship by inviting people to games.

Ollie Bloom awarded for being a kind classmate.

Ollie Bloom awarded for demonstrating kind leadership to his teammates during the cricket season.

Otis's big blue eyes gazed at Bee's, waiting for her answer. School and work, Otis and Tommy, Bee and Max. When you boil it down, were these pairings so different? School was a microcosm of the office, when she thought about it. To Otis, it was like Tommy had been promoted for his poor behaviour. Tommy was his mini version of Max Magnifico: a chameleon who changed his demeanour depending on who was around and what was at stake. Did he target weaker mortals in the toilets then suck up to the teachers to get what he wanted?

"Your kindness *will* be rewarded, maybe not this year as student representative, but it will. Trust me," she reassured him.

After dinner, Bee and Gus sat on the sofa watching TV. When the news headline *'CEO of Curban Capital Bee Bloom ousted for conduct issues'* flashed up, she sighed. "Bloody hell." Gus scrambled to find the remote control then quickly changed the channel.

"It's just one low blow after another. I don't know if I can just sit here and take all this. It's wrong."

Gus turned to her. "Bee, the truth *will* come out. You just have to be patient."

"That's easy for you to say. You're not the one whose name and reputation is being dragged through the mud." Her voice was snippy and she knew it. She looked over at him. "Sorry. I shouldn't be snapping at you. I know you're just trying to help."

His mouth curved into a sympathetic smile. "I *do* get it. And don't get me wrong, what they've done to you, how they've treated you, it's horrific. But the people who know you, who *really* know you, will see right through it all."

Despite feeling like she was on the verge of vomiting up her chicken curry, she forced a smile and nodded.

"There're a lot of people out there who love you, Bee. That's got to count for something. You've just got to focus on the voices that matter to you right now and mute the ones that don't."

That was also easy for Gus to say, but she wasn't going to complain again. She had made her point. At that moment, she wondered what Penny Pryor would be making of this saga. Would she be sitting on her own sofa in Melbourne rubbing her hands with glee? Or maybe not, seeing as Max didn't want her in the job either. She needed something to distract her racing thoughts. "How about we watch *Ted Lasso* again?" she suggested. "Scooch over a bit." She wriggled closer to Gus then rested her head on his shoulder.

It occurred to Bee that this was the first evening in years where she didn't have emails to reply to or conference calls to join. The transition to not working wasn't going to be easy because she was used to operating at full speed seven days a week. What was she going to do with herself? Savannah had suggested to get busy with *any* project, even one around the house. She told Bee to embrace not working because she would be snapped up, swiftly. However, being snapped up was the last thing on her mind. She was bruised, and like all bruises, she needed time to heal.

Chapter 31

The Financial Report, *Thursday, December 11, 2022*
Hugo Hamilton calls in the administrators

Hugo Hamilton's group of bars and restaurants has been placed into voluntary administration. Hamilton called in receivers this week, with his twenty venues closed until further notice.

Lucy groaned as she read the morning's news. It was official. Hugo was going belly-up! His life had become a living archaeological site with more and more skeletons unearthed by the day. Were there any left? For the girls' sake, she sincerely hoped not. Teflon Pamela had been calling and texting Lucy incessantly. Presumably she was going to say the administrators had it all wrong or that the receivership was someone else's fault. Lucy knew she would have to return her calls at some point, she just couldn't face it today. Today was dedicated to investing time in herself and her girls.

As she made her first coffee of the day, Lucy was aware of a lift in her mood. She felt lighter, as if she'd removed a pair of lead boots that had been weighing her down for years. She was relieved about not having to pander to Hugo. Nope, that was Erin's job now. How long would it take before Erin tired of her new responsibilities?

Lucy actually felt a bit sorry for her because, despite being a homewrecker, she could do much better. She appeared to be around twenty-two, three years older than Fleur. Fleur would never in a million years get mixed up with a middle-aged man like Hugo, because she was far too smart and sensible. How was Fleur going to handle this part of her father's drama, dating someone almost her own age? All would soon become clear when the girls returned later today. First, it was time for a walk with Bee at the dog park.

It was 7am when Lucy and Bee met at Tania Park. Rosie had said they needed to act like AA sponsors for each other. Having been a sponsor in the past for her ex, Rosie claimed everyone needs a support person when they are on a journey of "personal recovery". They were to provide guidance for each other, a sympathetic ear, encouragement and praise, honest feedback and look out for warning signs! Rosie was also deadly serious when she recommended that they follow the twelve principles of personal recovery—honesty, hope, surrender, courage, integrity, willingness, humility, love, responsibility, discipline, awareness and service.

It all came across as a bit serious and structured for Bee and Lucy, but they accepted the challenge and agreed to meet every weekday at 7am unless there was an emergency or major weather event.

"Is this going to be my new daily wardrobe?" Bee asked, pointing to her Stylerunner black tights and Harry Styles Love on Tour t-shirt.

"Some days, yes. It can be really easy just to live in active wear. But I think as sponsors we need to encourage each other to shower and get dressed, even put a bit of tinted moisturiser on, too," laughed Lucy as she launched a ball across the park for Beano and Garry. "By the way, I'm really flattered you agreed to this whole sponsor idea of Rosie's."

"Why are you flattered? Of course I would agree to it." Bee was surprised by Lucy's comment.

"Because you're a kickass leader. Don't you have people constantly asking for your support, professionally, I mean? And you must have lots of people to confide in yourself?"

"It might surprise you to know that it can be pretty lonely at the top, when you're the CEO," said Bee in a sombre voice as they sauntered along, side by side. "You have to keep a professional distance from your employees and your clients, you can't ever get too close. That's why I always had Stuart. He was really the only one that I could be one hundred per cent myself with."

Lucy's expression turned to surprise. Perhaps, like many who were not part of her industry, she had wrongly assumed that Bee could never be lonely in her busy CEO life.

"Oh, I see," said Lucy. "And what about friends, you know, outside of work?"

"I never really made that many when I came to Australia. It wasn't because I didn't want to, it was a time thing. Every moment I wasn't at work was dedicated to spending time with the boys."

Bee was taken aback by the sadness underlying the point she was making. She had devoted so much time to her work that she had sacrificed something crucial to happiness: friendships. She inflated her cheeks then let all the air out with a loud blowing sound. She didn't want to dwell too much on that point so she pivoted the conversation back to Lucy.

"Anyway, I'm excited about helping you find a new career. Have you had any thoughts about what you want to do?"

"Well, funnily enough, I've already been asked if I would like to put myself forward for something." Lucy launched the ball again and watched the dogs chase after it.

"This sounds exciting."

"It's early days so I'm trying not to get too excited. Do you know Bethany Byron? She's the lady loaning me her apartment in Manly."

"Yes, of course. Entrepreneur. Self-made millionaire. She's in the Women's Rich Lists every year."

"Well, she's looking for a new PR Manager." Lucy's face was excitement and trepidation all in one. "What do you think?"

"I think it sounds like an amazing opportunity. You would learn so much from being around Bethany. I've only heard great things about her. And even if it wasn't your *forever* thing, it could be your *now* thing. You know, to get your confidence back."

"You don't think she's doing it because she feels sorry for me? I mean, I'm not even qualified for the role, really, and ... and ... I haven't worked for so long, I don't know if I'm any good."

Bee recognised the self-doubt creeping into Lucy's thinking because she was the same—get excited about the role and then worry if you're good enough for it. It was, according to research, common in women. Bee had read a study from one of the major American universities about a 'confidence gap' where studies showed men *overestimate* their abilities and performance, while women *underestimate* both.

Remembering that piece of research, Bee said, "Okay, I can see what you're doing, and you need to immediately dismantle all those barriers because they're all up here." She tapped her index finger on her temple. "First of all, Bethany Byron is a shrewd businesswoman, not a charity. Second, she has asked you because she sees your enormous potential and third, you would be an asset to any company."

Lucy stopped her saunter and turned to Bee with an appreciative smile. "Bee Bloom, you are going to be the best sponsor a girl could ask for. I don't think anyone has said such nice things about me in years." She hugged her and whispered "Thank you" in her ear, then pulled away, saying, "Anyway, it's not a sure thing. There are others in the mix. But can you help me get myself sorted for an interview. I have no idea what to say. What to wear. And I have to submit a CV. I don't even have one."

"Easy. I can help with all of the above."

As they walked to the Mugshot coffee van, Lucy asked, "What's next for you? Or is it too soon?"

"Yeah, way too soon. I could be unemployable after all this. Did you see the headlines today? Bee Bloom exits suddenly over conduct issues."

She sighed.

"You know, Bee, being at home for a short period might not be so bad. You might enjoy it. Don't rush into anything."

Bee sat with the phrase "being at home". It sounded scarier than diving with great white sharks. But what was it that scared her most? Was it telling people that she wasn't gainfully employed? Was it because her self-worth was so intrinsically tied to her pay cheque? Or was it that she didn't know who she was if she wasn't Bee Bloom, CEO? She quickly concluded that it was all of the above.

Lucy ordered the coffees and turned to Bee. "You know how Rosie gave us those twelve principles to stick to?" she said. "How about for some fun we create twelve principles for Max and Hugo, six each. You go first."

"Erm, okay." Bee held out her hands and began finger-counting. "How about intimidation, lack of empathy, elitism, power, deceit, manipulation. Wow, that was easy."

"Okay, my turn. Anger, insecurity, control, cocaine, younger women, oh, and definitely chipolata." Lucy grinned then chuckled.

"So it's true. He does have a shrivelled chipolata penis?"

"Definitely, especially after a bit of coke. It's like a pebble in a pile of dirt. So much overgrown hair around it. Yuck. And all the time badgering *me* about one missed hair after a wax. To us." Lucy lifted her coffee cup to Bee's.

"To us."

When Lucy arrived home, she saw Pamela's green Bentley in the driveway. How the old woman was still able to drive was anyone's guess. That car had dings all over it, none of them her fault, *of course.*

Bloody Jocelyn would have let her in. Why couldn't Pamela just leave her alone? Could she divorce *her* too? She entered the house in stealth-mode and tiptoed to the kitchen doorway where she could just make out the two distinct and annoying voices of Pamela and Joceyln—Pamela's regal articulation and Jocelyn's squeaky high-pitched tones.

"You know she drinks about two bottles of wine a day? I see all the empties in the yellow recycling bin."

"Well, I knew she liked a drink and I always thought she was a sloppy drunk. She embarrassed me terribly at my seventieth birthday when she was intoxicated to the eyeballs and fell on the lawn in front of all my golfing friends. But this sounds like alcoholic behaviour. Does Hugo know?"

Lucy vividly recalled having just one glass of champagne at Pamela's seventieth birthday party, as she was the designated driver that day while Hugo indulged in heavy drinking and cocaine. And she had, in fact, tripped over a pair of abandoned sandals on the grass. However, Pamela's version of events seemed to be deliberately embellished to portray Lucy as a drunk.

"He knows a little bit. I've dropped a few hints. But she's mostly drunk during the week when he's not here."

"It wouldn't surprise me if that's why Hugo's business has gone belly-up. She's driven him away, you know, to live out of an apartment in the city when she should be looking after him and cooking him a nice, home-cooked meal. I mean, look at that fridge. There's no food in here."

Lucy couldn't stomach any more of this crap. She stepped forward to see Pamela sitting at the kitchen table in a pastel-pink Chanel suit, hair in an up-do, coffee cup in hand. Jocelyn was sitting across from her in her usual work attire of shirt and chinos, coffee cup also in hand. Jocelyn's face paled the minute she saw Lucy.

"What is it, dear?" asked Pamela. "You look like you've seen a ghost."

She followed Jocelyn's eyes and turned around to see Lucy standing only ten feet away. Unlike Jocelyn, Pamela appeared unfazed by being caught out.

"You pair of witches. GET OUT NOW!" screamed Lucy.

She had wanted to strangle Pamela in the past over various snide comments, but not as much as she wanted to strangle her now. If she knew what was good for her, she would take that saggy granny butt off her kitchen chair quick smart and zip it.

"Excuse me?"

"I said GET OUT NOW. Both of you."

Pamela set the coffee cup down on the table in front of her, stood up, straightened her skirt and jacket, and turned to Lucy.

"Now, you listen to me. I know you're probably drunk or hungover, but once you sober up, you'll realise that you've crossed a line. You can't talk to *me* like that." Her mouth snapped shut, contorting into a tight, pursed expression that resembled a cat's bum.

"Oh, yes I can. Now move it. Go on, get out." Lucy waved her hands at Pamela, shooing her out like a bad fart.

Pamela picked up her padded Chanel handbag from the dining table, hung the gold chain strap over her shoulder, patted her up-do and took small dainty steps towards Lucy. Now one metre away, Pamela tilted her head back, allowing her to peer down her nose at Lucy.

"Don't even think about coming after *my* money. You. Won't. Get. A. Cent." She poked Lucy five times in the chest then stuck her nose in the air and walked off. It was typical of Pamela to bring money into the situation. The tightest person on the planet, she was obsessed with her wealth and maintaining it. And even after twenty years as her mother-in-law, she still hadn't figured out that Lucy wasn't after *her* money, or Hugo's.

"You know money doesn't buy happiness, Pamela?" Lucy spoke to Pamela's back as she shuffled towards the front door. She then moved her eyes to Jocelyn, who remained standing, motionless, next to the kitchen table.

"Joycelyn, you too, get out."

Jocelyn coyly stepped past Lucy, unable to look her in the eye, and followed Pamela to the front door.

Once Pamela and Jocelyn had stepped out of the house and onto the front porch, Lucy shouted "Good riddance!" and slammed the door, before collapsing in a heap on the floor. The second her bottom touched the floorboards, she was startled by the appearance of Maya and Fleur, who were flying down the stairs towards her.

"Mum, are you okay? That was awesome. I can't believe you told the old dragon to get out." Maya bent down and hugged Lucy tightly.

Fleur wrapped her arms on top of Maya's and added, "It was so bloody cool, Mum."

"Where did you both come from?" asked Lucy in shock.

"We hid in our rooms when we saw the old dragon's car arrive. She's been texting us all bloody day, saying make sure you speak to Daddy, Daddy, Daddy, Daddy. Well, Daddy and her can piss right off," said Maya.

"And then we heard you come home and we've been at the top of the stairs listening to everything. Gosh, Mum, I didn't know you had that in you," added Fleur.

"Nor did I, my precious darlings. Nor did I." And in that instant, Lucy's anger and bitterness melted as she sat at the front door on the floor in a loving embrace with her girls.

Chapter 32

The Financial Report, *December 12, 2022*
Ex-Curban Capital CEO Bee Bloom calls in the lawyers

The former CEO of Curban Capital is understood to have called in the lawyers. Bloom is seeking compensation for what she considers unfair dismissal and a set-up by the new chairman Max Magnifico.

Bee engaged the most high-profile employment lawyer in Australia—Lucinda Brown of Brown & Partners—who came with an eye-watering hourly rate. *But if that's what it costs to take down Max Magnifico, then I'm gonna pay it,* thought Bee. The recommendation came via Savannah who, despite being London-based, owned a contact book packed with global connections. Bee had never met Lucinda (she considered that a good thing) but she had heard numerous stories of how she wiped the floor with corporate bullies and serial harassers. She was nicknamed 'The Tiny Terrier' because she was five foot one and, apparently, impossible to shake off once she sunk her teeth into guilty mongrels.

Lucinda came with a team of four lawyers who Bee met on the forty-five-minute initial consultation over Zoom. Lucinda did all the talking while the others typed away, capturing every detail of Bee's story. It was impressive how quickly everything was moving. Lucinda had already managed to secure a meeting with the Curban lawyers at her offices that afternoon. This first meeting was to present their counterproposal to what Lucinda considered "entirely unsatisfactory and flimsy terms" from the Curban camp.

When Bee told Stuart she was shaking in her Guccis about her first face-to-face legal meeting with Max, Stuart somehow redirected the conversation to fashion.

"You might be photographed. We need to think about this moment carefully. I know! You need pussybow power. Pencil skirt. Erm ..."

Before he could continue, Bee blasted, "It's not an Amber Heard and Johnny Depp courtroom appearance, Stuart. It's at a lawyer's office and it's confidential. No press will be there." Sometimes his obsession with all things fashion and gossip was entertaining but really, today of all days, when she'd just said how much she was crapping herself.

"Okay. I was just trying to help ..." Stuart's voice drifted off. He was upset. And, because Bee had known him for so long, she knew it wasn't just because of the tone she had taken with him.

"Thank you. I appreciate it. I really do. Now, tell me, how are you holding up? This is really tough for you too?"

"I told you. I'm okay. Well ... I'm sort of okay. Well ... if I'm honest, I'm worried about my rent and all my outgoings." Bee heard his voice crack.

"I know. And I'm speaking to the lawyers today about your employment terms too. Trust me. I'm going to fix this. For both of us."

Stuart's voice returned to normal. "And make sure they pay up. We've done nothing wrong."

Of course Stuart was worrying, even though he pretended to be fine. That was *so* him, to mask his true feelings. Like an onion, he had layers.

Gus offered to attend the meeting with Bee, but she wanted to keep it professional, not personal. That's why she asked Savannah to chaperone her. Savannah would act as her shield if things turned nasty. *Just don't look weak*, Bee told herself.

One valuable lesson she had learned in her very short time working with Max was that he was able to sniff out weaknesses and exploit them.

He was like a dog with olfactory superpowers, able to detect a human's emotional state by their scent.

When Bee and Savannah arrived at the offices of Brown and Partners, Lucinda was waiting for them at reception. Her demeanour screamed *capable* and *efficient* by the way she was poised at the ready with her manilla folders cradled in her arms. *Definitely a prefect when she was in high school*, thought Bee. Her dark hair was pulled back off her pretty but serious face into a tight bun. She wore a knee-length navy Scanlan Theodore crepe knit dress with a high neck and short sleeves and shiny black Mary Jane-style high heels. And she wasn't up for any chit-chat, which was fine with Bee.

"We don't have a lot of time to recap on our position, so let me just explain how the meeting will run." Lucinda's eye contact with Bee was intense and purposeful. She meant business with those eyes. "We'll be in that meeting room over there." She pointed to a large boardroom with glass windows. Bee shivered inwardly. "I will start the meeting with a few formalities, then we'll move to presenting the counterproposal. Ah, there they are now."

Bee shivered inwardly again. She turned and saw Max, Arthur and two men in suits heading towards them. Lucinda shook hands with the men and directed everyone to the boardroom. Bee moved quickly to be first. *You got this*, she said to herself.

The three women sat across the table from the four men. The beginning of the meeting was a blur as Lucinda stepped through the purpose of the session in legal speak. Bee reached for the glass of water in front of her and noticed her hand tremble as she lifted it to her mouth. She took a quick sip and set it back down, hoping nobody noticed. She locked eyes with Arthur and noticed a glimmer of softness, perhaps even a hint of regret, in his gaze. Max was as stony as ever. He strummed his fingers on the table, then yawned loudly.

"Are we keeping you up, Mr Magnifico?" Lucinda said abruptly while glaring across the table at Max.

"No, of course not. We're very keen to hear what you have to say," he replied in his best silky-smooth voice, which wasn't fooling anyone on Bee's side of the table.

"Our position, Mr Magnifico and team, is that your offer is completely unacceptable; it's actually laughable. In fact, it's *so* laughable that the only place for it is the bin." Lucinda then removed papers from her folder—Bee assumed it was her original 'deed of release'—and proceeded to tear up the pages. She then pushed the scraps of paper to the centre of the table.

"We are proposing the following terms which are much more appropriate." Lucinda retrieved four copies of stapled documents from her folder and slid them across the table.

Bee sat motionless, watching Lucinda out of the corner of her eye. She had such incredible gravitas. Even Max was now paying full attention.

"We believe it's in everyone's interests for this not to go to court; therefore, my client is seeking a swift and amicable resolution."

One of the Curban lawyers in a grey pinstripe three-piece suit was quick to set his eyes on the dollar amounts noted in his document.

"This is clearly much more than we initially offered," he scoffed. "We came here today to discuss amending *some* terms, but these look well outside the ballpark."

"Mr Baker," Lucinda addressed him. "This isn't a negotiation. Your clients have clearly done the wrong thing: leaking videos of my client to the press, besmirching her impeccable reputation with false claims of poor conduct. And as if that isn't enough, we have evidence proving Mr Magnifico was setting her up. Should I go on?"

"And going behind her back to strike a deal to line your own fat pockets," piped up Savannah. She had her game face on and Bee loved it.

"The deal to buy Curban is bloody genius and the shareholders are going to love it when we take it to them for a vote. But you're right about one thing: we *will* line our pockets, quite handsomely," Max gloated with a huge grin on his face. "And anyway, what are *you* doing here?" He glared at Savannah.

"I don't need to explain that to *you*." Savannah shot back a dirty look.

Smirking, Max assumed a childlike voice. "Did Bee call in Mummy to help her clean up her mess again? Shall we talk about how you helped cover up her cocaine habit in London?"

Savannah was having none of it. "That's precisely the kind of inelegant remark I would expect from someone like you, Max. You're nothing but a cheap scoundrel in an expensive suit. But seeing as you're intent on dragging us all down to your level, are you familiar with the saying you can't be rich *and* have a big dick, so seeing as you're rich, shall we assume ..."

"Can we please just focus on the current matter," Lucinda interjected.

Max curled his lip and Savannah sneered.

Bee was struck by Arthur's silence and quiet demeanour. It was like he was hanging his head in shame. This personal slanging and smear campaigning wasn't his style, she knew that much about him. Was it possible he *was* regretting the way everything was going down?

"We'll need some time to review all the proposed terms," said Baker.

"You need to move quickly. I'm sure you'll want all this cleared up before you take this *genius* deal to your shareholders," Savannah said.

"Why are you still speaking, Savannah? No one cares what you think," Max snarled.

"Actually, Max, a lot of people *do* care what I think. In fact, they care very much what I think, especially when I oversee their private investments." Savannah leaned forward and rested her clasped hands on the table. "One of my clients in New York happens to be the largest shareholder in Penfold Partners. And as his private investment manager, I may be inclined to advise him to pull his money and his vote. That might just scupper your deal." Her eyes sparkled as she delivered this bombshell.

"I seriously doubt you carry that much sway," guffawed Max.

"You can always see for yourself, Max. And maybe that will wipe that childish grin off your face."

"Can we please return to the terms. You have twenty-four hours to get back to us," demanded Lucinda efficiently.

"We'll come back to you overnight. But in principle we are open to reviewing the terms and we agree, we want to keep this out of court," said the second Curban lawyer. Baker nodded.

"Because what shareholder wants an employment dispute with a senior woman in the courts, and therefore in the papers?" Savannah smirked at Max.

Max stood up and, without looking at anyone, stormed out of the boardroom, slamming the doors behind him. "I suppose the meeting is adjourned," joked Savannah, laughing to herself.

As everyone else around the table stood up and prepared to leave the room, Arthur made his way towards Bee and put his hand out to shake hers. Bee contemplated it for a second then turned away. That would hurt him, but not as much as he had hurt her.

Chapter 33

"It's absolute bollocks, Jenny, and you know it," Rosie screamed down the phone as she crossed Martin Place. She was aware passers-by were staring at her, but her care factor was zero. It was necessary to scream because Jenny wasn't listening. And it wasn't uncommon for the pair to scream at each other in the heat of the moment, when the stakes were high.

"I'm just telling you that I heard Bee Bloom had a coke problem when she was working in London," Jenny screamed back.

"And again, I'm telling *you* that if you write that you're compromising your own journalistic integrity. It's defamatory and Bee's lawyers will wipe the floor with you."

"Listen, I'm not making this shit up, Rosie. I've got a verified source."

Rosie imagined that Jenny had shapeshifted into a bloodhound, her instincts honed and ready to sniff out any scent of a story. "For fuck's sake, we both know your source is a lying, vindictive psychopath. You have to wake up now, Jenny, and smell the coffee." There was silence on the other end of the phone. "You know I'm right. You don't want to be on the wrong side of this one," added Rosie.

More silence.

"I'll think about it," huffed Jenny before hanging up.

Rosie wasn't going to let her think about it, though. She would give her fifteen minutes tops before calling her back. That was just how this cat and mouse game worked between PR pro and journalist. It was a game they played time and time again where they know they need each other, yet constantly try to outmanoeuvre one another.

There were many times when Rosie *had* lied to Jenny to save a client's skin, but this time she *was* telling the truth.

Bee had told her all about Ben Taggart and that Christmas party all those years ago. And Jenny, well, she was letting her desire for some good old clickbait cloud her better judgement. Forget the cost-of-living crisis and economic downturn, what people really wanted to read about was how a female CEO could be shafted by a male chairman in 2022. Jenny knew she was just one click away from having the most read article of the month, maybe even the year. Hell, the story was playing across all the mainstream TV news channels. Bee had become a household name and Rosie was buckling under the incessant enquiries from media asking for comments and interviews. After this Bee case was over, she was bloody well going to Fiji.

When Rosie arrived at her office, she checked with Paula if Curban had settled its outstanding monthly retainer bill of fifty thousand dollars. Rosie just had a horrible feeling that if she didn't get the dollars through quickly that Max would put a freeze on all payments. Paula checked the accounts ledger, and the answer was "no". She told Paula to just keep ringing Curban's accounts department until she got confirmation of payment.

Next, Rosie called an urgent meeting with Simon and Jazzy to discuss if there was anything they were working on that could be shared exclusively with Jenny in exchange for burying Bee's coke story. It was unfortunately a case of throwing someone else under the bus to save Bee. She just hoped that when Reid & Co Counsel restructured, there would be less of this grubby game-playing.

Jazzy practically skipped into the meeting, the way people do when they're in that bonking-all-night phase of a relationship, while Simon dragged himself in with a face like he was chewing on a wasp. If their facial expressions and body language were a barometer for how much sex they were having, then Simon wasn't getting any. But then neither was Rosie.

"Okay, I just want to make this a quick meeting. We've all got loads on our plates. Have either of you got anything, and I mean *anything,* that we can use as a trade for keeping something about Bee Bloom out of the papers? Simon, any sexy government goss?"

Sexy and government didn't quite go in the same sentence, it was just to butter Simon up, make him feel special. Rosie's body language was hurry, hurry, *hurry.* Her legs jigged up and down under the table and she tapped her pen impatiently on her notepad. Jenny was a slippery operator and if she *did* just go ahead with the coke story, then it would spread like wildfire and Rosie would be pedalling backwards for days, maybe weeks, to reverse the damage. And Bee's reputation would be mud.

"What about Bill Sykes? Could we say he might be replaced soon?" suggested Simon. "We could say that management aren't happy with his performance."

Simon's years of working in ministerial offices had made him into one of the best schemers Rosie had worked with. He had no problem throwing *anyone* under the bus. It almost came naturally to him. *I suppose, in politics, if you can backstab a prime minister then anyone is fair game.*

"I couldn't do it to the man. He's super annoying but he doesn't deserve a move like that. What else?" asked Rosie, speedily. She checked her watch. It was approaching fifteen minutes since hanging up on Jenny. Her legs jigged faster.

"Isn't there anything about Hugo Hamilton? Surely there's a few more skeletons?" asked Simon.

"Possibly, but that's not Jenny's beat. Hugo is too tabloid for her," replied Rosie.

Simon sat forward in his chair, visibly thrilled with the idea he was about to share. "I know. How about the money side of his downfall? How much debt he's in, like he owes gazillions, the biggest bankruptcy of its kind on record."

Rosie shrieked, hands flapping in excitement. "Genius, Simon, bloody genius. OMG, yes, yes, yes. Jazzy, you need to ask Joe. And not tonight when you're in bed. You need to call him now." Rosie realised she was coming across as slightly unhinged, but the stakes were sky-high.

"Er, I don't know if I want to do that, Rosie. I don't really wanna mix work with, you know, pleasure," said Jazzy unenthusiastically.

Rosie reached across the table and extended her arms fully to touch Jazzy's hands.

"Jazzy, I *really* need this. Like, I *really* need this. We just need to know roughly how many millions he owes and who he owes it to. Can you just ask that, pleeeeeeease?"

Rosie pulled her arms up and placed her hands firmly together in the praying position. There was silence as Jazzy worriedly nibbled on her bottom lip.

"All right. I'll do it. But just those two questions. I don't wanna annoy him."

"I'm sure he won't mind, Jazzy. He was the one, after all, who told me about Hugo's debts in the first place."

"Yeah, but only because he was drunk."

"Okay, okay, good point. Can you just go and call him now, please?" Rosie's heart was in her mouth.

Jazzy left the room and returned one minute later saying Joe was in a meeting and couldn't speak for about two hours. Rosie could feel herself about to explode. She begged again and offered Jazzy an all-expenses-paid weekend away for her and Joe to the Emirates One & Only Wolgan Valley Luxury Resort. Jazzy's head jolted backwards and her eyes widened, shocked at Rosie's desperation. She let out an exasperated sigh, then walked back out of the meeting room. Simon looked over at Rosie and chuckled. He was enjoying her banshee behaviour.

"So?" Rosie stood up as Jazzy reentered the meeting room, her hands back in the praying position.

Jazzy looked down at her notepad. "Okay, so Hugo owes one hundred and twenty million dollars to creditors and fifteen million to employees."

"I owe you big time for this," Rosie yelled, rushing over to kiss Jazzy on both cheeks, then she high-tailed it out of the meeting room to call Jenny.

Jenny told Rosie she appreciated the information about Hugo Hamilton's dire debts and while it would do for now, she didn't consider it enough to make them even. *Sigh.*

Rosie left the office early for her appointment with Dr Preethi Kumar. It was the last thing she felt like doing after her exhausting toing and froing with Jenny, but she was too scared to cancel. Preethi ran her practice like a headmistress runs a school—organised, efficient and not accepting of any bullshit excuses, especially at the last minute.

Today Preethi was wearing a multi-coloured midi dress (of course) and gold ballet flats. It was the exact same outfit that Rosie had just seen on a mannequin in the window of Zara.

"How's your daily routine going? Are you swimming, making sure you eat at mealtimes, going to bed on time, leaving the laptop and phone outside your bedroom, all those things we talked about last time?" Preethi rattled off her routine questions.

"Yes, to everything," she lied, glancing down at her new Marni sandals.

"Good. So let's start with where we left off last session."

Rosie squirmed in her seat.

"We talked about your colleague." Preethi looked down at the notes on her lap. "Jazzy. You were going to think about the power imbalance aspect of any relationship?"

Rosie fixed her eyes on Preethi's bookshelf in the corner of the room.

Stacked with psychology books, Preethi often pulled one out and read paragraphs aloud to support her theories. Sometimes she offered to loan Rosie the book and Rosie would accept, then return it the following week unread.

Preethi followed Rosie's eyes and made her way over to the bookshelf. She removed a book with the title *How to Tell If It's Love or Friendship*. As she returned to her seat, Rosie said, "It's not love. I've already worked that much out."

"Oh, okay. Did something change since we last met?"

"I didn't end up saying anything to her and now she's seeing a rich banker." Rosie dramatically threw her arms up in the air. "So, there you go. Problem solved."

"And are you okay with that?"

"I suppose so." Rosie fidgeted, while Preethi sat motionless, staring at her. "Maybe I confused my feelings."

"Excellent. This is excellent," whooped Preethi, suddenly springing to life. "I'm so proud of you acknowledging this. You know, in this book"— she held the book out so Rosie could see its front cover—"Dr Engelhart talks about how it's hard to tell the difference between platonic friendship and romantic love. She talks about how it's important to rate the intensity of your feelings. Is this something you've thought about?"

"Sort of," replied Rosie. "I love being around her." She stared out of the window, searching for a more concise explanation. "I miss her when she's not around. And I think about her a lot."

"This is really good, Rosie," beamed Preethi, proud of her client's progress.

"But it's different to how I felt when I met Orlando. I don't desire her in the same way." She brought her eyes back to the room and to Preethi. "I can't explain it beyond that." She shrugged and looked down at her feet, as she always did when she was lost for words.

Preethi placed the book down on the side table and leaned forward.

"It might be that at this point in your life, and after everything you've been through, you're actually just looking for friendship."

Bingo! *Just looking for friendship.* Sometimes all Rosie wanted in return for her three hundred dollars was Preethi to endorse her feelings. She didn't want to read her academic textbooks or deep dive into the psychology of human relationships.

"Preethi, I just realised I have a meeting. Can we stop there, please?" she lied, again. It had been a really long day and all Rosie wanted was a Thai takeaway and to collapse on the sofa. And she bolted before Preethi had time to rise out of her armchair.

Chapter 34

Can you spare any time this morning to help in the canteen? They have record numbers of orders today. They would particularly like help at recess otherwise they might have to shut the counter. Thank you!!!

Bee stared at the message in Otis's WhatsApp class group-chat, paralysed by indecision over whether to put her hand up or not. There was no reason not to, she had nothing else planned this morning. She just wasn't sure she was ready to embrace the role of volunteer parent. There were days when Bee saw those messages pop up while she was in a meeting and imagined herself serving the students their fancy bliss balls. It was an appealing fantasy, particularly when she was in the thick of a stressful client transaction. *Fuck it.* As Savannah said—"Don't mope around."

Bee: I can help.

Billy: Wow, you sure, Bee???

Bee: Yes! I'd love to.

More like I feel like I should because I don't have work as an excuse anymore, she thought.

The decision of what to wear had her stumped, despite how simple it seemed. Stepping back, she let her gaze sweep across the full length of her wardrobe. It was replete with all her corporate outfits—dresses, skirts, blouses, shirts, jackets, and none of it was befitting of her new life at home. Although they were individual pieces, collectively they formed a uniform that had come to define her. The realisation of no longer needing this uniform, at least temporarily, felt like she was shedding a part of herself. She rummaged through her jeans and t-shirts which occupied just one of the twenty shelves in her walk-in-wardrobe. Jeans were only worn interchangeably with active wear on weekends, for an 'off duty' look. For now, she was permanently off duty.

Once dressed, and with thirty minutes to spare before her canteen duties, she decided to grab a coffee from the local New Street Cafe. She'd only ever driven past and was keen to check it out. Gus had taken the boys to their before-school activities, telling Bee it was best for them to keep their usual family routine as normal as possible for now.

As she pulled up outside the cafe, she was surprised by the number of parents who were enjoying pre-school coffees and milkshakes with their kids. Is this what parents do when they're not in a rush to get to the office? It was all very civilised.

With her face hidden behind Celine sunglasses, she timidly approached the serving counter, worrying that someone might recognise her face from the front pages. If only she had Savannah's confidence and carefree attitude, not giving a toss about what others thought of her.

"Hi, there, what can I get you?" asked the friendly bobbed barista sporting a red-and-white-striped matching shorts and shirt set.

"Flat white, please, large," said Bee, nervously scanning the faces at tables inside and outside the cafe. "I love your matching set. It's very cool," she rambled.

"Awww, that's really kind of you. Thank you. Just a cheapie from Cotton On," said the barista.

Bee smiled. It was exactly the sort of self-deprecating comment she would make. "I might have to get one for myself," she added.

As the barista moved across to the coffee machine, her eyes glanced back at Bee. "Have you just moved into the area? I'm good with faces, it's my job, and I haven't seen you before."

"No, I've lived here for five years. I would just normally be in the city working. But I, erm, yeah, I, erm, am not going in today, or tomorrow, or … the day after that." Bee stumbled over her words. It was the most inarticulate she had been in years.

"Okay. Well, I hope we see you again. My name's Bella, by the way."

"I'm Bee." She resisted the urge to divulge any more personal information. For now, it was refreshing that she didn't need to even mention Curban Capital.

"Here you go." Bella handed Bee her coffee. There was no message on the lid. *Sigh*. She was going to miss Luca's kind daily scribbles.

When Bee arrived at the school office, the efficient administrator behind the reception desk asked her to sign in on an iPad then handed over a lanyard marked 'visitor'. She was told to hand it back when her shift was finished then asked if she knew where the canteen was located. Too embarrassed to admit she didn't, she lied and said yes. It wasn't hard to find anyway. She caught sight of someone carrying a baker's tray full of bread rolls across the playground and followed them.

As she entered, she was immediately struck by the bustling atmosphere. It resembled a factory, with a line of mums (she presumed they were fellow mums) diligently working with their heads down, engrossed in their tasks.

"Hi, I'm Bee. I'm here to help this morning," she announced to the factory line. One of the ladies leaned back and shouted in a thick Scottish accent, "Follow me, let's get you an apron from out the back."

As they walked to the storeroom, the lady introduced herself as Linda and head of the canteen. She was more the age of a grandparent than parent and appeared to run a very tight ship, judging by her spotless storeroom with tidy shelves.

"We'll get you started on filling the popcorn bags." She handed Bee a blue-and-white-striped apron, then walked back to the kitchen, before coming to a stop next to the popcorn machine. "So you just fill each bag to about three quarters full." She demonstrated the task as she spoke.

"Leave enough room to be able to roll the paper bag closed."

"Got it," said Bee, immediately getting to work.

As she started scooping, she quickly glanced at the production line of mums, and it *was* all mums, busily getting on with their assigned tasks. There was chopping, baking, bagging up, washing up and no chatting whatsoever.

After finishing the popcorn bags, she was assigned to filling brown paper bags with recess orders. The choices read more like a healthy cafe menu than public school canteen.

Fruit cup, carrot sticks, yoghurt tub with Greek yoghurt and maple syrup topped with berries or granola, brownie cocoa cookie (with minimal sugar!), banana bread muffins—delicious homemade recipe, bliss balls— the best in Manly! A perfect healthy treat for your cherub! Frappe of the day. Watermelon and strawberry.

Blimey. Bee felt herself doing that thing that all kids hate—'in my day'. But back in *her* day the menu consisted of oven chips, baked beans, fried egg and greasy pizza that made a thud when it landed on the plate, all served up by dinner ladies with bat-wing cellulite arms. There was zero cellulite in this kitchen.

It was approaching recess time and Linda asked for everyone's full attention. Like a drill sergeant she issued instructions on where to find change for cash orders, how to handle Spriggy spending money orders and how to make sure the "wee scallywags" returned their Milo cups.

As soon as the bell sounded, Bee heard the stampede of feet heading towards the canteen hatch. Linda lifted the shutters to hordes of hungry faces and the calling out of orders. Most of the kids were polite with nice manners and Bee even recognised a few from Otis's cricket team.

"Next, please," Bee said, feeling like she was getting the hang of it.

"Aren't you Otis's mum?" asked a red-haired, freckly-faced girl, scrunching her freckly nose.

"Yes, I am. Are you in his class?"

"No. Duh, do I look like I'm in year six?" She rolled her eyes. "Anyway, my mum said you were in the papers for being naughty. Something like you got expelled from your job. Were you caught vaping? Is that why you're working the canteen now?" she sniggered.

This little carrot-top had Bee lost for words. And there she was, worrying what a parent might say to her; she never thought she'd be taken on by a child. "Well, that's not strictly true."

"Whatevs. I'll have a yoghurt tub with berries."

"Please."

"What?"

"Please. Say please, please."

Linda barged past Bee and leaned across the counter "Put your manners in check, Charlotte, and say please to the lady serving you."

Linda had just saved Bee from throwing yoghurt in the girl's freckly face. As she handed the tub over, Charlotte didn't thank her. Instead, she whispered to her friend standing to the side, then they both stared at Bee and started giggling. It was like being back in the playground. Little bitches.

"Hang on a minute," said Bee firmly. She exited the kitchen and made her way around to the front of the serving hatch. "Did you know it's really rude to whisper?"

"All right, Karen," said the friend. And both girls started laughing again.

"Excuse me?"

"Karen, I said Karen. That's your name, isn't it?"

Bee put her hands on her hips "I'm not a Karen, thank you very much. What's your full name? I'm going to tell your mum exactly what you just said to me."

"Go on, she won't care. She's not a loser like you."

"You little …" She stopped herself from saying *bitches*. "You little meanies. Who do you think you are? Do you think it's cool to go around speaking to people like that? I bet you think you're the queens of the playground. You'll never get anywhere in this world with an attitude like that." Bee was pointing her finger just inches from Charlotte's face.

"Don't push me," Charlotte shouted loudly, trying to attract attention and round up an audience.

"What? I didn't push you, you little liar," Bee snapped back. At that moment, a supervising teacher in a green high vis vest came rushing over.

"What's going on here?" she asked Bee before turning her eyes to the two girls.

Bee couldn't get a word in edgeways because Charlotte and her prickly little sidekick were too busy whining about how they had both been pushed. Before she realised it, Bee was being escorted to the principal's office while the mean girls were led back to their classroom. Thankfully, Otis hadn't been on the playground to see the whole thing. He would have been as embarrassed as his mum, if not more.

The teacher directed Bee to one of the small classroom chairs outside the principal's office. With her knees under her chin, she lowered her head in shame. The administration staff behind the front desk were discussing content for the weekly newsletter but Bee assumed their conversation would turn to her as soon as she was out of their sight.

The principal, Mr Norton, arrived five minutes later. He was a young principal, quite handsome with warm eyes and a kind smile. *Please be kind to me*, she thought.

"Bee, would you like to come into my office?" he said.

"Of course." She jumped to attention then followed him sheepishly.

He pointed to a chair across the desk from his own. She swiftly took a seat and placed her hands on her lap, palms facing upward, reminiscent of her school assembly days. With wide eyes, Mr Norton gazed at her, his hands tightly clasped and his posture impressively upright. *Can't spend all day telling kids to sit up if you don't sit up straight yourself,* Bee thought.

Bee was overcome with a burning sensation in her cheeks as she flashed back to her ten-year-old self, sitting in front of the principal of her North London primary school for flicking ink onto the white lab coat of the science teacher. She grimaced at the thought.

"I don't really want to go over the canteen business. I think we all know why you went off at Charlotte. She's a petulant child who needs to be taught a lesson, but don't repeat that, please. I just need to be seen to be doing the right thing."

She wasn't expecting him to start with that. "Okay," she said.

"Are we going through something at home?" asked Mr Norton like he already knew the answer.

"Ah, yes, there's been a change to my ... to my circumstances." She shifted on her chair. "Gosh, is it really hot in here?"

Mr Norton reached for a remote control on his desk and pointed it at an air conditioning unit on the wall. "You lost your job. I saw it on the news."

Bee gulped. Her cheeks burned again. He wasn't beating around the bush.

"And I don't believe for one second what they're saying about you."

She gulped a second time. It was another comment she hadn't expected from him.

"My sister Amy works in finance, and she gushes about you all the time. You're her role model."

Bee's face lit up. Gus was right, some people *would* know the truth among all the lies. "That's really lovely to hear."

"You must be feeling like you've entered a parallel universe. I mean, one day CEO, the next day serving bliss balls to spiky brats like Charlotte." His mouth curved into a smile as if he were about to laugh.

"I suppose so." *Where is he going with this?* she wondered.

"And I suspect you might be having an identity crisis. I see it all the time. I have spent twenty years trying to understand you parents—the ones that work and the ones that don't. All I hear is "I wish I had a job." "I wish I worked less." "I used to be this, and I used to be that," he said, flopping his head and hands from side to side with each statement. "You're all too hard on yourselves."

"I guess we are," Bee agreed. He was right. He had in that moment succinctly captured how Bee felt by working too much at times and how Lucy had felt for not working at all.

"If I can give you one word of advice?"

She gave a childlike nod, keen for any pearls of wisdom that he might have to offer.

"Just be kind to yourself and don't come back to the canteen for now," he chuckled. "But if you do have some spare time, we could use your CEO super skills elsewhere. Somehow though, I think you'll be back to running a business in no time."

She doubted that very much but enjoyed the compliment. Should she just ask quickly how Otis was getting on, because she actually had no idea? Or maybe she would save that for another time.

"Thank you, Mr Norton."

When Bee walked into the canteen to return her apron, Linda and her mum volunteers clapped in unison.

"You bloody legend," shouted Linda from behind the kitchen bench with a tray of bliss balls in her hands. "I'd have loved to tell that wee miss up herself to bugger off. Thank you from all of us because she's now banned for two weeks." And they all burst into fits of laughter.

Savannah: What did you get up to today?

Bee: I volunteered in the canteen …

Savannah: 😕 *What did you do that for? That wasn't what I meant when I said don't mope around!*

Bee: Yeah, well, I won't be going back so don't worry.

Chapter 35

"I've never taken so many calls for one client in my entire career," gasped Rosie as she sat at her desk, sipping on a sugar-free Sprite. "Not that I'm complaining, I love working for Bee, it's just relentless."

Rosie and Jazzy were the only two left in the office. It was 10pm. They had both just devoured McDonald's Quarter Pounder With Cheese meals and Rosie was already regretting hers. It had been Jazzy's idea to order Macca's because she was still feeling hungover from her 'date night' with Joe. So far, Rosie had managed to successfully extract herself from all conversations relating to Joe but at some point, she knew she would have to just grit her teeth and listen. After all, it wasn't very nice to act so uninterested in her personal life.

"Do you think Curban will settle soon?" asked Jazzy, moving from her desk to perch on Rosie's.

"I don't know. Max Magnifico is a complex individual, to put it politely. I don't think he gives up easily and he certainly won't want egg on his face." Rosie reached for her phone, remembering she wanted to share a meme of Max. It was of Max with his hands covering his eyes, accompanied by the words *What videos? Nothing to see here.* "Did you see this? I heard he was trying to get it taken down."

"OMG that's brilliant. I love it," laughed Jazzy.

"And what about this one? This one is *the* best." Rosie brought up another meme, this time of Bee, hands in the air, with the words *Ain't nobody like Bee Bloom!* "It's got up to two million views."

"She's definitely winning the hearts out there, don't you think?"

asked Jazzy.

It was hard to think about anything other than the Macca's taste that was repeating on her. "Yeah, but there's still *a lot* more work to do! We better crack on." They had at least another hour of work ahead of them. *Oh bring on Fiji!*

The next ten weeks

"Max Magnifico is a snake in a suit," says investment banking veteran Savannah Silva, December 13, 2022

In this exclusive interview, one of the industry's most high-profile women, Savannah Silva, says Bee Bloom was set up by Curban chairman, Max Magnifico. Silva, who is visiting Sydney from London, says Magnifico is the biggest snake of her working life.

Hugo Hamilton in trouble again for punching a camera person, December 14, 2022

Hugo Hamilton can't seem to keep out of trouble these days. He was exiting the Surry Hills headquarters of his now bankrupt business when a camera person tried to take a photo and was pushed by Hamilton to the ground.

"Wrongly dismissed," says Green Energy CEO John Piper, December 15, 2022

John Piper is the latest client of Bee Bloom's to come out in her defence. Piper says Bee Bloom is one of the most outstanding leaders he has ever had the pleasure of working with.

Lucy Love and Hugo Hamilton file for divorce, December 16, 2022

Lucy Hamilton has officially filed for divorce from her predator husband, Hugo Hamilton. Love, who has two children with Hamilton, is said to be moving on with her life while he shacks up with a staffer.

Ding, ding, the gloves are off in the Curban Capital ring, December 17, 2022

Max Magnifico has come out swinging, saying that the firm was absolutely in the right to step down Bee Bloom. Magnifico is refusing to settle with Bloom, prompting some to say the matter will go to court.

Lucy Love moves out of Hamilton family home, December 17, 2022

Removal vans have been seen arriving at the Avalon home that Love and Hamilton shared. The house is set to be put on the market with an asking price of around twenty million dollars.

Curban clients consider moving their business, December 18, 2022

In the ongoing saga at Curban, sources say that clients have grouped together to voice their unhappiness with Bee Bloom's departure and are considering taking their business elsewhere.

PR fixer Rosie Reid restructures her business, December 20, 2022

Rosie Reid, Sydney's best-known crisis manager, is reshaping Reid & Co Counsel, the business she has run for fifteen years. Reid said it was time for a change and that she will be pivoting her focus to female-led businesses.

Hugo Hamilton's victims will not press charges, seeking compensation, January 6, 2023

Hugo Hamilton's victims have announced that they will not press charges for fear of being dragged through the courts, but they are seeking compensation for trauma. How they will be compensated is unclear, given Hamilton is declaring himself bankrupt.

Lucy Love appointed PR Manager of Urban Style, January 10, 2023

CEO and founder of Urban Style, Bethany Byron, has appointed Lucy Love to the role of PR Manager for her multi-million-dollar business. Love starts her new role in two weeks.

Curban Capital staff go on strike, January 16, 2023

Staff at the offices of Curban Capital have walked off the job, demanding that Bee Bloom be reinstated. We usually see nurses and bus drivers strike, but this is an industry first for an investment bank.

Penfold Partners pulls out from buying Curban Capital, January 31, 2023

"The deal is off," says Ben Taggart from his Manhattan offices. Taggart said the drama surrounding Curban was damaging to the Penfold brand.

Rosie Reid moves into Surry Hills, February 10, 2023

The PR fixer, Rosie Reid, has moved from her CBD digs to Surry Hills, occupying a former terrace.

Bee Bloom finally settles with Curban Capital, February 15, 2023

After ten weeks, the ink is finally drying on settlement agreements between Bee Bloom and Curban Capital. Sources familiar with the situation say Magnifico was told to "pull his head in" so everyone can move on.

Suzy Scott, the former assistant to Max Magnifico, claims he's "a corporate psychopath", February 25, 2023

Max Magnifico's former assistant, Suzy Scott, has been described as brave for coming forward to share stories of his serial manipulation and conniving. Scott described Magnifico as a "callous, impulsive and cunning bastard who belongs in prison with other psychopaths".

Max Magnifico fired from Curban, February 25, 2023

After just three months in the job, Max Magnifico has been fired as chairman of Curban. Magnifico said Curban wasn't the right calibre of firm for a man of his exceptional talents while Curban said he wasn't the right calibre of individual for the firm.

Bee Bloom announced as the keynote speaker at Wellbeing Magazine's Women's Summit, February 27, 2023

Wellbeing Magazine *yesterday announced that Bee Bloom will feature as the keynote speaker at its inaugural Women's Conference on the twenty-third of March. Tickets to the event sold out within two hours.*

Max Magnifico in a scuffle at the chairman's lounge, February 28, 2023

It was the most cringeworthy moment of Max Magnifico's flying life when he was refused entry to the Qantas chairman's lounge today. Magnifico demanded Qantas CEO Alan Joyce come and speak to him personally while other lounge members, including Keith Urban and Nicole Kidman, stood and watched. Magnifico finally retreated after a bit of pushing and shoving with a burly Qantas security guard.

Bee Bloom seen drinking cocktails in Fiji, March 15, 2023

Bee Bloom has been spotted laughing and drinking cocktails at Fiji's Six Senses Malolo Resort with Lucy Love, Rosie Reid and her former assistant Stuart Sanderson. Bloom has a good reason to be laughing, after Max Magnifico was sent packing back to France.

"What is your usual occupation?" Bee was stumped by how to answer the question on the Australia landing card laid out on her tray table. Her Swarovski ballpoint pen hovered over the blank space while she deliberated whether to make something up rather than write the words 'unemployed'.

It was fair to say things had got off to a rocky start after her 'sudden departure from Curban'. After her canteen debacle, she dedicated her first week of unemployed life to tackling household chores. She started by vigorously scrubbing the stubborn urine stains off the herringbone tiles on the boys' bathroom floor, as if they were Max's smug face. With equal fervour, she proceeded to power wash anything in sight, finding the process as gratifying as squeezing the boys' blackheads or watching Dr Pimple Popper.

Once she'd scrubbed and power washed everything, she joined a new local gym and paid upfront for thirty sessions with a twenty-something PT called Tilly. Tilly whipped her butt three days a week while intermittently barking, "Yes, queen Bee, you're killing it."

And sandwiched between all those activities were lots and lots of flat whites at New Street Cafe while chatting to Bella, her new favourite barista, about fashion, art, nutrition and of course, Harry Styles.

The trip to Fiji was Bee's idea. She said they—Rosie, Lucy and Stuart—needed a break and the trip was all expenses paid on her as a thank you for their love and support. They just needed to bring their fabulous selves! Bee was aware that Rosie hadn't accurately billed her for the extensive work she had done in managing interviews and putting an end to the smear campaigns orchestrated by Max. This discrepancy was obvious to Bee, because she was used to reviewing Rosie's monthly invoices at Curban. She also knew that Rosie desperately wanted to go to Fiji but, like all workaholics, was petrified of being away from the office. Lucy needed a break after enduring the most humiliating and public divorce. Their sponsorship of each other had developed into a close friendship with laughs *and* tears shared at the dog park every weekday. And Stuart, well, he *had* to come. Bee missed seeing his face every day. He happily assumed the role of holiday planner extraordinaire, in charge of all the logistics from flights, hotel, helicopter transfers, spa treatments and daily yoga to Bee's paradise island stylist.

Six Senses Malolo Island was selected because, with just twenty-four villas, it was private. Stuart's over-excitement started the moment their transfer helicopter touched down. He couldn't contain his excitement, comparing himself to billionaire Kendall Roy from the TV drama *Succession*. "Bula! How fabulous are we?" he squealed while trailing the sarong-wearing porter with a welcome cocktail in one hand and a refreshment towel in the other.

They each checked into their own one-hundred-and-eleven-square-metre pool villa that beautifully blended Fijian and contemporary design. As soon as Bee found the outdoor shower, she speedily discarded her travel attire and positioned herself underneath the refreshing stream of cold water. She then unpacked her belongings, admiring each holiday outfit as she went, before sinking into the four-poster king bed. She let out a big *ahhhhhh*. No snoring Gus, no farting Garry, just her!

That first night, the group met in their fabulous island outfits for sundowner drinks at the hotel bar. They got talking to two couples from San Francisco. Bee chatted to Logan, a handsome man in his early thirties, who was telling her about the tech start-up he founded in Silicon Valley. And the conversation was bouncing along nicely until he asked, "So what gets you out of bed in the morning?" Bee froze. She was embarrassed and felt a flush coming on. How could she say "Nothing right now" to this inspiring young entrepreneur who was so passionately explaining his vocation?

"Well, I'm kind of in between things at the moment. I suppose you could say I'm exploring my options."

"Cool," said Logan, nodding his head.

Lucy must have had one ear on Bee's conversation and one on the three-way she was having with Stuart and Raja, Logan's Pilates instructor wife, because she turned around to Logan and said, "This amazing woman here is being *way* too humble. She is the former CEO of a *hugely* successful investment bank, she has paved the way for lots of young women who look up to her, and she is my amazing friend and sponsor."

Logan glanced at the cocktails in their hands.

"Oh, not AA sponsor, friend sponsor. It's a long story." And she turned back to her three-way.

"Wow. So cool. We should talk. I'm looking to raise capital for my business and would love your advice. I mean, if that's okay, seeing as this is your vacation and all?" asked Logan.

"I'd love to help," Bee replied. "Let's chat tomorrow." She was aware of a spring in her step after the conversation because for the first time in ten weeks, she felt useful.

The following day, as they lounged by the resort's pool, Lucy brought up Bee's uncomfortable encounter with Logan. "You know, I reckon Mr Norton might have been onto something when he mentioned the possibility of you having an identity crisis," she blurted out from beneath her oversized straw sun hat while applying her SPF 50 sunscreen.

"Pardon?" said Bee.

"We are a society that leans heavily into 'What do you do for a living?' to kick off conversations. It helps us situate ourselves in other people's universes, as well as our own. I read it somewhere," said Lucy, diligently rubbing the sunscreen into her thighs. "You were embarrassed last night saying you're currently in between jobs, but you shouldn't be."

"Nobody will judge you for being a lady of leisure for a bit," Stuart piped up from his lounger next to Bee's.

Bee jolted and turned to Stuart, staring him down with her meanest eyes.

"Just kidding, Bee. I know you hate that phrase. Maybe just say you're a homemaker instead then," he laughed.

"Not funny, Stuart. Do you know, I've been employed since the age of fourteen?" Bee said. It was true. She had seamlessly segued from student and part-time worker to full-time corporate ladder climber. "So no wonder it's not sitting well with me." It was also true that Bee had woken up to the fact that her self-worth had always been inextricably linked to a pay cheque. "Maybe I need to go on one of those new beginning type of self-discovery retreats."

"Oh yes, please," said Stuart.

In that moment, Lucy's face brightened and her mouth fell open. "I've got an idea. You should talk about all of this stuff in your speech next week." She sat up, pivoted her legs to the side of her sun lounger, and turned to face Bee. "It will resonate with everyone. Hell, I'm having an identity crisis of my own. After twenty years of being married to a chipolata, I'm on the hunt for a jumbo frankfurter." She laughed naughtily.

"Me too," chimed in Rosie from beneath her trendy Prada bucket hat. "Not the frankfurter part, the identity crisis bit. I've been halved, split in two. Now I'm known as Reid and Pincombe Counsel," she said, her face contorting into a grimace. "It was the only way for me to retain Simon Pincombe and his lucrative clients. And ... three months ago I thought I was a lesbian."

"WHAT!" shrieked Stuart, moving dramatically into a seated position.

"It's not a big deal, Stuart. I just confused my feelings." Rosie pulled her hat down to hide her face, refusing to be drawn into further detail.

"Do we reckon Max is having an identity crisis now?" asked Lucy.

"Abso-fucking-lutely," replied Rosie. "The only reason guys like him stay in the game as long as they do is for the power and to avoid relevance deprivation. He needs to just bugger off for good now and stick to crushing merlot grapes in his gladiator sandals, or whatever he does in France."

"Let's not talk about *that* man, please, peeps. It'll spoil our holiday," said Bee.

She didn't want to allow Max any more airtime. This break was for rejuvenation and positive vibes only. "Pass me the cocktail list, please, Stuart." She hadn't noticed until now that he was wearing Gucci swim trunks today. "All Gucci'd up over there, Stuart. That apartment won't buy itself, you know; just saying."

Hadn't he learned anything from his recent experience? Straight back into his old spending ways the minute he got his new job.

"Just saying," he mimicked. "Just saying, you're starting to sound like your kids, Bee. Anyway, I'm now on the discount list at Gucci after becoming one of their best customers, thanks to buying you and Savannah all those outfits. And let's just say it's *very* generous so I'll be back there next week."

He smirked while Bee lowered her head and peered over her Celine sunglasses, giving him a stern, teacher-like glare.

"What? There have to be *some* perks to the job. Now, what cocktails are we having?"

"Ladies and gentlemen, we are now preparing for our descent into Sydney. The captain has turned on the fasten seat belt sign. If you haven't already done so, please stow your carry-on luggage underneath the seat in front of you or in an overhead compartment. Please take your seat and fasten your seat belt. And make sure your seat back and folding trays are in the upright position."

Bee looked back down at the landing card on her tray table, twirling her pen around in her hand. That's it! She wrote 'Currently exploring options'.

Chapter 36

The Financial Report, *Thursday, March 23, 2023*

Bee Bloom speaking today at Wellbeing Magazine*'s Women's Summit*

After almost three months in hiding, Bee Bloom will today give a keynote speech at the inaugural Wellbeing Magazine*'s Women's Summit at the Crown Hotel in Sydney. Over one thousand attendees are expected at the event. It's not known exactly what Bloom will be talking about, although sources say she will share some insights into her very public showdown with Max Magnifico.*

"The car's ten minutes away," said Gus. Bee smiled and nodded. There was just enough time for one last read-through of her speech.

The summit had been Stuart's side hustle for four weeks. He worked in his new fashion PR role by day and put together *revenge* outfits by night. "Babe, you are dressing for revenge," he had said. "You know how after a break-up you want to show that dirty ex how fucking fab you are without them; well, this is your moment. And we need to make you shine."

Bee understood Stuart's dressing-for-revenge sentiment. She wanted to look fabulous, of course she bloody well did, but it was much more than that—she wanted to *sound* fabulous. Having maintained her silence for three months, she was well aware that attendees, including the journalists who had covered her story, would be hanging off her every word.

"Bee, it's perfect. You need to put the notes away now and get your game face on," said Savannah, who was sitting on the leather lounge in Bee's study. She had flown in yesterday from London.

"I agree, Bee. It's almost time to get going anyway," added Rosie, who was standing in the study doorway, on her phone.

Bee did a quick square breathing exercise—in for four, hold for four, out for four, hold for four—then stood up.

"Right, come on then."

Gus and the boys followed the three women out to the front gate.

"We'll see you there in about an hour, okay?" said Gus, stepping forward to kiss Bee on the cheek. "Remember, you know your worth. Don't second guess yourself for one second." Savannah and Rosie looked at each other and smiled at Gus's thoughtful words to his wife.

As she got into the waiting car, Otis and Ollie shouted, "Go, Mum." Her heart swelled with love and pride.

"I think I've outdone myself this time," shrilled Stuart when Bee, Savannah and Rosie walked into the hotel lobby. He had styled all three women from head to toe and was clearly ecstatic with the result standing before him. Bee was dressed in a Gucci tile print black and white maxi dress with a gathered waist and pussy bow, paired with Gucci patent leather stiletto sandals that tied around her ankles. Savannah was also in Gucci, sporting a black and white embroidered wool midi skirt and matching jacket with black Gucci mules. Rosie injected a splash of colour in a 16Arlington fuchsia-pink satin shirt dress with an exaggerated collar, matched with a pair of black Prada loafers.

"Lucy, get over here," Stuart yelled to Lucy who was quietly waiting on a nearby sofa. Dressed in a Zimmerman cream ruffled asymmetric silk-satin wrap dress and her favourite Jimmy Choo sandals, Lucy ran, yes, ran in sandals, over to the three women and hugged each of them.

"Right, get in, everyone. I want a photo," ordered Stuart. He clapped his hands together like a cymbal-banging circus monkey and ushered everyone into the shot. As he did, an incredibly handsome Crown employee dressed in black trousers and white shirt came towards him and suggested that he take the photo. Savannah gave him an obvious once-over, but the employee appeared to only have eyes for Stuart.

"How about we do some fun poses?" suggested the young man. The group began playing to the camera with a cross-arm pose, pouting pose, twirl pose, look-over-the-shoulder pose until another Crown employee, with a scowl on her face, approached the group to suggest they move to the green room.

"The fun police has arrived," whispered Stuart into Bee's ear.

The green room, so-called because it's where performers wait before they go on stage, was nothing special—it was a bland, windowless boardroom with a large round table, eight chairs and a few platters of canapés. Stuart offered around a tray of mini quiches, but nobody was hungry. Bee suspected everyone else was just as nervous as her but didn't want to admit it. "I can't believe one thousand people are coming," she said, allowing a touch of imposter syndrome to creep in.

"*Over* one thousand," corrected Stuart.

Bee nibbled her bottom lip. It was a sign of nerves which Savannah picked up on.

"And you'll be great, Bee. You won't even see most of the faces. Just keep your eyes on us"—Savannah pointed at herself, Rosie, Stuart and Lucy—"and your gorgeous boys."

Rosie and Stuart decided to check how the ballroom was looking. Stuart, the self-proclaimed perfectionist, didn't trust the Crown staff. He had taken it upon himself to micromanage everything from spacing of the chairs to flower arrangements. He said he also wanted to check if the new man in his life had arrived.

The 'networking' part of the evening was getting underway at six o'clock sharp. After one hour of cocktails, guests would be directed into the ballroom for the main event. Rosie instructed Bee to wait in the green room until there was a sufficient crowd gathered in the cocktail area. She didn't want Bee to be out there too early, looking all eager beavery. "We need to create an element of suspense," she had said. "But not so much suspense that you're like Beyonce at the Grammys and everyone thinks you're a diva."

Bee stared at the bottle of white wine sitting in a chiller and wondered if one glass would soothe or sink her.

"Do you fancy a wine?" she asked Lucy.

"Nah, I'm trying to cut back." Lucy made a sad face.

Bee opted for a soft drink. "Apple crisp kombucha it is then." She removed her speaking notes from her clutch and rehearsed her points one final time.

At six twenty Rosie returned. Around five hundred guests had arrived, and the reception room was nicely buzzing. It was time for Bee to make her entrance.

"Oh my God." Bee looked at Savannah with big eyes.

"We will be right by your side," Savannah said softly.

Flanked by Savannah, Rosie, Lucy and Stuart, Bee walked into the cocktail lounge adjacent to the ballroom. She was grateful for the soft lighting in case she felt a sudden flush of nerves. For now, she felt surprisingly in control, her breathing was normal, and her gut, which was where she held tension, felt knot-free. She looked out at a sea of smartly dressed guests huddled around high cocktail tables sipping on champagne. She estimated about seventy-five per cent of the crowd were female.

"Hi, Bee Bloom, I'm Nancy," said a young woman who had rushed over from one of the tables. "I'm a junior analyst at Morgan Stanley. I'd love to chat to you, if that's okay?"

As it *was* the 'networking' part of the event, Bee was happy to oblige.

"Of course, Nancy. Let's grab that table over there." Bee pointed to an unoccupied cocktail table and made her way over. She happily chatted to Nancy until Rosie pulled her away "to circulate". There was, apparently, a queue of young women who wanted to meet Bee. Rosie said they could have three minutes each, speed-dating style.

In mid-conversation with a young lawyer, Bee was stopped dead in her tracks; her jaw dropped to the floor. "Would you excuse me, please?" she said. She grabbed hold of Stuart who was in the middle of barking orders at a waiter. "What the fuck is he doing here?" she whispered angrily into his ear.

Standing in the entrance to the cocktail lounge was Arthur. It had been three months since Bee last saw the sneaky little hobbit in the boardroom showdown at Brown & Partners. The tension knots began firing up in her stomach. Arthur caught Bee's eye and began walking towards her. She steeled herself—he *was not* going to ruin her moment.

"Yeah, what *is* he doing here?" snapped Stuart furiously. "Let me handle him, you go and get yourself prepared." Stuart protectively stood in front of Bee. He puffed his chest out and lifted his head up with his nose in the air. "What do *you* want?"

Arthur attempted to look over Stuart's shoulder to catch Bee's eye. Stuart side-stepped to block him.

"I said, what do *you* want?"

"I just want to speak with Bee for two minutes," Arthur said softly.

"How dare you just turn up like this, you two-faced little weasel. You don't deserve to speak to Bee ever again. I didn't see your name on the guest list and we don't have booster seats so why don't you take your mothball suit and your combover and piss off." He folded his arms and shot him a simpering smile.

Gosh, Stuart could be harsh. His words were spiteful, and Bee was too classy for that. She stepped out from behind Stuart. "It's okay, Stuart." She touched his arm. "I'll give you two minutes, Arthur. That's all I've got. Follow me."

"Need me to come?" Stuart asked, casting his best *I hate you* look at Arthur.

Bee shook her head then led the way to the green room with Arthur two steps behind. Once inside, she didn't offer him a seat; she wanted to stand, just to keep it short and so she could tower over him in her high heels. She folded her arms and waited for him to start.

"Bee, I can't tell you how sorry I am. I was hoodwinked. I was a fool. I should have known better and I will forever regret how I acted." His voice quivered with every word.

Her kind heart *almost* felt sorry for him but her head still wanted to crush him. How could he be hoodwinked at his age, someone so experienced? She was still dumbfounded by how he'd played this so badly, and the rest of the board, for that matter.

"If I had my time again I would never have appointed Max. You have to understand, he completely pulled the wool over my eyes. And I hate myself for that."

Bee exhaled loudly to convey her frustration then glanced at her phone. "You've got one more minute." She wasn't going to make it easy for him; she wanted him to grovel.

He appeared panicked by the time restriction and started rambling. "Everyone misses you, Bee. I miss you, terribly. Please come back. We all want you back. Curban is just not the same place without you. In fact, Curban *is* you."

Everything about his demeanour was sadness and regret. He looked even smaller than normal, almost cowering, like a naughty toddler expecting a slap on the bottom.

Bee drummed her fingers on her arms to show her impatience and irritation.

When she didn't reply, Arthur said in a faint voice, "Bee, please, say something." Her silence and finger-drumming were unsettling him.

She moved forward and opened her mouth. Arthur perked up a

little, anticipating a response, but all she said was, "After you." Then she opened the door, gesturing for him to leave. Sadness returned to his face. He shuffled despondently towards the door before turning back to look at Bee.

"Goodbye, Arthur." There were so many things she could have said, so many hateful words that she'd thought of using while she lay awake at night ruminating about the whole ordeal. But in that moment, Bee decided that silence was golden.

"Ladies and gentlemen, would you please welcome, Bee Bloom!" said the drop-dead gorgeous editor of *Wellbeing Magazine*, after reading a gushing rendition of Bee's CV.

Bee made her way to the stage to an enthusiastic round of applause. *Don't trip, please, don't trip.* She placed her notes on the lectern's slanted surface, readjusted the microphone and looked out to the audience. Sat in the front row were Gus, Otis, Ollie, Rosie, Lucy, Savannah, Stuart and his new partner, Luca the barista, and VIP guests of *Wellbeing Magazine*. In the second row were Suzy, Davide, Jazzy, Maya and Fleur. They all gazed up at her with encouraging smiles. Beyond that, the rows became a sea of indistinct faces.

"Good evening, everyone." She began with an Acknowledgement of Country then thanked everyone for attending. She took a deep breath, looked down at her notes, and continued.

"When I was in school and complained to my father about bullies, he used to tell me *some people are born mean and to just accept it as part of life.* I didn't accept this advice back then, and I still don't now. Because to me, treating people with kindness, treating them the way you like to be treated, is one of the simplest acts whether you're on the playground or in the boardroom. It's so incredibly disappointing when I come across leaders who *still* believe that the only way to get ahead is by using *power* or *toughness*; leaders who believe business is all about the cut-throat, the hustle and climbing on the backs of the people you meet along the way. We seek out kindness, not toughness or power, in our personal relationships, so why shouldn't work be the same?"

At that moment, she caught sight of Penny Pryor in a fuchsia suit. *Breathe slowly,* she said to herself. Noticing Bee's eyes were on her, Penny smiled faintly and nodded her head.

"And being a kind leader doesn't mean you're a pushover or you're weak. You can still make hard and bold decisions with kindness. Leading with kindness is having the ability to do hard things in a human way, recognising that people aren't robots. Kindness doesn't replace anything in your leadership toolbox, it just adds value to what you already have. How do kind leaders deal with difficult situations? With authenticity and empathy. Toughness and power are a short-term way of looking at leadership because in the long term you need to build trust and relationships and you need to treat people well."

As she scanned the room, she spotted Jenny Wallis, who was frantically scribbling away on her notepad. She took a breath then moved to the second part of her speech, which had been Lucy's idea. "Now, most of us in this room are professionals—we go to work every day, we have jobs, jobs we love, jobs that allow us to live our lives to the fullest, jobs that give us purpose. But"—she paused for dramatic effect—"your job is *not* your identity. And if, like I used to, you think it is, then your world can come crashing down in an instant if you lose it.

"When I lost my job, I was angry, and I was embarrassed. But most of all, I was lost. Who am I, if I'm not Bee Bloom, the CEO? Who am I if I don't get up every day and put on my high heels? And as I found out recently, how do I fill in a landing card when arriving back in Australia when it asks "What is your usual occupation?"

She paused again while gentle laughter rippled around the room.

"I had to take a long, hard look at myself and learn to appreciate that so much of what's important in my life comes from other places."

She looked at Gus and her boys then waited in significant silence, as the eyes in the room followed hers to the front row. "If you take a tumble, and at some point in life we all invariably do, what matters most is that you are surrounded by people who love and support you. And as I discovered, love and support can come from familiar places *and* surprising places. For me, it comes first and foremost from family." She took another quick look at the important men in her life. "And from friends that I rely on wholeheartedly every single day." She looked at Stuart. Blushing, he held his head up high, his eyes shimmering with tears as Luca put his arm around him. Bee paused again, taking a moment to soak up the warmth radiating from the audience, before nodding with satisfaction and taking a deep breath.

"I'm fortunate to be surrounded by formidable women who have bolstered my self-esteem, reminded me what matters most and pulled me through some dark moments. I have been held up and cared for by new friends." She looked at Lucy and smiled. "By the women who genuinely wanted to see me be my best self." She moved her eyes to Rosie and smiled. "By the women who have always supported me, through thick and thin." Her eyes now on Savannah. She could see Savannah's lip was quivering. Stuart put his arm around her, and she let her head fall into his shoulder.

"The final point I want to make tonight is this—when life throws you a curveball, don't let it defeat you. Use it as an opportunity to learn and grow. The things that seem wildly important today may not be tomorrow. Because tomorrow is a new day and life goes on. And *always* stay true to your own values. For me, that means ..."—she paused meaningfully before leaning into the microphone—"integrity. Respect. And of course, kindness."

The Financial Report, *Friday, March 24, 2023*

Kindness over toughness, Bee Bloom makes an inspiring call to action.

In her first, highly anticipated public appearance since departing Curban Capital, Bee Bloom chose not to divulge the details of her showdown with Max Magnifico. Instead, she delivered a powerful speech on kind leadership, identity, friendship and values. The audience's resonance with her words was evident through the standing ovation she received. It seems everyone is cheering on Bee Bloom for whatever she does next.

The End

"Three things in human life are important: the first is to be kind; the second is to be kind; and the third is to be kind."

Henry James, American Author

ACKNOWLEDGEMENTS

Writing *High Heels and Low Blows* was a solitary experience, but the process itself involved a group of incredible humans who spurred me on, and there are many to thank:

Firstly, my publisher Bonita for taking a leap of faith and bringing the novel to life. You're a force. And Margot, your gutsy, furry friend, for bringing us together.

So grateful to Shannon M who did an awesome job editing my work.

I'm indebted to Iain because I couldn't have finished the story without you. Thank you for your genuine excitement, our weekly chapter meetings and yummy one-pan dinners.

Round-of-a-paws to my Tania Park doggy crew who always listened to my plot ideas at the crack of dawn, especially Kate, Helen, Billy and Pat.

Big thanks and love to: Kat for your inspiration and lending me *Bird by Bird* to get my juices flowing; Kristina who pumped my tyres up on days when they were flat; Juli, Jeremy and Sander for your support and wines along the way; Camilla, Shannon B and Jill for your friendship; and Sarah and Andrew who helped nudge things forward.

Thank you to my loved ones who put up with me every day: my partner Adam who radiates positivity and always puts me on a pedestal. You have so much patience and I don't have any! My gorgeous, kind boys, Max and Louis. And my dog, Alfie, who watched me write and made sure I took plenty of thinking-time walkies!

Lastly, but certainly not least, thank you to the readers. I hope you find as much joy in reading this story as I did in writing it.

MORE REALLY GOOD FOOTBALL FICTION FROM POPCORN PRESS

Jarrod Black

Chasing Pack

Anna Black

This girl can play!

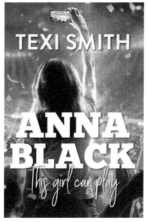

The End of the Game

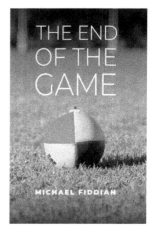

The Gaffer

Game

The Yawning Giant